About the Author

After thirty years as a high flying business executive for international corporations, Emma Bellemy decided to part company with her American Express Gold Card, and jet set life-style, in favour of keeping sheep and growing grapes in Devon. She abandoned the 'Good Life' when the call came to advise big businesses on using their resources to help charities and community projects. Now, Emma lives quietly as a writer between her homes in Sligo on the wild west coast of Ireland, the Cotswolds in the UK and her farmhouse in Brittany.

For Hayley, who waved her magic wand, and for George.

Emma Bellemy

LIVING WITH JUNO

AUSTIN MACAULEY
PUBLISHERS LTD.

ISBN 9781785543692 (Paperback)
ISBN 9781785543708 (Hardback)

www.austinmacauley.com

First Published (2015)
Austin Macauley Publishers Ltd.
25 Canada Square
Canary Wharf
London
E14 5LQ

Printed and bound in Great Britain

Acknowledgments

With fondness, love and grateful thanks, you all
know who you are.

1 – Sometimes ... you have to make a dash for it

My route to meeting Janie Juno began when I accepted a job offer for a responsible but dull position in Taunton, the county town of Somerset in the South West of England, famous for its cricket.

I was living an uninteresting suburban existence in the same West Midlands city I'd been born into almost forty three years earlier, a place that had been on the wane since its heyday of once being compared car wise to Detroit, and when an escape hatch of opportunity suddenly popped open, I swam for it like a spawning fish.

Being a baby boomer from Scottish immigrant parents, I was part of a generation that had been well educated and given opportunities which had allowed me to climb the career ladder from a relatively young age. By the time I was in my late thirties I had reached a level of seniority that had surprised me and I was, by a long way, the youngest executive at my current company. I lived and worked conscientiously and dutifully and was viewed both by my family and colleagues as a reliable pair of hands; a hardworking cog in the domestic and corporate machinery who had none of the undesirable traits of spontaneity or irrationality.

I'd applied for the new role in the South West with its eye watering salary on a whim from The Appointments section of *The Sunday Times* not really expecting to get it but a few months on, having scraped through the interview process by the skin of my teeth because of the nine points on my driving license – a near ban and a story for another day – I found myself flat hunting with a short list of criteria for my perfect location.

Over a wet weekend in early January, I'd pinpointed Exeter and made an offer on a waterside apartment with views across a small boat yard to the quay which allowed me to hear the clanking of the halyards in the wind and the caws of the sea gulls overhead. Together with the salty whiff from the water, it gave me a sense of the all-important living near the sea.

Several of those around me were privately very concerned about my bid for freedom including my current female boss Barbara who we more commonly referred to as Battle-Axe Babs. She was a no-nonsense unmarried shrewd operator who'd fought her way to the top only to hear the death knell of retirement which was proving to be a more slippery opponent than anything she had seen off in her rise through the ranks.

She was a big woman with a penchant for flowery blouses and elasticated waists which gave her an air of nostalgic reassurance, engineered to conjure up fond memories of how our grannies used to treat us. On her part, this was a carefully cultivated illusion to make us work hard to gain her praise but more importantly, it signalled that we could confidently spill our guts and she used the information gleaned to dazzling effect. It was clear to me, though not to everyone, that it had provided her with the political leverage to manoeuvre herself into a position that was practically unassailable, except for the small matter of the looming enforced retirement.

Barbara was clever alright but I always felt she afforded me a little more respect, guessing rightly that I had sussed her out, and whilst we'd never be equals she was mostly direct in her dealings with me. I say mostly because she was an operator after all. The word was out that she was more than a little exasperated by my desire to hurl myself onto the rocks and towards the end of my notice period she took me to one side.

Her enquiry began with a 'can you step into my office please?' but I sensed it wasn't to do with the standard of the work from the division I headed so I hastily tucked a strand of my blonde bobbed hair behind my left ear, took off my black rimmed glasses and followed her.

Once inside she asked me to close the door and take a seat, gesturing to the leather sofa against the wall. It was late on a Friday and she'd taken her shoes off so I thought it only polite to do the same. As we sat on the sofa (trying to ignore each other's black scuff marks that shoes leave on your tights, squashed up toes and faint cheesy odours that were gaining in strength) she came to her point.

'Gina, I know this is a really big move for you so how's it going? I'm guessing by the look of you that it's all under control as usual and your things are neatly stowed in labelled boxes. I'm right aren't I?'

She sounded almost motherly.

I took a deep breath and tried to convey an air of being organised when I knew that, as far as my 'really big move' went, all I had in fact were two retro Space 1999 bar stools, a wicker laundry hamper and three ubiquitous Habitat storage jars with round lids, having left everything else with the ex.

'Oh you know, lots to do, but the lists are slowly dwindling.'

There were no lists.

'How are the boys taking it?'

She was referring to my sons aged sixteen and eighteen.

'College and university beckon so we've agreed they'll stay with their dad and visit,' I replied neutrally to gloss over the fact that I'd turned myself inside out before finally concluding it would be in their interests.

'Did you buy your new furniture and arrange for the moving man?'

I pretended to study her career photos on the wall while I bought time to let my voice drift upwards in search of a level of cheer I didn't feel.

'Oh yes, everything's ready,' I squeaked. 'All good to go, I think you would say.'

As there was no furniture, there was no man and I would be porting my stuff in the back of a small Mercedes, just to give you an idea of how little there really was.

'You'll be missed around here for sure Gina but not wishing to cast black clouds on your ... um, little adventure shall we say, if you find the change too disorientating, please give me a ring and we'll sort something out,' she said silkily.

My blood began to boil and when she leant over and patted my arm, I jumped like I'd accidentally been poked with an electric cattle prodder. I knew all of this was down to the problem she was having in replacing me and reasoned that her words had been carefully chosen in order to knock my confidence whilst her kindly pat and taking her shoes off were displays to make we waver between stable security and the dangerous unknown. When my number seven on the Richter scale of seismology had subsided, I gathered myself and replied neutrally, 'Thanks Barbara, that means a lot,' though in reality I knew wild horses would never drag me back once I'd left.

She signalled the conversation was over by standing up and squeezing her puffy feet back into their extra wide black patent shoes before returning to her side of the desk.

'Remember what I said, Gina, always here to help.'

Her smile was one of self-serving indulgence and her message of 'stay with what you know' was intended to instil doubt and confusion. If she was closer to the truth than she realised that was my business and a lifelong career in one place might be fine for her but wasn't for me. No thanks dearie and if becoming a Battle-Axe Babs was all I had to look forward to, I might as well chuck the towel in now.

To my credit, I'd anticipated and rehearsed for this moment and the look I had settled on was a Julia Roberts 'Boudicca on the chariot, hair in the wind, I will triumph' kind of thing wearing a Tina Turner Mad Max 3 impregnable 'nothing can stop me now' breast plate. I hoped Babs had appreciated it but wasn't so sure when all she did was to raise one of her pencilled in eyebrows.

Time for me to go.

Not retreat.

Just go.

Go South.

Her chat had only made me more determined to make a success of it, hinting as she had that it might be a step too far. A few relatives by marriage and some of my more 'settled' colleagues had echoed the same sentiment, but as their motives were also questionable I had chosen to set them aside too.

It wasn't a fear of the unknown that had stopped my own parents leaving the tenements of Glasgow in search of a better life and ancestry was on my side; if they could overcome fears and doubts then I could too. In an increasingly swelling sea of negative opinion the people around me could not understand.

It wasn't possible for me to stay.

It wasn't possible for me to come back.

I was convinced that once away from this faded, jaded, die hard conurbation and living somewhere exciting and stimulating, I could shake off the grey moribund treadmill of my life and grow a different one that was filled with new friends, new distractions and happy times. Like a plant, I wanted sunshine, clean air and access to water to allow the new shoots of my exodus to blossom and thrive. I didn't see myself as a needy hot house weeping fig but as something outdoorsy, exotic and compact like a Hebe which is easy on the eye and flowers occasionally. It also happens to be true that in Greek mythology, Hebe is the name of the Goddess of Youth.

I rest my case.

The day eventually came, not too long after my Battle-Axe Babs encounter, when it was indeed time for me to pack up and fly south. I received flowers, gifts and good luck wishes, said my goodbyes and without a backward glance headed down the M5. Fittingly, I left grey skies in the Midlands and arrived in lovely spring sunshine.

I first caught a glimpse of Janie Juno (though I didn't yet know her name) as I was unloading my meagre possessions and spotted her walking along the pavement on the other side of the road. Her shortish light brown hair, curling slightly outwards, bounced as she stepped lightly and her flouncy skirt swayed gently from side to side. She looked over and smiled warmly making it easy for me to do the same and my impression was one of loose familiarity, as if I might have seen her somewhere before. The idea departed as quickly as it had arrived and when she turned the corner out of sight I wondered if she lived in the same apartment block.

The next day I decided to explore my surroundings and the first thing I noticed was how bright everything was. Granted, it was a clear sunny day but I was instantly taken with the sharpness of the extraordinary light. A gentle wind furrowed the water and the slight wave tops glistened silver. People were milling around appreciating the day, eating ice-creams and stopping at waterside cafes. Everyone appeared relaxed and small children laughed excitedly. With some surprise, I had to root around for my sunglasses, such was the luminosity.

And it was warm.

I found an unoccupied seat at a cafe called Mangoes, ordered a cappuccino and removed my thick woollen jumper. The sun was strong enough to heat up my skin and I could feel it radiating. The water must have reflected it too and, given this was only the middle of April it was unheard of, at least for me, to be almost sunbathing.

I revelled in it.

The coffee arrived and as I took in the happy scene of people enjoying themselves against the quayside backdrop, I exhaled deeply. A little more than I'd intended because it made an odd gurgling sound and the man at the next table peered at me questioningly. I raised my eyebrows by way of apology but from the moment of my spontaneous exhalation, my tensions began to ease.

'Excuse me but are you alright?' next table fifty something man asked me in an anxious tone.

'Erm, yes thanks. I have a bit of a cold, I'm afraid. Sorry about that.'

Good quick thinking.

'It always happens when the seasons change, but these occasional sunny days coming early like this are gifts from the winter god, don't you think?'

His accent had a hint of Devon drawl and he smiled with an easy charm. I noticed the eyes beneath his thick, fair fringe were brown and friendly and he had a boyish way of turning slightly away from you, then lowering and tilting his face upwards when he spoke. It made him appear shy which was attractive as well as endearing, if not a little practiced for my taste.

'I'm Maxwell, Max, how do you do?' He proffered his hand and I shook it lightly, feeling the skin dry and not too soft.

'Hello Maxwell-Max, I'm Gina. Pleased to meet you,' I smiled back.

I couldn't help it.

'The rowers are having a good outing today. I've been watching them practice and compete. It's fascinating. I used to do a bit in my time but those days are long gone. How about you, have you ever rowed?'

'Me?' I spluttered into my coffee, blowing some of the foam onto his grey cashmere jumper.

He took it well, dabbing himself off with the paper napkin that he hastily grabbed from beneath his saucer and laughed, showing a decent set of teeth that I took to be his own.

'Listen, Maxwell-Max, where I come from, the nearest you get to rowing is your fiver's worth on the boating pool in The Memorial Park. Two laps and your number's called in. By loud hailer.'

'You look like you could do it, Gina. The rowing club is just over there.'

He pointed to a single storey brick building across the quay with huge doors onto the water which happened to be two hundred yards from my place.

'There's a class for novices starting on Wednesday. Why don't you give it a try? I'll be there and can show you the ropes, well blades actually.'

I must have looked askance because he added hastily, while putting a reassuring hand on my back I noticed, that blades were oars. My relief was instant and palpable. He'd leaned forward when he spoke and together with the hand action I got the impression that his complete focus was on me, to the exclusion of all else. That day I was flattered but in time I would come to realise that it was a bedside manner he had perfected for the benefit of his clients in his role as a senior partner in a London-based law firm; his speciality being commercial property.

'Get there for 6.30 and I'll arrange for you to go out in the playboat, so called because you can't sink it.'

That's what he thinks, was my first reaction but to be fair to him, he seemed genuine if a bit smarmy and the idea of being on the water had as much appeal as being by the water. The rowers looked elegant, toned and fit as they glided along with the swans and though it was a tad early for the swallows to be darting for their flies, they would come soon enough. And so, because the sunshine-filled happy day made me feel lighter than I had for years, I found myself saying, 'Ok, you're on. But I warn you. They said the Titanic was unsinkable.'

We sat in the sun for a few more minutes and I explained about my new job starting the next day. He told me he lived alone but provided no explanation and gave me his mobile number saying to call him if I fancied a chat or changed my mind about rowing. I swallowed the dregs of my coffee, careful not to get a creamy moustache, and went to get up from the table.

'See you on Wednesday. Bye Maxwell-Max.'

'Bye Gina. Look forward to it.'

He stood up when I did and shook my hand again. For a second, I thought he might try to kiss my cheek but when the moment passed, I wondered if I had imagined it. I reflected on our exchange as I walked along the quayside and thought how easily he had scaled my carefully constructed and heavily fortified battle-weary defences, the ones that made Fort Knox look like a chicken coop. I was no newcomer to male charm but my experiences were largely in the course of my work and whilst I had managed

Max's attention professionally, outwardly appearing calm and relaxed, inside I was having kittens.

He was skilled if he could mount a challenge in a matter of minutes that had me saying yes, yes and yes but on the plus side, he might be able to help me settle into the area because of his obvious resources and contacts. My best bet was to keep him as an arm's length 'friendly professional' and I was relieved when I settled on this as a label for the tone of our dealings. I re-secured my defences and when I saw that the little rope ferry was open I paid the 20p fare and stepped aboard.

Minutes later I was on the opposite side of the quay strolling across the main square when I caught another glimpse of Janie Juno with a dark haired girl as they walked past the big window of the Italian bar.

She was laughing at something and turned just at the moment a sunburst caught her hair and gave it a halo effect. I blinked at the trick of the light and shielded my eyes so I could see better but she had already disappeared inside. Coincidentally, later that evening I received a message welcoming me to the area, also mentioning the Rowing Club and saying that she would be there on Wednesday if I was free.

Later on, as I lay in my strange bed in my strange room, I felt the first glow from the embers of new beginnings being gently fanned by the experiences of the last few days. My face was hot and smooth from the glorious weather and I felt proud I had made two new contacts, both of whom were steering me towards the possibility of doing something that was both outdoors and mercifully, involved being close to the water. A little closer than I had imagined as it would turn out but when these thoughts trickled through my mind, the West Midlands began to seem like a lifetime away.

2 – Sometimes ... you have to hold your hands up and play the game

By lunchtime on the first day of my new job, I knew I had made a grave mistake when I realised that my colleague, Freddie the Finance Director, was a misogynistic psychopath who was entirely ungovernable by the CEO (who was my boss too).

This was a world that Max was familiar with and because of the seriousness of the matter, I didn't feel he would look upon my call as a come-on. I needed his professional advice and nothing more, I tried to convince myself as I began to dial his number.

'Hi, Max, it's Gina.'

'I was just thinking about you.'

He sounded pleased and I thought, "were you now?" but let him go on.

'How did the first day go?'

'Very illuminating, Max, is all I can say.'

I heard him suck in his breath.

'Interestingly, when I went through all the hoops of the recruitment process, I was never introduced to the FD and now I know why. I'd asked several times for a meeting with him but for one reason or another it had never been possible and in retrospect I feel I was fobbed off.'

I heard him groan as if he already knew what I was going to reveal.

'Gina, who managed the project before you?'

'Good question. My PA, Susie, told me her name was Amanda. She had been good at her job and was about the same age as me. Susie also told me in confidence that in her opinion Amanda had been reduced to a near nervous breakdown and was sure some kind of payoff had been affected. She had seen a non-disclosure agreement.'

'More like a gagging order,' he chimed in.

'I might be in the proverbial merde, Max.'

'I didn't know you spoke French,' he laughed but now wasn't the time to tell him I'd slaved in Brussels for five years.

'You're going to need to keep your wits about you girl.'

'I know. It already feels that what should be a straightforward nuts and bolts project role is taking on the dynamics of the equivalent of a 3D game of chess – every minute of the day. He's tried to ambush me several times already and it could be exhausting. I tell you, Max, the politics of both the organisation and its network of associate companies could trump Westminster any day and I reckon progress has been slow as well as expensive because of the sheer resources needed to make a dent on the institutionalised cronyism.'

'You don't strike me as being a shrinking violet, Gina, but you might be advised to keep your head down.'

'As far as the earth's core at this rate,' I quipped and he laughed again.

'Psycho-Freddie has definitely got issues and you need to play the long game until you can find an Achilles heel.'

His tone was matter of fact and scarily pragmatic but I knew he was right. 'And besides, you've got your rowing on Wednesday and that might help.'

I failed to see how but as my life by the sea was changing at a rate of knots, the best thing I could do was to tread water and go with the tides. No puns intended.

We said our goodbyes and after he made me promise to go to the club, I rang off. With my phone still in my hand, I sat on my space 1999 bar stool and looked out into the darkness across the water. On the other side of the quay I could pick out the illuminated spire of the old church and the swaying fairy lights of the bars. I put the phone on the worktop and looked at it thoughtfully. Max was right and had definitely been the person to talk to but I still couldn't help wondering what on earth I'd done in taking the job in the first place.

I raided my fridge for some humus and momentarily reflected on how nice it was to be free to suit myself with what and when I ate, remembering my ex and our set meal times. And now, because I only munched when I was hungry, I had lost weight and it added to my pleasure of the moment.

Returning abruptly to my little work problem, the words of Battle-Axe Babs rang in my ears and for a split second I conceded that I might actually have bitten off more than I could chew. I had to quickly reinforce that going back was an impossibility and consoled myself with the fact that it was still early days. Let's see what Wednesday would bring.

And unlike the previous night, I didn't go to bed glowing. I went instead with a gnawing anxiety and dreamt of Nightmare on Elm Street. It must have been the Freddie effect.

3 – Sometimes ... having long nails draws blood (yours and others')

On Wednesday, I left my office at 5.45 on the dot and if anyone frowned at my perceived mid-afternoon departure, they said nothing to me. A quick dash home for a change into Lycra shorts, vest top and hoodie and I made it to the club on time where Max was already helping a few others get their sleek boats out of the shed. When he saw me he excused himself and started to walk towards where I was standing.

In the distance I saw Janie Juno in a boat with three other girls; one with her dark tresses tied up in a bright pink top knot, another with short blonde hair who was fiddling with something and a girl at the back, sporting a cap. All four looked competent and elegant as they rowed together in time facing forward while the voice of their cox drifted across the water issuing instructions I did not understand. As I watched them, transfixed by the moving tableaux they presented, I was oblivious to anything and jumped when Max spoke.

'Hello there. Am I pleased to see you or what?'

His smile was broad, if not quite direct as I explained earlier.

'How's work been? Things any better?'

'So, so. Psycho-Freddie is still on my case but I've let it be known that I don't intend to tread the same path as my predecessor which put the wind up him a bit and is buying me some precious time. I really appreciated speaking to you the other night. This is a big move for me and I want to be grown up about it. Crying down the phone to my folks will only get me a 'we told you so' which won't help.'

'You're welcome and glad to be of service.'

He gave me a funny little salute which, despite myself, made me laugh.

'Are you nervous about any of this?' he asked, raising an eyebrow and taking in my body and clothes.

Not that it was obvious. No, no, he was Mr Smoothy himself but check me out he did; in spades. He obviously liked what he saw because he licked his lips for a split second which was not lost on me. Wasted perhaps, because of my decision to stay 'friendly professional', but definitely not lost.

'No, not really,' I lied.

The night before, as well as having nightmares about Psycho-Freddie the FD, I had dreamt I was drowning. Soon I'd have bags under my eyes bigger than Dot Cotton's.

'I've arranged to meet Janie Juno here later. Do you know her? She was rowing just now with three others.'

He thought for a second and brushed his fringe to one side as was his habit.

'No, I don't think so but as I said, I haven't been here for a while and members come and go all the time.'

I concluded that if he'd met her, he would have remembered so I didn't pursue it and looked instead at the heavy fibreglass boat he was leaning against, guessing correctly it was 'the one'. It looked to be about twice the width of Janie Juno's and was clearly for learners. Luckily, it was a clear still evening and I was told that it could be launched when the more competent crews were all clear in their pairs, fours and eights. I could only guess at the terminology.

In truth, it was a sight to behold and reminded me of a scene from one of the epics where the Roman/Greek/Enemy fleet is lined up ready for battle, but minus the fluttering pennants. Everyone was focussed, good-looking and fit and I got the impression this was a professional set up. Welcome to Exeter Rowing Club Gina, I thought as I listened to the polished accents and took in all the beautiful people around me. 'I think I'm going enjoy this.'

True to his word, Max helped me launch the playboat and introduced me in turn to Pete O'Mara, the coach who was going to preside over my first outing. I'd made Max promise he wouldn't watch and said I'd meet him later in the bar for a drink. So off he went in search of a pint and left me in the capable hands of Pete, a veteran rower of some thirty years who reassured me that nothing could go wrong. He had a lilting Irish accent and was stocky but not fat with a full head of thick greying hair and looked to be around late fifties. There were a few broken veins around his nose which suggested he liked a tipple but he gave off an air of knowing what he was about.

'Now, Gina, you need to lose some of the tension in your shoulders and warm up before we start. I won't make you run twice around the quay tonight as we're short of daylight, but next time, limber up and it'll make things easier.'

At first I thought he was joking but his expression was in earnest and added to my sense that this was something to be taken seriously.

I made my first mental note.

'It's right hand over left hand as far as pulling on the blades and get a feel for the connection between the boat and the water.'

I was wobbling like a good 'un. With blades flaying, boat swaying and a few bashes against the quayside, it was not a pretty sight. My fingernails were digging into both my palms and my right hand was catching the top of my left, lacerating it to a pulp. Too late to do anything about it now as I looked down and saw blood, red blood, dripping down both hands. The only saving grace was that I was actually beginning to get the knack of it, to feel the boat move through the stroke and the more I concentrated, the better I became, as long as I ignored my bleeding hands.

Pete O'Mara was shouting through his loud hailer which prompted me to think again about the boating pool in the park. The memory of it compared to what I was attempting now made me chuckle and in that one lapse of concentration the boat shot backwards at full pressure, rammed the pontoon and capsized, throwing three things into the freezing murky water.

Me, my pride and whatever dignity I believed I had.

'Oh bejesus!' Pete screamed through the loud hailer. Then, 'Help! Mayday! Man down. Woman in water!'

The alarm in his voice was unmistakable, even if the words had come straight out of a cheesy war film, but it was the last thing I heard as I felt myself sinking slowly into the quay with the darkness closing around me. I had the presence of mind not to panic and waited until I hit the bottom, feeling the soft mud, before allowing myself to float back up to the top. If I had wanted a rescue crowd I would have been delighted by the mob but as I wanted to die with shame, I would have preferred there to have been just a few.

On breaking the surface, someone threw a life ring which hit me on the head leaving a nasty gash but at least I was able to grab hold of it whilst the mob on the quay pulled me to safety. Strong male arms leant over the edge to haul me up and amongst them, through my streaming slime gunged hair, I recognised Max.

'Oh bejesus. Oh bejesus!'

It was Pete again.

'The playboat's never gone over before. We'll have to amend the Health and Safety policy again.'

I heard Max say in a steady and calming voice, 'Forget the policy, Pete, is she alright? Are you alright, Gina?'

I stood dripping and shivering on the quayside with blood running down my face and my hands cut to shreds. Though my courage was about to desert me in place of howls, I squared my shoulders, parted my hair and replied, 'Yes thanks, never better.'

This, I could see, made Max's eyes crinkle in merriment and without a backward glance I did the best catwalk flounce that the squelching would allow for back to the ladies changing rooms where I bawled my eyes out at the ignominy of it. By the time the other crews had come back I was already showered, changed and drinking my first glass of wine at a table in the far corner of the bar. The big plasters that Max and I both wore on our hands, arms and my forehead were the only tell-tale signs that something had gone awry but as the rowers were more interested in their timings for the forthcoming head race, they only asked whether we'd been fighting.

I was on the look-out for Janie Juno as she was beginning to intrigue me and at nine thirty she appeared at the other end of the bar laughing and chatting happily with the three girls I'd seen her in the boat with earlier. One of the men's eight had just bought her a drink and she was quickly surrounded by people who wanted to say hello.

Her hair was still slightly damp from the shower but her cheeks were rosy and the figure she cut in her blue jeans and simple white shirt was effortlessly chic. People were flocking and I watched her take time to pass a few words and decline several more offers of drinks before finally spotting me. She grinned cheerily and gestured with her glass which I took as an offer but I had to decline due to work the next day. I gave her a small shake of my head and an apologetic smile and she nodded in understanding before slipping from view as the throng closed around her.

I could see it would be tricky to be introduced and decided it would wait for another time. Max hadn't noticed the exchange as he was in deep conversation with the men's captain but as I couldn't grasp what they meant by skulling, and was more than a bit out of it, I sat quietly sipping the last of my drink and tried to resist looking under my plasters. I really needed to get back and when he walked me to my apartment block he kissed me gently on the lips as we stood on the steps. No surprises, no fireworks, no alarms, no tongues, no clinches – just a manly natural kiss which I surprisingly enjoyed and I could see that he did too. It had felt right and my 'friendly professional' stance was beginning to come under threat as I sensed he might be about to breach my ramparts.

'You need to get some rest Gina after tonight's pal larva. I'll call you tomorrow and we'll do something at the weekend if you're free.'

'Thanks Max, I don't have any plans and that would be nice. You were a real hero back there and I hope the scratches get better soon.'

I saw his eyes crinkle again in the half light.

'Gina, it was a pleasure and I wouldn't have missed it for anything!'

He burst out laughing.

Humph, I thought. So much for good professional impressions but it clearly hadn't put him off and he seemed keener, if anything. I let myself in and waved him off, knowing that I now stood on the threshold of a reluctant life.

When I had said yes to his invitation I'd tried to hang it on my sense of obligation for tonight and the work advice but in reality I knew I was approaching a line in the sand. I could feel my inner pendulum of fear versus loneliness beginning to swing and knew that our date would necessitate some serious door opening.

I was referring to my heavily bolted, triple padlocked, emotional, million-year-old, oak-studded one, in case you were wondering.

And that was assuming I could locate the key.

4 – Sometimes ... a knock on the door is life changing, but you have to open it first

A few days later on the Friday night, and not having seen anything more of Janie Juno, I was preoccupied with the date I had for the next day with Max. He was going to take me out on his speed boat from Teignmouth, on the south coast of Devon about ten miles from Exeter, to a seafood restaurant across the bay in Lyme Regis. I was carefully laying out my clothes for the trip when I heard a tap on the front door.

The lack of the buzzer meant it was someone already in the block, but eleven thirty at night was a bit on the late side and because I still didn't know many people, I was on the verge of ignoring it. Concern that someone might be needing help got the better of me and I tiptoed to the spy hole to see if I could get a glimpse. I recognised Janie Juno's profile immediately but hesitated.

It had to do in part with preparing for my date with Max but more than that, I sensed another point of no return. I said earlier, that one of my aims in relocating was to make new friends but the reality was that I wanted to make 'some' friends. I was technically Gina No-Mates who in the Midlands had kept socialising down to a quick drink with a colleague and conversations to matters of business. The gentle art of chatting was as mysterious to me as the Loch Ness monster.

Outwardly, especially at work, I appeared to be socially well adjusted and popular but the truth was that I carefully hid behind my job to avoid getting close to people who might see my sensitive nature and exploit it. For years, I had cultivated a hard outer shell to protect my insides which I perceived to be made of delicate pink marshmallows.

Not white ones.

Easygoing and casual social contact of the sort that Janie Juno engaged in seemed like a different planet to me and I didn't have a clue as to how I might get there. Deep down, I admitted I was lonely but the act of cutting back the overgrown brambles I had deliberately allowed to spring up on my pathway to personal friendships seemed thorny at best.

I had taken a very small step and cut down six inches when I had leant on Max for advice regarding work but that had been out of necessity and not out of choice. His kiss had terrified them into re-growing because of the conflict it created between wanting his support to help me get established in the South West and rejecting his attention because I was too afraid of the consequences.

Faced with Janie Juno's interest in me and a chance to get the secateurs out, I wasn't exactly brimming with confidence that I had what it took to enter the land of Gina Some-Mates and a dive under the duvet wasn't beyond the pale at this point. However, the emotional part of my brain helpfully gave in to the persistent tap, tap, tapping of the rational part and I was served up a succinct dish of options.

If I didn't open the door, there would be no second chance.

If I kept the chain on it and only opened it a fraction, there would be no possibility of it opening further.

Logically, it therefore had to be either opened wide or not at all.

I heard the ticks of the clock in the hallway and knew she wouldn't wait there forever.

'Just turn the handle and open the door,' a female voice impatiently hissed in my ear, loudly and firmly and so clearly that I had a quick look around to see if anyone else was in there with me.

Nope, I was definitely on my own.

'Just open the bloody door!'

It did an 'Italian Job' and I was too startled to disobey. I also felt a little push from behind which propelled me forward but I swear there was no-one else in the hallway with me at that point. Best we don't go there.

So I did.

Open it, that is.

I opened the door as wide as it would go.

In fact, I threw the door open with all my strength and ushered Janie Juno in.

Then I firmly closed it behind her.

The voice didn't congratulate me. In fact it said nothing, having presumably grown bored.

Until now remember, there had been no chance to talk let alone look one another over properly but here we were, in my hallway, facing each other, for the first time ever. To say that we were immediately at ease would not be true.

'Oh, Hi. You're Janie Juno, aren't you? I'm Gina, I saw you at the Rowing Club but I'm really sorry I didn't say anything. Um, really sorry, I didn't want to seem rude or um ... I mean to say that I would have liked another drink but you know, with work and everything and ... and ... and here we are then. Come in, come in and ...'

My words tailed off as I ran out of breath and I felt awkward and stupid. Most of what I'd just said was gibberish even to my own ears but I was so nervous and out of practice, I couldn't help it.

She laughed a little uncertainly but thrust her hand forward. 'Nice to meet you, too, Gina. I've been seeing you around all over the place and I'm really pleased that we've finally met. Glad I caught you in but I'm not interrupting you am I?'

She gestured to my bedroom where she could see a pile of discarded clothes.

'Oh, no. Not at all, I've got a date with Max tomorrow, the guy I was at the club with, so I was just trying to get organised.'

Seeing her close up, we weren't too dissimilar with both of us being quite tall, around the same age and of the same build with blue eyes. My hair is coached to a straight blonde bob and coiffed to within an inch of its life while Janie Juno's was a sort of sun streaked very light brown and shoulder length, curling slightly outwards. I had on trademark black tailored trousers topped with a crisp white shirt and discrete pearls in my ears and she had on jeans, a fringed woollen wrap and gold dangly earrings that looked like falling leaves. Whereas I appeared severe and all angles, she looked fluid and casually elegant, pretty much like the other times I had seen her.

'Listen, I'm sorry if I was a bit gushing, it's just that I'm not very good socially.'

I surprised myself by being so open but it was down to her easy unhurriedness, in taking time to talk to me that was drawing me out.

'Hey listen, Gina, you're not on your own there. If I'm honest, I struggle to get to know people and I still get a few butterflies when I know I'm going to meet someone new. Usually I've got trepidations as well because you can't be too careful in this day and age. It's a dog eat dog world and you're never sure who you can trust. I think it's normal to be like that, in fact I think it's better to be like that.'

Had she just admitted that she shared my concerns, the ones I'd had before I opened the door? I stood rooted to the spot in surprise as if a bolt of lightning had zapped me because the message was that I wasn't a freak; I was only being cautious, and cautious was good.

'Take you and me for example, Gina,' she carried on. 'I've come in and clearly you weren't expecting me and I was a bit nervous and you were a bit taken aback but we've managed OK haven't we? These little conversations will help us to get to know each other, they'll be like stepping stones and we'll hop across the divide together, a stone at a time. That's what I always do with people I like.'

Her voice was light and girlish but she spoke common sense, kindly and honestly. Though you can't set aside a few decades of reclusion in a few minutes, I felt she had handed me the equivalent of a very sharp and effective pair of secateurs, some safety goggles and a suit of protective clothing in which I could start to recover my overgrown bramble path. And I was grateful.

In her reference to us crossing the divide together, I realised she was looking for something from me, too, and I resolved to provide whatever it was when the time came.

I'd been struggling for a while, plagued by a feeling that there was something unsavoury and unpalatable about me, that when people discovered it they would run for cover. It was something illusive but I sensed it was to do with the ending of my marriage and the shame of having no friends. Now, in the hallway with Janie Juno, she was telling me that she liked me and I began to see that if she did, others might too. Perhaps then, it was only a matter of time before I would begin to like myself and these dark feelings of self-loathing would subside.

I suddenly felt lightened, as if I was looking into the mirror at an altered image of myself but it had been a strange half an hour or so with voices and pushes and bolts of this and that so I gave myself over to it, feeling safe and secure that Janie Juno was one of the good guys and I was at last on my way.

'The idea of the stepping stones is a lovely image and I think I'd very much like to move onto the next one,' I said laughing lightly, feeling that the helium bottle could not be far away.

'Me too, Gina, so how about on Sunday night, we go to the Blue Fat Fish?'

'The where?' I croaked and she chuckled.

'It's a music bar in town. I think Bella and Lou will be there, you've seen them. They were in the rowing boat the other night.'

'Bella being the one whose hair was in a pink top knot, and Lou who had on a cap?'

'That's them alright! I'll call round for you at seven thirtyish.'

She opened the door to go out.

'Which flat is yours?'

'It's at the very top. I'll show you one day. See you Sunday and I'm happy we've finally met. I think we're in for some good times, Gina.'

I watched Janie Juno skip up the stairs two at a time and I went back to laying out my khaki shorts and cream Guernsey jumper for the speed boat adventure the next day, along with the particularly seductive pink and black lingerie that I had seen fit to buy earlier. As I did so, my mind was able to wander away from our conversation to the not unpleasant possibility of having a romp with Max.

If I could open the door to Janie Juno, I had a good chance of being able to do it for others.

5 – Sometimes ... laughter can get you out of a tight spot

Max had given me instructions to drive over the long bridge that spanned the River Teign then to turn left at the junction. He had told me his place would be easy to find from there as his Porsche would be on the drive and the house was a pale shade of pink in the shape of a helter skelter.

The sun was climbing as I started my car and drove in the opposite direction to the weekend traffic that was descending on the quayside for morning coffee. There were a few light clouds flitting across the otherwise clear blue sky and the day promised warmth.

On arriving, I felt I had stepped back in time to a little seaside town unchanged from the fifties and a warm feeling of nostalgia enveloped me as I recalled family holidays in Weymouth when I was small. Following his instructions, I drove by a quaint ice-cream parlour selling Knickerbocker Glories in traditional tall glasses and stripy sea-side rock that wouldn't have looked out of place in an Edward Hopper painting of Coney Island.

I was swiftly brought back into the twenty first century however when I noticed next to it, the very slick office of a fancy London Estate Agent. I had no clue that this place was a honey pot where a ten by ten beach hut sold for the price of a three bed-roomed semi in the provincial suburbs.

A few minutes later, I easily found Max's house which turned out to have stunning views across the bay and he had the front door open when I pulled onto his drive. He was dressed in cargo shorts and a loose fitting black polo shirt and when he smiled and kissed me on the lips I felt the stirrings of arousal.

'Welcome, welcome. Come on in. Did you find me OK?'

He dangled his arms loosely over my shoulders and when I looked into his normally guarded brown eyes I saw, without question, desire there too. His look, though swift, had been loaded but then, to my surprise, he let me go and busied himself with putting the kettle on for a cafetiere of coffee. It thankfully gave me the chance to take in the surroundings and to steady my legs.

'What? Yes, it was really easy. You've got a nice place here, Max.'

Understatement.

Back in control.

'Thanks. It suits me well. I grew up not far away and my dad used to bring me here fishing. When the tide went out we collected cockles from the sandbank which they call The Salty and I knew that one day I would live here.'

'Did you buy it like this or build it?' I asked glancing around at the muted tones and white curved walls.

'There was originally a dilapidated house here with a large garden that I bought at auction with the idea of demolishing it and selling off half the land. With the proceeds, I commissioned an architect to build this one and the money I made from splitting the plot covered it all. I guess I got lucky.'

Astute more like, I thought, but well done to him anyway. It was very tastefully furnished with no obvious scrimping and the internal lines were aesthetically gorgeous.

'You said you lived alone, how come?'

'Well, it's the usual story, I'm afraid. I was married twenty years ago and have a son called Charlie who is at university. His mother and I divorced when he was small and I've been a bachelor ever since, but not a monk though!'

He laughed with his eyes crinkling at the corners in that very attractive way.

'Have you ever been married, Gina?'

'I have but we divorced three years ago. I have two sons, one at university like Charlie and the other who is at college.'

'You don't look old enough,' he teased, handing me a cup of freshly brewed Blue Mountain and gratefully didn't pursue it.

'Let's go out onto the terrace. I've set up the garden furniture for the first time this year. I think it'll be warm enough.'

The view with the tide in was of little boats bobbing on their buoys in the slight breeze, glinting here and there where the sun alighted on metal. Looking down river, the hills of Dartmoor reared up to the sky and unconsciously, I sighed at all the natural beauty.

'You like it?'

'What's not to like, Max? It's gorgeous.'

'I've booked us in at an Oyster and Fish place on the harbour in Lyme for one o'clock so if we get going while the tide is in our favour we'll have no problem. Our transport is just there.'

He pointed in the near distance to a small but sleek speed boat that I could just make out was called Tarzanah. I almost had to pinch myself to be honest and the whole scene in front of me seemed a world removed from the grime of the industrial Midlands. As each minute passed, I felt my emotional trust growing and I resolved to be open to the possibilities of spending uncomplicated time with him.

'We'll drink this and get going,' he said cheerily.

At this stage, I knew absolutely nothing about sailing or cruising. I'd had my near drowning experience in the quay the other night but aside from my boating pool attempts, I hadn't been on anything seagoing except for a cross channel ferry. I therefore put myself in his trusting, capable hands and we made to go.

On the beach, we launched the small tender and rowed out to Tarzanah. Once aboard, we tied the tender to the buoy while carefully unhitching the speedboat and reversed it gently out into the open water.

So far, so good.

With both of us in casual shorts, woollen Guernseys and sharp sunglasses, he powered the boat to full throttle and we set out towards Seaton. I could feel the sea spray on my face and taste the salt in the air. Overhead, seagulls flew nonchalantly and without haste, enjoying like us, what the day had to offer.

About half way across the engine started to splutter.

'No problem. I'll check the fuel.'

The fuel seemed OK.

'No problem. I'll put on the spare outboard.'

The spare wouldn't start.

'No problem, I'll put a call in from the radio.'

The radio didn't work.

As he went through the motions of checking boat's things, I realised we might be some time. Our predicament pointed to Max not being quite as on top of things as I had given him credit for, having assumed that being a hotshot lawyer required thoroughness, and I was beginning to feel a creeping uneasiness.

Not knowing very much at all, it seemed to me we were in a tight spot and from films, I knew that people sent out distress flares if all else failed.

'Do we have any flares?' I asked with a sinking feeling, although sinking was the last thing I wanted to conjure up, raw as I still was from my rowing escapade. By deduction, I already knew the answer to this question given everything else so I was not surprised, if a little exasperated, by his 'No, I don't think so. Sorry.'

'What are we to do?' I asked trying to stem my panic.

'Oh, that's easy,' he replied a little too breezily. 'We'll wave and shout for help.'

Nooooooooooooooooooooooooooo! I screeched in my head as I gritted my teeth. This can't be happening to me! Not again. Not in the space of a week.

To cut a long story short, we attracted the attention of party on a ritzy yacht who were out for a day's sailing with better things to do than rescue a lawyer and his bint, but rescue us they did. They unceremoniously tied us to their stern and radioed to the coastguard who in turn radioed to the diving boat who in turn came and collected us on their way back into Teignmouth, complete with twenty or so divers in full regalia hanging over the rail heckling us, in an almost friendly way.

After what seemed like excruciating hours, they dropped us on our mooring and carried on. When we arrived back on the beach in the tender, the coastguard was already there to greet us, also in full regalia including an official looking cap. Even with my lack of experience in these matters I knew the cap meant trouble and when he stuck it on his head, I knew it was serious.

He helped us ashore and then took out a notebook.

'Welcome back,' he said in a clipped formal tone. 'Glad you're safe.'

Both of us looked down at the pebbles on the sand and said nothing.

'I have to take some information as to what happened. Did you do a pre-sail check?'

'No.'

The coastguard carefully and slowly wrote this down.

'Did you have fully functioning emergency equipment on board?'

'No.'

He licked the end of his pencil and wrote this down, in capital letters which he went over twice.

'Do you keep your engines routinely maintained?'

'No.'

He looked at Max as one might look at a foul smelling dog turd recently expelled from an animal other than your own.

'Consider this a formal warning and bring your papers to me no later than Monday 5 p.m. Skipper's name, please.'

Max quick as a flash said, 'Gina Jarvie.'

I looked at him in horror, eyes agog, speechless.

'First mate, please.'

'Maxwell Trent.'

'Thank you, sir, and now for the rollicking. You were both very stupid to go out there under-equipped and without ensuring the safety of your vessel and crew.'

The coastguard was looking at me and I went pink with indignation. Now wasn't the time to protest my innocence.

'You, first mate, are also to blame and this incident will be included in the Inter-coastal broadcast along with your names as a warning to others not to be so foolhardy.'

He wasn't lying.

'Yes, sir.'

Max tried to look abashed. Tried, I say whilst all I could do was shuffle my bare feet in the sand.

'OK. Be on your way. See you on Monday.'

He stomped off along the beach, angry at our stupidity and angry that he'd missed his afternoon cuppa. For a few minutes we stood in silence, thoughtfully watching the retreating back of the coastguard in his official cap.

'I blame you, Gina,' he laughed as he grabbed my arms to protect himself.

'Me?' I shouted, incredulously. 'What has all this got to do with ME? I am an innocent bystander. I trusted YOU!'

I was apoplectic and having no success at wriggling free.

His grip was firm and he brought his face closer to mine.

'You are such a gorgeous distraction that I've thought of nothing except you all week.'

He kissed me. Long, hard and lingeringly with warm salty lips. I felt his hand come up and stroke my breast with such a lightness of touch that I almost missed it. So that's how it's done, I thought, after more than twenty years of being out of the loop. I broke off from the kiss though we still held each other and our reflected smiles were warm and inviting.

And then we began to laugh.

Our first chortles quickly gave way to side splitting mirth as we began to see the funny side. We wiped our tears with the backs of our hands and leant amiably into each other. When one of us managed to stop, the other started up again and our laughter was drawn out, welcome and unbridled. Passers-by must have thought we'd been at the rum when they saw Max and me that day in our bubble of happiness and we were still chuckling when Max said,

33

'Come on, Gina. There's an excellent fish and chip shop round the corner. I'll treat you!'

For all his 'Grand Designs' house, his flashy Porsche and his hotshot lawyering, Max had shown a fun-filled, devil may care side to himself that conveyed both genuineness and humility, and I began to love him for it.

6 – Sometimes ... a chaise longue is a nice place to recline

We ate the fish and chips from their papers sitting on the wall at the back of the Knickerbocker Glory ice-cream parlour looking out to sea. It was an effort to keep the more brazen sea-gulls away but Max showed me how to make a hole in the paper and tug the chips out one at a time using the wooden forks.

'Let's go to The Anchor next. I think we deserve a drink and the sun's over the yard arm now. I believe there's live music later so we can check it out.'

'Fine by me!' I said between vinegary mouthfuls.

They were delicious and probably tasted all the better because of being by the sea.

'I didn't see Potato Scallops on the menu in the Fish Shop. I would have had one otherwise,' I remarked as I idly dangled a chip.

'Never heard of them. What are they?'

'They're thick slices of potato fried in batter. You can have one or two of them, instead of a pile of chips.'

'Must be a Midlands thing but I don't think you'll find them down here. You'll have to make alternative plans.'

He raised an eyebrow questioningly and plunged two chips into his mouth. I looked around me at the gorgeous views and the bright light.

'I'm prepared to make the sacrifice Max, but just on this one occasion,' I laughed.

The pub was crowded when we got there and someone had scrawled on the blackboard outside that Hogwash were playing.

'They're a great local folk band. Are you into that type of thing?'

'Not really to be honest. I've got a wide taste but folk isn't my thing. I like the vibe of live stuff though, so why not?'

We fought our way to the bar and ordered pints of real ale before squeezing onto the corner of a large occupied round table and squatting on a pair of low stools. I took a sip and it was rich and fruity, very unlike anything I'd tasted before.

'This is a lovely drop of beer, Max. Who makes it?'

'Bootley Ales. It's owned by a mad brewer in his mid-sixties called Lord Mortimer Dunseford. He's very high profile, not just because of his name but because he's a walking billboard for his brand. He uses pigs on his pump clips and vans, all very distinctive. Whenever you see him he's usually wearing something with his logo prominent. You can't miss Mortimer, big bloke with a beard.'

'No harm in standing by your product.'

I quite liked the sound of him.

'None at all and CAMRA, the real ale people, love it. He has a long suffering wife and an even longer suffering French lady-friend. Rumour has it that if you look closely you can see the lady-friend's face in the beer clip image he started off with which he aptly named, some would say, Jiggy Piggy.'

'No!' I gasped, almost choking on my laughter. 'How does he get away with it? Is he a real Lord?'

'Difficult to tell but he's got the toff accent and is eccentric enough to be one so I wouldn't put it past him. They make it out in the Teign Valley, on the edge of the moor, west of Exeter. The Brewery is open occasionally for a tour and we'll drop in one day but there's also a beer festival held every year in Newton Abbott and I'll find out when the next one is.'

'Pick me. Pick me!' I grinned and we chinked our beer glasses.

The musicians had started to warm up and I took in the two guys with beards on guitar, the baldy with the fiddle and the girl on the bodhran Irish drum with her hair tied up in a pink top knot. As I looked closely, I was sure she'd been in the boat the other night with Janie Juno.

'Max, see that girl there playing the drum. Does she belong to the rowing club?'

He looked to where I gestured and put his hand affectionately on my arm.

'Yes, I'm sure that's Bella. She's a great rower and I'd heard she was into her music but didn't know she played with Hogwash.'

'I'm supposed to be going out for a drink with her tomorrow night to the Blue Fat Fish. I hope she won't mind if I go over in the interval and introduce myself. What a coincidence?'

As I sat huddled closely into Max, the music swept over me; a mixture of jigs and ballads and it felt right for the location. Dartmoor was just few miles up the road and had a great tradition of folk music that radiated throughout the area. I enjoyed it more than I imagined and at the interval, even if I was a bit anxious, I made a point of standing next to Bella when she was buying a drink at the bar. She was the same height as me with brown hair and the biggest, loveliest dark grey eyes I had ever seen, framed with lashes made thick with mascara. When she asked for a coke she spoke with a London accent which surprised me.

'Hi, are you Bella by any chance? Are you going to be at the Blue Fat Fish tomorrow night?' I asked uncertainly.

'That's me. Bella by name, Bella by nature!' she laughed. 'Glad you can make it, the more the merrier. Lou should be coming along as well. There's a tribute group playing, the Red Mock Chilli Peppers. Write ups are good, but it'll be different to Hogwash,' she smiled as she sipped her drink and I immediately felt at ease, glad that I'd had the courage to speak to her.

'Did I see you rowing on Wednesday?'

'You did. We were practising for the head race tomorrow. If you're not doing anything, come along and watch. Might see you there but if not, I'll be in the bar at eightish. Sorry, gotta dash. We're back on.'

With that she was gone and I spent the next hour hooked, watching her playing and singing. Her eyes seemed to dwarf everything and I liked her quiet confidence when she looked out at the crowd. Whilst the music was good and absorbing, Max and I had other things on our minds so when our drinks were finished we decided to go back to his for a nightcap.

Outside the pub, he put his arm around me and gave me a kiss on the top of my head. I put my hand on his waist and we sauntered up the hill to his house talking animatedly about the music with me thanking him for an introduction to it. Still holding on to me, he took out his key with his other hand and opened the door. We stepped inside and he closed and locked it behind us.

We made it as far as the bedroom where the large full moon lit up the river, casting silver shadows on us and the reflected shards of light on the black harbour water added to the silhouette. A statement designer red and chrome chaise longue had been positioned to great effect in front of the main window and it was here that he slowly and gently removed my clothes, kissing me on my mouth and neck and moving down to my breasts. When he put his hand inside my flimsy knickers and felt my eagerness, he emitted a groan.

He deftly pulled them down and did what chaise longues were designed for, whilst I held his head with my hands, pulling him deeper inside me as I laid back on the soft leather and enjoyed being pleasured. He murmured and held me firmly by my hips.

When he surfaced, I took off his jumper and felt the warmth of his chest where our bodies met. I unbuttoned his shorts and slid down the zipper, using my foot to drag them and his boxers to the floor. He was hard and big and I had been made ready so I guided him into me and he pushed and pummelled before exploding, though not before I had the chance to hear the waves crashing metaphorically speaking, as well as actually hearing them from the bay. We collapsed onto the chaise longue, panting and sated and lay there looking out at the stars. Words were not required, as I stroked his head which lay across me.

Eventually, because of a problem with his foot, we pulled apart and I hopped into the king-sized bed whilst he went in search of some whisky. For a few moments I lay star shaped in the middle looking out of the window and reflected on how uncomplicated the sex had been. I had worried that my body was no longer in the first flush of youth and with certain areas losing their battle to gravity, I'd felt anxious in the preceding days knowing that we were headed in this direction. After not having anyone else during and after my ex, as well as bearing two children, I counted that it must have been twenty years or more since I'd been with a new lover and I relished the strangeness and newness of Max. Whilst he was in pretty good shape, his body also showed the normal wear and tear for his age but we had accepted each other for what we were and had given ourselves over to the moment. When it had come down it, none of our real or imagined imperfections had mattered and we'd had a good time. In cricketing terms we were close to notching up a century between us but the stumps had yet to fall!

I moved my arms and legs angel style, impressed to feel that the sheets were crisp. When I peeled the duvet back, I could also see faint creases suggesting they were new. Good on you, Max. He'd obviously given some thought to it I mused, as I settled myself in for a night of passion and fun.

From downstairs, I suddenly heard the clatter of breaking glass followed by a string of swear words and went quickly to the top of the stairs.

'You OK, Max?'

'Arrrrrrrrrghhhhh,' came the muffled reply. Then 'put something on your feet if you come down.'

I slipped into my boating shoes and arrived in the kitchen to a strong smell of single malt and to see him peering at his left foot propped up on the table. The three smaller toes looked swollen and red.

'What happened? Are you hurt?'

'I stubbed my bloody toes on the metal leg of the chaise longue earlier just before I went on my knees but thought I'd be alright. Besides, we were too far along to stop. Just now my foot gave way and I dropped the whisky bottle.'

Not bad going I thought, a performance like that from a man with stubbed toes. If that was what he could do under injury, what was he capable of at full pelt? The groan I had heard earlier hadn't been ecstasy after all but he could be forgiven.

'You poor thing,' was the best I could come up with and asked if he had any frozen peas.

He hopped to the freezer and opened the bottom drawer.

'In there I think. You're going to have to get them, Gina. I'm sorry.'

So that night, instead of us being curled up in each other's arms and whispering in the dark, he was on the brutalist chaise longue with his packet of peas while I slept the sleep of the recently shagged silly in an enormous bed in paradise.

At A&E the next day, they confirmed he had broken two toes and recommended that he desist from any more bedroom gymnastics for at least a week or two. The young male doctor in attendance, who turned out to be the son of a friend, dined out on the story for weeks.

7 – Sometimes ... superheroes are not as bright as we give them credit for

Janie Juno and I decided to walk to the bar in town because it was a dry and clear evening and as we climbed the hill I asked her if she was seeing anyone.

'Not as in a relationship,' she quipped and laughed enigmatically in a way that made me feel it wasn't a topic she wanted to stay on.

Instead I went over the speedboat meltdown, the luscious romp and the broken toes. We had a good laugh but just as we were about to go in the bar, her tone altered and she stopped. She turned to look at me and placed a friendly hand on my arm.

'Gina, you're going to need to exercise caution as this guy seems highly eligible but has remained single for twenty years. Have you asked yourself why? Is it because he's unwilling or unable to settle for one chocolate in the box when he can eat them all?'

'Maybe he just hasn't found the one that tickles his taste buds.'

I tried to make light of her words.

'Seriously, do you know anything about the others before you, who they were, how long they lasted and why they broke up?'

'All he said was that he hadn't been a monk,' I replied, ignoring a small doubt that was beginning to take hold.

'It's possible that he's banking on the fact that you don't know about his past or his reputation to lure you in when you otherwise wouldn't touch him with a barge pole. His type of property lawyering involves chasing and closing the deal then moving swiftly on to the next one and he obviously has a talent for it, but he might be the type who does the same to his women. I would keep him dangling until you can find out more.'

'By the short and curlies?' I was still trying for the lightness thing.

'Not exactly Gina, but make sure he's begging for mercy next time you get him on the chaise longue,' she chuckled and became thoughtful again. 'Have you factored in too that he might be having a problem with his ego because you're not actually fazed by the lifestyle or boys toys and he knows he can't impress you with them? He's a clever guy, this one, so go easy or you might get singed.'

'I'm as rusty as an old nail at this game but it's helping me to talk it through with you.'

'I know, Gina. That's what I'm here for. I guess things are still hard for you after your divorce.'

'You can say that again! I've lost confidence in myself to recognise emotional pitfalls let alone climb out of them. I feel as if I've been reduced to a quivering lamb born in the winter that's lost in the snow. Get my drift?'

I couldn't resist the last quip but the picture was a grim one.

'Do you know the old Chinese proverb that in the dark you must move slowly?'

'No, but I understand what you're saying, Janie.'

'Good, then in that case let's get inside this bar and get us a drink. I could do with a large glass of something cold and alcoholic and I'm guessing that you could too.'

'Thanks for the heads up and I'm sorry it's hogged our walk because I wanted to find out more about you.'

'Well you'd better prepare yourself, that's all I can say and don't worry. We've got loads of time ahead of us and you'll be bored silly when I've finished. I might even tell you about my 'non-relationship' with Gaz if you're lucky!'

She laughed her throaty laugh, removed her hand from my arm and tugged open the door into the bar where the noise of the throng swept over us like a wave.

Bella appeared without the pink top knot, her hair hanging down in long thick loose tresses that the Venus de Milo would have been proud of and I could see it wasn't brown so much as a rich auburn colour. She had on a pair of flattering grey cargo trousers and a pink tee-shirt that when she raised her arm, revealed a perfectly toned and flat brown stomach. What I wouldn't have given.

'Hi, come on in. Glad you could make it.'

Kisses all round.

'Lou is getting drinks and if you're quick to the bar she'll get one for you.'

I recognised Lou from the boat, minus the black cap, and went over to introduce myself, with only a slight hesitation, feeling safe that Janie Juno was within arm's length.

'Good to meet you, Gina. I saw you at the club last week, how did you get on?'

'Oh you know ...' I wondered if she had heard and blushed.

'We're looking for someone else for our boat so if it does turn out to be your thing, with a bit more practice, we'll take you.'

'Are you serious?' I asked wide eyed in disbelief, my heart pounding with excitement.

'I sure am. Your ending was a bit unexpected,' she laughed kindly, 'but Pete O'Mara who coached you, said he thought you had what it took and was worried that when you fell in you'd give up. He blamed himself.'

'Are you sure he meant me? It wasn't his fault at all and I'd just assumed I wasn't any good when I didn't see him afterwards.'

'He was too embarrassed but you should speak to him next time and hear it for yourself. I'm deadly serious about that offer and if you can build up stamina and technique, you're in.'

Buoyed by her surprising feedback and the idea that I might make it into a real crew, I began to relax and think about how it could help me.

'Anyway,' she added. 'It should be fun tonight. Are you into the Chillis?'

'I've heard them on the radio but that's about it. I like live music and it's a chance to check out the bar. How about you?'

'My last boyfriend got me into them when we went travelling around Australia for a year. I got back three months ago.'

'Are you still with him, your boyfriend?'

She laughed out loud as if I had said something funny.

'Not any more given that he announced he was gay as soon as we got home and took up with a fireman. I never saw that one coming, but hey, you only get one life. I'm single again and he was never 'the one' anyway so I'm back playing the field, just exploring my options as they say.'

Lou had no bitterness in her, just an easy, natural manner and if the fireman had caused her a problem, she'd opted for pragmatism over self-pity. This girl was open and straightforward and I liked her already.

'What's your poison, Gina?'

I asked for white wines and took the time while she was being served to notice her properly. Lou was a bit taller than me and looked to be in her late twenties. Warm hazel eyes and highlighted honey shoulder length straight hair that looked velvety, she had a sporty vitality about her and a quiet reserve though she wasn't shy. I got the impression she was a watcher rather than a plunger but it also turned out she was a surfer.

We carried on chatting while waiting for the drinks and I became conscious that I had settled into the easy banter and was enjoying it. Lou's style was friendly and sincere and I felt confident I could drop my guard, if not completely, then at least a little just to see how it felt so I decided to share a long held dream.

And a frustration.

'I've never been to Australia and would love to go but it's not possible to take the time out to do it properly so I can't see it happening.'

The words tumbled out more easily than I'd expected, with no spontaneous combustion or other nasty side effects. It hadn't been so bad after all but if I'd been hoping for tea and sympathy, it wasn't what I got.

'No excuse,' she said firmly but smiled. 'If you really want to do something, Gina, you've just got to find a way. I'm Exeter born and bred and we're not generally known for striking out to see the world but I gave up hairdressing to go travelling and have never regretted it.'

'Is that what you do?'

'Not anymore I don't! I gave it up because it didn't interest me. I vowed that when I came back I'd change direction and look for something that fired me up and I've just landed a dream job with a surf gear company. I learnt how to ride a board in Oz and a crowd of us go regularly to Croyde on the north coast. My uncle owns a bakery in town and he's let me have the flat above it for peanuts so all told, life's not too shabby now.'

By her look of sparkling contentment, I could tell that it wasn't.

I realised I had been given a lesson in openness and positive thinking as I took the glass of wine she gracefully handed me. If I hadn't told her about my dream, I would never have heard her message.

'What brings you here to the South West, Gina?'

'Change of heart, change of scenery, change of job.'

'Ahhhhh, I think I see. Do you have any kids?'

'Yeah, two boys, sixteen and eighteen. One's at Uni, the other's with his dad.'

'Blimey. You don't look old enough!' Her surprise was genuine.

'Thanks, Lou, I was in my mid-twenties when I had my eldest which was young by today's standards but not back then.'

'Seriously, girl, you look pretty up together and I never saw that coming either! I take it there isn't a Mister Gina from your change of heart comment?'

She leant in, cocking her head inquisitorially with a raised eyebrow and a cheeky grin.

'There was, but now he's ex Mister Gina,' I grimaced.

'I see. Same as Bella then but I'll shut up and say no more in case I spoil the night. Speaking of the devil, let's go and find her before she dies of thirst.'

Lou passed Bella her drink before disappearing off to talk to someone she knew and Janie Juno did the same, leaving us on our own at the end of the bar.

'How did you get on with Max the other night?' Bella asked me casually.

'I didn't realise you knew him. We had a great day despite a few dramas.'

I rolled my eyes and laughed giving her a quick summary of all that had occurred. I had deliberately told it with humour so I wasn't prepared for the reaction that followed which saw Bella sucking the air in between her teeth and puckering her lips slightly. Not her, too, I thought, anxiously, and braced myself.

'Oooooh, you're going to need to watch out, Gina. I don't know him well but he does come to the club now and again in search of, er how shall I put it delicately,' she looked upwards as if to pluck a floating word from the air. 'Company. Know what I'm saying?'

Her eyebrow began to rise.

'He has a reputation for not sticking to one woman for very long so my advice is to hold on to your heart ... Tightly.'

I felt uneasy that she had guessed rightly about my embryonic feelings and I was also beginning to be slightly unnerved by the warnings, two now in less than an hour. These girls were opening my eyes to the reality of the situation I was in with Max but taking their advice was going to be easier said than done because I really liked this guy and he was fun. However, as much I didn't want to, I had to acknowledge that some of the evidence pointed to him being an enthusiastic player in the game of "chase the ladies" and I would have to find out what I was dealing with. Wanting to park my creeping concerns about Max and get on with enjoying the night, I steered the conversation back onto safe ground.

'I liked the band the other night, Bella. I'm usually more bluesy than folksy but I thought the mix of lyrics and honest music was heady. Everyone played brilliantly but you were the real star.'

'I love my music and it wasn't always like that you know. I had a messy divorce ten years ago, from a bloke with more money than manners and hid myself away in my cave for a long, long time. It was the music that gradually restored me to the person formally known as Bella and ultimately gave me the change of direction I needed.'

She scanned the crowd over the rim of her glass and I could see the memory of it still hit home. A bit like me then, I thought.

'Have you always played an instrument? The only thing I've ever picked up is a tambourine.'

'I taught myself to play the guitar and the fiddle but I play the Irish drum with the guys because they need one. There's a jamming session next Friday at the Crown and Sceptre, a pub on the way into Torquay. Why don't you come and stay over at my place on the moor. My daughter Izzy is spending a bit of time with her father and his new family before she goes to university so you can have her bed. You'd be very welcome,' she smiled eagerly.

Given that I barely knew her, it was a generous offer and I quickly realised that whilst her invitation was genuine and warm, it wasn't something she did lightly, or frequently. Her reference to her cave left me with a strong impression that her home was her sanctuary and it was flattering to think she was willing to admit me. My normal misgivings and anxieties about invitations like hers hadn't materialised, I was pleased to note, so I instantly said, 'Thank you. I would like to very much.'

'I'll email you the directions to my place and I'll drive us to the pub. You'll get to meet the guys in the band and I know they'll like you!'

Did I just pick up the very faintest, almost indiscernible inkling of relief in her voice that I had accepted? I strained my senses to get a precise fix on her tone and it occurred to me that, because she wasn't generally open in this way, a polite decline might have been taken as a mild rejection. I sensed a well-hidden vulnerability but it was there if you knew where to look, as I did. So you, too, I thought. We're both just as scared deep down but we've taken the plunge and I recalled Janie Juno's stepping stones. We would soon come to discover we had more in common than either of us had imagined, not least the fact that we were around the same age.

I immediately got out my diary and wrote 'JAMMING WITH BELLA!' on the Friday space, acting decisively to show her my thanks, understanding and commitment. I saw her moment of apprehension melt away as we chinked our glasses and laughed spontaneously.

'To Friday!'

'What are you two cackling about?' Lou had come back. 'Has Rob turned up?'

I saw Bella narrow her eyes.

'Uh oh! You haven't told Gina why we're really here, have you?' She smiled foxily but Bella wasn't going to be drawn and scanned the crowd, studiously ignoring her.

'Well, I will tell you then, Gina. But first, try to guess?'

Bella looked like she could playfully murder Lou.

'Not the music?' I asked puzzled.

'Partly the music,' Lou grinned.

'Er, to meet up and have a good time?'

I was struggling.

'Of course. But haven't you wondered if there might be a man involved?' Lou asked, slyly, and Bella still said nothing, continuing to look the other way.

'A man!'

It came out as if she'd said 'ET' and she laughed at my expression. Whilst Bella pretended to look bored.

'A real man, Gina. One who I happen to know is called Rob and who plays for Exeter FC as well as being good with a ukulele. He's recently joined the rowing club for fitness and is mad for Bella. Isn't he, Bella?'

'Right, I'm not putting up with this froth any longer. There are more interesting conversations to be had in the ladies.'

Bella flounced off, but I could see the edges of the smile she was struggling to hide. Left on my own with Lou, I felt I could voice something that was niggling me.

'Doesn't that make him quite a bit younger than her, Lou?' I asked falteringly.

'Gina, get with the programme!' she said in an exasperated, though kindly voice. 'Their fifteen year age gap is only stoking his interest and between you and me, Bella's hoping he'll invite her back to his. I also happen to have seen a tidy little overnight bag in her car.'

Lou tapped the side of her nose when she said this and laughed gleefully.

'I hope he knows what he's letting himself in for and his policy is up to date. That's what she does you know, she underwrites sports people and musicians, events too. Maybe that's her plan, finish him off and put in a claim!'

'Lou, you little devil!' I burst out laughing.

These last few weeks were breaking new ground for me in all directions and my previous assumptions, boundaries and fortifications were toppling like a house of cards. If I had initially questioned the age difference between Rob and Bella it had quickly become irrelevant knowing that Bella was fundamentally a moral, responsible and genuine person. So why shouldn't she cross an awkward taboo and have fun? Who was to say it was wrong?

Tonight I had gained new insights into the way these girls chose to live. That is to say, really live, embracing life, living it to the full, having it all without the need to justify or be concerned about conformity, whatever that was. They were united by their sport and their outlook on the world and were thriving on it.

On their terms.

Myself, Janie Juno, Bella and Lou were all getting on like a house on fire and I knew I wanted these girls to like me and to become part of their group. They were easy and fun and broke the moulds without being conscious of doing so and without apology. I would come to reflect more on this theme in the coming weeks.

Meanwhile, the band eventually came on and the playing drowned out the possibility of us chatting further. Rob had turned up and spotted Bella, whisking her on to the dance floor where they treated everyone to some seriously up close and personal dancing. The air was charged with their sexual chemistry leaving no-one watching in any doubt as to the night they would go on to have. They were captured in the single dance floor spotlight and it accentuated their movements which were mesmerising and spontaneous, each of them responding naturally to the other. It was balletic and infectious.

We saw Bella only briefly after that as Rob couldn't get enough of her and when it was time to go, she gave us all a quick peck on the cheek and called breezily over her shoulder that she'd see us on Wednesday at the club. We looked at each other knowingly, linked arms and set off to walk back to the quayside where Lou's current boyfriend Jonnie had a room in a shared house.

As we got closer, the smell of the river rose up around us and we stood under the old covered market taking in the ripples of the water made by the wind that was getting up. The Victorian streetlights along the edge threw out a warm orange glow.

'Lou, do you see what I see?'

I pointed to two figures perched on a pontoon dressed as Batman and Robin. We looked closer and sure enough, two young guys were laughing and helping each other to struggle out of their bulky costumes. As we watched, they took everything off and framed in the street light, we could see they were stark naked. Nice bodies though.

'Yours looks good,' Lou pointed and laughed. 'I reckon they're drunk. This always happens at night on the quay! Idiots.'

And she calmly made off towards the life belt that was hanging next to them on the pontoon.

'That's not a good idea,' I heard her shout above the wind. 'The river is nearly in full spate and you're likely to drown.'

Lou was standing with her hands on her hips, serious whilst appreciating the view. I was in fits and enjoying the spectacle not believing they would actually consider jumping in.

'We know you're superheroes,' I managed to quip. 'You don't have to prove it!'

They were having none of it and took the plunge, yelling at the shock of the icy water. Lou threw out the life belt which they grabbed and she hauled them onto the pontoon where they looked more like drowned rats than guys who could save the world, their manly bits having been reduced to the size of fishing bait.

'What is it about water that makes people end up in it?' I asked shaking with mirth, and then Janie Juno reminded me of the playboat, so I shut up and squirmed quietly instead.

8 – Sometimes ... a pair of unlikely earrings can send messages to the universe in a way that lipsticks can't

Max had to stay in London on business for a few weeks and we kept in regular contact via email or phone and occasionally used the webcams on our laptops. He called me at my office late one night and because I was on my own we switched to camera. Mid way through our chat, I began to very slowly unbutton my shirt and when it was undone I opened it with a flourish to reveal a sexy black bra.

I was laughing as all this went on but I carefully clocked his reaction which was priceless. When he'd seen me unfasten the first button he wore an expression of such wide-eyed disbelieving anticipation that I knew I was taking him into new realms. He looked eager and animated as if he'd been ushered into a showroom of Ferrari's and asked to choose one.

When he requested me to pull the cups down and show him my nipples I obliged and if he hadn't been in such good physical condition, it might have finished him off. We'd had a bit of phone sex, too, where we had got down and dirty with each other, and ourselves, which had been good fun and I got the feeling he was missing me.

Perhaps it was the prospect of more webcam voyeurism or perhaps it was out of a genuine fondness for me but, either way, he announced during one of our calls that he would take me to Barcelona in the autumn. As this was still some months away it added to my sense of a future with him and helped assuage my doubts and the warnings of my friends.

I was beginning to believe he was a changed man who was ready to settle down.

With me.

***

The life that was shaping up with him would require additions to my wardrobe by way of cocktail dresses and ritzier casual clothes so it was time to go shopping and I wondered if Janie Juno would like to join me.

'Sorry, Gina, but I've got to finish some work. How about I call in later for a coffee?'

'No worries. I'm off to buy some new lipsticks because rumour has it they're discontinuing my colour.'

'Not your famous red Chanel number 36 Russet Moon!' she gasped mockingly.

'You don't understand. I can chart my victories, and one car crash, by my lipstick moments and it's a looming crisis. I bet Marilyn Monroe never had this problem,' I said defensively. 'Or Lucille Ball!'

'I can't imagine they did.'

'Do you not realise that I would have to go cold turkey to be weaned off them now? It's that serious.'

'I'm sure it is.'

'Bah! You're just humouring me, and you can say what you like but I'm going to hot foot it into town and buy up all the stock I can find. Is there anything you'd like me to pick up for you, even though your lack of compassion doesn't warrant it?'

She knew I was being light hearted but there was some truth in my panic.

'Not really but maybe some dangly earrings if you see anything going cheap that I might like. I'm actually on the lookout for something big and round in mother of pearl.'

'Sounds very specific. What are you up to?'

'You'll see. I'll tell you later.'

I browsed in a few department stores without much enthusiasm and had a coffee outside The Clarence Hotel because the day was fine, sitting at a table overlooking the majestic Gothic cathedral. A recent fund raising drive for its five hundredth year anniversary was under way, incredibly half a millennium, and I imagined for a moment the changing life it had witnessed.

As I sat there, I looked closely at the details of the facade; the gargoyles, saints and other biblical scenes that the stonemasons of the time, and since, had created so perfectly whilst casually observing the mixture of tourists, locals and students looking at it too.

A chap was busking with his guitar and I wondered idly if he was someone famous getting back to his roots because the playing was so good and when I stood up and put some change in his cap on the floor, he began to play a current song that I recognised.

It was possible.

I had managed to buy six Chanel Russet Moons and a pair of earrings for Janie Juno that I thought fitted the bill but as they hadn't cost an arm and a leg, unlike the lipsticks, I decided they would be a present and had them wrapped with a bow. I was looking forward to our time later because I hadn't seen much of her outside of the rowing club.

I made my way back down to the quay via Fore Street and saw the river sparkling in the sunshine. As I walked, I felt light on my feet and the few bags that I had swished gently against me as I strolled along. I said hello briefly to some people I knew and let myself into the apartment block and into my flat. I had just put the kettle on when Janie Juno appeared and we decided to sit on the balcony at the small black metal table and look out onto the water in the late afternoon sun.

'I've got something for you,' I said as I rummaged for the little black box tied with a pink ribbon. 'I hope you like them.'

When I handed it over, her face lit up and she clapped her hands.

'Ooooh for me! For me!' she squeaked and ripped off the ribbon quickly to open the box.

Her eyes widened and she put them on before going to look in the mirror. Her reaction was childlike and heart-warming and I remembered with a little stab of sadness that I couldn't recall the last time I had given anything to a friend.

'They're perfect, Gina. What lovely taste you've got!' she laughed knowing, they had been to her own specification.

'Glad you like them and they look lovely but why do you want them?'

'I've been invited to talk about my recycling project and I want to wear things in that theme. Because mother of pearl is the inner layer of a shell, I thought it would be fitting to show that you can make something from another material that's been discarded.'

She wasn't wrong there.

'What is it that you actually do?' I asked, eager to know.

'I run my own small marketing agency that specialises in helping organisations with social and community aims. Ethics play a big part in it and I stay clear of anything that has faceless shareholders who confine their interest to the bottom line.'

'I've been reading about the rise of social enterprises, is it that the kind of thing? There was an article about a chocolate maker in the papers last week, about how they plough their profits back into the communities they source from.'

'They're actually one of my clients,' she laughed and her face glowed with pride. 'Along with a giant futuristic exotic garden dome and of course, my recycling project which is state of the art. The stats are amazing and that's what I'll be talking about. They've asked me to visit schools and large employers to outline the benefits, not just to mother earth but to describe the feel good factor when you begin to recycle more than you throw away. It's very powerful Gina. They think my strange sing songy voice, no don't laugh, will come over well on the radio and some interviews have been arranged. One is with Jenny Murray on Radio Four's Woman's Hour and I can't wait to meet her, such an icon!'

I knew about recycling of course, but when you thought about it in those terms it started to become personal.

'I make sure we do as much as we can at work but why don't you come in and talk to us too. We'd love it. What made you set up on your own?'

'I did a course in textiles and design at college and started off in retail, working for a natural cosmetics company but because I came up with some good ideas for a marketing campaign they moved me out of branch and into HQ. I think I must have had a good eye for detail and straplines and because I believed passionately about nature and being ethical, I started to define the brand along those lines at a time no-one else was doing it. I encouraged the buyers to go out and look for products around the world and to bring back their stories which I had printed up professionally including photos so that our customers could see what they were buying into.'

'I know the shops you mean. They were really ahead of their time and I went there because of the values they stood for. Was that down to you?'

'In part, but it was a team effort. The woman who headed it was a legend and I got to meet her a few times, she was tiny with a sensational aura. Don't get me wrong though Gina, we had a business to run and margins were tight so I also got involved with pricing and supplier negotiations because we could only continue to support projects if we made money. The time came for me to leave when two things happened within weeks of each other. There was a boardroom coup where I felt the new owners didn't properly understand our core values or connect them with ringing tills, and I had a surprise op.'

'You sound as if you nailed the creative stuff while having a good head for business which makes you a bit of a rare beast.'

'Maybe ... I've never regretted it but the op coming out of the blue when I was in my early thirties was a setback. I went to the doctor for a twinge only to have it turn into something major and I was rushed into hospital to have my ovaries removed. No time to freeze eggs and it was touch and go for a while. It changed my perspective on life and I resolved to do more community based work.'

'You didn't have any children before your problem came to light?' I asked gently.

'No. I was too engrossed in work.'

Her voice was tinged with a resigned sadness.

Janie Juno's face had become animated when she had described her role, revealing both her idealistic nature and the importance she placed on doing something for a higher cause. When she talked about her health, she had become fleetingly wistful and I could see that her career had taken the place of children and her business had become her baby. I didn't want to pull her down so I veered away from the subject when I could.

'Is it hard being a lone worker and not having the security of a salary?'

'I'm hardly ever on my own, technically, and I love the independence of it. I live within my means but manage quite well on the fees I earn. Take shopping for example, I hardly clothes shop, preferring to get stuff from charity shops and use the time I save to go rowing on the water.'

I was genuinely surprised by this because she always looked so well turned out. She had a distinctive style but everything she wore was tasteful and complementary. Incredible to think that it was all second hand but I guess that was part of her recycling ethic too.

'How about you, Gina? You've never really talked about your work?'

'Well, compared to you, it's as dull as ditch water. I'm currently on a project for a large organisation to implement a business control system across all departments supposedly to make things easier but I'm having awful problems with a colleague. Max has been a brick and has contacts that can help, but it's not good.'

'Can't you do something else? Have a change of tack?'

'I think it's too late because it's all I know. In the past I was given a project working with schools to encourage fourteen year olds to think about their own business as a career choice which was fantastically rewarding but it's a long way from what I'm doing now.'

'How did you get into it? Surely you were given careers guidance,' she asked, picking up on my frustration.

'Ha!' I laughed derisively. 'They pushed me down the accounting route because I was known to be good with numbers. No-one ever put my creativity to the test except a big American logistics company that spotted my talent for operational and financial planning in the late eighties and installed me at the heart of their European HQ in Brussels, where I never saw the light of day for five years.'

'That's sad. What did you do, though, I mean actually do, Gina?'

'I covered everything from forensic accounting in tracking down spirited away private jets bought by rogue Italians to creating flight paths for cargo planes on a board like they did in old war films, but for cost optimisation rather than Bomber Command.'

She laughed at my comparison but she was smart enough to realise that it had left me unfulfilled and straining at the leash for a change.

'How long is your project going to last? Is there a way you can take time out afterwards or think about starting something new that you can dovetail and run with when it's over?'

I really hadn't considered anything beyond the end, which was in eighteen months' time, as my energy was going into my day to day mind games with Psycho-Freddie the FD but she had planted a tiny seed in my head nonetheless.

'Shall we open a bottle of wine, Gina, could this be a cause for celebration?' she looked at me lopsidedly.

'I don't know if I would go that far but you've got me thinking and thanks,' I said as I heard the sound of rusty cogs straining to turn in my head.

'Don't be silly, that's what I'm here for. Anyway I meant to say that I'm going to Topsham on my bike next week. It's on the Exe estuary, really pretty town with lovely shops and cafes. Do you want to come?'

All this, I thought, on the back of giving and receiving an inexpensive pair of earrings. My pride had matched her pleasure and the small exchange had given rise to another round of enlightenment. If this is what present giving achieved, I would do it again soon, and often.

9 – Sometimes … secret weapons come in disguises but not the ones that immediately spring to mind

Bella, true to her word sent me detailed instructions on how to get to her place. It had come from her work email address and I noticed she was 'Director of Specialised Insurance Services, Music & Sport.' I took a moment to consider this because there had been nothing about her manner that had hinted at high office responsibility and though Lou had dropped in about her insuring things, it could have meant anything.

She was obviously doing a role that reflected her interests in rowing and playing with the band and somewhere along the line she had a talent for risk assessment. I wanted to find out more.

I arrived at her house on Friday as agreed and knocked on the elegant front door. She turned out to live in a beautiful Victorian terrace on a pretty side road off the high street in a traditional market town located on the eastern side of Dartmoor.

'Oh, Hi, Gina, come on in. I'm about to get my instruments together.'

She busied herself with zipping her drum, guitar and music into their cases and was dressed in jeans and cream jumper with her hair tied up again, for practicality she told me later.

'You found me OK then? Welcome to the madhouse! At least Izzy is away so things are less frantic. Would you like to meet Merlin?'

Nice name for a cat I thought as she led me into the kitchen where I saw a very large and elaborate cage that reached nearly up to the ceiling and was about four feet wide. What kind of cat would need to live in a cage like that I wondered? Eventually it was the noise that gave it away and I could see it was a beautiful blue and yellow macaw parrot who was squawking happily.

'Merlin, say hello to Gina, good boy'

'Hello, Gina'

The parrot spoke with Bella's distinct London accent. I was momentarily stunned to silence then laughed at the surrealism.

'And why exactly have you got a parrot, Bella, I mean aside from it being good company?'

'That is a very, very interesting question. He belonged to a neighbour who had to go away but couldn't take him so she asked me if I could help out for three months. That was eight years ago and we're inseparable. He's very intelligent and beautiful, too, don't you think? You're beautiful aren't you, Merlin?'

She fed him some nuts through the bars of the cage.

'You're beautiful, you're beautiful,' the parrot said in response.

'He comes out and sits on my shoulder if I'm practising my music or watching TV and is really very affectionate.'

If she hadn't been talking in earnest I might have thought it was a joke but she was deadly serious so I dismissed the quips that had fluttered into my head (no pun intended) because I could see I might cause offence, such was the admiration she had for her feathered friend.

'Right then, let's get going. Bye, Bye, honey bun,' she said to the parrot.

'Bye, Bye, honey bun,' the parrot said to Bella.

And I had to bite my lips to stop my laughter erupting.

***

In the car on the way to the pub I asked where her accent was from.

'London, East. Your next question will be how I got here, right?' she smiled.

'Well, I did wonder, because I'd picked it up in the bar the other night.'

'There's not much to tell but I joined a specialist group of insurers straight from school and learned the business from the bottom up. I was always sporty when I was younger, mostly swimming and athletics, competitively so, and I gravitated towards their sports section where I worked my way up the ranks. There was a big reorganisation about seven years ago which coincided with me taking up music to get over my divorce and when they decided to relocate the office to Exeter because it was cheaper, they asked me to head up the division.'

'Did you have to think long and hard about it?'

'For all of five minutes you mean. It was a no-brainer, Gina, and the music and rowing scene here is perfect for me. I travel up to London a couple of times a month to head office but I get to live in the rural splendour of Dartmoor and have a great work life balance.'

'Lou said you underwrite events and people.'

'That's true and I work a good deal with concert promoters and sporting fixtures in case they have to give everybody their money back or get sued. It's fascinating and I enjoy seeing the organising that goes into it. I don't get involved myself but I have to understand it because of the possible risks. If I was ever going to do anything on my own, it would be to set up an events management company but for the moment I'm very happy where I am. Until Izzy finishes her first year at Uni I want to keep things stable as it was tough when her father and I split up.'

So she, too, was happy at work. First Janie Juno, then Lou and now Bella, they were all apparently thriving whilst I was currently stuck in the monotony of dutiful line towing. The dark night cloaked the little car as we crossed the moor, cocooning us in the interior space. The light from the dashboard cast cosy shadows and I faced up to the fact that a plan was needed. Whilst I was considered to be pretty expert at it at work, in my personal life I was rubbish but that would change now I was beginning to get a sense that I might be the organ grinder instead of the monkey. I parked it for later because I needed to think more and besides, I wanted to know what Bella's thoughts were on me and Janie Juno getting to know each other.

'I think she's very good for you, Gina and believe you were destined to meet!' she laughed while looking in her rear view mirror and indicating to avoid a pony. 'She talks common sense and if she's willing to share her insights, which are usually on the nail, you should listen to what she has to say.'

'I'm really grateful to her because I tend to keep people at bay and shy away from making friends because I'm anxious.'

I kept my eyes on the windscreen as I said this.

'Firstly I don't think she wants your gratitude, Gina. She'd prefer you were equals and will do what she can to draw you out of yourself. We're not stupid you know. Coming from the place you've been takes its toll. She'll always be there but remember it goes both ways and she gets a lot from knowing you too. Your take on the world is original and funny. I'm not sure you realise it.'

'My ex once described me as humourless,' I said flatly.

'You! Are you sure? I find that very hard to believe.'

I thought she was exaggerating to be kind.

'Generally I never engaged in having a laugh at work and seeing as on the outside I had no occasion, I just assumed I was.'

'What about your friends?'

I took a deep breath. 'I've struggled to make them. Janie Juno is the first.'

She kept her eyes straight ahead and thought for a second or two before she spoke.

'And she's helped you to come out tonight hasn't she?'

'She talked to me about small stepping stones and it gave me the confidence to take up your offer.'

In for a penny, I thought and blamed it on the cosy car.

'So would you say she did the mirror thing to show you what the rest of us sees?'

She sounded thoughtful.

'Maybe, but it's still early days.'

I recalled the moment in my hallway.

'I can tell you now Gina, you're one of the most relaxed and happy people I've met in a long time. You've made it very easy for me to invite you and chat and I think you've worked out that I'm choosy.'

'I got that feeling but I'm glad you did it. You're like an onion I think, lots of layers of original and interesting things to discover and I'm looking forward to knowing more.'

'Well in that case, when we get back from the pub I might tell you about my secret weapon at work and maybe even about Rob. I know you're dying to ask!' she laughed as we turned into the car park.

I helped her with her drum and guitar as we pushed open the heavy door and almost fell in. The pub was a traditional spit and sawdust with real ale and pewter tankards and a huge fireplace with burning logs that dominated the room. The lighting was low and came from red satin covered lampshades with tassels that were hanging from brass wall lights amongst pictures of hunting scenes in gilt frames with green borders placed haphazardly around the walls that looked to be Georgian.

The guys were playing together in one of the corners and raised their heads briefly in greeting when they saw Bella. I bought us a pint of Bootley and a slimline tonic water and we went over to join them.

'Hi, Gina, Bella said you might come. This is Chris, Tim, Phil and Phil. I'm Bob. Are you going to play anything?'

'Me!' I spluttered, this time spraying Bob with foam.

I made mental note seventy three to stop this habit.

'The only thing I've ever picked up is a tambourine that I used to bash my brother's head with. Last year.'

'You should ask Bella to let you have a go with her spare drum and join in.'

'Maybe another time Bob but for now I'll let you pro's get on with it tonight.'

'We'll hold you to it, won't we, fellas?'

They all nodded in unison.

Better practice.

Made mental note seventy nine.

The pub had filled up and by closing time there was a great crowd. I was a bit the worse for wear because of the lost count number of pints I'd had, along with some pork scratchings and was grateful when Bella took charge and got us both home.

We sat in her kitchen with a pot of coffee and some toast whilst the parrot slept beneath a cover over his cage.

Fair enough.

I was feeling more sober, or at least slightly less drunk, when I remembered her cryptic comments from earlier so I thought I'd start with work and leave the subject of Rob well alone.

'What's your secret weapon then?' I asked, hearing my own slurs.

'It's not common knowledge but I believe I can trust you. I can, can't I?' she was checking me out.

'Of course! Whatever you tell me stays between us. In all likelihood I'll have forgotten it by morning anyway.'

I yawned.

'OK. What I'm about to say must be taken at face value, yes?'

'Yeah, yeah. Whatever you say.'

Of course she had the advantage of knowing what was coming and was enjoying the fact that I didn't.

'OK, brace yourself.'

'Yup, look at me, I'm in position.'

I crossed my arms as in the brace-brace flight safety instruction guide which I always read.

'I can see the future.'

I sat bolt upright and my mouth must have dropped open because she gracefully extended one of her beautiful pointed nails to just under my chin and gently closed it again. Never mind the brace-brace, my arms flopped on the table but my ears pricked up and I instantly became alert.

'What do you mean you can see the future?' I whispered in awe.

'My mum Davina is a clairvoyant and my grandmother was, too. Izzy has the ability but she and I don't use it to tell people's fortunes, though it's possible. I deliberately close myself off to those channels with friends and family but it comes in very useful sometimes at work.'

She smiled slyly.

'Because you can see what's going to happen,' I asked wide eyed and breathless.

'Occasionally, yes. So armed with my statistics and trends for risk assessment, I bring a little extra something to the party.'

She was really laughing now and so was I.

'Bloody Hell! That was the last thing I thought you were going to come out with. What was I saying about you being an onion? Look there goes another layer! Is there any point in me asking about Rob?'

'Not really,' she smiled serenely. 'There's no future in it.'

Bella picked up her cup and drained the last of her coffee whilst I was relieved she hadn't offered me tea.

10 – Sometimes ... you're secretly pleased when your friends take all your valuables

'Hey, Gina, what do you think of us going out in a double and learning to skull, you know, row with both hands instead of one? My dad's single is gathering dust and I'd like to do it for his sake.'

Lou's dad had died suddenly about six months ago and I knew the family were devastated. This was a big thing and it would help her to move on. The trauma had been compounded because it had been Lou who had found him slumped after a massive heart attack and nothing could be done. In his early sixties, he had supposedly been as fit as a fiddle and was one of the longest serving members of the club.

That she asked, made me proud and bolstered my confidence, even though I was still trying to go easy up the slide to take the catch, both to do with coming forward to row, and still had a lot to learn. I desperately wanted to be in the girls' boat and if I could skull I would be able to go out on my own and practice more, which would speed things up for me.

Pete O'Mara thought it was a great idea and agreed to coach us for our first outing. It would involve the infamous loud hailer again and him riding his bike along the towpath

71

next to the canal shouting instructions, but I was prepared this time.

We got on the water on a lovely summer's evening when the quayside was full of people enjoying the weather and everyone was laid back in that typical South West manyana spirit. There was hardly a wind, only a gentle breeze, and we couldn't have wished for better conditions.

'OK, Lou and Gina, take your time to sit the boat and keep it steady on the water. If you can, lift your blades up.'

Wobble, wobble. No good. These things are made of light fibreglass and have sliding seats. Sitting in one is like balancing on a wooden lollipop stick in a swelling sea, my point being that it looks a lot easier than it is.

'OK, try it again.'

His Irish accent was more pronounced when it was magnified.

Better this time.

'Right, come forward to row and practise taking off at the same time. Gina, you follow everything that Lou does and keep to her timing. As you don't have a cox it will be down to Gina to keep looking behind and steer it using the blades. OK, give it a go.'

We got off to a juddering start but picked up the stroke and before long were actually moving in a reasonably competent manner. With both of us in vests, shorts and sunnies and me in a bandana, we rowed elegantly and in unison. Pete was still shouting instructions and I could see that we were attracting admiring glances from the people sitting outside the pubs and the bars.

Up and down we went, careful to duck the low hanging cable for the rope ferry and managing to stay pretty central so we didn't ram the pilings opposite The Prospect Inn.

So far, so good.

We lost Pete a couple of times as he struggled to cycle around the masses who were taking in the evening sun but our confidence was growing and we felt we were mastering the fine boat on which we were precariously perched.

We decided to take a short break at The Port Royal end of the stretch so I whipped out a Chanel lipstick from my cleavage, where I kept it for safety, and did a quick refresher; always important to keep up appearances, especially since we were getting some appreciative looks. After quick sips from our water bottles, we manoeuvred the boat around to go back up river and I saw Pete beckon us over.

'You're both doing very well and I'm going to let you go up and come back on your own. I'll see you later in the club for some pointers. Is that OK?'

'Yeah, we'll be fine. See you later Pete.'

We watched the happy couple, him and the loud hailer, cycle away.

'Hey, Lou, he wouldn't let us do this if we weren't any good would he?' I spoke to her strappy back.

'I think you're right, so how about we start to build up speed and do a few at full pressure.'

'OK, I'll give the nod. Right are you ready? Come forward to row. Row!' I shouted as Pete had done.

And off we went lickety split, easy up the slide, taking the catch, focusing and watching. As we came alongside The Waterfront we could see the admiring glances and as I turned slightly to look over at them, I forgot about the ferry rope and it smacked me on the back of my head. I stopped my stroke in mid flow, which is called catching a crab in the trade, but not before Lou had carried on and the effect destabilised the boat which tipped us into the water bang in the middle of the quay.

The people watching were either horrified or shaking with laughter, take your pick, but no-one could help. Pete had drummed into us that it was essential to stay with the boat for safety so we swam out to where it was floating upside down and managed to right it, treading water as best we could. The blades were still intact because they were secured with screw shut rowlocks so at least that was something.

A group of young guys started to wolf whistle and heckle but we studiously ignored them.

'You alright, Lou?' I asked, holding on tightly

'Yeah. How about you?' She was laughing.

'My pride took a hit but other than that I'm fine and I've still got my lipstick thank goodness!'

'Stuck down there it's going to be as safe as houses. Let's act like this is part of the drill. What do you say?'

'Anything to get us out of here.'

We pushed the boat to the side but still no-one asked if we needed help and they continued to point and laugh. 'OK, OK. The show's over!' Lou shouted back at them. 'Get on with your own lives! Gina, you go first and keep it level so I can get in then we'll get the hell out of waterfall alley and go and find us our own drink. Are you ready?'

I climbed in gingery and tried to hold on to the edge of the river bank, very different from a purpose built pontoon. As Lou stepped in, I lost my grip and the boat tipped over a second time and threw us in again. This time, because we were so near, everyone was dangling over the edge to watch the spectacle, still laughing, jeering and wolf whistling.

'OK, folks, I have to tell you, this is a practice safety exercise so you can all be on your way now, but thanks for your help anyway.'

Lou fired off sarcastically.

We managed to get away on our third attempt but the sun had lost its heat and we were cold and shivering. On the run back to the boat house, we rowed like we had the devil on our tail because ... we ... were ... freezing!

When Pete saw us arrive he rushed out on account of us being late but when he took in our soggy states, his concern turned to amusement.

'Oh dear, what happened? Did the ferry rope accost you?' he laughed gleefully.

'Yup,' we replied in unison.

'Ah bless! Enough said; it happens to us all. Get yourselves warm, showered and changed and I'll wait for you here. Everyone else has gone so it's just us now.'

His lilting accent made him sound like Terry Wogan and though never a massive fan, it was comforting.

The showers were fine in the club but as my place was over the road and I had two bathrooms, and fluffy towels, we decided it would be quicker. I used the en-suite while Lou took the bathroom and we shouted to each other as we got clean and warm.

'Gina, we rowed quicker than Steve Redgrave in the Olympics getting back.'

'I reckon we did too and if it had been official, we would have picked up the gold!'

'Do you think anyone on the quay will recognise us? Seriously?'

'Maybe you, Lou, but I had on my bandana so I'll be fine.'

'Thanks, Gina. I knew I could rely on you.'

Changed and showered we went to find Pete and saw him outside the boatshed locking up.

'Gina, Lou. I'm pleased to see you've changed colour from pale blue to rose pink!'

He was laughing at his own joke.

'Humph, you could be more sympathetic.' I feigned a sulk.

'Gina, I know you're a survivor from our playboat session so I wasn't in the least bit worried about you being alright. And, Lou, I knew your dad for forty years and you're his daughter so I wasn't worried about you either. Aside from providing the drinkers with entertainment did you have a good time or has it put you off?'

He looked from one to the other of us and smiled knowingly.

'We're made of sterner stuff!' I said striking a Mr Universe pose.

Throughout the banter, Pete had his back to the boatshed doors and I was facing him with the quay behind me. Lou stood off to my left.

'Did I see you, Gina, whip out a lipstick at The Port Royal?'

He raised an eyebrow cheekily and took a step forward.

'Moi?' I asked, puckering up my lips and feigning surprise. 'No. That must have been Lou.'

'Gina, I bet you did it when I couldn't see behind me!'

'I'm saying nothing,' I said silkily and took a step backwards.

Keys in one hand, mobile in the other, Cartier watch on my wrist and my favourite Ray Ban's on a rower's string around my neck.

Straight into the quay.

Splash.

I heard their gales of unbridled laughter as the water closed over my head.

Being a veteran of quay encounters, I let myself sink until I stood on the soft mud then bounced back up to the surface. When I eventually broke water, they were leaning over the side rendered almost helpless by their howls but were at least willing to help. I held up my arms to be rescued but was too low down to be hauled up so instead they stripped me of my valuables, the ones I'd had the presence to hold on to, and left me to swim the fifty meters to the pontoon where I could climb out.

So much for friends, I thought.

I dripped over to where they were still holding onto each other wiping their tears and announced that from here on in they were officially no longer my friends and if they attempted to be nice to me at any point in the future I would remind them of their hapless mirth in my moment of need. This set them off again so I stalked off with my nose studiously in the air.

During the session I had gotten to know Lou better and I suppose Pete O'Mara, too. Though we'd fallen in the water, me more than Lou as I just explained, I'd had a lot of fun and made some progress. My friendship with her was turning out to be different to that which I had with Janie Juno, which was different again to Bella. Each was unique in its own way but the common thread was that I felt valued and cared for. When I tried to imagine my bramble infested overgrown path, all I could see was a beautiful walkway strewn with wild Lilly of the Valley and I considered myself lucky. There were no sides or asides to these girls and though I was closest to Janie Juno, Bella and Lou were completely behind my friendship with her and it never precluded any of us from being with the other when we felt like it.

As I squelched into the flat for the second time that night and took a moment to reflect on my quay exploits, I smiled.

I never had this problem back in the Midlands.

11 – Sometimes ... a brooding duck wants nothing more than a tasty cheese sandwich

Psycho-Freddie continued waging internal war against me and managed to find ever more creative ways to derail my project. My theory was of a frustrated mind imploding in on itself, no longer content with his own work he had a perverse need to destabilise me and create dramas where none existed. But there was also the faintest whiff of a sexual undercurrent, which I can honestly say I'd never encountered before, that was fuelling his animosity towards me because I was out of reach. If he couldn't have me, he would bury me.

One day, I found on my desk a three hundred page internal contract from him for the provision of IT (a department which he controlled) for my project. As I scanned it at home later that night, I concluded sadly that it had been intended to be unworkable in order to kill me off in typical psycho style. Effectively, everything would grind to a standstill and it was beginning to get serious as I was falling behind schedule and The Board were asking questions.

The one card I had up my sleeve was a partner of Max's who was an expert in employment law though I sincerely hoped I didn't have to use it, even if things were looking bleak and I was carrying a lot of responsibility. I'd had no luck in finding any leverage against Freddie and I was beginning to privately lose faith in my professional self and abilities.

But just as I reached my darkest hour, the sun began to rise on the horizon.

The Achilles heel that Max had told me to look out for eventually came from an unexpected source when we began applying for our Investors in People award; a straight forward exercise of evidencing positive support and commitment to the staff through our everyday behaviour and procedures. It entailed an impartial consultant coming in who would randomly select people for interview, compile answers to the set questions and report back. If the answers matched the criteria for best practice we would receive the accreditation. It was to be an open and transparent process.

We were mid-way through it all when I was called unexpectedly into my boss's office, who was the CEO of the company. I was still grappling to make sense of Freddie's behaviour and hadn't as yet said anything to anyone because the attacks had been so insidious. Besides, I was the new girl on the block and complaining was only going to get me labelled unfairly as being whingeing, bossy or nagging and as none of these were helpful I had stayed quiet.

When I walked into the palatial chrome and leather office, the CEO was behind his desk wearing glasses and reading a report. He was fantastically ambitious and was called Derek. Originally from Liverpool, he'd left school at sixteen and set up his own market stall which had expanded into a good business. Having tired of it, he'd sold up and funded himself through university and two Masters degrees which wasn't bad going for a boy raised on a council estate in Toxteth.

He stood up and took his glasses off, suddenly looking older than his mid-forties. Quite a handsome chap; tall, dark hair, lean from marathons, he had piercing blue eyes that he had to adjust to kindliness. He'd been open in the interview process but since then had retreated behind his public persona which I found unsettling. He called the shots as to the tone of our engagements and I simply followed, though rarely did we ever discuss anything personal.

He knew about my rowing which he had no choice other than to publicly endorse though I think he resented my early departure twice a week. We kept banter to a minimum and remained professionally focussed on the business whenever we were alone together.

'Hi, Gina, thanks for coming up.'

His office took up most of the top floor whilst mine was a tiny hovel at the back next to the car park. As there was no lift, going up and down six flights of stairs in the mock castle turret wearing Kurt Keigers was no mean feat but thanks to my rowing and my newly applied lipstick, I was composed.

'Take the weight off your feet, sit down.'

He motioned to the chair on the other side of the desk and smiled, without sincerity. His attempt at light heartedness put me on alert and I watched closely as he retook his seat.

'How's it all going?'

He knew from my regular updates that we were falling behind.

'On the whole, I'm hopeful we can still bring it in on time. We're losing ground on IT but I'm confident we can pull it back from other activities at the point of roll out.'

This was true.

'How do 'you' think it's going, Derek?' I asked him pointedly.

'I'm impressed that you're making headway with Freddie. I know he's not always easy but he means well.'

More like he makes it easy for you I thought. As long as you let him do his own thing and the figures continue to add up, you're free to do what you like doing best which is getting your face out there and playing the big shot. I didn't reply.

'Have you spoken to Maggie, the Investors in People consultant?'

He knew that I had.

'Yes, she saw me last week, routine questions that I answered honestly if a little strategically.'

'She was very impressed with you.'

I had been impressed with her too, but chose to remain silent.

'But a problem has come up.'

He continued looking down at the report.

'Something she's never encountered before and feels duty bound to bring to my attention before she makes her final recommendation.'

He was shuffling his papers nervously, interspersed with the odd chin rub and I smelt a rat. A big black hairy one and I steeled myself.

'Maggie has shared with me informally that she believes there is something akin to a fifth column snaking its way through the organisation that is intent on destroying someone. That someone is you.'

Well there's a surprise, I thought, and then the seriousness of the situation kicked in as I realised someone was deliberately out to harm me. It was the stuff of Michael Crichton horror and I felt sick. Not queasy or faint or light headed, properly sick, to the very pit of my stomach. With a herculean effort, I managed to re-arrange my features so that when he eventually looked up, my emotions were back under control and my face was expressionless.

'How has this come to light, exactly?' I asked coolly with a well-placed note of sarcasm that I didn't feel.

'She said that when she had been speaking with Freddie's staff, everyone at the end of their interview, when she had asked if they wanted to add anything, had been negative towards you and your methods. It was the consistency of the words they used and the vitriol with which they spoke that alarmed her. Already concerned, it came to a head when someone admitted they'd been given a note that instructed them to say bad things about you under threat to themselves.'

This time I couldn't contain my disbelief, or anger.

'You're joking!' I spluttered as the weight of the implications hit me. 'Who would do such a thing?' I gasped.

He looked uncomfortable and I saw a thin line of sweat break out on his upper lip which he tried to surreptitiously wipe away.

And then I understood.

He had set his jaw to steady himself, knowing as he did, that he could no longer duck the Freddie problem. The Investors award had just evaporated and The Board would want to know why.

I calculated quickly that if I could get Maggie to go on record and get copies of her interview notes, I could sue. Max's partner would have a field day with this; an organised smear campaign against a legally responsible director of the company with individuals being threatened if they didn't partake. It was the stuff of tabloids.

Alarming to think that whilst I had been diligently trying to get on with the job I'd been hired for, dark forces were at work to derail me. I felt a whisper from Machiavelli reach through time and I adjusted my position to cover an involuntary shiver. I swallowed and moistened my dry mouth before I spoke, lest I croaked.

'Derek, have you given any thought as to how you want to proceed?' I asked carefully, wanting to hear what he was thinking, knowing he wouldn't have called me in without having considered his options; he'd been around too long not to be battle-ready.

I also knew that his biggest problem was his ego and the tacit agreement that existed between him and Freddie which allowed Derek to lord it over his cronies whilst Freddie took control of the pennies. Think Tony Blair and Gordon Brown here (Ex British Prime Minister and the Chancellor/Prime Minister in waiting) and you get it. Who exactly was pulling whose strings?

Now, I'm no schemer but I was so angry that I became determined to get something out of it. I had been made to lose sleep and question my professional abilities at a difficult personal time. I had uprooted myself to a different part of the country to take this job knowing I could do it standing on my head only to find it was being made un-necessarily arduous by a despot.

My Scottish protestant ethic, inherited from my parents, believed that hard work paid dividends and I actually liked working, being the sort who preferred to add value by creating new things and opportunities, not by swishing around the same money or fancy accounting. Anyone could turn a profit with numbers and history had plenty of corporate collapses who had failed to innovate except in the one area of financial reporting.

I waited to hear what he had to say.

'Well, Gina. That's a good question.'

Too right it was.

'Freddie is really good at his job. He's been in it for forty years and knows everyone there is to know. It's been useful to the business especially in helping me to get established in the right networks quickly. He's been an asset.'

Interesting, but I had already worked that out for myself.

'He's due to retire in a few years and perhaps the strain is getting to him.' He spoke slowly but each word had been carefully chosen and rehearsed. 'How would you feel if we put this behind us and he apologises to you?'

Never accept the first offer.

'I think it's a bit more serious than that, Derek. There is tangible evidence that he has tactically undermined a new female colleague and possibly her predecessor. My reputation in delivering this project on time is at stake and has been threatened by his actions.'

Negotiate, negotiate, negotiate.

'I see what you're saying but I guarantee you will have all the necessary resources at your disposal to meet the deadline.'

Good offer, getting close but no cigar.

'I think a bonus would be in order, too, Derek with half now and half on completion.'

The bonus idea, rather than compensation would be face saving for him and avoid awkward questions so I knew he would be prepared to pay more for it. My heart was pounding but I remained outwardly calm noticing he didn't flinch. The barrow boy in him had planned for this eventuality and he had a number in mind. My challenge was not to sell myself too cheaply and I quickly did the maths on a tribunal payout, along with the adverse publicity. I noticed ironically from the big calendar on his desk that the date was Friday the thirteenth.

'Yes, I've been thinking along similar lines. How about fifty grand paid as you say, half now, half at the end?'

His eyes narrowed and he looked at me piercingly. The smile was crocodilian.

'I think a year's salary is closer to the mark.' I said easily as I crossed my legs and carefully folded my hands in my lap so he wouldn't see them trembling.

'Ah, Gina, you fight a hard bargain but I think we can just about stretch to it.' His tone was oily. 'I'm going to propose that the three of us go out to lunch at The Castle next week to set the scene for going forward. The food is excellent there.'

'I don't think so Derek.' I stood up, smoothing down my black pencil skirt and picking an imaginary speck of fluff from it. 'It's your job to explain the finer points of this to Freddie.'

I made towards the door and began to open it.

'Oh and by the way, if there is the slightest and I mean the slightest return to his previous outlandish standards of behaviour or any of you for that matter, I'll see you in court. Thanks, it's been very illuminating.'

I opened the door and closed it quietly behind me with a gentle click.

My heart was racing descending the stairs and I needed fresh air desperately. Dropping back into my office, I quickly told my PA I was going out for a sandwich, grabbed my mobile and headed off to the park to sit by the river and take stock.

I found a bench in the sun where a mother duck was leading her ducklings to the water and watched as she gathered them, the mere sight of it lifting my spirits and re-settling me. The air was still and I breathed deeply before calling Maggie.

'Hi, Gina, I thought you would be in touch. I guess you've spoken to Derek. This is honestly the first time I've encountered such pre-mediated destructive intent. Are you alright?'

'I think so and thanks, Maggie. It was a bit of a shock between you and me but I'm over it now and Derek is in the process of making changes.'

I didn't elaborate on what they were. That was between him and me.

'Can I help in any way? I was personally appalled. You are such a professional and your enthusiasm for your staff was a credit to you.'

'Would you be prepared to go on record, put it down in a private letter to me?'

'Of course, Gina. I'll do it straight away given the seriousness of the situation. Absolutely. You do know it's criminal?'

'I do indeed. Could you send it to my home address please Maggie, in Exeter.'

'I didn't know you lived there. I do, too. Let's meet up for lunch one day, soon.'

'I'd like that but let's promise not to talk about this or it'll likely put us off our food!' we both chuckled.

She agreed to get something in the post that night and I rang off.

The next call was to Max.

'Dinner on me tonight, I've had a bit of luck.'

When he asked why, I told him it would keep but to take it easy for the rest of the afternoon to build his strength up for later. Down the phone, though he said nothing, I could hear his thoughts and smiled knowingly to myself. We said our goodbyes and arranged to meet at his place.

When I went over the events of the last half hour they seemed incredible but the thing that struck me the most was that I'd had the courage to stand up for myself and use the situation to my advantage; to take something from it on my terms. This shift undoubtedly had its origins in having the support of a tight network of strong female friends outside of work to draw on.

In Derek's office, Janie Juno, Bella and Lou had all stood figuratively alongside me and I had negotiated from a position of our combined strength to achieve significant concessions. It was a revelation to me that our connectedness could wield more power than the sum of our individual parts as I totted up my gains. I had Freddie off my back, a limitless deadline budget to protect my reputation, and a windfall I would bank most of to give me a financial cushion and new possibilities.

Not only had I survived the actions of a warped individual intent on bullying me for his perverted gratification, I had triumphed.

With little appetite for the sandwich in my hand, I fed it instead to Lucky Ducky and opted to take the rest of the day off to make a long weekend of it. I would take some time to prepare for the night ahead where Max would be the happy beneficiary of my undivided attention and to visit the stationers to pick up some folders for an idea that was beginning to form.

And if I happened to be passing the Merc garage on my way, I might just drop in for a little look.

12 – Sometimes ... when someone calls you darling you think of tasty crabs

We caught the small ferry across the water to Teignmouth and only remembered that the jazz festival was on when we saw the world and his dog spilling out from the bars and pubs along the old back quay. We were headed for The Ship where Max had luckily booked a table for eight o'clock. I had decided against telling him about the shenanigans at work as I needed some respite for a few hours and didn't want it to dominate our time together, it would easily wait until dinner.

The evening was warm and the sunset down river towards Dartmoor was a majestic spread of all shades of pink. We got off the ferry and walked along the back beach seeing little boats bobbing optimistically as the waves gently lapped the shore. I loved it here because the houses that fronted it were all shapes and sizes, bunched in together and very slightly down at heel. People lived there year round and the lifestyle was casual and unhurried. It was a place that was comfortable with itself and different to Salcombe, forty miles along the coast, where houses were the second home play things of investment bankers who did them up with more money than taste.

Opposite The Ship was a crab shack where you could order and collect but they also sold pots of fresh crab meat practically straight off the boat. Mitch, the owner had told me once in the pub about supplying it for a US President's visit but had signed something to prevent him from saying. Just another tall story perhaps but I knew he had a couple of boats and made a fortune selling into London's Borough Market which was frequented by the top chefs.

Max seemed happy and was appreciative of my (no bra needed) secret support vest and (no knickers wanted) casual shorts. It had turned him on discovering I was wearing very little during a passionate kiss earlier when he'd glided his hands over my body. His good mood was further helped because his toes had healed and I liked to think he was looking forward to our night together.

'What'll you have, darling?'

He had his arm around my waist, pulling me into him and had whispered in my ear.

Had he just called me darling? My brain and heart did somersaults at the very idea and I was momentarily stunned as if an electric current had passed through me. Incredibly he had, and my shock gave way to a warm flush of happiness.

'Pint of Bootley please, Max. I'll save the wine for dinner.' I smiled lovingly at him.

'Good idea and I'll do the same. Be right back and I'll check in for the table, too. I think we were lucky to get it.'

He kissed me again then started for the throng at the bar.

I stayed outside in the last of the sunshine, where the music floated above the people noise. A jazz quartet on a raised make shift stage between the crab shack and the place that made the odd little stone statues was banging out a John Coltrane number and despite it being a complicated piece to play, it sounded good.

My mind wandered invariably to Max and I thought about the 'darling' of just now, knowing that I had definitely heard right. Could this be it? Could he be the one? I looked over at the sky and when a doubt appeared in the form of a small black cloud, I reasoned that Janie Juno and the girls didn't know him as I did so their warnings couldn't be valid. I threw caution to the wind and sought any excuse I could find to ignore the advice of my friends.

He'd been kind and attentive and the previous week had taken me to a Summer Ball where all the great and good of the local property market, from estate agents to developers, had gathered. Everyone had been dressed up to the nines but had let down their hair in spectacular fashion, with amongst other things a full-sized authentic fairground dodgems ride. These guys really knew how to party. His firm had taken a table and around it were some of his other associates and their wives. Surely he wouldn't have invited me unless he was serious?

Max emerged and I parked my musings as it was still too early for us to broach the future but in our contentment of the moment I was confident it would come soon.

'Here's your pint, Gina, and the table is confirmed. We've enough time to savour it and take in the music. Good?'

'Excellent and glad we didn't miss it. I'm enjoying myself.'

I leant into him and watched as he drank, handsome in sunglasses, and saw others looking at us admiringly which added to my sense of having a place at his side. A slight wind had got up, and with the sun dipping quickly, it had grown cold and I shivered.

'Take this.' He handed me the jumper he was wearing loosely around his shoulders. 'Let's go inside.'

As he guided me forward with his hand in the small of my back, we were shown to a cosy table in the middle of the heaving restaurant. It had been done out in stained pine and old fishing nets with kitsch sailing memorabilia hanging on the walls and lighting that came from hurricane lamps. Everyone was animated and the atmosphere was buzzing.

'They get their crab from Mitch next door so I'll go for one of those. What about you?'

'Same here and, Max, as this is on me, I propose we go for a bottle of Pouilly Fume. No expense spared.'

He looked confused for a second then thumped his forehead.

'Sorry, Gina. You said you'd had some luck and it went completely out of my mind. Did you get a pay rise?'

He laughed, knowing how unlikely it was given what I had already told him about Psycho-Freddie.

'Well act-u-ally.' I pronounced each syllable slowly, 'I did, sort of. More like a bonus really.'

'Are you sure?'

He became suspicious as his lawyer's nose began to twitch and he looked at me with a raised eyebrow. I told him the whole sorry tale and when I'd finished he puffed up his cheeks and blew out some air.

'How confident are you of getting the letter?' he asked shrewdly.

'Highly. It's winging its way as we speak.'

'Would you like Beth, the employment partner at the firm to take a look and hold onto it for safe-keeping? The office in London is secure you know.'

'Yes to both ideas. It makes sense in case I need to use it.'

'Have you earmarked the money for anything?' He asked a little too casually.

'Funny you should ask me that.'

I laughed and took a big swill of my wine to prolong the moment.

'Well, have you?'

I could see the suspense was killing him.

'Yes, I put down a deposit on a silver CLK convertible at the Merc garage. All being well, I collect it at the end of the month. Cheers, Max!'

I raised my glass to his look of incredulity, without mentioning my other idea.

He whistled through his teeth. 'I've got to hand it to you, Gina, it took guts to stand up to them and you dealt with it smartly. I propose a toast to Gina, The Invincible.'

'And to absent friends.' I said, thinking of the girls.

We laughed until the waitress looked at us disconcertingly then we put our serious faces back on and laughed again at our studied expressions. It was a companionable moment where we were united in our playfulness and with each passing second, I hurtled closer to the abyss.

I felt my story had earned me respect. After all, he was a man of money, in a world of money where deal making was the Holy Grail. In having the presence of mind and corporate know how, I had hammered out my own deal with the toads of Taunton (Derek and Freddie) and shown my metal. They had seen I wasn't someone to be trifled with and I hoped it would work in my favour with Max.

Our sex that night was more akin to love-making because of how I felt about him. Whilst enjoyable and prolonged, it was less hurried and our bodies responded with familiarity. He had entered me as we had stood in front of the bedroom picture window and I had placed a foot on the sill to be better able to accommodate all of him for our mutual pleasure. We had also made love in the shower where we had soaped each other before hopping into the big bed and falling asleep with arms and legs entwined.

Breakfast the next morning was a leisurely affair at the Coffee Rush where we sat outside in the sunshine and ate croissants. He'd been carrying a magazine which now lay casually on the table and with his mouth half full he opened it to a page earmarked for a forthcoming jewellery auction at Bonham's.

'You like your jewellery, Gina, and they've got some lovely things coming up. Look at this one here.'

He jabbed his finger several times on a picture of a pretty ruby ring in the shape of a flower.

'I was thinking of going myself. Will you join me?'

He had finished chewing and was wiping his mouth.

What was there to say? Wild horses wouldn't have stopped me and my heart was pounding with giddy excitement. In truth, I was thrilled beyond words. Was this his way of telling me he was feeling the same and wanted to give me a wildly extravagant love token as a sign of his commitment?

'Of course, it would be my pleasure,' I finally managed to get out once I trusted myself enough to speak.

13 – Sometimes ... a nightdress travels from Tara to Topsham

After Max had shown me the photo of the ruby ring, I was floating on a cloud of possibility and I struggled to reign in my emotions and stay grounded. It was difficult when everything he was doing, saying and suggesting was adding up to a life of companionable times ahead and my imagination was crammed with images of us in the future; laughing, talking, making love, socialising and travelling.

He was perfect for me and I considered myself lucky on many levels; the main one being that he had led me across the emotional quagmire of my divorce to the promised land of lasting love and contentment. He had made it easier than I had expected and my gratitude was fuelling my love and optimism.

All the pieces seemed to be fitting into the picture of us living happily ever after and a flicker of warm affection that started in my heart pulsed steadily and slowly around me.

I was standing in the kitchen looking out the window at nothing in particular as these thoughts and feelings surfaced but then I abruptly remembered the time. I was due to meet Janie Juno in the bike storage shed in ten minutes for our ride to Topsham so I carefully re-wrapped my musings in their pink satin ribbon and added them to my burgeoning virtual pile before going to the bedroom to dig out some shorts.

***

'Hi Gina, seems a while since I've seen you.'

She was energetically inflating her front tyre with a hand pump and was a little breathless, 'another beautiful day! Do you know the way?'

'I've only been by car, so not really,' I said unlocking my own bike.

'It's pretty flat you'll be pleased to hear. We follow the canal to the swing bridge then take a path along the edge of the estate to the outskirts. From there we can cycle on the main road into town and hope the museum is open because of a nightdress I want to show you.'

'Why?' I drew the word out as an image of a pink floral winceyette thing sprang to mind.

'No patience, that's your problem. You'll just have to ride quickly to find out.'

'If you say so,' I shrugged, thinking it strange but then Janie Juno wasn't your average travelling companion so there must be more to it and only time would tell.

We set off in bright sunshine, cycling side by side, and when the path became too narrow, she took the lead. Along the canal we saw birds and wildlife and stopped to watch as a cormorant did battle with an eel. At one point the eel got away but the bird was determined and we rooted for both of them because of the good fight they put up. Sadly there was no happy outcome and eventually the eel tired and got eaten.

I saw a tiny corn bunting further ahead and we stopped to watch it clinging onto the swaying reeds but other than that we were mostly silent as we focused on not falling off. The gentle breeze kept us cool and the path was easy. Half an hour later we arrived at The Lighter, a pub on the wharf next to the old warehouse which was now an antiques centre.

We sat on a bench table in the sunshine looking across to the other side of the estuary where the ferryman would go if you paid him, and drank large glasses of chilled wine which were refreshing in the heat.

'It's so peaceful here and the incoming tide will cover the mudflats soon. I like it when it's full of water.'

'Me too, Gina, but those bird watchers will have to keep an eye out or they'll be stranded.'

She pointed over to the hordes of twitchers who were looking at something intently.

'Are those Avocets?' I asked incredulously, knowing they were almost extinct in the UK.

'They certainly are. We're lucky don't you think?'

'Reason one thousand and sixty seven to be down in the South West. I wonder if Max knows. I'm seeing him later and I'm sure he'll be interested. What are you up to?'

I glanced at my phone and saw that Bella had rung.

'I'm meeting up with Gaz,' she laughed but didn't look at me and sipped her wine.

Because of the sunglasses it was difficult to fathom her expression.

'Someone from work?' I asked but the name rang a bell.

'No, not work. He's er, he's a sort of friend. He lives on the quay on the opposite side to us.'

'Do I know him?'

'Not sure. He drinks in The Sailor's Inn. Tall, blond, fortyish, very good looking but wears a tracksuit along with some dodgy white trainers, a bit chavvy and not my usual type. He's a labourer on a building site.'

My curiosity was rising like the mercury and I could barely contain myself but let her go on.

'We got talking about three months ago when he recognised me in the pub as one of the rowers he admitted to having the hots for, and asked if I lived close by. I pointed to the apartments and the next day he pressed the entry buzzer. I let him in and we sat on the sofa ... you're going to love this, Gina. Are you ready?'

'Of course, of course! Spill the beans, I'm all ears.'

'As we sat there with a cup of tea, he told me he had a hard on that was pressing uncomfortably against his trousers, no preamble, no guile, nothing and then ... are you definitely sure you want to hear this?'

She was still laughing.

'I do, I do ...'

'Are you certain?'

She raised an eyebrow, taking her glasses off and pretended to wipe them, being deliberately playful.

'Just tell me!' I shouted and saw people raising their heads.

'He unceremoniously whipped his willy out.'

'He did WHAT?' I gasped, in a mixture of horror and salacious curiosity.

'Well, as you can imagine, Gina, I was more than a little surprised but it was one of the friendliest and biggest I've ever seen and within minutes we were in a clinch. He deftly got rid of my clothes but for some reason that I can't remember, I'd put on some white lace French knickers that morning which he loved.'

She had leaned in closer and lowered her voice in response to the keen interest the guys at the next table were taking.

'So what did you do?'

'What do you mean, what did we do?' She rolled her eyes. 'I'm going to tell you this but you must promise not to tell a soul because there's quite a bit more to it.'

'I promise, I promise,' I squeaked and crossed my heart with my fingers.

'I'll hold you to it or I'll think of something really horrible to do if you don't!'

She finished off the last of her wine.

'OK then, if you're sure, but let's get another drink first.'

I trotted off to the bar for what would be our third large glass and nipped to the toilet, predictably reeling from what I was hearing. There must be a reason for her telling me so I would just have to stay with it to the end.

I checked in the mirror that everything was safely re-secured in shorts and vest and applied a new coat of lipstick. I managed to carry our drinks back to the table, even if I was swaying slightly and saw Janie Juno cut a glamorous figure sitting there primly with her dark glasses, looking fit and tanned in her cycling gear. No-one could have guessed what was on her mind.

'Thanks, Gina. This is slipping down a treat,' she said slurring her words. 'Cheers!'

She swallowed and coughed as it went down the wrong way and was starting to develop a slightly feral look, as was I. She hiccupped and carried on, wiping her mouth roughly with the back of her hand.

'We moved to the bedroom and had a lot of fun watching ourselves in the sliding door mirrors. In fact I'd go further,' she leaned in again. 'We adjusted our positions so we could get a better look and had some of the best sex on the planet, ha!'

She banged the wooden table with the palm of her hand laughing loudly and then people really did start to look at us.

'Shush! We'll be asked to leave.'

I gave my best indulgent and knowing smile to the surrounding tables and noticed her glass was empty again.

'So he could fully appreciate my knickers, the white French lacy ones ...'

'You already said that.'

'Oops, sorry. Did I? Well anyway, to give him a better view, Gaz asked me to get on top with my back to him so he could see them on my bottom as he did his thrusting. He eased me up and down until I squealed and gave me more orgasms than either Linda Lovelace or Emmanuelle had in their whole careers! He was so straightforward about everything with no hang-ups and in the course of it all he told me I was a brilliant fit and could feel my, you know, er fanny muscles which he put down to rowing. He also said that I had the prettiest box he'd ever seen.'

She was convulsed and wiping her eyes.

I wasn't sure what she meant so I stayed quiet, in mesmerised stupor.

'Gina, I didn't know what my box was,' she blew her nose loudly. 'So I asked someone who explained it was my front bottom.'

'Is that what you call it?'

I was in fits.

'Well don't you? I was always taught to, at school and at home.'

She was serious.

'I've heard it called some things but never a front bottom!' I giggled.

'Anyway, he eventually ran out of steam, but because I didn't rush off to the bathroom it turned him on and we did it again. That night I had to run a salt bath and walked like an Egyptian for days. At one point I even considered going to A&E,' she whispered conspiratorially and reached for her wine.

Realising it was all gone she grabbed mine instead and downed it before I could say anything.

'Gina, your face is a picture! You look like someone who's just walked in on their mum and dad for the first time.'

I shook my head in absolute incredulity at what she'd just told me and tried to assimilate my thoughts.

'So do you go out with him or what?'

I still didn't get it.

'God no! There's no conversation, it's simpler than that. We meet up now and again and have an afternoon of no strings sex at his place, and sometimes his mate joins in.'

Her expression was defiant but skittishly challenging and she knew she'd served up a plate of something I'd never eaten before.

'So what do you think of that then?'

She was revelling in my bewilderment and incomprehension.

'Is that all there is to it? Don't you feel anything for him?' I spluttered.

'He's quite funny and we have a good laugh, but neither of us is interested in anything more. We've agreed to end it as soon as one of us finds someone else but for the moment the two of us, or sometimes three,' and here she grinned suggestively, 'take it for what it is.'

I tried to put aside the various images that were popping into my head and realised I felt the stirrings of pity because she was missing out on the joy of real lovemaking, the sort that I had with Max.

'Would you ever consider having a proper relationship?' I asked evenly.

'Like you, Gina, you mean?'

She raised an eyebrow. 'I've had people in the past who were important but it would have to be someone pretty special to put myself through the trials and tribulations that you do with Max. I just prefer things uncomplicated, at least for the time being.'

'What do you call him?' I asked as I tried to appear worldly.

'Gaz of course! But what you really mean is what label do I give him? Assuming I want to.'

'He's not your boyfriend?'

'Definitely not! But if I had to Gina, I'd call him my shag buddy. There, I've said it.'

She started giggling again and I understood what she meant by her 'Non-relationship' status. As I absorbed her behaviour and rationale my thoughts began to realign in a shift of attitude. I slowly grasped that the two of them had cooked up a simple arrangement which provided mutual satisfaction without the huge emotional investment of becoming attached. They were connected, but that was different.

If it went against the perceived wisdom that sex without love leaves you empty and hollow, I reminded myself of my own marriage and wondered who had been kidding who? Janie Juno might be on to something and having a good bout of sex at least once in your life was no mean thing, so who was I to judge?

So I didn't.

The nightdress we eventually got to see, after several strong coffees, had been worn by Vivien Leigh in Gone with The Wind. Her first husband's sister, unlikely as it seemed, had lived in Topsham and there was a room in the museum dedicated to the actress. The gown was displayed on a headless model in a glass case and was off white silk with a ruffled neck, tiny and exquisite.

I loved the movies, and knew the film, so was more than a little star struck. It affected and excited me in the same way that seeing a pair of Dorothy's ruby slippers had done some years before and though I didn't have any inkling, my own Hollywood moment lay just around the corner.

14 – Sometimes ... James Bond doesn't have a license to kill just when you need it

When Maggie's letter arrived, I decided to do as Max had suggested and lodge it for safekeeping with his employment lawyer. It contained a frank and to the point summary of what had occurred. I let Derek and Freddie know it existed by dropping in a few words casually at our next meeting but received only the slightest nod of acknowledgement. I also made a point of telling them it wasn't kept at my home as I didn't put it past either of them to burgle me Watergate style.

With work now re-stabilised, albeit because of the 'smoking gun' letter, I had more time to focus on my personal life and decided to throw a party. Throughout my marriage, there had been no such desire, let alone opportunity so this was a big departure for me.

I gathered the girls together and we chatted over coffee in Mangoes, the cafe on the quayside.

'I'm thinking of holding a soiree,' I announced grandly with a flourish, and more confidence than I felt.

'Oh yes please!' They echoed as one.

'When are you having it?' Lou asked, taking a mouthful of chocolate brownie.

'What about to coincide with the fireworks on the quay at the beginning of the Festival?' Bella said excitedly. 'The flat will have the best views in town. It'll be perfect.'

'Me and Janie Juno had a quick chat earlier,' she nodded enthusiastically, 'and we've come up with a James Bond theme. What do you both think?'

'It's a great idea and I already know what to come as,' Lou said gleefully. 'You might regret inviting Jonnie and me because we're going to look so good.'

She struck a theatrical pose.

Janie Juno had told me privately that she'd had an idea too but wanted to keep it a secret so I steered the conversation away from costumes.

'How about we make it a cocktail party,' said Bella. 'I know how to make a mean Marguerita.'

'And there's a book at M&S I could look through for ideas.'

Lou was clapping her hands together happily.

'Who do you think we should invite?' I asked.

'Only beautiful and interesting people,' said Bella and Janie Juno agreed. She'd been urging me to do something so she could invite her eclectic mix of friends that included Pablo the starving artist and a children's author called Mike.

'Let's make a list and think about invitations. We'll need to get cracking because it's only three weeks away,' Lou said as she went to the counter for paper and sat down thoughtfully.

'So who do we know who is beautiful and interesting?' she asked chewing the end of the pen. 'You first, Bella, you know everyone.'

We managed thirty names, some who we all knew from the rowing club like Pete O'Mara and others who were friends of one or other of us. I had Maggie on the list because she had gone out on a limb and of course Max, whom I pictured myself with; our arms entwined sharing cocktails and laughing at a private joke, everyone commenting on the lovely couple we made.

Janie Juno got Pablo and Mike on the list while Lou offered a musician who'd made it big with a song about clocks whose family had known hers for years and a young female soul artist she'd been to school with; Jess or Joss somebody or other. We also agreed to ask Joanna, a successful business woman who lived in the apartment block and who was an older very elegant lady but fun loving. Lou's widowed youthful mum Stephanie, who also knew Joanna, was invited as well.

I had kept in touch with Kasim, an ex-colleague of mine from the Midlands, whose family had come over from Pakistan just after the partition in the late 1940's. A sweet and lovely man a few years younger than me, we spoke regularly on the phone and he'd been a great support when I split from my ex. I still confided in him but was careful as I knew he hoped for more than friendship and it was only my circumstances which had prevented it. I was married when we met, then the upheaval of the divorce and now Max. We were just good friends with a long standing date for him to visit on the weekend of the party so it all tied in together nicely.

All told, we had a broad spread of interesting and unusual people and with cocktails a plenty plus the fireworks, it had the promise of being a good night.

I had seen Max when I could but he had been busy and my rowing was taking up weekend time which didn't appear to be a problem for him. Thanks to my extra skulling practise I was miraculously in the boat with Janie Juno, Bella and Lou. We were training with Pete O'Mara and they were all helping me to catch up on technique. I was seeing a lot of them and our friendship had accelerated in parallel to us coming close to winning our first few races. I was changing shape rapidly and had dropped another dress size. My complexion had lost its office greyness and had taken on a healthy hue, just like Lou's when I had first encountered her and all things considered, I was feeling healthy and happy.

The party in truth had been Janie Juno's idea and once she understood that I hadn't been to or given one in decades, she threw herself into the organisation even though I knew she was busy with her own work.

The build up to it proved to be enjoyable and was an absorbing distraction so the time passed quickly between our early inklings and it actually happening. Between us, we printed and sent out invitations featuring the famous 'down the gun barrel' image and set about perfecting our cocktail making. It had been easy to decide on Vodka Martinis (shaken not stirred) along with Margueritas and Prosecco for those who fancied fizz.

Janie Juno had kept her outfit a surprise but I had chosen to go as Rosa Klebb (From Russia with Love), the KGB spy with the spikes on the back of her shoes which I had coincidentally seen on a trip to New York.

The shoes not the spy.

I had adapted an old pair of my own to good effect and sexied up my potentially staid outfit by cutting a big slit in the skirt to offer a glimpse of black lace stocking top and thigh.

Kasim, who had arrived the night before, had decided to put on his tux and come as James Bond himself. Though his Asian colouring wasn't quite authentic, he nonetheless looked striking, having a touch of the Omar Sharif's about him and I hoped he might meet someone tonight.

Janie Juno had arranged to arrive earlier than the others to help with the set-up so when I opened the door and she stood there looking astonishing in a black ring master's outfit (Maud Adams, Octopussy), complete with top hat, whip and fish net tights I was rendered speechless. She laughed at my awe struck expression, flicked her hair and asked if I was going to invite her in.

As I stood aside, she strode forward and looked around, asking eagerly where Kasim might be hiding as she wanted to meet him. It was fair to say that when he emerged from his room and they clapped eyes on each other, there was no going back. I smiled to myself as I realised that Gaz was about to become history and watched from the other side of the room as he kissed her politely on the cheek, while his eyes roamed over her in delight. I left them to answer my mobile phone that was ringing insistently.

'Hi Gina, how's it going?'

I could hear Max was phoning from a travelling car.

'All good here, we're waiting for the first guests. How about you?'

I began to get a sinking feeling.

'Well, to be honest I'm stuck in traffic on my way back from visiting Charlie at Uni in Bath.'

He hadn't mentioned he was seeing his son today. 'I think I'm going to be very late, if I get there at all. I am so sorry. You will forgive me, won't you?'

I couldn't make out if this was a request or a statement but what could I say? He knew I viewed family visits with children as sacrosanct and so not wanting to appear trite, I kept my voice light.

'Oh dear, poor you. Nothing to apologise for and if you're unable to make it, I understand completely. Do feel free to drop in though, time permitting. You know you're welcome,' I said in a forced syrupy tone that almost choked me.

Alarm bells pealed and I questioned whether his timing had been deliberately chosen to coincide with everyone's arrival so I would be powerless to respond. I felt he'd manipulated me and was indignant at being wrong-footed.

'Thanks Gina, I knew you'd understand and if I don't make it, I'll phone tomorrow. Must dash, coming up to a roundabout.'

And with that he was gone.

I struggled to understand why tonight of all nights he had chosen to absent himself when he knew I wanted to introduce us as a couple. I was heavily tempted to drive over to his place to check if he was lying but dug deep for some self respect and held out against demeaning myself. The people would be here in a matter of minutes and I needed to focus and calm down.

I went to the kitchen to check on the food, feeling rattled that he'd pulled a fast one and had out-manoeuvred me, and annoyed that he had made me question his behaviour. When I opened the window for air, I felt trust fly out and anxious suspicion blow in.

'Are you OK, Gina, you look a bit pale? Has something burned in the oven?'

It was sweet Kasim who had disentangled himself from Janie Juno where they had wasted no time in canoodling on the sofa. He must have sensed trouble.

'Ah thanks, Kasim. You really are Mr Lovely and I'm fine but Max can't make it. I'm sorry you won't get to meet him, after all.'

I saw a smidgeon of smugness flash across Kasim's face for a nano-second before he gently patted my hand, looked into my eyes and said, 'Never mind, Gina. I was rather hoping I wouldn't.'

He grinned broadly showing his beautiful white teeth that contrasted perfectly with his smooth dark skin.

Despite my consternation, I laughed and wagged my finger at him in the naughty boy fashion I knew he adored. The door bell ringing brought us back to the party and within minutes the place was buzzing with the beautiful and interesting while Shirley Bassey belted out theme tunes at full pelt.

Lou and her boyfriend Jonnie had come as Pussy Galore and Odd Job (the heroine pilot and the Chinese guy with the killer bowler hat from Goldfinger). Bella was dressed as Honey Rider (the bikini clad Ursula Andress from Doctor No) complete with impressive hip dagger and her figure was glorious thanks to her rowing. Rob, the footballer had on a shorty wetsuit, flippers and a diving mask, which we all argued about as it could have come from any of the films.

When Bella and Lou asked me about Max, I laughed it off though I knew it wasn't lost on them and was grateful when no more was said.

As I took in the room of people, the low lighting and music, the balcony doors wide to the twinkling lights against the darkening sky, I felt I was in a different dimension looking down on myself. Had I really facilitated this gathering, encouraged by my friends who were fast becoming like sisters? It didn't seem real and I had to pinch myself. My brief reverie ended when Kasim handed me a cocktail and guided me towards the open doors.

'Mishter Bond, licensed to kill, at your service, ma'am.'

He spoke playfully in a put-on Scottish accent then stretched his arm around me and we leaned companionably over the balcony looking out onto the water.

'I could easily do it you know, Gina. I've been in secret training,' he said, cocking his head slightly and winking.

I was slow at first to pick up his reference to Max, who at this moment seemed to cloak me in uncertainty. I tried to laugh lightly but it came out as a vindictive snort.

'Oh dear, poor Gina. You really have it bad don't you?'

'I'm afraid so, Kasim, but I was warned. I thought we could have been a great team and I so wanted to get back into the land of 'coupledom' and be normal like everyone else.'

'What! There's nothing suburban about you, Gina. Haven't you realised that yet? You're not made for that kind of life. We've only known each other for a few years but in that time, I've seen you do so much. Look at how you've spun your life around from those miserable years turning yourself inside out over your marriage. This is your time now and you don't need anyone like Max to make you stand tall. You do it by yourself.'

'Honestly, is that what you really see? Inside, as much as I hate to admit it, I've been empty for years. With Max, I felt he had rekindled something that I had thought was long dead. I was sure I could feel the first flickers of a desire to be alive again, which didn't seem possible back in the Midlands.'

'The flickers aren't only to do with Max, Gina. Look at the friends you've quickly made. They love you and want you to be happy. They're not stupid.'

'Janie Juno says the same but I have too many battle scars, Kasim and the world as I know it is spinning. I've also fallen in love,' I whispered.

'Ah. Now we're getting to the crux of the matter. Do you think he's sensed it and has backed off?'

'Yes, I think it's possible.'

I pursed my lips and nodded my head reluctantly. 'He knew how important his being here tonight was for me and his last minute call stinks to high heaven. How could I have got it so wrong?'

I felt tears threaten and swallowed them quickly.

'He might be telling the truth. Have you thought of that?'

'But why didn't he warn me earlier that he might be late, or worse, not even make it? I feel strongly that he's lied and set me up.'

'Gina, it's not your fault. He's led you along. When we spoke on the phone you were full of the great places he's taken you to and the hints and suggestions he's made. He's a charmer. He knows what to say. How long has he been a bachelor?'

'Twenty years,' I sniffled.

'Well, what does that tell you?'

'But I thought I was different, that we were different. Everyone said how good I was for him and what a great couple we made.'

'That word again, couple. My advice is to let him go. See him here and there if you want to, for fun, but only if you can hold onto your heart. You'll never pin him down. And anyway, I'm always here if you change your mind.'

He kissed me lightly again on my cheek and gently squeezed my waist.

Janie Juno joined us on the balcony from where she'd been hovering to let us have our moment together and I could see that her play for him had paid off because he lit up when he saw her, reminding me of what I'd passed over. He really was a dreamboat; tall, cultured, successful in his field (which ironically was Taxation) and charismatic but it hadn't been meant for us then and Max had seen to it that it was impossible now. I hugged them both and went back to the party.

The sight that greeted me was of dancing and laughter. I could see Jaws (The Spy who loved me, Moonraker) in a clinch with a girl clad in a gold lame body suit (Goldfinger) and Blofeld (the super villain) getting up close to Miss Moneypenny. Everyone was having a great time, though I think the strength of the cocktails had something to do with it.

At ten o'clock we all huddled outside to watch the firework display and cheered, woohooed and clapped as the rockets exploded dazzling the sky with great spheres of colour, like enormous flower heads bursting and fading and bursting again. No-one had scrimped and the display lasted for half an hour. I was enthralled and for the moment my thoughts of Max melted like the dead fireworks into the quay.

The party began to wind down in the early hours and the guests fell out the door, and some down the stairs, on account of the deceptively innocuous drinks. Everyone was laughing and singing Burley Shassey, her new nickname, as they tumbled out onto the pavement, thanking me for a fantastic night.

Bella and Lou said they'd see us the next day and finally we were on our own in the flat, me, Janie Juno and Kasim. She had no intention of leaving and when she took Kasim by the hand into his bedroom, I merely raised my glass to them both. I staggered into my own bed, leaving the party aftermath for tomorrow and tried not to think about Max.

Faintly, from next door arose the sounds of loving; whispers, laughter, rhythmic squeaking and the odd scream from her, and him, interspersed with periods of quietness then more of the same.

I thought of them together and knew I should be pleased – having some of Janie Juno was good for him – but a tiny, tiny part of me resented their fun because I had been rendered so miserable by Max. As they started up again, it only served to highlight my sense of abandonment and though I had downed my share of cocktails, they hadn't anesthetised my pain.

I lay there thinking over the things that Kasim had said about my desire to return to being in a couple and his conviction that it was only because I knew nothing else, gradually conceding he was right.

In his quiet way, he had brought me round to rejecting the belief that identity, status and security could only be achieved by having a significant other. He had shown me that my assumptions were profoundly flawed and would not deliver the lasting happiness I sought. What had he said about me not needing anyone else in order to stand tall? With a clarity of thought you wouldn't normally associate with a dozen Margueritas, I concluded that 'safe' and 'same' would not set me on the right path and steeled myself to explore what else was out there.

But it was with a deep and genuine sadness that I reluctantly accepted Max wasn't the one for me after all and imagined him slowing drifting away on an outgoing tide.

15 – Sometimes ... having good sex makes it difficult to sit down

I slept surprisingly well after reaching my decision and got up early feeling fresh and eager for the day. I attacked the debris from the party and within an hour, the place looked like somebody actually lived there.

I was on the balcony having a coffee in the sunshine when Kasim appeared in his grey silk dressing gown, looking boyish in a languid, relaxed manner that gave me the impression he had spent a very satisfying night. He was unshaven and his hair, normally slicked back to straightness, was unruly but his dishevelment only added to his attractiveness.

'Any more coffee in the pot, Gina? I'm gasping.'

'I'll bet you are. Did you enjoy yourself?'

For a moment he mistook my question and shuffled slightly as a faint blush crept up from his neck.

'The party, Dumbo?' I added quickly and his relief was palpable.

'Oh yes, wasn't it great? I think Janie Juno enjoyed herself too.'

He looked at me shyly.

'She always does,' I said laughing. 'She's gone off to organise brunch at Mangoes for the crowd later. We're all supposed to be rowing this morning but I guess like me, the others aren't going to make it.'

'I'm not sure if she's physically capable of sitting down,' he said absently as I handed him a cup and he took a sip. 'Are you OK with the fact that we erm, made a night of it?' He couldn't avoid it any longer.

'Delighted, Kasim, what are your plans when you move to Paris in the New Year?'

'I don't know but we'll discuss it later. Before I go, I'm hoping to come down for the odd weekend and Joanna said I could stay with her if it's a problem. I think she took a shine to me.'

He was talking of my elegant older lady neighbour who I had seen at the party batting her eyelashes at him. She had come as Solitaire, the fortune teller from Live and Let Die, though I know Bella had been tempted.

'You're always welcome to stay here but you are a very naughty boy,' I said, wagging my finger at him. 'I leave you alone for five minutes and you've got a harem on the go.'

'I should be so lucky, Gina.'

Still laughing, he turned his gaze towards the water.

'How about you? How are you feeling about Max this morning?'

He carried on looking out at the quay.

'I had a text from him to apologise for not coming. Because of the late hour he decided to call in at some friends who lived en route and then stay the night.'

Even to my own ears it sounded fabricated, but Kasim, to his credit, said nothing.

When my phone pinged an hour ago, my heart had skipped though Max's message had only added to my growing sense of having been put in my place. I hadn't as yet replied, preferring to think carefully about what I was going to say, but in the instant Kasim asked me I made up my mind.

'I'm going to wind things down with him and will probably send a letter. It's better than a text or a meeting. I'm going to do it this week.'

'Really?'

He raised an eyebrow and I squirmed because I knew he was going to hold me to it. I would therefore need to be strong.

'Absolutely!' I said with a conviction I didn't feel.

Before Kasim had a chance to say anything else, I stood up to get fresh coffee and left him to take a shower.

***

He emerged half an hour later fresh and composed, with a twinkle in his eye and a spring in his step. It was approaching eleven so we set off for brunch on the other side of the quay.

Mangoes was one of those timeless places with comfortable vintage sofas that you lounge around on and they served the best coffee for miles. We liked the relaxed scruffiness of it and the hand drawn murals of mermaids on the walls. They'd been there for years apparently and were peeling off and fading in parts, but it only added to the charm of the place.

When we arrived, some of the crowd had already pulled tables together and were tucking in. It was a rowdy affair as we stuffed our faces with freshly made bacon rolls washed down with hot drinks and everyone was animatedly chatting about the previous night. There were many 'thank you's' for the hostess which was warming and made me think I would do it all again, in the not too distant future.

Kasim sat between me and Janie Juno and for part of the time they spoke in low whispers which I took to mean they were making plans to see each other, and he was telling her about his contract to work in France.

Joanna sat on the other side of me and it was the first time we had a chance to chat because the previous night, I'd been flitting about like a butterfly. She was petite and of indeterminate age, keeping her youthful looks with regular Pilates and had an attractive face with carefully applied make-up that accentuated her dark brown eyes.

Her clothes were tasteful, expensive and very well cut and though still attractive now, I got the impression she had been a looker in her youth. She leaned into me and slowly placed one of her perfectly manicured hands on my arm.

'Thank you for last night, darling. I haven't had so much fun at a party since I can remember.'

'You're welcome.'

I meant it sincerely as I had been curious about her, especially when Kasim had asked me who she was after spotting her in the car park next to my flat.

'Your Asian friend seems very nice. What a gorgeous man, such lovely manners. I do believe he might have got himself hitched but be sure to tell him that if it comes to nothing, I'd be very pleased to have some of his company.'

She laughed daringly, in a pleasant tinkling way and I feigned disapproval at her flirting but giggled along with her.

'You little devil, Joanna. Do you have anyone special in your life? That is besides Kasim,' I asked smiling, knowing she wasn't married, drove a top of the range BMW and had a very successful care home business.

'I used to, but we parted. Best thing that ever happened really because now I'm free to live life on my terms. Here on the quay there are plenty of people to keep me company and I'm never lonely. I'm so pleased you've moved in. You're just the sort we need around here.'

'That's very kind and I'm enjoying it, too.'

'You seem to work long hours. What do you do?'

I gave her a summary of my project but, like everyone else, the shutters came down in less than a minute, such was its dullness, and she quickly but politely cut me off.

'Would you like to join me at a ladies club supper on Dartmoor next Monday? I think you might enjoy it. We'll take a guided walk then eat in a pub on the moor. The ladies are all professional but very interesting and friendly and most are around your age.'

'That sounds lovely and thank you, Joanna. I'll be there.'

I got my diary out and made a note.

Looking at all the scribbled entries, I realised how full life was beginning to be and recalled, for a brief moment, a time in the Midlands when the pages had been blank. If Janie Juno was lucky in having Kasim, I was lucky in having these people.

How easy the linkages to friendship now seemed to be, and how easy it was to accept these offers. Just as the pages of my diary looked different to a few years ago, so did my approach to meeting people and having fun. Whereas once I would have been reluctant and anxious, now I was relaxed and eager, feeling that I had at last mastered the gentle art of chatting.

When Jonnie, Lou's boyfriend, suddenly bellowed to me from the other end of the table, he gave me a start.

'Gina, I know you're into your art, there's a private showing at the iStorm gallery along the way on Friday. Would you like to come with me and Lou, eight o'clock suit you?'

'Thanks, Jonnie,' I managed to shout above the hubbub. 'Sounds perfect!'

I got my diary back out.

'Oh and don't forget the Autumn Ball at the end of the month, we're all going. I'll book you a place and you'll need a nice dress.'

This came from Bella.

I hastily entered the various dates and with events like this to keep me busy, I could see a possible pathway to extricating myself from Max. He wasn't my only ticket to good times and he was beginning to slowly but surely fade, surprising given that it was less than twenty four hours since he had let me down so badly.

I knew, without doubt, that I'd read the situation with him correctly and buoyed by Kasim's advice which echoed Janie Juno's assessment, I also entered a note to write to Max and end it quickly, before I ruminated further.

When the brunch came to its natural end we all went our separate ways. It took a while for Kasim to say good bye to his new found friends, including Joanna, though eventually it was just me and Janie Juno who waved him off. She turned to me as his brake lights disappeared around the corner out of view and asked me honestly how I felt about the two of them getting together.

'Truthfully?' I said smiling as I linked my arm through hers. 'It's worth a try!'

16 – Sometimes ... the writing on nice paper does not always entail happy news

Dear Max, I began and stopped, chewing on the end of the pen in my mouth. I had bought some high quality writing paper and was in the process of compiling my letter. I had deliberately not texted or phoned him, waiting to see how he was going to play it. As there had been no contact between us for nearly a week, I concluded it was the long game.

Dear Max, I read at the top of the blank sheet.

Dear Max, nothing I thought.

He's not dear Max.

He's a ... he's a ... slimeball!

And despite myself, I laughed at the word and the picture it conjured up in my mind of him being a cross between the Ghostbuster's green dripping ectoplasm and a six foot bogey.

Then I sighed.

How hard could it be?

'Ok, focus. Write the bloody letter and post it, Gina,' I said out loud.

So I did.

I kept it short and sweet and said what I wanted to in eight well-constructed sentences.

"It's been lovely but I want to concentrate on work and rowing, blah, blah" that type of thing followed by a final 'Thank you'.

I resisted adding a "Goodnight and good riddance" and hastily signed it with two kisses (one would look begrudging and three would suggest possibility) before stuffing it into the envelope. I licked it twice for good measure and banged it sealed with the side of my fist. I scribbled his address on the front, pressed a fluff covered stamp angrily on the corner and went to rid myself of it on the square. I put my ear to the post box and listened to make sure it had dropped then flip-flapped my hands as if I had just handled something particularly unpleasant.

I knew deep down that expecting Max to fling himself to the ground and proffer his undying love was at best delusional but his response, when it eventually came a few days later, was a cause for concern to say the least. He phoned.

'Hi, Gina, Max here. How are you?' His tone was sing-songy.

'Fine thanks, and you?' My voice deliberately held an edge.

'Oh you know, keeping busy, working on the new shopping mall development in town.'

'Ah yes. I read the article in the paper. Good that you've got a slice of it.'

'There are a few of us in a consortium. One of my clients has given me an in.'

'Isn't that a bit risky?' I asked knowing the need to stay professionally clear of anything that gave you an insider interest or else it was curtains.

'No, not if you play it right,' he laughed dismissively.

'Did you receive my letter?' I held my breath.

'Yes. That's really why I'm ringing.'

My heart quickened, still hoping.

'I'm relieved,' he said and sounded it.

My first thought was that he had me down as a stalker and I felt my anger rising. And then I considered his odd choice of word for a moment. He had said 'relieved' and it pounded against my brain for comprehension. I felt my face reddening as the tentacles of painful prickles that started somewhere on the top of my head slowly slid down my face and gripped it like a vice.

Why wasn't he sad or sorry or upset? Why was he ... relieved as in (quote) "someone no longer feeling distressed or anxious; reassured. Similar words being, thankful, grateful, pleased, happy".

Of all the things I thought he might say, this was not one of them and it sent me into a tailspin of Celtic fury. I bit my lips in outrage but remained silent in order to draw him further.

'Hello. Are you still there, Gina?'

'Yes, yes. I'm still here,' I said breezily then fell silent again, beginning to taste my own blood.

'I was worried that you were getting in too deep and I was going to have to let you down gently.'

The arrogance of the man was breath-taking after all he'd said, done and hinted at but his choice of word had inadvertently galvanised me because now I was under no illusion as to exactly what he was. How on earth had I allowed myself to fall into the clutches of someone like that?

In that instant I took stock of myself, pretty much as I had done at work when confronted with Psycho-Freddie's outlandish deeds and I rose up and gathered all of my strength, self-respect and dignity. Images of my friends standing beside me shoulder to shoulder also flashed quickly in and out of my head.

'I don't think so,' I replied evenly though my heart was thumping. 'It's possible you've mistaken my generosity of time with you for something else and I've been worried by your growing dependency on me, especially for your social functions.'

Clipped and pointed.

'Ah yes, you always did scrub up well, Gina, and were an easy choice for those pressing-the-flesh boring but necessary events. I received several pats on the back for having you in tow.'

Bizarrely, he chuckled.

'Everyone thought you were accomplished and charming.'

As his words emitted from my phone like poisoned arrows, I quickly grasped that I had been nothing more than deal making arm candy, there to help him open doors and now I was expendable. The realisation almost knocked me off my feet and I wanted to sit down before I collapsed in a heap. This wasn't easy given that I was in Marks and Spencer's food hall in the basement, coincidently by the fish section, where the glassy dead eye of a whole salmon stared out at me balefully which added to my sense of the macabre.

If I felt confused by our relationship (me and Max, not the fish), he had just shown me a side to him that was as cold and calculating as any user in history and I had heard enough. I didn't want to prolong our connection for any longer than the time it would take me to say goodbye.

I set aside his turgid, unworthy of a response comments and said with more breeze than I felt, 'Time to go I reckon, Max. It's been fun. Thanks.'

'Can we still be friends and go out for dinner, Gina? You really are one of the most fascinating women I know.'

Someone to add to your little line-up you mean, I thought disgustedly, listening to his upbeat tone which made it sound as if we were having a game of musical chairs.

'Not sure I'll have time to fit you in, Max, but thanks all the same. Must dash. Things to do, places to go. Goodbye.'

'Oh, OK, Gina. Bye then.'

His voice trailed off, small and puzzled at the other end as I deaded the phone. His invitation to stay in touch, his words and positioning were textbook client management and his careful handling of me, his bedside charm and his silky manner were all grounded in his methods of lawyering. He'd been at it so long he'd lost the ability to know the difference between deal making and personal integrity. The lines had become blurred then non-existent.

He was a player of the very worst kind who misused his skills, resources and insights to manipulate situations and those who put their trust in him. A more morally and emotionally bankrupt person I have yet to meet but in time he would be called to account for his conduct, though not in a court of public opinion but in a court of law.

Perhaps he should have listened to my warning about insider dealings and client privilege.

17 – Sometimes … you have to sing to get rid of your fluffy slippers

How do I lick my wounds, let me count the ways.

The day after the call from Max, I decided I would have a period of official mourning and thought a couple of weeks ought to get me over the worst of things. During this time I would give myself permission to cry my eyes out, wear fluffy slippers, put blankets around me and eat soup curled up in the armchair.

I was gathering together all the necessary paraphernalia like tissues and rugs and tin openers when Janie Juno tapped on the door and came in. Never one to miss a trick, she took in the random items and guessed what had happened.

'He got the letter?'

'Yes.'

'He called you?'

'Yes'

'He didn't beg you to reconsider?'

'Yes.'

I couldn't look at her and fiddled with opening a packet of Handy Andies.

'I'm getting a little confused here. He did or he didn't?'

'Er, he didn't. But it was the way you asked the question,' I said defensively.

She narrowed her eyes. 'So how did he take it?'

My words tumbled out too eagerly. 'Really badly, he was very upset.'

And then she knew I was lying.

'Oh dear, that bad.'

'That bad. Very bad. The worst you could imagine.'

'Did he tell you he was already married?' she asked incredulously.

'Worse.'

'What can be worse than that?'

'He told me he was relieved,' I said it quietly, pulling out a tissue, getting ready.

She brought her lips together in the shape of an 'O' and sucked in some air. Her expression was enough to convince me that I hadn't over reacted to the word and she took my hand.

'I'm sorry, Gina. That's so unfair of him. Did he say any more?'

I didn't want to go over the rest in detail because it still smarted, but she was due something at least.

'He gave me the impression I'd been good for his career.'

'Oh, you poor thing. I guess he wanted to keep in touch then?'.

'Yup, but I declined.'

'Were you on your own when he said all of this?'

'Nope, I was in the basement at M&S and had to sit on the steps leading up to the Pants Department with the old dears asking me if I was alright. One of them eventually got an assistant who wanted to showcase her recent first aid training but I managed to slip away before any harm was done.'

'Can I do anything? I see you're settling yourself in for the long haul eh?' She gestured to the items on the worktop.

I nodded.

'Have you spoken to Bella and Lou?' she asked with concern.

'No. Not yet.' My voice grew small and I coughed to try to stem my emotion. 'I'm struggling to face them if I'm honest because like you, they warned me and I could kick myself for having invested so much in him. You must all think I'm stupid for allowing myself to be ... to be ... carried along.'

A little sob escaped and I looked away.

'Gina, he encouraged it and you can't blame yourself for gravitating towards being in a couple again. It's a state of mind that feels familiar and safe to you and he knew it and lured you in for selfish reasons.'

'But why play with me in that way? I could have made him happy.'

My voice trembled.

'This guy is the complete opposite of you and needs constant reassurance of his ongoing attractiveness. It starts with the chase then the winning-over followed by the boredom before finally the moving-on.'

'I don't think the women are sequential,' I said flatly and she narrowed her eyes. 'I have a sense that there is, or was, some overlap when I think back to his absences and unavailability.'

I snivelled.

'Well there you have it then, my hunch was right but none of us judges you and we only want to help. All we did was give guidance, the decisions are yours to make.

'Telling' isn't our style and neither is being critical of what you do. You are your own person Gina and we are your friends as you are ours.'

She hugged me and when the tears flowed, she gently dabbed at my eyes.

'You've had a lesson with this guy and you've experienced something that was beyond your understanding of how the world worked. Isn't that valuable in some way? Why don't you think about it in that light and use what has happened to better equip yourself for the future?'

I knew it was good advice but my emotions were a cauldron of bewildered confusion and she saw it in my face.

'I don't think me staying here any longer will help you so I'll go now but will catch up again tomorrow.'

She kissed me briefly on the cheek and closed the door quietly.

Left on my own, I slinked away to bed where I hoped that sleep would bring some respite from the pain of my humiliation, but I was wrong.

***

Safe to say, for the next few weeks I was not myself and it was thanks to Janie Juno, Bella and Lou that I ate and dragged my sorry self through the motions of daily living. Judging from the synchronicity of their enquiries in terms of who called when, I guessed rightly that they had agreed between them on a round the clock vigil.

Lou had taken to phoning me daily around mid-afternoon.

'Hi, Gina, how you doing?'

'Oh you know, getting there, Lou.'

My voice was sad and low.

'Did Bella phone last night?'

She sounded like I hadn't sussed the vigil thing.

'Yeah, we had a good heart to heart.'

'What's her take on it?'

'She's going for the 'best got rid of him' approach telling me to buck up. But my heart has been torn to shreds and it's so bad I've been thinking of having a go with Gaz myself. It might cheer me up. Lou, you're not laughing are you? I'm in distress here you know, real full blown practically jilted at the altar type distress.'

'You're such a drama queen, Gina. You know Max studiously avoided the subject of marriage.'

'Well he hadn't actually said the word but he gave me the impression it was only a matter of time.'

'That was his MO and you know that, too. Have you seen him?'

'Absolutely not! I'd rather stick pins in my eyes.'

'There you go again, drama, drama. What you need is to get yourself done up and come to the Autumn Ball on Saturday.'

When I started to protest she talked over me.

'For goodness sake, stop this right now. We've bought you a ticket between us and it will be great, I promise. Just pull a new face on, one that's different from your current scowling 'woe is me' and get back out there. Honestly, you're acting more like your dog's died than someone who's had one of the luckiest escapes of her life ... from Mishter Schlimeball.'

She drew out the words making it sound like one.

Funny that the name had stuck and I had to laugh.

For the first time in ages.

'OK, OK. You've worn me down. I'll sort myself out and put something nice on.'

'You'd better. This is the social highlight of the year and you're not going to let the side down or I'll push you in the quay when you're not expecting it even though I know you're already well acquainted,' she cackled, referring to my little encounters which put me on the back foot.

'You're sitting there in your fluffy slippers with a blanket round you, aren't you?' she suddenly said accusingly.

'Nooooh,' I squeaked and quickly looked away from them in case she could see telepathically.

'You are. I can tell. You better not wear them on Saturday night, I'm warning you!'

'Lou, you are so cruel. In my moment of need, you are not my friend. If you were, you'd be giving me the attention I'm obviously seeking.'

'Of course I'm your friend. That's why I'm dragging you to the Autumn Ball, Cinders. Now shake a leg!'

She rang off.

Feeling cheated and slightly peeved by her lack of sympathy but starting to get bored with the Max thing myself, I elected to forego the second week of my mourning and I threw off the blanket. I opened the last bottle of our party Prosecco and when I decided that my elegant champagne flute didn't go with the fluffy slippers, they went too. By the time I'd finished the bottle half an hour later, the world didn't look so bad after all.

When Bella rang me (tea time call) I was watching The Sound of Music and singing along. I remembered once that I had been to a big screening where you got to dress up as your favourite character and I had gone as a goat on a hill. I had stood out a treat from the nuns but was usurped by a group dressed in matching curtains.

'Gina, who is in there with you? Not Max I hope.'

'No,' I sighed a little wistfully. 'Only the Von Trapps.'

'The Von Who? Gina, are you drunk?' she asked me in tone that was more exasperated than concerned.

'No. Not really.'

'You bloomin' well are. Hopeless. I rang to stay that I'll drop round for you on Saturday but am staying at Lou's so you'll have to make your own way back from the Ball.'

'Who said I was going, Bella?' I slurred with a note of petulance, still attention seeking.

'Not that again. Yeah, I've spoken to Lou. She told me and I'm not going there. Just make sure you wear that off the shoulder slinky Katherine Hamnett you showed me. Don't think of putting anything else on or I won't let you in the car.'

'It's too big.'

'Well, get it altered, you've still got time. Take this as a real threat, Gina, or as well as not letting you in the car, I won't let you in the boat!'

First Lou and now her but I knew she meant business. Not being in the boat would kill me so I quickly thought, dress or boat, dress or boat ... and knew when I was beaten.

'I told Lou she wasn't my friend and now you're not either. You know just where to hit me hard don't you?'

'Bah! You're definitely drunk and I've had enough of this. Go and take a cold shower to sober up and get that dress to the little man on Cowick Street. I'll pick you up at seven and don't forget to tell Janie Juno that you're going. I'm sure she'll be relieved.'

She rang off before I could say anymore and I sat bolt upright. Better not mess with Bella. It would be easier to wrestle with crocodiles than to take her on so I went straight to the wardrobe and rummaged about until I found the silk dress that I had stored carefully in a zipped hanging cover. I removed it and swished it in front of me on the hanger, watching the light pick out the crimson threads as I let the fabric fall in silky folds.

Better try it on.

The dress wasn't as big as I'd feared and alterations wouldn't be necessary. It had long sleeves and was cut straight across at the top to reveal bare shoulders, fitted over my hips and straight to the floor. It wasn't flared but had a long split on one side up to my thigh and I had last worn it on the night of Max's Summer Ball. I had found it too painful to look at since then because of the memories it evoked and had stuffed it at the back deliberately.

Seeing the dress again now, I sighed for what might have been but given the threats of my friends, I knew I needed to get over it, get out there and lay his ghost to rest. I hung it on my bedroom door to reinforce my determination and decided to call it a night, what with the Prosecco and all.

I slept well and it was the first time in a long time that I didn't have sweats about Max. Instead I dreamt of me, Janie Juno, Bella and Lou coming first in our class at the Exeter rowing regatta which would be held in a few weeks' time.

18 – Sometimes ... a bunch of balloons can make you fly

In the week leading up to the Autumn Ball and with the threats of my friends ringing in my ears, Janie Juno dragged me to the hairdressers where I had my hair re-highlighted. Next, she sent me to the beauticians where I had my bits waxed as well as my legs and I came out feeling proud I hadn't screamed too loudly. Last time, the girl from next door had rushed in to check I wasn't being murdered but personally I think you're permitted to make a noise when you have hairs ripped out by their roots in one of your most sensitive areas. Either that or they give you a wooden baton to bite down on.

The beautician had also plucked my eyebrows to within an inch of their lives and Lou had given me some of Bella's special face cream to put on each night before going to bed. The effect wasn't too bad as I looked at myself in the mirror. The back view seemed alright, too, because my bottom had toned so the dress fitted better than before and I wasn't unhappy with the results, in fact I was almost cheerful.

A knock on the door and Janie Juno nearly fell in as her heel caught in her dress.

'What do you think?' she asked, gaily striking a pose as I tried to take in the apparition in front of me.

'Wow, you look ... stunning!' was as much as I could splutter.

She wore a simple black velvet, ankle length fitted dress with cream silk straps, very plain at the front with no cleavage on show.

'Watch this,' she shouted as she ran across the room and I saw straight away that the back was striking.

The bodice had been interlaced with more cream ribbon but the best part of all was a perfectly proportioned train of black netting that was attached at the waist and tumbled as far as the hem. It rose gently up behind her when she walked, like a peacock, to reveal a long sexy split which showed off her shapely legs. There wasn't an abundance of netting but just enough to create this astonishing effect and the dress went from elegantly plain to stratospheric. I had never seen anything like it and then I noticed she had on a pair of long black gloves.

She laughed at my incredulity and gently put her finger under my chin to reclose my mouth.

'It's a copy of a Givenchy. A friend of mine bought it on a cruise, wore it then gave it to me because it's too small for her.'

'It's one of the most beautiful and interesting dresses I've ever seen and it suits you down to the ground. It could have come straight out of Breakfast at Tiffany's and you look wonderful.'

In that moment, we spontaneously embraced and when we pulled apart, we both had tears in our eyes.

'Why are we crying like this, aren't we silly?' I asked her whilst dabbing delicately at my face, trying to preserve my make-up.

'No, we're not silly. We're just pleased for each other that's all. Come on, Gina, let's show 'em what we're made of.'

And we hugged again.

At the sound of Bella's honking horn I waved from the balcony to let her know we were on our way. As we closed the door, we laughed, held hands and ran down the stairs onto the street. Bella smiled when she saw us.

'What a sight you are, gorgeous, gorgeous! And glad you could make it, Gina, you are a changed woman.'

I thought it best not to get on to the subject of Max so I took her compliment for what it was. We chatted mostly about the rowing club on the way and, when we had to park the car some distance away, attracted the admiring glances of people in the street.

Bella had on a full length black sparkly number that was clingy in all the right places but which fell away at the back to just above her bottom with the thinnest of black straps that criss-crossed her beautiful toned back. Her hair was down and her eyes glittered to match her dress.

As we handed over our tickets, we spotted Lou inside by the door talking to a chap and sipping champagne. Her hair was up in elaborate curls which showed off the curve of her neck and she had on a strapless brown chiffon dress with a heavily beaded bodice of tiny pearls and button sized emeralds that shone when the light caught them. She had added a tasteful thick gold choker and had made her eyes up more heavily than usual which added to the sophistication. Always a graceful mover, her hand elegantly lifted the flute to her lips and she looked timeless.

'Hello ladies.' She gave us the once over and nodded approvingly. 'I don't think you've met Adrian, he's with the Fleet Air Arm.'

A very good-looking fair-haired guy of around thirty, dressed in a black tux and sparkling white dinner shirt extended his hand to us formally.

'Pleased to meet you.'

You too, I thought and winked at Lou behind his back as he talked to Bella. She licked her lips like a cat expecting smoked salmon and narrowed her eyes with an expression that told me she wasn't planning on playing dead later on. I smiled knowingly and shook my head at her.

A glass of champagne was thrust (a little too easily) into our hands and we started to mingle. I spotted Pete O'Mara and made my way towards him.

'Hello Pete, I wasn't expecting to meet you here all done up like a dog's dinner!' I teased him.

'Well, hello Gina, I could say the same.' His eyes twinkled. 'It's a pleasant change to see you in something other than your soggy shorts and I'm very relieved that we're nowhere near the water!' His Irish lilt made it sound funny and I laughed too.

'Listen you,' I wagged a finger at him. 'I still haven't forgiven you for not fishing me out when I fell in and before you ask, my mobile phone and heirloom watch are fine thanks but I've got a lonnnnnnng memory and I'm going to keep an eye on you Pete O'Mara so you'd better behave.'

I punched him playfully in the ribs.

'Have you brought your missus?' I asked, looking around for one.

'That would be a thing seeing as how I haven't had a wife for over twenty years. I'm divorced and single thank the Lord! And planning on staying that way. Where have you the idea I was married?' he laughed heartily at my look of confusion.

'Sorry Pete, I just assumed. Who are you here with then?'

'Two very good and longstanding friends of mine. Henry has gone to the bar but let me introduce you to Jago.'

He tugged the sleeve of a man who was in conversation with someone else off to the left.

'Jago, come and meet Gina. She's a rower in the crew I was telling you about, well that's to say she tries to be when she can manage to stay in the boat,' he chuckled.

I was about to make a quip when a man of about fifty turned around and shook my hand. He was a few inches taller than me with fair greying hair that was longer than your average but not massively so and he had a neatly trimmed goatee beard. He was deeply tanned with a weathered ruggedness that made me think of the sea, and impossibly blue eyes that became even brighter when he smiled. He had a touch of the Richard Branson's about him and when he spoke, it was difficult to detect an accent.

'Nice to meet you, Gina. Pete here was just saying how pleased he is with the progress you're all making, especially you.'

I looked over with narrowed eyes but Pete had deliberately turned his head away and was talking elsewhere.

'Are you sure he was referring to me, Jago?' I asked with disbelieving sarcasm.

'Definitely you,' he smiled warmly. 'Are you enjoying it?'

'One of the best things that's ever happened to me.'

I raised my glass as if in a toast.

'Yes, I took a turn when I hit forty and was at a bit of a loose end. That's how I met Pete, we were in the same boat and we've stayed good friends ever since. He's trying to talk me into having a drink with him soon at the club so perhaps we'll meet again.'

He looked at me questioningly.

'Any friend of Pete's is a friend of mine, Jago,' I said lightly, steering the conversation back round even though I was curious about his loose end.

'He's been brilliant with us and I can't thank him enough.'

'I think you'll find the pleasure has been his, but don't tell him I said so.'

'Said what?' Pete had rejoined us.

'Oh nothing, I was telling Gina how pleased you are with them.' Jago winked and grinned at me conspiratorially which made me smile.

During our short exchange I noted he was self assured as opposed to cocky, with a strong but polite presence that gave me the impression he was comfortable with himself, and his place in the world. Despite the formal evening attire, I sensed he was a free spirit, a non-conformist who didn't follow the herd. Perhaps it was because of the way he chose to wear his hair, which really suited him, or perhaps it was something more oblique. Either way, he wasn't someone you'd forget bumping into in a hurry.

And I didn't.

'It's been nice to meet you, Jago, and I'm pleased to see you too, Pete, but they'll be wondering what's happened to me. I'd better go. Enjoy the Ball.'

'Before you disappear, Gina, I'd like to say that the rowing is seriously coming on a treat and I'm delighted with you all as a crew. Keep it up.'

The pride in his eyes was obvious and I went a bit pink because he was never lavish with praise so his words were all the more touching. The girls would be thrilled to hear it and I knew we would try harder than ever.

'Thanks, Pete, but it's down to you and we're very grateful for all the coaching. I'll see you next week with the others.'

Thankfully my blush started to recede. Jago shook my hand again and Pete gave me a chivalrous peck on the cheek. As I walked away, I heard Pete shout over my shoulder, 'And tell them not to drink too much either. I'm watching every glass!'

I was laughing as I started to make my way back towards Bella and noticed Janie Juno's dress was causing a stir, catching the attention of all eyes as she came forward to speak to people, her train slightly billowing up behind her. Women, and men, were nudging each other approvingly such was the impact but as she moved through the crowd there was nothing vain about her. If she realised she was one of the most attractive women in the room that night, her behaviour suggested otherwise and it only added to her charm.

'I'm so glad I came, Bella, I wouldn't have wanted to miss this.'

'I'm only grateful you found something other than your furry slippers to step out in.'

I gave her a nip on the arm.

Champagne and canapés gave way to a formal six course meal at large round tables clad in white linen that sparkled with silver and candles. In the middle of each was a big bunch of helium filled balloons and in the background a string quartet played Bach. We sat next to each other so we could chat, first Janie Juno, then me, Bella, Lou and finally Adrian who had managed a quick change of place names to squeeze in. A magician was doing tricks amongst the tables and came over to ours.

'Excuse me, madam, do you believe in magic?' he asked me.

'I do, I do!' I clapped my hands excitedly, entering into the spirit of things.

'Then in that case, please choose a card.'

He offered me a spread pack and I picked one at random then looked at it before sliding it gently back in. He then did an amazing high shuffle but instead of catching the cards they landed on the floor and my disappointment that the trick was a joke was writ large on my face.

He apologised profusely but grinned and asked me if I would be so kind as to look in the evening bag I'd placed on the table next to my glass. Sure enough, to my complete astonishment, there was my card.

My look of bewilderment made them laugh spontaneously.

'How did you do that?' I asked breathlessly.

'Aha, you said you were a believer and if you truly were, you wouldn't question it. It's magic!'

And with that he produced a squished plastic bouquet from mid-air and presented it to me with a flourish before moving on. My delight was unsophisticated in contrast to my glamorous outer self and I believe my friends saw a moment of naive vulnerability that surprised them. If I was honest, my unguarded response surprised me too but I reasoned quickly that I was in safe company.

After dinner, a nine piece blues band struck up and Maggie Reader, a local singer, joined them for a few songs. We all knew her from the Havana Club on the quay and clapped and cheered loudly in our applause.

The band had got the crowd to their feet and we all gave it what for. Guys asked us to dance and we were up there for a good couple of hours. There was a casino going along the way and we also dropped in and had a flutter. It was the first time I'd ever played roulette and was worried I'd become addicted and lose my new car, so I restricted myself to twenty pounds.

Which I lost.

Quickly.

Never again.

The car was safe.

At around one in the morning a man in a stripy apron with a pork pie hat served us bacon rolls from a shiny American Airstream, complete with neon sign. Adrian for some reason was wearing a trilby and the light from the diner cast an edgy shadow on his face making him look like a Private Investigator from an old movie. Standing next to him in my red silk dress, I was easily the femme fatale and all that was missing from the scene was a sultry cigarette and a photographer with an old school flash bulb camera who would take our picture and use it for blackmail.

The cigarette funnily enough materialised when Bella stopped munching and sniffed the air. 'I smell joint!'

'I do, too. Not far away either but no good to me, it sends me doolally.'

Lou pulled a gargoyle face.

'And I'm not touching it in case I start smoking again.'

Bella had recently given up.

'I get routinely tested so I'll have to pass.'

Adrian said wistfully.

That left me and Janie Juno.

'I wouldn't mind a puff but I haven't had any since I was a student,' I piped up. 'If I find it, you're sure you don't want any?'

'Certain!' they said in unison with a knowing look.

'I'm off now anyway and will see you in the week. Bella, you can let yourself in to my place, here are the keys, I'm staying with Adrian tonight.'

Lou's look was loaded which caused him to raise an anticipatory eyebrow and grab her.

We waited until they were all far enough away then tracked down the source of the sweet smelling aroma to a spot behind the casino where two young chaps were sharing a toke. When they saw us, they instantly offered and I took it first.

I inhaled deeply a few times until I felt it kick in then passed it around. When it took hold of us, the world became a peaceful and happy place, man, and I spent the next half hour arm in arm with Janie Juno chatting breeze about the beauty around us, that is if you ignored the bins we were stood next to.

We were now in the main car park trying to dial up a taxi, no mean feat if you can't read your phone, when a well-dressed man, portly and in his late sixties, came out of the main entrance. He was clasping a very large bunch of balloons in each hand.

'Seems such a waste, I thought you might like these.'

And just like that he presented them to us. With his generosity coming on top of the toke we struggled to speak but I eventually managed to thank him.

'Are you stuck for a lift?' he asked, taking in the innate mobile.

'I think that might be the case,' I said, clutching on to the last of my sensibilities as well as Janie Juno.

'Where do you live?'

He seemed genuine, though his mouth was twitching with polite amusement at the little scene playing out in front of him.

'On the quayside.'

'If I drop you at Maplins can you walk from there?'

'Easily, it's only a short distance and if you can provide safe passage kind sir you will be a knight in shining armour,' I slurred and nearly tripped.

He laughed heartily and pressed his key fob to peep-peep the lights on what looked like a large and swish Jag. I managed to get in the back easily enough but Janie Juno needed help so he gathered up her train carefully and stuffed it in along with the balloons and drove us to Maplins. He stopped the car, got out and opened the door gallantly, standing off to one side. We clambered out, though sadly not in the Lucy Clayton legs together, swing of the hips, composed and demure method of exiting, but more of your Essex girl staggering, tripping, getting caught up in things style of exiting; miraculously still attached to the balloons.

He was struggling to contain himself but in between chuckles he managed to say 'Thank you, it's been a pleasure' and gave a little bow.

Such rare courtesy we didn't deserve.

'No, no thank you. You've been a hero.'

I breathed toxic fumes all over him as he got back into the car and left us at some ungodly hour in the morning under a star filled early September sky; standing on the corner in a red silk dress and a Givenchy look-alike, holding onto our two large bunches of balloons.

'Come on, Gina, I'll race you.'

She already had her shoes in her hand and had started to run bare foot along the quay side, her train and balloons rising up behind her and the glee on her face plain to see.

Not wanting to be left behind, I started to run, too, and as I did so, I became my younger self, the little girl skipping wild and free in the fields. The wind was warm on our faces and it blew us effortlessly along the edge of the almost black rippling water as we ran and ran and ran. The balloons were bobbing and jostling and our dresses were flaying and rustling. The orange glow from the Victorian street lights cast a shadow and I could see Janie Juno perfectly silhouetted with her arm held high holding on to a string of round shadows that danced on her tail.

Almost breathless, we arrived at the apartment block and let ourselves in, struggling to get up the stairs before bursting through the door to my flat and collapsing in fits on the sofa.

'Well, that was good fun, wasn't it? This evening, Gina, you realise we have been ... lapsed adults.'

She emphasised the words and laughed her throaty laugh.

'Lapsed what ...?'

'Lapsed adults. A friend of mine coined the phrase when he laughingly told me I was having far too much fun, behaving like a seventeen year old rather than a woman with 'responsibilities'. He thinks that now and again when no-one is looking, I throw all my adult rules into the quay and "stop practicing" being grown up.'

'Like lapsed Catholics do when they don't believe anymore or can't be bothered or something like that.'

I was a little puzzled.

'Exactly, except we're not talking religion here. I think being a lapsed adult describes me to a tee, and now you, too!'

She pointed a gloved finger at me and threw back her head laughing, sprawled out against the corner piece, her hands holding onto her stomach in mirth.

'Tonight we've allowed ourselves to play like we did when we were small and have the good times we had in our teens and look at how happy it's made us.'

When her meaning had sunk in, it was pretty heady stuff. She was saying that we didn't need permission from anyone, except ourselves, to lapse back into playfulness and do non-adult things. It made me feel mischievously naughty and I giggled at the thought, as if I was skulking round the dorm after lights out.

'With magicians and balloons and all our mad running, I get it. I haven't felt like this for years and if that makes me a lapsed adult, too, then so be it!' I started to hiccup.

As she made to go home, she stuck her head back round the door, almost as an afterthought.

'You should try it more often, Gina, it suits you!' she said as she disappeared with a quick à bientôt kiss.

When Janie Juno had gone, I slipped out of my silk dress in the lounge, threw it over the armchair with a flourish and danced into bed. The last image that floated joyously into my head before Mr Sandman visited was the pavement silhouette of Janie Juno running barefoot in the breeze with her train and balloons billowing behind her.

19 – Sometimes ... sunflowers make an easier present to accommodate than a trampoline

The Autumn Ball was a watershed in many ways, but particularly in my relationship with Max because it opened my eyes to what was rock solid real – hard to imagine after the sprint along the quay, I know – and what had been nothing more than castles in the air; the one being my true friends and easy fun times and the other being grounded in innuendo and game playing.

Back in May at the Blue Fat Fish, when Janie Juno had warned me that I might get singed, I had dismissed it on the basis that she didn't know Max as well as I did. With the benefit of wonderful hindsight, I wished now that I had been.

Singed.

Only singed.

As opposed to fried.

Singed would have been far less serious.

Beneath the glamour of my red silk dress, I had gone to the Ball with the equivalent of a plaster on a gaping wound but had come away miraculously with only the faint remains of a tiny silver scar. This had happened because I was surrounded by the warmth of genuine friends and I had been enthralled by wonderful scenes and experiences. Whenever I re-ran the evening, I found myself smiling at all the small details and bit by bit, my feelings reached a tipping point that would forever become known as AB, After the Ball.

In the week that followed, I felt stronger but I was reflective on why such a night had been presented to me out of the blue. Why, when my instincts had been to squirrel myself away, only to be dragged kicking and screaming to the Ball, had I gone on to have one of the most memorable nights of my life?

There had to be a reason, if you believed in the laws of the Universe.

***

The following Saturday, as I was getting ready to meet my friends at The Waterfront bar on the opposite side of the quay, Janie Juno appeared at the door.

'Sorry, Gina, but I can't make it. There's a last minute glitch in the new publicity for one of my clients and I've got to iron it out.'

'I know that feeling! Is there anything I can do?'

'Yes, if you can completely re-organise the launch of an event that has been brought forward by three weeks, including an entirely new venue which is fifty miles away from the original one.'

'I might be able to do something because I've got a head for planning and if you like, I can help you later, and tomorrow after rowing.'

'OK, you're on! Tell the others that I'll see them in the boat in the morning and that I send kisses. See you later Gina. You're a godsend.'

I put on a black sleeveless linen dress and headed out. There was no sign of Lou but Bella had grabbed a table and

147

appeared remarkably fit and fresh in her cargoes and a tee-shirt, a look she always carried well. Her dark glasses were on and she was absorbed with the menu so that she didn't see me approach.

I waited until I was almost at the table before I shouted 'Boo!'

She jumped and her glasses fell off, spilling her drink and a little Jack Russell dog barked and pulled at his lead that nearly knocked a big woman over who almost fell on a cyclist who was riding too close to the edge. It was a miracle no-one got crushed or wet so I quickly pointed to a small boy and laughed in the hope they would think it was him and not me, but it didn't fool anyone.

'For god's sake, please just sit down, Gina, and don't touch anything.'

'OK, OK. Have it your own way. It was just a little joke.'

'Yes but you've unsettled everyone, they're all looking at us apprehensively now.'

'You're imagining it.'

'Is Janie Juno going to be joining us, or is she elsewhere today?'

Bella dabbed at her spilt drink while the big woman was being helped.

'She's got to catch up on some work but I'm going to give her a hand later.'

I explained about the event.

Bella looked thoughtful, 'Well, see how you get on. You know that's something I'm interested in doing, Events Management.'

'Yes, I remember you said. It would be good to chat after rowing tomorrow, when I know a bit more.'

'Feel free. I'm not sure Lou is going to make it either today. She was with Adrian again last night, that guy she met at the Ball.'

'What about Jonnie?' I asked, looking out at a pair of swans gliding nonchalantly along the calm river.

'I think you'll find he's old hat,' she laughed. 'Lou's young, free and single, with a great job and her own place. She had a hard time after that creep ditched her when they got back from Oz, but she's turned it around and is motoring now.'

'It's hard to believe Lou ever gets down about anything.'

'That business with her dad was hard too and she had to lean on me for a while, as did her mum. But that's what friends do, don't they? Anyhow, she's back on the right path now and having the fun she deserves. She's wild you know.'

We both laughed because there was a devil may care streak in her but Lou never needed to apologise or justify herself to us, her mother perhaps, but definitely not us.

'What about Rob, have you seen anything more of him?'

She'd put her sunglasses back on so it was difficult to gauge her reaction.

'Oh you know, here and there.'

She pretended to study the menu to distract me.

'Well? Spill the beans. Don't be shy.'

I snatched it out of her hands and nearly sent her drink flying again. Oops.

'Gina, you're impossible! That's my business, but yes, if you must know, he stayed over last night after the jamming session at the pub. Can't you tell?' she smiled suggestively.

'What does your parrot have to say about it?' I tried to keep a straight face.

'He called him Pretty Boy.'

She wasn't so much proud as squirming and I couldn't contain it any longer.

'Pretty Boy!' I got out between my choking laughter

'Well, you know ...' she actually looked embarrassed. 'That's what I call the parrot so it was only natural when he saw Rob.'

'I see.'

Now it was my turn to study the menu.

With our order taken, we took a moment to lift our faces to the sun and I judged the time was right to ask her about what was bothering me.

'Bella, I had a fantastic night at the Ball but can't understand where it came from. I was determined to stay indoors and keep the world at bay and I have to pinch myself that it actually took place.'

She leant forward kindly and took off her glasses. 'Oh, Gina, sometimes you really are an innocent abroad. Can you not see that you were being shown something, perhaps several things? Do you have any ideas or tell me, what sticks out the most for you?'

'I've thought about it a lot but I guess the key things were that I managed to enjoy myself amongst good friends and didn't need or want a man in tow. I didn't think of Max at all and didn't rely on him to create an opportunity to socialise; you all did it for me. And I met Jago.'

'Ah yes. I saw he was there but didn't clock you talking to him. I've only met him to say hello to a couple of times but he hasn't been near the club for years. He's a sailor, goes all around the world I believe and crews as well.'

'That explains a lot. He had a rakish salty sea-dog look that gave me the feeling there was more to him than met the eye. It must have been the sailing. He suggested he was going to come to the club soon, for a drink with Pete, and might see me there.'

She narrowed her eyes with a look that was so spookily intense that I thought perhaps she was seeing something awful she couldn't tell me about, and I caught myself in a moment of panic.

'What did you think to that, Gina?'

'I changed the conversation because I'm not interested in becoming embroiled with anyone else. I went straight from the frying pan into the fire, from my ex to Max, so I'm going to do a Pete O'Mara and devote myself to being single. These things always seem manageable at the outset then boom! You're in over your head. No thanks, Bella. It's not for me.'

'Well, there's your answer then. Just focus on rowing and give yourself time to properly enjoy being single, because you haven't really done that, have you?'

She knew in the Midlands I'd been head down after the divorce, choosing to work long hours to avoid dealing with the emotional upheaval, and then down here, pretty much from the beginning, Max had done his worst.

'The Ball showed you the value of friendship and of being independent. Take it for what it is and don't dwell on it. Are you OK with that?'

I nodded

'Good. Then go from there. While it's in my head, I've been meaning to ask you about Kasim?'

'I spoke to him last week and he was Mr Lovely as usual. He sweetly sent me a bunch of sunflowers to work with a note saying he would bring a trampoline when he comes for the Regatta so I can regain my bounce. I don't know if he's serious but he doesn't normally make empty promises.'

She laughed and shook her head.

'That's all we need! Where are you going to put it for heaven's sake?'

'In the garage, because the rafters go up quite a way. I could always stick up a bit of foam just in case.'

'Gina, the chances are you'll knock yourself out at the first attempt and lie there for days. I hope he was joking.'

'Janie Juno is keen to see him again and Gaz has been kicked into touch but did you know he's moving to Paris to take up a new post after the Christmas holidays?'

'No I didn't. How lovely. Will you go over to see him?'

'Do bears do their business in the woods, Bella?'

'I believe so.'

She kept her face straight.

'A trip's being planned for April so it'll be Paris in the springtime and all that. He'll be living in the 16th Arrondissement in a fancy apartment, the top floor of a house built during le Belle Epoque, lucky devil. Wild horses won't stop that visit, I can tell you, but before then I'm off to Barcelona.'

'Not with Max,' she said in alarm because she knew he'd asked me.

'No, definitely not with Max. I'm actually going on my own. I've always wanted to and I thought yesterday in my office, why not? The Ball made me realise I could do it so I booked a last minute flight and get back the night before the Regatta. It's only for a few days but Kasim will be there on business at the beginning and has asked me to lunch.'

I jiggled smugly in my seat, feeling quite proud of myself and her smile told me enough.

'I think that's one of your better decisions and you'll have a great time. But you'll definitely be back for our race at 1.30 won't you. Pete thinks we're in with a chance so make sure you get some fitness training in when you're away but then again, I imagine you'll be doing a lot of walking.'

'Don't worry, Bella. I wouldn't miss our race for the world and I'm confident we can pick up a pot, too!'

At that moment, we spotted someone sparkling in the sunlight sauntering towards us. Dressed in black trousers and black diamante night club top, with hair that looked like it had seen some action, it was Lou.

'Hello ladies. Sorry I'm late but you know how it is.'

We did a double take as she settled herself at the table.

'I really must try harder. This walk of shame stuff doesn't suit me but hey I made it, better late than never. Will Janie Juno be coming?' She asked as she grabbed a menu.

'No, she's working. Where have you been exactly? You certainly don't look like it was bed!'

It was me who got in first.

'Oh you know, here and there,' she replied breezily. 'But I could do with a strong coffee before anything else. Gina, quick here comes the waitress. Grab her for me.'

She really did look wild. Her mascara had run and her normally velvet hair was standing up in clumps. People were beginning to nudge each other but she couldn't have cared less.

'I'm going for the smoked salmon bagel. Have you already ordered?'

'Just, but we'll get them to hold it so we can all eat together.'

'Sure, great.'

It was the last thing she said before falling asleep face down on the table, leaving Bella and I grinning at each other over the top of her head.

20 – Sometimes ... you share your dreams when you sit under a big fish

I was staying in a hotel directly on Las Ramblas, the busy street in central Barcelona, popular with the locals as well as the tourists. It was a tree-lined pedestrian mall that stretched for three quarters of a mile and connected the Plaça de Catalunya, with its Christopher Columbus monument, to Port Vell. La Boqueria, the fantastically noisy and delicious food market was just across the road and Le Cafe de L'Opera with its dated facade and elegant turn of the century mirrored interior, was a bit further down on the left. The location was perfect to explore everything from the Gaudi architecture to the tapas bars, plus a few galleries that had caught my eye including the Miro at Montjuic, as much for its views across the city as for its art.

Nothing you read in guide books ever prepares you for the richness of humanity that unfolds at any given time in a big city and my senses were awash with sights, sounds, tastes and smells; all the feelings you experience from becoming a small thread in the weave of its fabric. I was filled with excited curiosity and took pleasure from people watching as much as cathedral watching, eating small perfectly formed plates of strange food and buying sweet smelling dried peppers to take home with me.

A living statue of an angel, in an unlikely corner of the street, made me jump to the delight of others, when it reached out and touched me. For all the world, she looked like she was made of aged stone, and once I'd recovered from the surprise I laughed and threw a few euros into her chalice.

Today, I was heading south towards the seafront where I'd arranged to meet Kasim for lunch at the Hotel Arts. He'd said that I couldn't miss it because of some big copper fish but I thought he'd been at the sangria when he'd told me about it last night on the phone so I wasn't too hopeful.

I had put on sensible shoes because the walk was a couple of miles, which would keep Bella happy, and the day was warm with a gentle wind coming up from the port. I meandered along in the shade of the trees and had on a modest black halter neck top with grey silk flared trousers. I carried a light cardigan in case it became too breezy at lunch and looked forward to seeing Kasim; it was amazing and exciting that we were here at the same time.

On reaching the coast, I turned left and walked idly along the port and the seafront. Sure enough, the big fish was visible from a good distance and I had no trouble in finding the restaurant. I spotted him sitting elegantly outside on the terrace with his legs folded and sunglasses on, reading a Spanish magazine.

He stood up when the waiter showed me to the table.

'Hello Gina!'

He kissed me European style on each cheek.

'Hi Kasim, this is a lovely surprise and thank you.'

The waiter pulled my chair out and seated me, draping a crisp linen napkin on my lap with a practised flourish.

'One of those lucky coincidences and I have good news. I've finished what I came here to do and don't fly out until tonight, so this afternoon I'm at your disposal.'

He smiled gleefully, showing his perfect pearly whites.

'Well, wouldn't you know it,' I raised an eyebrow, unsure of whether he'd planned it all along. 'In that case, let's play at being tourists. I was thinking of going to the Gaudi park at Güell as I've not been before.'

'Perfect, then we can see it together as it'll be a first for me, too. You like the big fish?'

He pointed upwards.

I looked with shielded eyes such was its size, and the way it sparkled in the sun. It was positioned so that it faced the sea and I thought it one of the most beautiful pieces of public sculpture I had ever seen.

'Aha! I can see that you do. It was designed by Frank Gehry for the 1992 Olympics and is credited for being a big part of the re-generation of Barcelona.'

'It's massive.'

'I can tell you that it measures thirty-five by fifty-four meters which is about 120 by 180 feet and is made of stone, steel, and glass.'

'You've been rehearsing this to impress me, clever dicky.'

'Actually, it's all in here.'

He showed me the article he was reading.

'I didn't know you understood the language.'

'Enough to get by on.'

He proceeded to order our aperitifs in perfect Spanish, always a dark horse, Kasim.

'How are you enjoying the city, Gina?'

'It's beautiful and vibrant and I have delusions about living here,' I said wistfully.

'Why delusions? It's not beyond your grasp if you wanted to.'

'It's only a pipe dream and to be honest, I think I would prefer to live somewhere a little quieter, not too out of the way but a place that's less built up and possibly a little less frantic. It must be my age.'

'Come and see Paris. Maybe northern France is more practical for you.'

'Maybe.' I thought idly and looked out across the terrace to the shimmering sea.

'How are you feeling, dare I ask, about Max?'

'A lot better than I was expecting to and it's because a couple of things have cropped up pretty much at the same time. First there was the Ball that I told you all about. Then I helped Janie Juno with re-organising an event which got pulled forward and now, being here in this fabulous city. It all adds up to a sense of new horizons and I think it's been my saviour.'

I sipped my ice cold Cava and took a little piece of Morcilla black pudding.

'Did you enjoy working with her?'

'Very much and I was able to make good suggestions that allowed us to take short cuts without compromising on quality so we saved money, too. The event took place last week and was flawless. The client was delighted and she's asked me if I'll help her with some others before Christmas.'

'I'm not surprised you're good at it, Gina, because of your talent for planning. Can you make a business out of it, do you think? You've only got twelve months left on the project which will pass in the blink of an eye and if Janie Juno needs help in organising events, then others will too.'

'It's possible, Kasim, and interestingly, I might have dismissed it out of hand as much as three years ago when I believed that people who walked away from their professions and took right hand turns in life were reckless, but I feel differently now. All of them, Bella, Lou and Janie Juno, do things they care about and have a passion for, so why not me?'

'Have you talked to Bella or Lou about it?'

'Bella dropped in ages ago that she'd love to do events and she did a bit for Janie Juno's thing. She and I were a dream team and Bella knows everybody, and I mean everybody, in the South West.'

'Gina, it sounds a winner. You both have the skills. She has the contacts. You have the money from your bonus. Why don't you go into it together and start small. If the business takes off, you can leave your jobs and the timing could work because of your project finishing this time next year.'

'It could also be good for Bella because her daughter will be established at Uni,' I said thoughtfully. 'There's another aspect of it that really lights me up too but promise you won't laugh.'

I looked at him shyly, not sure if I was ready to admit it.

'Whatever could that be?'

He raised a jokey eyebrow.

'You are laughing at me! I'm not going to tell you if you look like that.'

I folded my arms and sulked for two seconds.

'You know I'm only playing. What is it? I'm all ears.'

'Kasim, I want to do something that involves being with people. In the past you know I've always shied away and kept myself to myself but I don't want to be like that anymore.'

I looked for his reaction and he gently covered my hand with his.

'Do you really think I can't see that? Despite your glitch with Max, and that's all it was, you are thriving in every direction. I knew there was another Gina in there somewhere and here she is. Let me introduce myself to this new Gina. Hello, my name is Kasim.'

He stood up and gave a bow which made me laugh.

'Hello, Kasim! I'm glad you're my friend and we're here in this lovely setting. I feel happy and relaxed and am excited about seeing the park. It's turning out to be a very nice day indeed. Who would have thought it?'

'Me,' he said and smiled.

***

Lunch became a two hour gastronomic marathon of Olympic proportions which almost did for us both. We opted for Iberian ham and a Lobster ravioli followed by John Dory with calamari risotto for Kasim and Sole with seasonal vegetables and meunière of fennel for me. Everything tasted fresh and delighted our palates so that it was with reluctance when we finally got up from the table. Normally, I would have walked or taken the metro but because we were stuffed, we flagged down a taxi and in less than half an hour we were at the park.

We climbed the white steps by the cave structures onto the big terrace with the fluted pillars and played a quick game of hide and seek until Kasim panicked when he thought I'd done a runner after hiding myself in a bush. So not wanting to cause any further upset, I suggested we went up to the next level instead.

A continuous banquette covered in tiny bits of different coloured ceramics snaked its way around the space and people were sitting on it here and there taking in the architecture and the magnificent distant views. It was technically Carmelo Hill which belongs to the mountain range of Sierra de Collserola and the park is located on the northern face.

We managed to cram ourselves into a small space that had been vacated by an orthodox Jew and looked about us.

'I love the patterns and curves don't you, Gina? And look how the sun picks up the pieces, so they glisten individually.'

'See over there, too, the little turrety things. You wonder where Gaudi got his ideas from. Have you seen the Cathedral Kasim, the Sagrada Familia? It looks like it's made of melting wax.'

'I have, but the scaffolding is a shame. Do you know that work started on it over a hundred and twenty years ago and it's still not finished, or ever likely to be?'

'Isn't that part of its charm though, that it's still evolving. The Cathedral in Exeter is a bit like that. They're always undertaking new repairs and whilst they try to blend the old with the new, they also contrast it so you can see it's a work in progress. That's life. Nothing ever stays still.'

Sitting with him in the late afternoon sunshine and still full from my large meal, I felt sleepy and laid my head on his shoulder. I must have dozed off but came to when I'm certain I felt him kiss my hair. When I glanced at him, he was casually looking in the opposite direction and if he had, he wasn't saying. Even though Janie Juno was now on the scene, she could never come between us and I was certain that the friendship he and I shared, which had already endured, would continue. But, and a very big but, if I had nothing to offer him before Max, I was beyond empty now and was grateful that at least with Janie Juno he had found someone that interested him. I didn't believe she was a second best, I just knew he was fond of me.

When he looked at his watch, it was with regret.

'Gina, sadly this is where we must say goodbye. If I go now, I'll be able to make the flight. I can grab a taxi back to the hotel, collect my bag and go on to the airport. It's been a perfect day. Thank you.'

He stood and took my face in his hands but instead of kissing me on the lips, his mouth lightly brushed my forehead which made me almost melt with gratitude. Still holding me, he looked deeply into my eyes and I stood motionless not trusting myself to speak, feeling lost and small again. He had asked nothing of me in all the time I had known him and today he had been honest, supportive and funny. He hadn't mocked my business idea, in fact he had actively encouraged me, but as was always the case, circumstances conspired against us.

He had seen the momentary confusion and emptiness in my eyes, and hugged me, before turning on his heel and making a dash for the stairs. At the top he turned quickly and shouted, 'I'll see you in a few days' time at the Regatta, with the trampoline.'

His laughter bounced around the ceramics and landed happily on me to the extent I decided to buy an ice-cream. I sat quietly waiting for the sun to set and with the dying of the day, banished any further thoughts of what might have been.

21 – Sometimes ... chatting about Oscars leads to a honeymoon of sorts

Today was Friday, my final day before flying back to Bristol at 1700 so I had time to buy the gorgeous cream zipped coat and lime green kitten heels I'd spotted, have lunch at Els Quatre Gats and visit the Miro museum.

The regatta was tomorrow and increasingly, as I wandered around the city my thoughts strayed to our race and how we would fair. I had already seen and bought a black headband that would be perfect for keeping the hair out my eyes, but everything else we wore was strictly regulated. A crew could be disqualified for not being properly attired in correct club colours and both the men and women had custom made Lycra all in ones, in a bottle green colour with white stripes down each side. Admittedly, they sometimes showed off more down below than we would have liked, think camel toes here, but our only saving grace was that they gave the men a touch of the Linford Christie's, if you remember his famous sprint when he picked up Gold for his 100 meter dash, here in Barcelona.

I checked out of the hotel, leaving my trolley bag behind the desk, and headed out to the Avinguda Portal de l'Àngel which was a two minute stroll away from the restaurant at the Carrer de Montsió. I'd made a lunch reservation for 1.30 so I could browse and shop for a few hours.

Luckily, I got the last coat in my size and knew it would be a winner in Exeter. It was cream wool, knee length and fitted but with an A line flair. The collar was the real style cue because it was a high funnel neck with two belted ties and looked like something Barbarella might pitch up in. Now in spending mode, I also spotted a ritzy dark blue sleeveless top as I was about to exit, so that was given a new home too.

In the next mall along, I swooped on the lime green kitten heels like a falcon, having dreamt about them since I arrived. They were highly impractical, but when has that ever stopped us, and the assistant wasn't overly surprised when I decided to keep them on for my lunch. She politely wrapped up my sensible ones and I handed over my credit card, justifying the extravagance on the basis that the exchange rate would be kind to me.

As I toddled off down the road, I was distracted by my new footwear and didn't see the little bow-legged old lady dressed in black. The unexpected collision caused her to drop the bag of oranges she was carrying and they rolled in all directions, making it tricky to gather them up before a dog made off with a few. I apologised profusely and guessed by her bewildered expression that she was from the countryside, where you don't see many pairs of lime green shoes.

It was possible.

The restaurant was situated in an ancient side street and the entrance was via a pair of ornate steel and glass doors set into a red bricked facade which curved upwards to a pointed arch. An old lantern hung above the doorway which was lit, despite it being warm and sunny.

I was welcomed in and shown to a discrete table on the gallery so I could look down onto the main dining area with a good view of my fellow diners. It was a fascinating place and everywhere I looked there were paintings and posters. Picasso used to come here before he was famous and one of its claims was that it hosted his first exhibition. The restaurant had been going for more than a hundred years as an all-round artistic space and centre of Modernista – my kind of place – and you could sense its past seeping from the walls.

I noticed a framed illustration from the turn of the last century of two men on a tandem with the one in front smoking a pipe and appearing to do all the work. It reminded me of Lou and I in our boat and I smiled inwardly at the sentiment. It was a striking, light hearted image and was said to be a self-portrait of a previous owner, him being the man at the back.

I ordered from the set lunch menu, tasty portions of Catalan and Mediterranean cuisine and took time to enjoy the atmosphere. I was no stranger to dining on my own after my five years in Brussels and everyone around seemed as relaxed as me.

I finished off with a cheeky Carajillo, an expresso with a dash of brandy, because I knew their coffee was the best in the city then paid the bill and got on my way. My plan was to take the metro from Placa Catalunya south to Paral·lel station and the funicular to the Miro at Montjuic. The station was about fifteen minutes away on foot so I sadly changed back into my sensible shoes, carefully re-packaging my precious kitten heels.

When I arrived at the square, a young Catalan woman with long black wavy hair, tied off her face with a decorated Spanish comb, was standing in a star in the centre of a large paved circle with fountains behind her acting as a natural backdrop. She was singing soprano to the accompaniment of a portable CD player and was dressed completely in black; a chiffon wrap over a long dress which contrasted magnificently with her flawless olive skin.

There was something proud but vulnerable in the way she sang her songs, one after the other, with genuine feeling, alone in the circle and I was moved not only by the music but by her passion and natural shyness. Her talent was obvious.

It's a busy old place at the best of times, with fast flowing traffic all around, but that day her voice transcended the revs, the horn blowing and the blasts of music that occasionally escaped through open windows, almost as if the city took a breath and stopped to listen to her beauty.

I'd intended to hop on the metro but instead found myself sitting amongst the tourists and locals alike, enjoying the impromptu performance. The music, I discovered after buying her CD, was mostly old classical Spanish by a composer called Manuel de Falla, one of Spain's most important musicians.

Her name turned out to be Pilar Rodriguez and when she sang a song called Nana, people were visibly sniffling. When she followed it with a finale of Puccini's 'O Mio Babbino Caro' they openly wept into their bocadillo sandwiches then stood to applaud loudly, while others threw flowers recently purchased from La Boqueira for their grandmothers. The fountains themselves had appeared to be choreographed to the rise and fall of the music and added to the sense of harmony and unity that she bestowed on Barcelona for the duration of her songs.

I was able to thank her only briefly for the wonderful performance because she was mobbed, so I stowed the CD carefully with my shoes and went down the stairs to the contrasting gloom of the subway, albeit dragging my feet after what I had just been exposed to.

It was a straight forward journey to the Miro museum and once there, I put my packages in a locker and the key in my purse. I didn't bother with an audio guide as I preferred to amble about, following my nose, and very soon I was looking up at a huge mobile suspended from a fifty foot high ceiling.

'Do you like it?'

The man standing to my right suddenly spoke and I looked around in case he was talking to someone else.

'Yes I do, but I think it's loaded with innuendo.'

He laughed and I turned to look at him properly. His accent was unmistakably English and he was a man of about seventy, dressed dapperly in blue blazer, white shirt and a slightly lopsided authentic red bow tie.

'Not many people seem to get that about Miro. Interesting,' the dapper man said.

'It's the first time I've seen his work at first hand so I hadn't fully appreciated the sexuality until now.'

'I see.'

At this point someone came up to him, had a few words, he signed something and they went.

'Would you like me to give you a tour? I'm quite well versed in his art.'

Why not? I thought. Nothing could be worse than the audio babble.

'I'm Alan and you are …?'

'Gina. Gina Jarvie. I'm in Barcelona for a few days and fly back tonight to Bristol.'

'Is that where you live, dear?'

'No, I actually live in Exeter.'

'I'm in a village on Dartmoor, about ten miles from there.'

He told me which one but it meant nothing to me and then someone else came over, had a few words, offered him something to sign and went away.

'What line of work are you in, Gina?'

'Dull as ditchwater, I'm afraid. Finance and systems. Most people are asleep by now.'

He laughed.

'How about you?'

Before he could answer, an American couple approached. The man was wearing cowboy boots and a Stetson whilst the woman was struggling to walk upright under the weight of her blonde wig and boob job.

'Hey, excuse me, are you Alan Lee, the guy that worked on the Lord of the Rings films?' he asked in a drawl that only confirmed my Texan hunch.

'Yes, I am.'

'I said Carla-Jean it was likely him. Would you mind signing this here flyer for us, Mr Lee. We're real big fans and our kids, too. When's your follow-up coming out?'

'As a matter of fact, I've recently been over in New Zealand to help with the final touches but it won't be up to me I'm afraid.'

'Well, all the best to you anyways. I'll leave you in peace now, and thank you kindly sir, once again.'

He tipped his hat.

'Excuse me Alan, but did Mr Cowboy Boots over there just ask you about Lord of the Rings?'

He chuckled. 'He did Gina. I drew the illustrations for The Hobbit when it was re-issued and Peter Jackson asked me to help out with the artistic direction on the films so I said I'd be happy to. It's been very enjoyable.'

I suddenly looked at the time and realised it was marching on.

'I would really love to stay and continue this conversation Alan, but unfortunately I have a plane to catch.'

'That's a shame Gina, because I'm enjoying your company but here take my card and we'll have a coffee when I get back from The States.'

'Is it more film work?'

'You could say something like that.'

He looked embarrassed but my curiosity was piqued and it made me brave.

'Is it a secret? Are you not supposed to tell anyone?'

'Oh, why not,' he declared, throwing his hands up. 'You only live once! There's talk that I might be up for an Oscar.'

'Oscar!' I shouted.

'Shush ... keep your voice down.' He looked around quickly in case anyone was in earshot.

'I'm sorry Alan but I wasn't expecting that. Anyway listen, good luck with your 'thingy' and I'll try to give you a call. I'm afraid I really must go. Sorry again!'

I looked once more at my watch and saw it would be tight but do-able, realising I had lost track earlier when I was distracted by the music. I got to my hotel around five which gave me two hours to get to the airport and I did a last minute check for tickets and passport. Yup, all there but then something made my stomach flinch like it does when you eat ice-cream too quickly.

1700 isn't seven o'clock.

1700 is five o'clock.

I threw my head back, let out a long sigh and said to no-one in particular, 'I've done it again!'

With a reputation for this particular trait of dyslexia (not bad for an accountant with a history of aircraft scheduling) people around me normally checked the tickets, but as I was on my own it hadn't been possible. My watch now showed quarter past five so I'd already missed the plane and the next thought that popped into my head was of Bella. She would throw me in the quay for sure but perhaps there was another flight or another airport or someone like Alan Lee who could nip me back in his private helicopter. I fingered his card in my pocket but I didn't know him well enough yet to ask for a lift.

'Excuse me please but can I use the computer?' I asked the small greying man in a porter's uniform behind the desk.

'Si Señora, he just here. I give you password. You have problem?'

'Oh no, thank you. Everything's fine and dandy,' I replied breezily.

'Qué? Me no understand what is this you say, 'fine and dandy'. You me explain.'

'Another time, Manuel.' I could only guess at his name.

The next flight to Bristol was first thing in the morning and it would get me in for our race by the skin of my teeth; no time to practise but I would have to step up. I checked other combinations of routes but as there was no advantage, I re-booked my ticket.

And then I phoned Bella.

'Gina, you've missed the flight haven't you?'

I'd forgotten about her psychic powers.

'How did you guess?' I said lightly trying to make it sound normal.

'I knew this would happen! You mixed up the times again, didn't you?'

No point in arguing, she'd got the eye on me, even if I was in a foreign country.

'Sort of, but the good news is I'm booked on another one.'

'But it doesn't get you back to Exeter until one o'clock. That's right isn't it?'

I did a quick eyes to the left and eyes to the right in case she'd landed on her broomstick.

'Possibly,' I said, hedging my bets.

'Oh, for god's sake, just get here when you can. I'll do a ring round and get a replacement for you in case you don't make it and we'll speak tomorrow.' She hung up, leaving me staring at the grumpy phone.

Oh well, I had been stuck in worse places.

'Manuel, yes you, I need a room.'

'We have only honeymoon room now with big bed and bath but will let you have it very good price.'

Just my luck after what I'd gone through, a honeymoon for one.

It was only my fear of Bella that stopped me crumpling into a tear-fuelled sodden mess and I squared my shoulders and told Manuel that my husband would be along shortly. I hoped it would get lost in translation given his obvious limitations but when he winked at me lasciviously I made sure I slept that night with my bag firmly propped up against the door.

Alan Lee thankfully was not blighted with my particular form of dyslexia as he seemed to be on time a few months later when he collected his Academy Award for Best Art Direction for The Lord of the Rings: The Return of the King, the third in the film trilogy.

Phew.

22 – Sometimes ... you find just the occasion for the ritzy new top you've been dying to wear

The plane landed on time and because the traffic was lighter than expected, I made good progress and arrived at my flat an hour before our race. I guessed Kasim was around somewhere from the small trampoline that stood triumphantly in the middle of the lounge, but there was no time to look for him.

I had already phoned Bella and got messages to Lou and Janie Juno so my stand-in was relieved of her duties. After a quick change, and a hunting down of the new hair band, I tucked my lipstick inside my cleavage and sprinted across the road.

Pete O'Mara, dressed in a green club polo shirt, was running round like a demented leprechaun but his smile was genuine when he spotted me.

'Why did you do this to us, dearest Gina?' He laughed as he embraced me.

'Yeah, sorry about the little hiccup, Pete. I was having too much of a good time.'

'Welcome back that's all I can say and you're very lucky not to have been anywhere near Bella when the news broke. I was with her in the boatshed when you called and I thought she was going to combust!'

He was laughing again.

'What's the mood now?' I asked bravely.

'Calm and focussed. They've got the boat on the water and Vicky has been helping with the warm up. I'll grab the loudhailer and we'll swap you in. Now, just do the best you can and enjoy it. It's not a long race, only five hundred meters, and you're up against Exmouth, Bideford Blues and Bideford Reds plus Totnes and Paignton. We're in with a chance here so I hope you've put on your lucky drawers.'

How did he know I wondered, thinking about the big padded knickers I wore to prevent blisters on my bottom. People are under the impression that rowing is elegant but I've still got the scars to prove otherwise.

'Sure thing! And, I've got my lipstick.' I brought it out with a flourish.

'Forget your frigging lipstick. I want that pot, do you hear? Do you hear, Gina?' He bared his teeth.

'Yes, boss! The pot!' I hastily stuffed it down into the darkness again, regretting my moment of frivolity.

'Right, let's go. Are you ready? And please, please, just try and stay in the boat!'

He rushed to the quayside and bellowed, 'Exeter number two, come in. We have a new crew member'

Their faces showed their happy relief.

Followed by daggers.

Better brace myself.

The cox brought them gently onto the pontoon and Vicky jumped out while Pete held the blades down for me to get in. Bella glared at me for two long seconds before breaking into a big welcoming smile and said 'Gina, you are one on your own. Get in the bloody boat and help us to win this thing. Am I glad to see you or what?'

Spontaneously, they all cheered including our tiny cox Ruthie who was never known for making anything other than barking noises when we fell behind.

'Sorry about that folks,' was the most I could manage because of the lump in my throat.

'Never mind, Gina. This win will be for all of us, but for Pete especially. Kasim is sat with my mum and Joanna about half way along.'

Lou was beaming.

Janie Juno only rolled her eyes and joined in the nervous release of laughter. Within minutes we were focussed and adjusting before setting off for a very quick practise to sit the boat and go over our tactics for getting away first, and keeping the lead. Pete had drummed it into us that Bideford Blues were the ones to watch because last time they'd narrowly beaten us by a boat length. The tankard we were after was all the more important to us because we were on home ground, or water, so to speak.

Ruthie shouted her instructions and we did a few racing starts that went smoothly enough and some full pressure work, but not enough to tire us out. We made our way to the start and had time to take a few sips from our water bottles, and for me to do a quick flick of lipstick, before we were called to the line.

'Exmouth, come back five strokes and Totnes come forward four strokes.'

I recognised the voice of Johnny, one of our officials who I knew from the bar and it gave me the confidence to believe we could actually do it. He was arranging a fair line up for the start. None of us said a word as we kept the boat as still as we could and then Ruthie spoke into her mic.

'OK, ladies. This is an easy stretch. We're going to do it text book style and use everything we've practised. I want that tankard as much as you and if you listen to me, we'll get it. Understood?'

'Yes cox.' We shouted in unison.

'I'm going to call you off now, starting from bow. Are you ready bow?'

'Yes,' from Bella.

'Number three?'

'Yes.' Me.

'Number two?'

'Yes.' I heard Janie Juno.

'Stroke?'

'Yes.'

This came from Lou, who sat opposite the cox.

'Good, we're all ready.'

Johnny shouted through the loud hailer, 'Come forward to row.'

My nerves were taught and I had the heavy wooden blade in my right hand, feeling it warm and smooth beneath my sweaty fingers.

'Row!' Johnny commanded above the crack sound of the starting pistol which pierced the air and galvanised us.

My heart was pounding as we got cleanly away and I could feel the power coming from Bella rowing behind me. We had to follow everything that Lou did to the second and we kept our heads facing forward at all times, even though the temptation to look for the other boats was burning. I knew all eyes from our club were on us and I could feel Pete O'Mara bearing down.

The quayside was lined with spectators and people were cheering and shouting as we edged our way along the river in the direction of the finishing line, out of sight around the corner.

I heard someone shout 'Come on, Gina. Come on Exeter number two. You're ahead, keep going' but could only guess who it might be. I could see Bideford Blues gaining ground but the others seemed much further back. Ruthie continued to bark instructions and goad us forward but Bideford started to come alongside until we were neck and neck.

I could hear their cox saying they had us and I thought it was all over, but Ruthie calmly instructed us to full pressure so we pulled harder and lengthened our stroke. Again, I could feel Bella's power behind me and miraculously we started to pull away, first by a person then by two until we were a boat's length ahead. How much further could it be? We were at full pelt but our boat was smooth and the blades came cleanly out of the water so we kept our momentum.

We turned the bend in the river and Bideford tried again because they had the advantage of the line but Ruthie deftly steered us over and they had to go wide. In the few precious strokes they lost, we pulled further ahead until we were two lengths apart and my confidence grew. My breathing was laboured and my legs were feeling the burn but I rowed as if my life depended on it.

As we approached the finish line, with fifty meters to go, Bideford made a last minute attempt and Ruthie took us back up to full pressure. It was so close I couldn't bear to look and shut my eyes for an instant to concentrate on the technique.

It was only the noise of the crowd erupting that told me we had won.

I opened them again to cheering faces and waving banners that our friends had made with our names on and leaned forward panting across my blade. I felt Bella pat me gently a couple of times on my right shoulder but we were still too breathless to speak.

'Well done girls!'

It was our friend Dave, the club President, from the safety boat moored at the end, before the weir.

'Thanks, but it was a close call.'

Bella was still trying to get her breath and it was Ruthie who congratulated us next.

'That was a great race and I'm proud of you all. Did you feel the turbo kick when we upped the pressure? They couldn't match us and I knew it from earlier so I saved the best spurt for last. Well done Bella for power and Lou for pace, you were a great team!'

I was grinning like the proverbial Cheshire and we all began to reach across to one another as best we could without destabilising. I saw Pete on the quayside trying to push through the crowds to get to us. You couldn't miss him in his green gear waving and shouting, not so much as a demented leprechaun, but as a man who'd just been delivered of a son after seven daughters and couldn't hide his delight.

Ruthie took us to the side, to below where he was standing, and he leaned over, his normally composed face beaming from ear to ear.

'Ladies, ladies! You were fantastic out there! Bloody fantastic and you've made me very proud. It's a great day for us all and I thank you from the bottom of me Kilkenny heart.'

His voice sounded more Irish than ever and when he suddenly blew us lots of air kisses, we all laughed as he was never one for spontaneous displays of emotion, which made it all the more poignant.

'And one more thing, Gina.'

Oh here we go I thought, what did I do wrong this time and my heart sank a little. At this point he threw himself on his knees and lifted his arms out to me, 'Thank the Lord above that you didn't fall in!'

Everyone sniggered as the adrenalin took hold and I pretended to sulk for a nanosecond before my smile reflected his and I punched the air.

'Bring it on, Pete!' I shouted as we started to turn the boat around to row it upriver.

***

At the club house we were welcomed back like conquering heroes with everyone complimenting us on the race. To be heralded by both our peers and the hierarchy was a proud moment but our win also initiated us firmly into the inner fabric of the club where we were respected for our achievement.

I felt light as a feather as we washed and stowed the boat with all of us talking excitedly over each other, re-running our win. When everything was put away, we stood in the sunshine on the pontoon and had a group hug. Our shared experience and triumph had only strengthened the already tight bonds between us and I felt the warmth of these friendships course through my body. Reluctantly, we pulled apart and decided to go in search of Kasim, Joanna and Lou's mum Stephanie, who had thoughtfully brought us a picnic.

We found them sitting on deckchairs with a bird's eye view of the river and as we made our way through the throng, still dressed in our club gear, the spectators parted which added to our sense of accomplishment.

As soon as Kasim saw Janie Juno they got into a clinch with lots of kissing and laughing and we left them to it.

'Well done girls! It was one of the most exciting races of the regatta.' Joanna carefully and elegantly tucked a loose strand of silken hair behind her ear.

Today she had on her diamonds which sparkled when she moved.

'I've brought some smoked salmon bagels, I know they're Lou's favourite.'

Stephanie was busy unpacking the picnic while Bella and I were reminded of the last time we had seen Lou with a bagel, face down fast asleep on a table actually not too far from where we now stood. We gave each other a look that Stephanie noticed but couldn't gauge and we smiled when Lou decided it would be a good time to gaze into the far distance.

When Janie Juno and Kasim eventually unstuck themselves, he came over and kissed my cheek.

'Gina, I am so proud and happy for you. Did you see the trampoline?'

'I did,' I said laughing. 'You were serious then?'

'Always am. It's a good job you gave me a key to let myself in but I'm sure Joanna would have helped.' He winked at her and she giggled, very girlishly. Tut, tut.

I knew this was his way of bringing the subject round to the missed flight so I took a deep breath.

'It was the timing problem.'

'Not again!' He squawked. 'You didn't mix up 1700. Not again?'

I looked down and shuffled a bit as he put his arm around my shoulder and squeezed it.

'It's a good job we love you, is all I can say.'

And everyone raised their bagels in a toast.

'Which reminds me. I have a special little something I need to get from the flat. Won't be long.'

He excused himself to the sound of us hungrily attacking the carbs.

The day was growing warmer so I took a few minutes to stretch out on my own on the edge of the quay, and though the adrenalin from the race was no longer there, my thoughts had decided to stage their own high octane competition.

Janie Juno came and lay down beside me.

'Did you enjoy the race?'

I felt the second lump of the day come into my throat as I struggled to harness my emotions, not only from winning, but from everything that had led up to this moment. I had on my sunglasses and was still wearing my all in one but she obviously sensed my state of mind and gently took my hand.

'We really showed 'em didn't we? Those Bideford Blues girls are crying their eyes out back there. One of their crew should have gone to Barcelona!' she quipped which made me smile.

'I wouldn't have wanted to miss this for the world and I'm sorry about not getting back on time. It was a really stupid mistake to make.'

'It happens, but the main thing is you got here and we won. Pete's reaction is beyond anything I could have imagined or hoped for. Difficult to believe that we lit him up like that, isn't it?'

'A very happy man. When I tried hard, it was as much for him as for any of us.'

'Me too, Gina.'

'On days like today, with this tide of good feeling all around you and your own sense of pride, it's difficult to imagine why you'd lock yourself away from it.'

'People have their reasons ... ,' she said quietly, letting it drift along with the water.

I sighed and wiped away a stray tear from under my glasses.

'But look what happens when you turn the key, Janie. Every ounce of me feels truly alive, even more than the night when we ran with our balloons. I thought then it was a pinnacle but things just keep getting better. All of this today,' I swept my arm round in a broad arc, 'shows me that life is filled with happy possibilities. You only need to know where to look.'

'That's true Gina, but you also have to be prepared to take a punt and venture down a few dark tunnels, where the light isn't always visible. It shouldn't stop you from entering them though.'

'Not unless the 17.53 from Carlisle is coming in the opposite direction!' I smiled through my tears.

'Now, would that be the 5.53 or the 7.53, Gina?' she raised her eyebrow questioningly and grinned. 'You rowed every bit as well as the rest of us today and, considering you only started a few months ago, you've proved yourself to be a worthy member of this team, by any measurement. Do you remember the time when Lou invited you in the boat back in April and you thought she was joking?'

'Yes, I do.'

'But just look at what you've done. I mean, really look at what you've done and how far you've come, Gina, in such a short while. If all those doubting Thomas's you've told me about in The Midlands could see you now, five months on, what would they think?'

'I'm unrecognisable,' I said in a whisper of revelation. 'Almost to myself.'

'So you were right to come down here and have a love affair that would end badly so you would throw yourself into something new and excel at it?'

'It looks that way, doesn't it?'

I gave a small laugh at her succinctness.

'What's next then, Gina?' She jumped up and brushed a speck of dirt from her thigh.

'I think I'm going to enjoy the afternoon sun before I shower and put on my blue ritzy top for the award ceremony later on. How about you?'

'I think I'm going to do exactly the same. But my top is fuchsia pink.'

'And here's a bottle of Dom Perignon, ladies, to toast your success!'

Kasim presented it with a bow and began the process of popping the cork, as the eager hands of the winning crew held out their flutes. He always did have an aptitude for injecting a little glamour and some style into an occasion.

23 – Sometimes ... you can keep your hat on

The autumn inched slowly forward and the lock to the river closed, which restricted our rowing to the canal. During the week, because of the diminishing daylight, our sessions were shorter. At weekends we had the opportunity to go further on, away from the congestion of the other boats, as far as The Double Locks pub or further still to The Turf Hotel that marked the beginning of the wide Exe estuary.

We had some lovely outings on early winter mornings, when the sun was low on the horizon and mist swirled on the water. The grass was white with frost which hadn't yet melted, and the shadows were long. If it was nippy when we started, after a few minutes the layers came off and soon we were down to our tee-shirts. The water was still and the wildlife sleepy, including the swans that could be seen snuggled down in their nests.

We'd taken to going for coffee after these sessions and were now a regular fixture in Mangoes. On any given Saturday, we could be found there slouched on the vintage sofas catching up with each other and sharing our news.

'Have you given any more thought to the pre-Christmas fundraiser party?' Lou asked as she bit into her chocolate brownie.

'No time,' Bella had her mouth full of croissant. 'Lou, tell Gina.'

'Tell Gina what?' I asked, digging out the pink marshmallows from my hot chocolate.

'One of the crews organises a party and serves the food. You charge by the ticket, normally five or six quid, then you deduct costs and whatever's left goes into the boat fund for new ones. They aim to make around three hundred pounds.'

'Who's been chosen to do it this year?' I asked innocently.

'Oh, didn't you know? We have. I thought I'd told you.' Lou popped the last of the brownie into her mouth.

Bella nodded, so she obviously knew.

'Us!' I cried louder than I meant to.

'Shush, keep your voice down Gina. They're looking at you again.' Bella was licking her fingers. 'They seem to think we're organised, can cook and come up with something that's never been done before. Word must have got out about your events, Gina.'

Janie Juno nodded thoughtfully. 'We can easily do it. There's three weeks to go and people have already saved the date so it's just a case of thinking of a theme and maxing the profits.'

'How about Heroes and Villains so I can go as Lara Croft?' Lou stuck out her 34EEs a bit further than normal and I knew she'd be in for a good time if she went dressed like that.

'It's a great idea,' I said. 'And food wise, if we keep it simple and do a meat chilli, a veg chilli plus a few nibbles everyone will get a good meal. It won't be much work and costs will be low.'

I was already determined to give everyone a night to remember and to double what they normally took, so in my head I set a target profit of six hundred pounds.

'Bella, how are you fixed for time?' I got out my notebook

'Sorry, Gina, I'm up to my eyes in it.'

'And I know you are Lou because of your busy retail period. That leaves me and Janie Juno.'

'Sure you can manage?' Bella looked apprehensive.

'Absolutely! That's settled then. Heroes and Villains it is. I'll make the tickets this afternoon and put them on sale. Lou, you're queen of the cocktails. Come up with something we can sell to boost the takings.'

'Yes, sir, Gina! I'm on the case!'

Once we had the idea, the plan flowed like clockwork and that night Janie Juno and I printed the tickets. Over the next few days we bought and made decorations until the small hours and I dovetailed the party with another event she had asked me to take on in the unlikely setting of the Botanical Gardens in Shaldon.

It had involved the transformation of a derelict stone folly at Homeyards into a fairy tale castle, complete with braziers and dragons, for which I had hired a top notch chef and delivered a gourmet, once in a lifetime party for fifty of the county's movers and shakers. It had meant using some of my precious annual leave but when the party had made it to the society pages of Devon Life, I was delighted. My hard work had got me some recognition, especially as getting the permissions on the back of the rigours of health and safety hadn't been easy. The client had paid me a thank you bonus and I now needed to seriously think about which way to take things.

For our own Heroes and Villains, I kept a daily count of ticket sales as I'd numbered each one (sorry, but that's the accountant in me) and watched as they approached the one hundred mark. I had calculated that to meet the target we needed to sell another twenty, but I did have a trick up my sleeve.

***

On the day of the party we decorated the club house and I extracted the chilli I'd made the week before from the freezer so as not to be chained to the kitchen. Lou had perfected a cocktail she was calling 'The Mummy Returns' but I dreaded to think what was in it.

At seven o'clock, that would be 1900 hours, they started to arrive and we were there to greet them and get the music going. Lou, as predicted, came as a stunning Lara Croft wearing her Aussie gear and big boots. God knows where she got the guns from.

Bella, with her long flowing tresses and sleek black dress, had come either as Morticia Addams (hero) or Lady Macbeth (villain) take your pick, while Janie Juno had opted for a contemporary Britannia look, complete with a brush for a trident, a turban for a helmet and a union jack umbrella for her shield.

The mind boggled.

I had decided to go as Dorothy from the Wizard of Oz, my favourite heroine of all time, and I managed to find a little dog like Toto for my basket.

Not a real one.

The room had filled up nicely and the smell of the cooking chilli added a homespun nostalgia. The cocktails were slipping down a 'ker-ching' treat and a few stragglers at the door without tickets had mopped up the spares, so it was all coming together.

Initially, it had been difficult to spot Pete O'Mara because most of them were unrecognisable, but I eventually worked out that he was the Uncle Fester talking to Bella, who was obviously Morticia at this point.

I was kept busy in the back for a while waiting until everyone had eaten before coming round to the other side of the bar, and it was the first chance I had to take in what we had done.

Dave the President had come with three others as the Steve Redgrave winning team decked out in GB all in ones. They wore gold discs the size of dinner plates around their necks and stood on portable podiums which they lugged about with them. There were several Superwomen and Catwomen, a Cruella De Ville, a mummy (we were bang on with the cocktails!) another James Bond and some that I wasn't so sure about, like the tomato for instance.

When they started into the dancing, I judged the time was about right to retrieve my concealed chalk board from its hiding place and rang a bell. From their various corners I could see Janie Juno, Bella and Lou looking quizzically at me.

'Attention! Attention, please!' I shouted above the noise and someone quickly turned the music down.

'As we all know, tonight is in aid of new boats'

'Hear! Hear!' they all shouted, as new boats meant quicker times that translated into more wins.

'So listen up everybody, I have a suggestion to make.'

Now, before I go any further with my story, you must understand that in the world of rowing there are some you might say who are proud of their muscles and show them off at every opportunity. Dave the President, surprisingly for a man of nearly fifty, was one of them and it was this trait that I was counting on for my little ploy. As it happened, I wasn't wrong.

I rang the bell again, for effect.

'Ladies and gentlemen, Heroes and Villains, and the tomato over there, I am opening, for one night only, a tote where you may lay down good money for those of us you either love or hate to treat you to their finest strip-tease!'

I had barely, excuse my expression, finished and the room erupted.

It went wild.

I mean wild.

London zoo had nothing on these guys and gals.

'Order! Order!' I had to ring my bell again.

'This blackboard here,' I pointed to my blackboard. 'Will be used to record your pledges, and by that I mean you can pay me a pound to nominate a person of your choice to bare their ... all! I'll keep it open for thirty minutes and at the end of that time, the three Heroes or Villains with the highest number of nominations will go forward to the final round of pledging which will cost you another two quid a pop.'

While I thought it might have been a good idea, nothing prepared me for the stampede of African wildebeest proportions and money changed hands quicker than at the Harrods sale. Each time a pound was donated, I put a chalk stick mark against a name and very quickly three people jumped into the lead. As the stick marks increased, the face of one of them started to look pale even under his carefully applied white face paint.

Pete O'Mara.

The other two names belonged, unsurprisingly, to Dave and one of the female rowers who made Jessica Rabbit look like a twig. Now, please believe me that my intention wasn't to humiliate anyone, it was to simply raise money, and I could already see we were on course for several hundred pounds. It was time for me to do a bit of fixing and schmoozing so I glided over to Pete, leaving Bella in charge of the Tote.

'Gina, I really can't take my clothes off in front of them all. I could barely do it with my missus, when I was married. You've got to help me here,' he laughed, but nervously.

'Don't worry, Pete, I've got a plan. Just stay with it because you're making us a fortune. I promise, you won't have to remove a thing. Cross my heart.' I crossed my heart.

'Bloody hell, Gina, where do you get your ideas from? We've never seen anything like it!'

'Aha!' I said tapping the side of my nose and sauntered back over to help Bella out.

'Gina, I reckon there's nearly three hundred quid in this pot. Look at all the chalk marks! It's brilliant, you're a genius.'

'OK, folks. Attention! Attention!'

I rang the bell again.

'As you can see, the three finalists are, in reverse order.'

A slight pause and a cough for dramatic effect.

'In third place is Superwoman Miss Victoria Bentham. Step forward Vicky and take a bow!'

She was beaming and gave a twirl with a sexy wiggle.

'Second is our very own President, Delectable Dave aka Sir Steve.'

There was no stopping him and he made a show of starting to rip his clothes off there and then.

'And finally! The person here tonight that is leading the first round is none other than Uncle Fester, Pete O'Mara, the only Irishman outside of Ireland who can get away with drinking Bootley Ale instead of the Guinness.'

All eyes turned to Pete and big cheers went up. While he smiled and bowed, I knew he was on the verge of a nervous breakdown.

'OK, folks, next round. Get your money ready, two quid this time. Off we go!'

I rang the bell again.

Business was brisk and I made sure it was me who manned the board and placed the marks. For every one we got for Pete, I added one to Dave and nobody noticed because of 'The Mummy Returns'. However, after fifteen minutes, there was no denying that Pete was still the forerunner.

Time for plan B.

I dimmed the lights.

I had already primed Dave, but the fact that Pete had won threw a spanner, albeit a small one, into the works. I whispered into his ear, and as Tom Jones' began to belt out 'You can leave your hat on' Pete braved the stage and started swaying his hips and undoing his buttons.

For the second time that night, they went wild.

The cheers and whistles were deafening and Pete was making a good fist of dancing, while not actually taking anything off. Another minute of gyrations continued before the Steve Redgrave lot, including Dave, jumped on the stage and shoved Pete unceremoniously out of the way before they promptly disrobed.

Everything.

Nothing was left on.

People were screaming and holding onto each other in hysterics and Pete was laughing, fully clothed, in the wings.

At the end of the performance the guys made a bow, to the front thankfully, picked up their gear and covered their bits modestly with the gold medal discs before flouncing off the stage, one after the other, to wild applause.

Job done!

Afterwards, people came up to thank us for one of the funniest nights they'd had in a long time and myself, Britannia, Morticia and Lara had another of our group hugs as we posed for photos. It was while this was going on that Janie Juno whispered into my ear that it was time for us to add another notch to our piece of lapsed adult driftwood, and when I nodded enthusiastically she couldn't stop herself from laughing again.

The night went down in history for two reasons.

We made a record thousand pounds profit for the boat fund, and I had my first ever one night stand.

Albeit unintentionally.

24 – Sometimes ... a packet of Hobnobs is enough to satisfy your appetite

Unlike the surreal tomato, which had us all guessing, he had come to the party dressed as an unmistakable Nelson in period British naval costume with distinctive hat and hair, including a ponytail.

Generally speaking, the rowing club was always a hotbed of romance and who could blame them? They were young, fit, healthy and toned and thought nothing of having flings and jumping into bed with each other as and when the opportunity arose. Some ended in marriage, though not straight away, and for generations people met their future spouses while posing at the bar wearing very little, such was the nature of the sport.

Being older than average, with two sons who were only slightly younger than some of the guys, I always made a rule of avoiding being the subject of gossip by studiously rising above the ever present hormonal swirl that seemed to ooze from the very walls.

When I had first joined the club over eight months ago I was with Max, who had come and gone with the seasons, and since the beginning of August I was firmly unattached. They egged me on here and there, more out of playfulness than by way of a serious proposition, and I wasn't unaware of the book that the younger ones ran which offered good odds on several of the seniors doing the business with me. I took it in the spirit it was intended but never let my guard down.

I had got talking to him outside the club house by the water when I'd gone to cool down after dishing up the food, to decide when best to pull out my blackboard. Someone had handed me a very large 'The Mummy Returns' cocktail which I was eyeing suspiciously.

'You're Gina, aren't you?' came a voice from the darkness behind me before it stepped into the light.

'Well, technically yes, but tonight I'm Dorothy, as you can see.'

I looked down at my shoes and clicked them together.

'Pleased to meet you, I'm Mr Nelson but you can call me Horatio or Harry if you like.'

He took off his hat and made a sweeping bow. A good bit taller than me and very handsome in a dark and brooding kind of way, he made a very good Nelson indeed.

'I've never seen you before at the club, Harry. What brings you here?'

'Matt and I were at Uni together and because I was visiting this weekend he asked me along.'

I knew Matt from the senior crew so that made Harry about thirty.

'Are you a marine biologist, too?'

'No, nothing like that. Have a guess.'

He smiled and his teeth were white in the semi darkness.

'Tinker, tailor, soldier, spy ...?' I was trying to remember the rhyme.

'Where did that come from?' he asked incredulously. 'But seeing as you're very, very close I'll tell you. I was in the army and now I work for MI5.'

My surprise was an understatement and I looked sharply into my cocktail, wondering what she'd actually put in it.

'You're joking, because you're not supposed to tell anyone.'

'That might be the stuff of George Smiley but we're a bit more out there since Stella Rimington took to the lecture circuit.'

'Funnily enough, I heard her speak once at a conference, but I still don't believe you.'

'Gina, I mean, Dorothy, I can't show you my ID if that's what you want. I'm in fancy dress for one thing but Matt will vouch for me.'

'I'm sure he will!'

'Seriously, I do work for them and I can tell you that much and no more.'

'So how did you get into it?'

'I was in the Royal Corps of Signals and it was a short hop from there because we were always being scouted.'

'Yes, but what's flag waving and semaphores got to do with intelligence gathering?'

It was a fair question and he laughed.

'It's a bit more hi-tech than that these days; think advanced IT systems, satellite communications and the like. I am, I mean, I was an expert. It still comes in very useful.'

'I'll bet. Listen, I have to go now as I'm about to unleash a goldmine for this club so you'll have to excuse me.'

He clasped my arm as I went to pass and lowered his voice meaningfully, 'Can I meet you later, Gina?'

His insistent grip and directness were audacious and incited me to throw caution, and anything else I might have been thinking of, to the wind.

It was powerful stuff.

'OK, Harry, if that's even your real name. I'll be the one collapsed in the corner, especially if I have any more of these!'

I gestured to 'The Mummy Returns' frothing dangerously in my glass.

In the quietness of our shared moment, and with everyone else indoors, he put his arms around me and we kissed furiously. I hadn't seen it coming and it literally knocked the wind out of me. It was a delicious kiss and he held me close and tight in a way that left me in no doubt what he wanted.

'Save yourself for me later, Gina, and I promise we'll have some fun.'

His look was lingering and I saw a daring flash in his eyes which made me heady.

'I'll meet you at the gate to the boatyard next door at midnight. It's opposite where I live. Alone.'

We kissed hard again and adjusted our clothes before returning to the party.

During the evening, we exchanged a few more words and each time we touched, my excitement grew.

I would like to say that alarm bells rang but it wouldn't be true and, if anything, I was already aroused, and determined to see it through. I wanted no counsel and had intentionally said nothing to no-one, though I knew Bella had seen us briefly together.

After the group hug with the girls, I had five minutes until my rendezvous and imagined us like spies in the night, our faces lit from a match he held to my cigarette.

I said my goodbyes and scanned the room.

He wasn't there.

Outside, the night was crisp and clear as I walked the hundred yards to the gate, carrying my ridiculous basket with the toy dog in it; my ruby slippers glistened under the street light. The Wizard of Oz meets The Third Man was all I could think of as I clip-clopped along.

'Gina!' His voice jumped out of the darkness, again.

'Yes,' I whispered huskily.

We kissed and he put his arm around me as we crossed the deserted road to the apartment block and I let us in. My flat was in darkness but the lights from the quayside threw shadows on to the floor and I used them to guide me to the fridge for a bottle of wine. I noticed he took his boots off as soon as we entered the hallway and put them neatly to one side, but the rest of what followed is a little hazy.

We made it to the bedroom and shut the door, ripped each other's clothes off with an urgency that left us both panting and set about having energetic sex, lots of it, all night.

His body was toned and beautiful and if he hadn't been a spy, he could have modelled for Calvin Klein.

At one point, we broke the bed. At another, the lamp toppled over with a crash and I heard the bulb break. The piece de resistance however, was when the picture hanging above the headboard fell down on top of us, caused by the incessant vibrations of our banging against the wall. I have no idea what the people below me thought was happening because I went out of my way for weeks to avoid them.

We slept intermittently and had to straighten the linen several times after getting knotted up and covering it in crumbs from the packet of Hobnobs we'd scoffed after our herculean efforts.

In the very early hours, when only lovers are awake, I snuggled in against him and he drew me near.

'Since when did Dorothy wear lace-topped stockings?'

I could sense his smile in the darkness.

'And when did Horatio ever do what you did to me?'

'Oh, I think you'll find that he and Emma Hamilton had a good time between the sheets!'

'Harry, if you really are a spy, what does your family think?' I asked gently.

'We're not really in touch, Gina. My father was a career diplomat and I was shipped off to boarding school. They divorced and have new families so I hardly see them now but they were never interested in me anyway. I'm not married and have no-one I'm close to so my work is perfect. I travel a lot and settling down isn't something I've ever considered, even if I could.'

He sighed but I didn't know why, then kissed me tenderly on my forehead before leaning over to look at his watch.

'I have to be away in an hour. I wish I could stay longer.'

'You don't have to say that. It's been great, I've enjoyed it.'

'I've already got your phone number and address, and I'd like to stay in touch. I can't promise dates or times, or even when I'll be in the country, but what do you say?'

'How have you obtained this information, exactly?' was all I could think of and he laughed.

'I told you I gathered intelligence. I see it all around me. I bluetoothed your phone and made a mental note of the road name, apartment block and your flat number as we came in. It's what I'm trained to do. Do you believe me now?'

'You're scary, do you know that?'

'Over coffee, before I go, I'm going to give you a crash course in personal security and I want you to listen carefully. Do you understand?'

'Yes sir, no sir, three bags ...'

'... I'm serious but before then I'm going to give you a beasting. Don't look so alarmed, it's what we call a very hard run in our full kit, so come here now.'

And I did.

***

I must have nodded off but the beeping of a very distant alarm, somewhere out in the far reaches of the universe, brought me slowly back into the day. I saw he was already out of bed and buttoning up his breeches, looking for all the world like a contemporary of Nelson's who was about to set off for war, which in a way I suppose he was. My heart lurched as it travelled back hundreds of years to a different parting.

'I'm sorry, Gina, that it must be like this. Go and make some coffee while I finish off and I want you to take on board what I'm about to say.'

I got up, put on my robe and walked gingerly into the kitchen where I boiled the kettle and made us a cafetiere, before returning to the bedroom with two mugs. I gave him his and climbed back into bed, watching as he sat next to me and pulled on knee high shiny black boots, his linen shirt still hanging loose.

He held my hand and imparted gently, but firmly, information on staying safe that I still use to this day; each time I transfer my keys from my handbag to my pocket on a deserted street, I think of Harry.

When it was time to go, I let him out with a lingering kiss and pulled back the curtains to watch as he strode in the early morning mist along the quayside in his period naval uniform to wherever he was going. He turned round once and waved quickly before continuing on his journey and I held my hand up, leaving it there for several long seconds while I shivered at the sudden chill his departure had wrought upon me.

A week later, I received a case of Bollinger from Fortnum and Masons with a note simply addressed to Dorothy, love H. There were a few phone calls and even a dinner in Bruges, horribly just after a shoot out in a square when a man jumped from the clock tower, but we never had the chance to get physical again.

A year or so later, I bumped into him literally outside the back entrance of Liberty's in London where I almost didn't recognise him. I was walking along Kingly Street, which runs parallel to Carnaby, after buying some purple suede boots and was laden down with several shopping bags. Out of the corner of my eye I saw a man running towards me and had to step out of the way to avoid him. There quickly followed another man with a beard, dressed casually in jeans and a leather jacket, who was giving pursuit and I realised with a shock it was Harry.

Idiotically, I called out his name which stopped him dead in his tracks and I watched as an expression of horror seeped slowly across his face. I was ten feet away when he looked uncertainly at me then back to the man he was following. As quick as lightening, he bounded over and touched my arm.

'Gina, I'm sorry. I can't talk now. I'll phone you.'

I nodded, stupefied by what I was seeing, and gaped as he sprinted off down the road. Feeling the need for a drink to steady myself, I dived into The Clachan, a pub along the way, and ordered a Jameson's with a dash of water. I got my phone out to be ready when he called.

It eventually rang an hour and another whisky later, and I snatched it up.

'Hi, Gina, apologies for back there, but I was on a job.'

'I know and I feel stupid that I didn't see it for what it was. Are you OK?'

He laughed, 'I'm fine, it was nothing. It's good to hear your voice. Are you here for long?'

'Only until tomorrow. I have a ticket for a concert later. But it's sold out.' I added hastily, thinking that he wouldn't have been able to join me even if he'd wanted to.

'No worries. I'm sorry.'

'There's no need. You never made any promises, Harry.'

'Gina, I miss you, there's something ...' The line went dead.

And I never heard from him again.

***

The day after the Heroes and Villains party and despite Lou's now famous cocktails, we were due out on the water for eleven. Miraculously a hot bath had almost done the trick and along with my lucky padded knickers, I was able to sit in the boat, with Bella behind me.

'Good night last night?'

I heard the wiliness in her voice and turned round sharply which was fine because we were still waiting for Lou and Janie Juno to get in, and Pete had hold of our blades on the pontoon.

'Yes, it was excellent thank you. Did you enjoy it?'

I decided to play along.

'Probably not as much as you.' She rolled her eyes upwards and smiled in feigned innocence.

'Yes, I'd forgotten you were the all-seeing one,' I said with a note of sarcasm which she ignored.

'It wasn't so much that, as the neat pair of boots I almost fell over when I gently opened the door to drop in some plates you'd forgotten.' She grinned smugly.

'Military man was he? They always leave them by the door, in case of a quick getaway.'

How did she do it, I asked myself for the hundredth time.

'You could say something like that,' I replied breezily. 'But he didn't need to beat a hasty retreat.'

Her laughter could be heard for miles and eventually Pete got fed up holding the shaking boat and told the others to get a wiggle on, before it wrenched his arm off.

25 – Sometimes ... you get to lie in a marble bath when you're least expecting it

'Gina, I've got you a present, but you can't open it until Christmas day and don't go shaking it. I'll give you a clue. It's something for your new events business.'

Janie Juno and I were treating ourselves to a slap up lunch at Gidleigh Park on Dartmoor before she went to Paris the next day to help Kasim settle into his new swanky apartment. Neither Bella nor Lou had been free, and not wanting to miss out before she left, we had decided to come on our own.

We were sitting in the wood panelled dining room at a table overlooking the terrace and the croquet lawn. In the summer they did an old fashioned traditional afternoon tea there but on this chilly winter day we were glad to be snug inside, at least for the time being.

'Thank you, that's very sweet and I hope I can still pick your brains.'

'Of course, Gina, and we need to get out our diaries because from now on I will be using you, and only you, to organise all of my client events. I've already passed around your business cards and pointed people to the new website and testimonials. I think you'll find you're going to be kept busy. Here's to you!'

She raised a flute of the champagne that we had recklessly decided to splash out on.

'And here's to you, for making it possible.'

We chinked our glasses.

The other diners, sensing a celebration was in order, looked over, smiled and nodded. I loved it here because there was never any stuffiness but the service and food were off the scale and deserving of the two Michelin stars. I hadn't been for a while so the treat was all the more enjoyable, and audacious.

'How did you get on with adjusting your hours in Somerset?'

'Easier than I'd imagined and it might have had something to do with the good progress I've engineered, having a fantastic new deputy project leader and oh yes, the smoking gun letter that I didn't even have to wave under their noses. Both Psycho Freddie and Derek Dastardly were like putty in my little angel hands.'

I held them up for effect.

'So it's Monday to Wednesday on your project and Thursday to Sunday on your events?'

'That's about the long and short of it but I can swap days around too, if it suits a client.'

The waiter came and explained the lunch menu in detail and I was hard pushed to choose between the Ravioli of Brixham crab and the Devon quail with truffle risotto to start with, followed by either the Cornish bream with saffron sauce or the Partridge and braised chicory.

In the end, we had it all.

'How's the money situation shaping up, Gina? I know you were worried about not having a regular salary?'

'With the bonus I negotiated and the bookings I already have, I'm ahead of my earnings target and can help Bella if necessary when she comes into it in May. Izzy will have finished her first year at Uni and she thinks the time is right. I love working with her, she sees things differently.'

Janie Juno laughed and looked around to make sure no-one was eavesdropping.

'Has she ever said anything to you about your future?' she whispered across the table.

'No, not that I can remember.'

I could hear my heart beginning to thud.

'Oh, I thought she might of.'

She stroked the stem of her glass thoughtfully.

'Why would you think that?' I asked casually, not comfortable with where the conversation was heading.

'Do you want to know?' She leaned in conspiratorially.

'I'm not sure'

I felt goose pimples on the back of my neck and shivered, despite the warmth from the open fire.

'I won't tell you, if you don't want me to, but it could be important.'

She had hooked me, intentionally or not.

'OK, spill the beans. Out with it.'

'She sees us both in France!'

'What, for a holiday?'

'Don't play dumb, Gina, it's me you're talking to.'

'I just can't see how, that's all. Maybe you with Kasim in Paris, but not me, surely?'

'Definitely us both, together. How about that then?'

I sat back on my chair to mull it over but could only think she'd crossed her wires somewhere.

'I've just started a new business venture which will be based in the South West, maybe as far as London, which will require both Bella and I on the ground. How will all of that stack up with us being in France?'

'Well, tuck it away and let's see what happens. I think it's exciting but maybe we should top up our French.'

'You can next week and though mine is a bit rusty, I did alright in Brussels,' I said grumpily.

'There you go then. If you can speak a language, why would you move to a different country and have to start all over again.'

She was smiling broadly.

I could see her logic, but moving to any country seemed about as unlikely as me planting a vineyard so I put it down to the champagne. All the same, something began to gnaw away at me, something unsettling.

I had just undergone a period of rapid change and needed to come up for air. If I looked back only as far as twelve months, my life had altered on so many levels and I wanted a period of relative stability. I was enthused by my new work direction and thriving on being surrounded by fun and interesting people, but to contemplate even more change was exhausting. It had taken me years to get to this point, finding true friends at last, and the idea of running away from it all left me cold.

'I don't think I want to know anymore. When are you coming back?' I spoke firmly, mainly out of fear.

'Not until the middle of January. He doesn't take up his new post until then so we'll have time to explore the city. I haven't seen him for three months since the regatta and Gaz keeps calling me.'

She made a little grimace, but I got the feeling she'd been tempted and was sounding me out.

'Kasim's had a lot on with work and the move.'

I had spoken to him myself a few days after our Heroes and Villains epic, being careful to avoid any mention of Harry. Only Bella knew what had happened and I wanted to keep it that way.

'How would you feel about another go with Gaz?' I asked evenly.

The question had been hanging in the moment, waiting to be plucked and aired.

'I nearly did before our party but I put myself in Kasim's shoes and didn't want to confuse things.'

'Sounds like it might be serious if you resisted a roll in the hay elsewhere.'

I laughed in an attempt to instil some lightness into a situation which was obviously making her anxious.

'There are times like now, when I haven't seen Kasim for a while when I think it might have legs and with the backdrop of the apartment in a stunning European city, what's there not to like?'

She sighed wistfully, pursing her lips and looking down at the table, her finger idly toying with the hem of the tablecloth.

'But something's missing, isn't it?' I asked gently.

'I think so and I feel torn. Deep down, I believe that either the spark's not strong enough or I'm just not made for long term relationships.'

'They can be very rewarding, a shoulder to lean on, a problem halved, sex ...'

I drained my glass and looked around for the waiter.

'But I have all of that with my friends and Gaz. I'm not convinced that you don't lose yourself in a couple Gina, that your identity isn't slowly eaten away. What's that poem by Ted Hughes that in the morning they wore each other's faces? Don't you think all relationships end up that way? You ultimately forego things that are unique and important to you and merge into something that ends up as a mass of nothing but compromise and resentment.'

'I think the trick is to work hard to maintain your individuality while you knit together your common areas and remain open to whatever the other brings to the party. Anyone who wants to change you, or be changed, is heading for malfunction junction, but Kasim's not like that.'

'No, but for me, it's more a case of whether I want to take things to the next step of us becoming an item.'

'Has he said anything to you?'

'No, but I'm expecting something in Paris next week.'

'You, of all people, know the history between Kasim and I where we tell everyone and each other that it was only circumstances that conspired against us. The truth is, at least for me, I believe we never had what it took so now I stick to the line that we are better off as friends and am honest.'

'Gina, I'm going to go out there and take a long hard look at everything. I know you and I are planning to go over in April for the spring but don't bank on it is all I'm saying.'

'If things don't work out between you, it won't preclude me going but as I've committed to organising a big beer festival in Newton Abbott at the end of April, I was going to delay the visit anyway.'

'I'm relieved to hear it, because I was feeling under the cudgel and didn't want to let you down.'

'The best thing you can do is to go over and enjoy the experience. Don't look for problems that aren't there. He hasn't offered you, or asked you, for more than you both have already so it's not as if he's waiting for an answer. Take it as it comes and when you come back, I'll share my ideas for the big garden event and some thoughts on the launch of the new talking chocolate bar.'

'You're right and discussing work is putting me back on terra firma, I feel calmer already. It's a place I know and where I'm control. Thanks for understanding, Gina.'

'Janie, I don't like the sound of that. Work, as we both well know, is not the answer. There are times when you have to confront and fix, even when what you really want to do is to lock the door and throw away the key. Promise me, you won't duck this issue with Kasim.'

'I promise.'

Her smile was small and it tugged at my heart to see her so troubled but I would help where I could. She sat up straight and visibly adjusted her mood.

'Let's talk about your boys. What are they doing at Christmas?'

I grinned broadly at the thought of them and the heavy atmosphere that had descended on our alcove began to dissolve.

'They're coming to Exeter and we're having lunch at Bella's with her family and afterwards we've been invited to Lou's mum's. I'm grateful I have something to offer them away from The Midlands and grateful I have friends around me who will be welcoming. It should be fun.'

'I'm pleased that the dust has settled, I know it's been hard.'

'You can say that again, but there is definitely light where none existed. A great big beacon of a lighthouse light that I can see for miles and miles!' I laughed as I reminded myself of how far I had sailed on my perilous ocean.

'Let's finish our coffee and go for that walk we promised ourselves by the river. It'll blow a few of the cobwebs away and make the drive back easier. What do you say, Gina?'

'Did you remember to bring your walking boots?'

'I did.'

'Me too, and if we drop in at Moretonhampstead on the way, we might be in time for a pie and a pint at The White Horse.'

'Are you mad? I don't think I could face another plate of food for as long as I live!'

***

I had rung ahead yesterday to ask if there was a small room where we could change and of course there was, and it would be no problem. After paying the bill and retrieving our bags from the car, I presented myself at reception.

'This way please, Miss Jarvie, we'll let you into one of our unoccupied suites.'

Janie Juno and I exchanged looks as we were led up to the first floor and shown into a sumptuously decorated but cosy lounge that was chintzy and welcoming. I could see the marble bathroom through an open door and to the right of it was the master bedroom with enough plump cushions on the bed to fill a small car.

'This is Gordon Ramsay's favourite. Come down when you're ready, and take your time.'

The house keeper smiled warmly as she closed the door gently behind her and we stood gaping at each other.

'Blimey! I've stayed in some places but never anywhere as grand as this. I wonder how much it costs?' I said, running my hand across the surface of an elegant teak sideboard.

'Come and see the sunken bath, Gina, it's beautiful.'

I followed the sound of her voice and found her lying fully clothed in an oblong marble tub that wouldn't have looked out of place in a Roman Senator's villa. She was picking up the bottles of Molton Brown that were liberally sprinkled around, opening them and sniffing.

'Take a picture of me. I want to show Bella and Lou what they've missed!'

She struck a pose with one arm behind her head and because of the large mirror I got into the photo too, accidentally. We were giggling like a couple of demented hyenas and took our time getting into our trousers and thick socks. It seemed a sacrilege to put on our boots, but luckily they were clean.

'Stand in front of the window and I'll take one of you too.'

The sun peeked out from between the clouds, as if on cue, and threw shafts of light into the room that drew out the perfume of the fresh lilies in the vase. As I looked out at the gently sloping gardens, she snapped me in profile. We stood in silence for a few moments, marvelling at the beauty and tranquillity of the scene. There were evergreens here and there and the still day brought out the smoky colours of the deciduous trees to present us with a rainbow of muted winter colours.

'Not too shabby eh, Janie Juno?'

'Not too shabby at all!'

We high fived before picking up our rucksacks to head reluctantly back down the stairs.

'Have a good walk and thank you for visiting us.'

'Thank you!' we both beamed and pushed our way out through the big oak door.

We put the clothes in the back of the car and zipped up our jackets against the cold.

'Now, that's what I call service,' I said as we strolled arm in arm down the driveway in the direction of the river to pick up the path.

We walked in companionable silence for a while, each of us reflecting on the things that had cropped up over lunch but I had an event idea that I wanted to sound her out on. The woods were quiet with the barest of birdsong and the damp leaves beneath our feet threw up their mustiness as we walked. The sun was low and made the wilting bracken glint like gold against the green moss covered stones.

'Janie, your work with community organisations has inspired me to use my events and the website to raise the profile of good causes.'

'I wondered if you would.'

She sounded pleased.

'It's all come from the fairytale castle event in the Botanical Gardens, do you remember?'

'How can I forget? It was stunning and I think it launched you.'

'The Devon Life people want me to stay in touch and let them know if I do anymore.'

'I'm not surprised.'

'I've been thinking about putting one together on The Salty, the sandbar that gets exposed when the tide goes out in Teignmouth. Have you seen any of Jack Vettriano's paintings? There's one of a man in a tux dancing with a beautiful woman in a red evening gown on the beach, while the butler holds the umbrella.'

'Yes, I have and I love them but what have you got in mind, exactly?' She asked slowly and I could see it had caught her attention.

'I would like to do a dinner in that style, to coincide with the ebb and flow of the tide. Something that pops up, with elegantly dressed people at a fine dining table, then pops down again when the sea returns, leaving no trace. I'm in talks with the Harbourmaster who, amazingly, doesn't think I'm nuts and hasn't dismissed the idea. There are two dates in July and August next year when it might work and he's asked me to submit a plan.'

'Blimey, Gina, it sounds fantastic. How do the good causes fit into it?'

'I'll sell tickets and donate a chunk of the proceeds to the Lifeboats and to Clic Sargent, a children's cancer charity, by making The Salty 'Open for Dinner' for one day only! My idea is to encourage other people to stage similar events in unlikely places which they can promote through the website and raise money and awareness for causes of their own.'

In the silence that followed, only the noise from the gently tumbling water over the boulders was audible.

'Well, what do you think? I haven't told anyone except you, notwithstanding the Harbourmaster of course.'

'Gina, it's a spectacular idea and one that you can count me in for! My head is already buzzing with thoughts and questions and I'll think about it while I'm in Paris. You are a genius.' She hugged me.

Her reaction had exceeded anything I'd hoped for and reinforced my instincts. I was taking a step closer to doing the meaningful work I had set my heart on and felt confident I could realise my plans on the back of the solid support network that had sprung up around me. It was totally beyond me as to why I would consider, even for a moment, giving it all up to go to France. She must have definitely misheard.

As we retraced our steps towards the hotel, Janie Juno disappeared into the bushes for a wee as a figure came walking towards me, wearing a bright blue jacket and black woolly hat. It was because of the hat that I didn't immediately recognise him.

'Gina?'

The voice was familiar but it took a few seconds to place it.

'Jago! What are you doing here?' I smiled in surprise.

'Same as you, by the looks of things, but I live nearby so this is something I do regularly.'

He was slightly breathless and there were steam clouds when he spoke.

'I'm out for a constitutional and this is one of my favourite paths by the water. What brings you here?'

I still couldn't detect an accent.

'Lunch at Gidleigh with my friend back there lurking in the bushes.' I pointed roughly to where she had disappeared.

'Good?'

'Excellent.' I patted my stomach.

'I'm sorry I haven't been into the club as I said but I've been out of the country. How about a coffee next time I'm in Exeter? Here's my card and if you've got a pen I'll write your number down.'

His smile was warm beneath a newly acquired tan and he appeared shy which suited the moment.

'I can do better than that.'

I fished out one of my new super duper business cards and handed it to him.

'Whistle Events? Is that you?' He looked at me closely.

'It certainly is.'

'Sounds interesting, but before your friend gets back, promise me you'll do coffee.' He looked into my eyes and held the contact.

'I promise. Call me and we'll meet up in the New Year.'

'You're on!'

'Merry Christmas, Jago'

'Same back, Gina. See you soon.'

I heard him whistling happily as he walked away and put it down to my new business name.

'Who was that?' she asked buttoning up her trousers.

'A friend of Pete O'Mara's, he was at the Ball when you wore 'the' dress.'

'I don't remember him.'

'Oh, you would have if he hadn't been wearing a black woolly hat, I can assure you.'

26 – Sometimes ... a boy on stilts, that he had for Christmas, delivers divine intervention

Christmas came and went in a whirl of happy social gatherings and my sons enjoyed meeting everyone before going back to spend New Year with their own friends.

Mine had been relatively tame, although I did manage to go around Exmouth dressed as a saloon girl, at least at the beginning. After parting company with my feather boa, bustle, garter and plastic pistol along the way, it was difficult to tell what I was meant to be; a bit like the conundrum of the tomato at our Heroes and Villains.

Other than that, it was quiet.

Janie Juno wasn't expected back for another week and I hadn't heard anything, but believing that no news was good news, I wasn't overly concerned.

Lou and I had rowed together a couple of times in a pair which we'd enjoyed and had gone as far as The Turf Hotel only to get stuck in the thick green pond weed that had taken hold over the winter. We'd had another close shave when our blades had got caught up in it but thankfully a passer by this time had helped us into the pontoon and we sorted ourselves out by rowing very carefully into the clear water to get us back without a dunking. I wouldn't have fancied our chances if we had capsized, because it was so cold and horrible in there.

The flat had been cleared of all festivities and I was now thankfully back in 'Gina Land', able to focus once more on organising the beer festival in Newton Abbott. This was to be my last single handed event before Bella came into the business part time on the first of May. She had been able to flex her hours, after another restructure had bizarrely merged her Sports and Music Division with the newly founded and unlikely Pets Insurance, which had made the parrot happy if no-one else.

For the festival, there were only two matters outstanding. The first was to organise the two hundred plus beers and the second was to finalise the entertainment from five pm on the Thursday to eleven pm on the Saturday, and yes I had checked the times with at least three people. There would be no more slip-ups like that from now on, otherwise Whistle Events would be whistling down the wind.

I had positioned my desk so I could look out on to the water and I sat for a few moments to reflect on the year that had just ended, which to my thinking had been split into three very different parts.

From January to April, my world had been cold, grey and lonely.

May to August were the Max months of sunshine, discovery and heartache.

September to December were playful and had passed in full Technicolor.

In terms of my personal achievements, I had made the successful move to a new location, managed my professional work problems in Somerset, took up competitive rowing in a crew and started a new business.

Emotionally, I had learnt lessons and had opened myself up to new experiences, none of which I judged myself too harshly for, thanks to the insights and confidence my friends had bestowed upon me. When Kasim had once said to me in Barcelona that I was a new Gina, I had played along with him, but now I really believed it.

And I liked this new Gina.

And I vowed that the old one was gone for good.

I had Jago's card propped up on my desk, against the stylish wooden calendar Janie Juno had given me for Christmas. It was made up of four separate blocks; one for the days, two for the numbers and one showing the months. His card was a terrible distraction because I kept glancing at it, then back to my computer.

There had been a missed call sometime over the holidays but not knowing the number, and because there was no message, I had ignored it. Only later, after scrolling through and checking did I realise it had been from Jago.

That was nearly three weeks ago.

When I had first met him at the Ball, and had spoken to Bella at The Waterside restaurant while we waited for Lou, I had told her about my fear of getting in over my head too quickly. It had happened with Max and I still wasn't completely confident that I could have a meaningful relationship without losing my heart. For all of my listed achievements and reflections, I was still vulnerable in matters of love.

I picked the card up, which was cream with simple black lettering, tasteful without embellishment, and flipped it back and forth between my thumb and index finger. I hoped that the action would provide divine intervention and waited to see if anything happened.

Nothing.

I did it again hoping, like the magician with his card trick, that it would take matters into its own hands.

Nothing.

OK, I'm going to flip it. If it lands face up, it's a sign and I'll phone him.

I threw it high into the air and as it fluttered slowly down to the floor, I put my hand over my eyes.

When I heard it land, I stole a peek through my fingers.

Face up.

But it could have been an accident.

I would need to do a best of three.

One up, two to go.

I threw it again, higher this time, but didn't bother with the hand over the eyes bit.

It landed face down.

Evens Stevens. The next one would be the decider, so I climbed up onto one of my space 1999 bar stools and dropped it from a great height, forgetting about the seat that swivelled.

I crashed to the ground in time to see the card flutter past me and land … face up.

Two ups, one down.

Perhaps I should do best of five.

When I got to about fifty three and had lost count several times, I was bored.

Should I or shouldn't I?

If the next person walking down the street is with a dog, I'll phone him.

It was a small brown sausage dog wearing a red tartan coat.

If the lights are on in the club house, I'll phone him.

Shazam! They all suddenly burst forth.

If there are two Hobnobs left in the packet, I'll phone him.

There were two in the round plus bits of a broken one with crumbs, so I wasn't sure if that counted.

I obviously needed something harder and flukier to make this work.

If Bella rings me in the next five minutes and a boy walks by on stilts, I'll phone him.

When my phone rang exactly a minute later, I knew it was her without looking.

'Hi, Gina, what are you up to?'

'Oh nothing really, just thinking about the beer festival.' I smoothed down my skirt.

'Are you sure? I had a strong sense you'd fallen.'

'Me?' I squeaked and tried not to look over at the stool lying on its side. 'Whatever gave you that idea?'

'Oh well, as long as you're alright.'

'Never better thanks, but while you're on, can you get your band to email confirmation they're still up for all three nights of the festival.'

'Sure, no problem. How's it going?'

'Getting there slowly, but there's a lot to it. I'm glad you're going to be playing though, as it'll be nice to have some friendly faces around.'

'Gina, you'll ace this and I can't wait to come into it with you. We're going to have a riot and that idea of yours for The Salty is a winner. I'm not surprised the tickets got sold in hours. I've got some four by fours lined up because we're going to need them to transport the paraphernalia across the shingle, and it won't be flat.'

'I hadn't got that far but yes, you're right. Let me get the festival out the way and we'll start work on it.'

'Are you sure you didn't fall, Gina?'

'Alright, you win. I was trying to decide whether to phone Jago.'

'And you fell over?' she asked suspiciously.

'Something like that, but I better go now. A boy's walking past on stilts.'

'OK, Gina, see you Wednesday.'

'Bye, Bella, lots of love.'

I watched as the boy of about ten walked carefully along the pavement on his brightly painted blue stilts and deduced they were a Christmas present he was trying out for the first time.

I sighed.

How hard could it be?

The button pressing was the easy bit.

My almost paralysing fear was of the passageway that lay in store on the other side of a door that would magically glide open once I entered a few numbers in sequence, and hurl me through time and space towards him; across this wide and darkening night.

I looked back at the boy with his focussed expression and watched as he got into his stride, admiring the determination and persistence. I knew by him simply appearing as one of the ludicrous conditions that my fate had been sealed and further procrastination was pointless. If a kid could learn to walk tall then I could too, so with one last look out of the window, and the phone still warm in my hand, I dialled Jago's number.

It rang six times and went to voice mail but I didn't want to leave a message and was about to ring off when I heard his voice.

'Hello, is that you, Gina?' He coughed slightly and I could hear wind rustling in the background.

'Hi yes, I'm not disturbing you am I?'

He had put my number in his phone, I noted.

'No, not really.'

I heard someone in the background shout 'pull in the mainsail.'

'Are you sure?'

'Certain.'

'Where are you exactly, if you don't mind me asking?'

'In the outer Hebrides, on a yacht belonging to a friend of mine. It's a miracle there's any signal.' I could hear whooshing now as well as rustling.

'OK, I'll make it quick. Would you like to come to a concert with me next Thursday, I have a spare ticket.'

'Absolutely! I'll be back by then. I'll call you and, Gina ...'

'What?' I shouted as if it was me in the storm.

'I'm really pleased to hear your voice.'

With that the phone went dead and I was left staring down at it.

In the time it had taken me to flip the cards and mess about it had become dark so I set about lighting the flat and hoped, after my rash invitation, that I could actually get a spare ticket to the Baroque concert in the church at the top of Fore Street.

I put the kettle on for a cup of tea and sat on the other bar stool, the one that was upright, and reflected on what had just happened. He had taken my call under difficult circumstances, which I viewed as a positive sign, and he had already stored my number. That was two things. And he hadn't needed to check his diary or come back to me, as Max used to do, leaving me uncertain. That was three things, and as three was my lucky number, at least for today, I'd better make sure I got him a ticket, first thing in the morning.

27 – Sometimes ... you never forget, for the rest of your days, a particular moment of hand holding

We had arranged that he would come to my flat at six thirty and I would cook us a light supper, before driving up into town for the concert at eight. I had decided to do a fresh tuna salad with some good bread and a crisp bottle of white wine, thinking that anything too heavy might have us nodding off accidentally midway through the performance.

It had been known.

He arrived on the dot and I let him in, taking in the old brown sheepskin flying jacket and the fine pale yellow woollen scarf draped casually but elegantly round his neck. His jeans were light denim and he had on a pair of brown calf leather ankle type boots that were tucked underneath. The tan was still there, but I would learn it was permanent from the amount of time he spent outdoors, from sailing and working in the family business. He still had a quiet assurance, which wasn't overbearing, and his eyes were by far the bluest I'd seen. He swept his hair of his face and everything about him was manly and rugged.

'Hello, Gina, I've brought some red wine and hope that's alright, because I wasn't sure what you'd planned. You look well.'

He kissed me politely on the cheek as he handed me a bottle wrapped in purple tissue paper.

'Let me take your jacket. It looks snug, very stylish and suits you.'

'I bought it from a charity shop years ago and, though it's seen better days, it's very warm.'

I liked his practical honesty and showed him into the lounge where he glanced at the table set for two, and the candles already lit. I made my way to the kitchen and heard him open the balcony door.

'You might need that jacket again if you go out there,' I shouted through as I began griddling the fish.

'You've got a nice place here. The view across the water is lovely. Is it yours or rented?' he asked, coming back inside and casually leaned against the worktop with his arms folded.

'I bought it with the proceeds of a house I used to own in the Midlands.'

'You'll never go wrong. Even if your plans change, you can always rent it out.'

'I wondered about that too, but I think I'm going to be here for a while with my new business and the friends I've made.'

'Pete O'Mara speaks highly of you, did you know? He still goes on about that win you all gave him at the regatta.'

'It was a pleasure. He's a great chap and you've known each other a long time, haven't you?'

'We have indeed. I got divorced about fifteen years ago, not long after I turned forty come to think of it, and rowing and Pete came to the rescue.'

'I know that feeling! Can you carry the salad please, while I bring in the plates? It's all ready.'

'Thank you, smells good. Living on my own, I don't always eat as well as I should, so this is a treat.'

Seeing that there wasn't an ounce of fat on him, I could believe it.

Over our meal, he told me he had two boys who were a few years older than mine and that he had a younger daughter from another relationship, who was coming up for fifteen. It didn't take a scientist to work out what had happened, but it was none of my business, and if you didn't have a past you needed to ask yourself why.

He told me about his sailing and when he saw I was interested, promised that when the weather grew warmer, he would take me out on his own sailboat and teach me the rudiments.

We kept it to a glass of wine each and I hastily cleared away the remnants of the simple meal before grabbing our coats and turning the lamps off.

His green Landrover was across the road and I clambered up into it, having never been in one before, but impressed him by knowing about the factory and a little about the engineering too, as it happened. We headed up into town and parked as close as we could to the church, which was further up on the right, and I put on my leather gloves because of the cold wind.

As we strode purposefully up the hill, hurrying against the weather, he held my hand.

The casual and easy way in which he had taken it, and the sensation of his around mine, made me feel safe and protected, taking me back with a contented nostalgia to a time when my father had done the same. These feelings of trust and security were powerful and the message Jago conveyed was that he could look after us both. Like everything else about him, his gesture was decisive and unambiguous, with nothing that suggested an attempt at forced intimacy. It was chivalrous, forthright and concerned only with my well-being.

That's how it was, and I've never forgotten it.

***

Inside the old church, hundreds of candles had been lit and the flickering flames picked out the texture of the stone, throwing eerie shadows across the faces of the statues in their various alcoves. People were sitting in the ancient wooden pews and we squeezed into one not far from the front, next to a large fluted stone pillar. It was well attended but not heaving and when the musicians started up with Bach, the music seemed to exude from every corner of the beautiful space, rising and falling as they played with fluidity and grace. Even I could see the instruments were old and I was puzzled as to why the tickets had only cost five pounds, such was the quality of what we were hearing. You wouldn't have wanted to miss a note, let alone fall asleep.

At the interval, sitting in the entrance foyer over a quick cup of coffee we had a chance to talk more.

'What brought you down here from the gritty West Midlands Gina?'

I knew he was playing with me because his eyes twinkled as he said it and I laughed.

'Work mainly, but I needed a change after my divorce and I wanted to make new friends. Actually that wouldn't be true.' I took a deep breath. 'Because of the way I was living, I wanted to make "some" friends.'

As soon as the words were out I marvelled at my own honest admission, which six months ago wouldn't have been possible. Being relaxed and open like this was now the norm and it was a moment to ring the changes.

'Pete had told me about your events business so, when you gave me your card, I sort of already knew. It's different isn't it, to your other job, the one you came down here for?'

'Chalk and cheese, but fingers crossed, I can make a go of it and hard work never killed anyone. But what about you, I know about the sailing, but do you work, too?'

'Yes, in a quarry and when I go sailing around the world, for months at a time, I leave my sons in charge. It's a family business that we've owned for generations and it gives me the flexibility to go away at short notice. The lifestyle suits me, though at times I feel my age.'

I had calculated earlier that he was fifty five, but he could easily have passed for less because of his hair and physique.

'You don't look it, Jago.'

He raised a doubting eyebrow. 'I feel it. Some days even older! How old are you, if I can ask?'

'Sure you can. I'm Forty two and a half!'

'The half is that important, eh?' and I nodded furiously, which he liked. 'I guessed you might be because of the ages of your boys, but you look younger too, even more so when you laugh. Did you know that when you do, the years drop away and we can see the younger, full of fun Gina?'

'Thank you very much Jago.' I proved his point.

'I'm serious. Whenever I've seen you, which I know has only been twice and here again tonight, you are laughing. Not a false or nervous one, that I would spot a mile away, but a real 'something is funny' hearty laugh. Not too loud and not too raucous, just right and it suits you.'

'Really? Are you sure?'

I peered at him as if he might have taken leave of his senses but then stopped the flippancy and became serious for a moment.

'If I told you that it wasn't always like that, would you believe me?'

'I would,' he nodded thoughtfully, 'because along with your laughter Gina, I see a look that crosses your face very occasionally, for a fraction of a second, where you are lost and far away.'

He went to cover my hand with his but I slid it smoothly out of reach, sensing that enemy territory was fast approaching and when I saw the musicians return to their places, I was relieved.

'Look, they're re-tuning ready for the second part. Let's go back to our seats.'

Jago guided me by my elbow and we settled ourselves, but his words had ruffled me. If I looked lost and far away now, after all the progress I'd made, then what did I look like before, when Max had gotten hold of me? Mr Slimeball must have thought I was easy pickings and in my fury I took another giant leap towards self-enlightenment.

The music was calming and I was grateful for the space it afforded to bring my emotions back under control. When the performance ended, I clapped my gratitude loudly along with everyone else and the musicians thanked us in turn which heightened my sense of connectivity with those around me.

As we made our way out onto the street, he determinedly took my hand, not willing to be fobbed off again as he had been in the foyer, and I knew it was pointless to deny us this moment. I hadn't put on my gloves and was able to feel the full warmth of his grip, which was even more powerful and reassuring as our flesh connected for the first time.

I did not let go until we reached the Landrover.

Hopping quickly up onto my side, I put the yellow paper programme from the concert on the seat between us before we chugged amiably down the hill.

'I play the fiddle, Gina, not as well as those girls back there but I can get a tune or two out of it. I promised myself after the divorce to do a few things and learning to play was one of them. Are you musical? I know Bella is.'

'I don't play anything, but I like all sorts. A few years back I would have ruled it out but since I'm thriving on lots of new interests, it's possible.'

'I always carry it to sea when I go, in a special waterproof case, and it's got us through some interesting moments. In a few weeks' time I'm off again, taking a tall ship across the Atlantic.'

'A pirate ship with all the sails, like the one in the Goonies? Are you serious? How long will it take you?'

This was very exciting.

'It does have lots of sails, you're right, and a few of the crew could definitely be described as pirates. I fly back at the end of March.'

'Two months is a long time but I guess you're used to it.'

I looked at my watch, yawning, and could see it was getting late, though out of politeness I asked if he would like to come in for a coffee. He raised an eyebrow at the age old clichéd double entendre, because we both knew that nothing was going to happen.

'Thanks, but I'll be getting back. It's a trek and a half across the dark, brooding moor all on my own to the sound of the high pitched howls, but don't you worry about me, maid!'

He had put on a rakish Cornish accent and the image of him running the gauntlet of the famous hound of The Baskervilles dressed as a pirate was funny. He had put his left hand gently on my shoulder, while his other rested idly across the steering wheel. 'I've really enjoyed myself tonight. The food and music were great but it was a shame about the company!'

He dodged the play punch I aimed at him.

'Me, too, and I'm glad we took some time to get to know each other.'

'Can I buy you dinner or lunch for tonight, before I sail away to distant shores?'

'I do have a lot on at the moment, but perhaps. I'll call you, if that's OK.'

'Make it soon, Gina, and don't forget me.' He kissed me lightly on my cheek before leaning over and pulling the door handle. 'Take care of the step as you get down. Pete told me that you weren't always reliable on your pins.'

'You tell him from me, that the next time he has something to say about me, he can say it to my face. Goodnight!'

I made a show of slamming the door but he had wound down the electric window and blew me a kiss.

'Sleep tight, Gina, and thanks again.'

'You too, Jago, and drive safely.'

He revved up the Landie and peeped the horn gently as he passed me at the entrance to the apartment block while I was putting the key in the main door. I turned and waved, let myself in, and walked slowly up the stairs to my flat.

Inside, I dug out the remains of the wine from the fridge, poured myself a glass and still with my coat on, went out onto the balcony to look up at the brightly twinkling stars in the crisp and clear night sky.

28 – Sometimes … you can't be held accountable for the actions of your big toe

A few days later, I awoke to no heating, or hot water, and whilst it wasn't exactly the North Pole, I did have a quick look in the wardrobe to see if there were any polar bears.

I pressed all the buttons on the boiler so many times that I couldn't remember which way round they worked then got out a big hammer and a screwdriver and waved them menacingly in front of it, by way of a threat.

Still nothing.

If I felt that my actions were conscionable, I didn't care, because as far as I knew, the National Society for the Prevention of Cruelty to Boilers didn't exist.

So I tried it again.

Still nothing.

I phoned Lou and got the number of the man who had serviced her mother, but when it went to answer machine, I knew I was in for a wait.

With my upstairs neighbour away in Paris, I decided she wouldn't mind if I helped myself to a bath at her place and went to hunt down the key she had attached to a sensible cork key ring. You can guess why.

I cheerfully gathered my things together and went up the stairs to her flat and let myself in. She had set the heating to frost watch and it had come on with the cold spell, keeping it warm and toasty. In the bathroom, I turned on the hot tap and poured in a good dose of her Jo Malone Red Rose bath oil then went to the kitchen to make coffee for my soak. I found the Blue Mountain she kept in the fridge and made a large cafetiere which I took back to the bathroom.

I poured out a cup and carefully placed what was left on the floor next to the bath oil, where both were within easy reach for refills. I turned the taps off, swished the bubbles around to spread them out from the mass at the tap end and got in. The water relaxed me and with a contented sigh, I let the warmth permeate my chilled body while I sipped my delicious coffee and steamed. The taps were mock Victorian with an attached shower head and were of a type that I could turn with my big toe, so when I decided on more hot water, I gave it a nudge.

And it fell off.

The whole tap system came away from the pipes, the shower pole, the lot and water gushed like a fountain. Jumping out quickly, I upset the cafetiere and bath oil on her new cream carpet and tried to pull out the plug as the bath rapidly filled close to the brim. I ran starkers to the kitchen for a jug to start emptying but I couldn't find one and grabbed a small bowl from the side instead. I bailed as quickly as I could into the sink next to it and when it was down to a manageable level I went to look for the stop cock. Because her flat had a different layout to mine it was nowhere obvious ...

Time to go for help.

I banged next door but they were slow to answer and I realised too late that I had disturbed them 'on the nest' because of his state of undress.

'Yeah, what do you want?'

He kept his door on the chain while I stood dripping with nothing more than a towel around me, not having time for a robe.

'Do you know anything about plumbing? The tap has come away.'

'That's what you get plumbers for, sorry.'

He closed the door.

I vowed I would keep my big broom to hand and next time they were at it, and she was screaming the place down, I would do some banging of my own. But then again, I couldn't talk as the only other people I could ask were the good folks below me who, since that night with Harry, I'd been avoiding like the plague.

No good, Gina, you're just going to have to brave it out so I rushed down stairs and banged on their door.

'Hello, Gina, are you alright?'

His tone was warm and concerned.

'Sorry, Bill, but can you help with a tap that's come away, it's a long story!'

'Of course. I'll grab a spanner and come straight up.'

I dashed upstairs and with help on the way, I did some more bailing and quickly pulled on my jeans and a jumper to look half decent.

Bless him. Bill was a retired vet and he and his lovely wife Linda were the quiet but reliable types, often giving me surplus vegetables from their small allotment across the quay. He located the stop cock in an obscure cupboard and turned it calmly off before venturing into the bombsite which was now the bathroom.

'Oh dear, how did it come away?'

He was scratching his head.

'Ah yes,' I said, stalling for time, as there was no way I could tell him that my big toe had caused it. 'It just fell off the wall I'm afraid, an accident waiting to happen.'

My voice was growing, even to my own ears and I wondered about my nose.

'Well, it's not good news, Gina. This lot will have to be replaced, but I'm sure the insurance will cover it.'

'Oh.'

'What on earth happened to the carpet?' he asked, horrified.

The black stain from the cafetiere had mingled with the Red Rose bath oil and looked like someone had bled to death. I ushered Bill out before he could ask any more awkward questions and set about cleaning up the mess. The bathroom, which had been functional, elegant and newly carpeted now resembled a crime scene that wouldn't have looked out of place in either Alfred Hitchcock's Psycho or Don Johnson's Miami Vice. If only he would come storming in and save me, my life would be perfect.

Don, not Alfred.

Instead, I took things into my own hands and seeing that it would be impossible to fix and clean before she got back, I resorted to plan B and got onto Fortnum and Masons. I ordered one of their swankiest hampers to be delivered on the day of her return, hoping that with the extra chocolates I asked to be included, she might actually speak to me again.

***

'Sorry I'm late Bella, I was just catching up with Janie Juno and taking delivery of a hamper.'

She peered at me with narrowed eyes. 'I'm sensing it's something to do with water.'

'Well, water is a big feature of our landscape and daily life down here.'

I didn't want to meet her look and be made to confess the mayhem I had created three days ago so I glanced around instead at the park we were standing in, which was the venue site for the beer festival. We had on our wellies and waterproofs because it was drizzling.

'And, I see blood on the carpet.'

If she tuned in now I would be done for, but she wasn't wrong as I had come very close to being in a lot of trouble.

'It wasn't blood, it was bath oil.' I hissed between clenched teeth, wanting desperately to change the subject.

'OK, OK, I don't see you going to prison so I'll drop it. Anyway, tell me, how did the Paris trip go with Kasim?'

'So, so.'

'Hmmmm, that doesn't sound too convincing.'

She re-did her top knot, tucking up some stray hair.

'Kasim had everything organised down to the last detail as you would expect. Tickets for the Pompadou, the Opera and Versailles, but the idea of taking it further is proving tricky. I think he's coming to realise that the women in his life prefer him to be their friend.'

'He's never been married, has he?'

'No, and I'm not even sure he's come close. I always try to avoid being sucked in by him, it's odd. I was very careful when I relayed the Heroes and Villains not to tell him about Harry, and he wouldn't have known about Max either, except that he sort of managed to wheedle it out of me.'

'That's why he's good at his job, he's thorough, and with his ever ready smile, people like him. Women especially. He's very charismatic and portrays himself as someone in need of mothering. Had you spotted that?'

'I can't say that I had, but now you mention it, I know what you mean. I've never been able to put my finger on exactly what it was that stopped me from taking it further with him because he's attractive, charming, intelligent, attentive and by any means successful but—'

'—he smothers you.' She finished the sentence for me. 'I think you turned away from him back then because, despite it being an easy solution to what was going on in your life, you managed to stay clear headed and follow your instincts. I know you tell everyone it was down to circumstances, and it's a nice get out, but I for one was suspicious and I know that others saw it as a smokescreen too. Lou had it sussed when she first met him at the James Bond party.'

We stopped walking and I turned to look at my wise dear friend.

'None of you ever said.'

'We didn't need to, as you'd got there for yourself, and second time around with Janie Juno it looks as if it's going the same way.'

'There's a possibility of a house over there, Bella.'

I looked at her closely for a reaction, but her face gave nothing away.

'Not Paris.'

I noticed it was a statement.

'In Brittany.'

'Why there?'

'Kasim suggested a visit to the coast for a few days and you get a lot more for your money out there. From the prices in the estate agents' windows, it's possible to buy a large stone farmhouse for half the cost of one of the flats on the quay.'

'Interesting.'

She rubbed her chin thoughtfully with her beautifully manicured hand, the only one of us to have decent nails and no calluses.

'Will you hold the end of the tape please while I quickly measure this section.'

I walked the ten or so paces and wrote it down on my clipboard before rejoining her.

'What's the next step, Gina?'

'I said I would go over to Brittany after the festival to take a closer look but an area around Quimper has already been identified for its access. It's about an hour south of the port of Roscoff, where the ferry from Plymouth docks. Janie Juno's really keen and if it's something that needs a bit of work, the price might be lower still.'

'How does that sit with Kasim?'

'I think he feels he's about to land himself a cushty holiday home.'

'And that's not on the cards, is it?'

Another statement posed as a question, her voice was measured with just the faintest note of steeliness in it.

'Definitely not,' I exclaimed. 'Maybe for a short visit but as I said, I don't believe he can ever be anything other than a friend, to any of us.'

'Good.' She absently flicked the nail of her little finger with her thumb and I noticed her lips were pursed as she mulled something over.

Bella had a way, aside from her psychic abilities, of getting you to work things out for yourself. I had observed and come to understand this only slowly, when she had chosen to reveal herself to me a layer at a time, like the onion I had joked about when I first met her.

She had a knack of affirming the direction you were heading if she felt it was the right one and guiding you subtlety if you were in danger of going down a cul-de-sac, without ever telling you outright what to do.

I sensed she was doing this now, with her insightful questions and one word responses, and it had been a revelation that she had been aware of the esoteric dynamics with Kasim. I remembered the times when she had already known I had missed the plane, or fallen over, and countless other seemingly inconsequential happenings, and smiled to myself. She used her talents sensibly, and today she was conveying that the idea of a place in France had merit.

Well, what did you know?

I recalled my lunch at Gidleigh Park and was eager to tell Janie Juno that Bella had already worked out what we were up to, gleeful at the prospect of seeing her face when I sprung the surprise. It would be my turn to give her the goose pimples that once again had begun to prickle the back of my neck and I hoped she had started into the chocolates.

29 – Sometimes ... a pint of Jiggy Piggy leads the way to new friends and apples

When Bella and I left Newton Abbot we travelled for twenty minutes and went for lunch in the Teign Valley, the area stretching from Bovey Tracey in the North to Kingsteignton in the south, where the river grew wide to become the big estuary that ran down to the sea at Teignmouth. We were on the valley road from Chudleigh Bridge and I had chosen the pub from the guide I'd been given by a local rep from the Campaign for Real Ales (CAMRA). It was so far off the beaten track that we only managed to get there by following detailed instructions.

The pub didn't look much from the outside but inside, it was traditional and welcoming with flag stones on the floor and a lot of old dark wood. On the wall were typical country scene prints and some fine line watercolours of farming through the ages. A few locals were propping up the bar and had given us city folk the once over before dismissing us accordingly.

'What'll you have, Bella?'

'A gin and tonic wouldn't go amiss and I'll take the fish and chips.'

I turned to the barman. 'A pint of Bootley please, Jiggy Piggy if you have it, a G&T and two fish and chips please. We're over there.'

I pointed to the corner seat by the roaring fire that Bella was busy settling herself into.

'That'll put hairs on your chest, madam!'

A loud clipped and cultured voice, semi hidden in the other corner, boomed out at me and I turned around to find its owner.

A very big man, who was possibly in his mid-sixties, was sitting relaxed with his stomach resting on the edge of the table. He had on a blue French beret and what looked like a fisherman's smock with the big pig logo of Bootley Brewery embroidered on the front. His face was ruddy and I could see that beneath the hat, his hair was brown. But his beard, and what a beard, was as white as the driven snow and his eyes were lively and vividly blue beneath brown bushy eyebrows.

Was it really him?

I recalled the night with Max when I had first tasted the beer and the description he'd offered of the brewer, Mortimer Dunseford. Looking at this chap, it fitted him perfectly and it was inconceivable that there could be two of them.

It had to be.

He was the sort who would have been handsome in his youth but the beer had taken its toll and I imagined that the only thing he could pull these days was the handle of one of his pumps, before I remembered the lady-friend and looked closely at the beer clip. Sure enough, the Jiggy Piggy was female with a suggestive glint in her eye and a massive décolletage that was barely concealed by a red poker dot blouse.

'You're not by any chance, Mortimer, Lord Dunseford, are you?' I asked falteringly.

'Moi! Who wants to know?' The big booming voice again. 'Do I owe you money? Or more to the point, do you owe me money?' He laughed and the noise matched the voice.

One of the locals nodded at me then pointed to his own head, making a couple of slow circles with his index finger to suggest that yes it was him, and yes, he was barking. It was nothing less than I had expected but the beret threw me.

'Put their drinks on the slate, Benny, and you two young ladies come over here and introduce yourselves. I would have done it myself but, as you can see, I'm settled in for me dinner now.'

He patted the huge stomach that went with the voice and the laugh and the beard.

Everything about him was larger than life.

We moved over to where he was sitting and I took a long swig of the beer, wiping away any traces of froth on my mouth surreptitiously.

'Why aren't you drinking my nectar of the gods?' He bellowed at Bella.

'I'm afraid I don't like beer,' she laughed and lifted her glass in a 'cheers'.

'Don't like beer? I've never heard such nonsense. You just think you don't like it. Here, have some of this. It's called Snout About Nothin' and I've entered it into the Newton Abbott beer festival. We've just started brewing it. Tell me what you think?'

Bella, being the good sport that she is, took a mouthful and pronounced it excellent to which he snorted.

'Well, you know my name so it's your turn. You are ...?'

'I'm Gina Jarvie and this is Bella, my friend.'

'Gina Jarvie, Gina Jarvie. Help me out here, where do I know that name from?'

'I'm organising the beer festival and I've been sending out emails,' I said with a touch of pride.

'Oh, that's right, now I've got you but we don't do emails. We don't do computers full stop. Can't you ever pick up the bloody phone and speak to us instead? What's wrong with doing that? What good's a bloody email to me?'

It was a parody of pompousness, and not pompousness itself, and I could tell he was enjoying the banter and testing me, unaware that I could handle anything he cared to throw at me after my running battles with Psycho Freddie and Dick Dastardly, the scoundrels of Somerset.

'It's useful when I'm dealing with over fifty separate breweries but I'll call you next time, seeing that we've been properly introduced and are now on first name terms.'

I gave him a lascivious wink, which he loved and howled at.

'I like the cut of your jib, Gina Jarvie. Have you visited my brewery?'

'No, I haven't and you're the first brewer I've ever met. Are they all like you?' I raised a teasing eyebrow, enjoying the sport with him.

'Good heavens above! What's the world coming to? Never met a brewer in her life? Are they all like me?'

He made a show of shaking his head and putting it in his hands.

'You lot, yes you at the bar, she's asking if all brewers are like me. What do you think?'

'No, Mortimer.' They all chorused flatly.

'Ha! Benny, give them a drink and put it on the slate!'

'Yes, Mortimer.'

I waited until he'd taken a bit more of his beer and said silkily, 'But if ever there is a chance to see it, I would love to.'

'Yes, I bet you would.'

'We've just come from the festival venue, after running through a couple of things, and it all looks to be progressing as it should.'

I changed my tone to one of officiousness so he would know he was in safe hands.

'I wouldn't have expected anything less from a city slicker like you, but seeing as how you came in and ordered a pint of my beer straight away, once you've troughed your chips you can follow me down the road and I'll give you both a personal tour.'

He didn't wait for a reply, downed his pint and held it aloft for Benny to bring him a refill.

I looked to Bella for her thoughts and when she nodded enthusiastically, I said, 'You're on. Are you nearby?'

'Of course, I'm on! You'd be bigger idiots than I thought if you declined my most courteous offer. This lot here,' he pointed a stubby finger at the poor locals, 'would love to get an invite, isn't that so?'

'Yes, Mortimer.' They echoed without joy and carried on with their drinking and conversations.

'And it's not far, a short way down the road in fact. About ten minutes at the most. My piggy van is outside round the back so Mrs Bootley Brewery, or Lady Dunseford to you, doesn't know where I am, but all you've got to do is follow me.'

'Have you been brewing all your life?' I asked, making mental notes for my marketing blurb.

'Since you were in your pram, by the looks of you, but in answer to your question, the brewery in one form or another has been going for over a hundred and fifty years, though I've only been at it myself for thirty odd.'

'So I'm guessing the building is quite old.'

I was itching to take out my pen and write it all down but I didn't fancy my chances so I stuck to my questions and hoped Bella would recall the finer points when we were on our own.

'You could say that, but you'll see for yourself in a few minutes. It sits on a bend in the river, in the middle of an old orchard planted by my ancestors which is the bane of my life. I'm not permitted to touch any of the buggers thanks to the helpful conservationists at the planning office, and all this despite our exuberant and regular correspondence which I now frame and put up in the bog. Ha!'

'Can you use the water, like the monks do at Buckfastleigh for their famous Buckie Tonic?' Bella asked with a hint of mischief because it was a thorny issue that we'd only been discussing the week before.

'What! Infamous more like!' He looked like he was fit to burst. 'Those thieving brothers. How they ever managed to pull that one off is beyond me. Not only can they take the water from the Dart, they've got a hydro-electric plant to boot so they get free effing power when mine costs me an arm and a leg and is another matter of correspondence.'

I imagined him writing his 'Sirs' letters to the editor of The Telegraph or Spectator and signing himself as 'Disgruntled from Dunseford, Lord.'

'So where does your water come from?' Bella asked tongue in cheek.

'I can take pleasure in informing you madam, that it comes from our very own spring and I'll do more than that, I'll show you. Drink up. Benny, tell the cook that the feed was better than that tripe she served up yesterday. See you tomorrow.'

Mortimer heaved up his six foot six, twenty stone frame and waddled out the door with us closely behind, looking for all the world like his brood.

He drove perilously along the road at high speed and we had trouble keeping up with him, especially after getting stuck behind a huge tractor, but the road was straight and he was difficult to miss. In several miles, we turned left at a junction then another quick left into a complex of old barns that provided a setting as timeless as a Constable painting. He screeched to a halt and got out of his van, gesturing for me to park in the corner near the two flatbed delivery trucks with the brewery logo on the side.

Further on, I could see a lovely old manor house that looked to date back to Elizabethan times, set in a beautiful garden with topiary hedges, which I took to be the family home. He was right about the orchard; there were apple trees everywhere and even though they were leafless, I saw by their shape and pollarding that they were well cared for.

'Come on, Gina, I haven't got all day.' He shouted over his shoulder as he waddled in the direction of the biggest stone barn.

We hurried after him and went past a smaller, open one where I saw an ancient round fruit press with a large black central screw and a handle. It must have measured five feet across and the whole thing was set into a granite-lipped trough with a chiselled spout from where, I surmised, the juice was collected. Next to it stood a large and proud oak barrel, almost blackened with age.

'Is that where you press your own apples, Mortimer?' I asked, gesturing to the machinery.

'Shush, you're not supposed to see that. I'm a real ale brewer, not a cider maker.'

'Is that what's in the barrel?' Bella asked laughing. 'You old rogue!'

'You ladies are far too sharp for your own good. If word gets out that the county's favourite real ale brewer, Lord Mortimer Dunseford, is making cider, the CAMRA lot for one will have my guts for garters. It's my twin sons what do it guv! That's my story and I'm sticking to it, so there. But yes, if you must know, we squeeze the apples the first weekend of October, put the juice in that there barrel and leave it for six months until the first of April, an apt date for cider drinkers, wouldn't you agree?'

'Do you have to add anything to make it ferment?' I asked innocently, not being from the trade.

'Now, you're being ridiculous! Of course we don't add anything. It ferments itself, you silly girl.'

He laughed till he had to mop his eyes, while Bella and I looked at each other and shrugged.

'Is it strong?' Bella asked.

'You could say that. At home we use it on everything from the family silver to treating the dogs, speaking of which, meet Denzel.'

A shiny black cocker spaniel was licking him furiously, obviously pleased at being reunited with his master.

'Down boy, down boy.'

But I could see by the gentle way he patted the dog that the feelings were mutual.

'So how many pints are in this barrel?' Bella knew all the right questions to ask.

'Pints! Pints! Do the maths yourself, there's sixty gallons, and I know it's nine per cent in answer to your previous question. I can honestly tell you that it's the juice of the devil himself and I'm doing the world a big favour by sitting on it. As you seem to be so interested though, each year I invite my friends and neighbours, including that lot from the pub, for the first ceremonial tasting, so make sure you come. April Fool's Day is easy to remember so take my card and call me. Don't bother emailing, as I rip 'em up.'

He gave one to each of us which we quickly pocketed and exchanged eager looks, for a second time.

'Right, unless there are any more facile or banal questions on my effing cider, can we get on with what I brought you both here for, which if my memory serves me correctly, is beer. Thank you.'

He was one of the most eccentric and oddest people I had ever met but his passion for his beer was undeniable and if I hadn't been driving back to Exeter, someone would have needed to carry me. He took time to show us the various stages of the brewing process and how he operated a gravity fed system, where the maltings and hops went in at the top and after the mashing, the beer drained downwards into the next tank and so on. When he spoke, he was animated, intelligent and hilarious, whether intentionally or not, and I liked him.

Just before we got back into my car at the end of the tour, I remembered to ask him about his beret.

'Oh, that,' he said putting his hand on his head as if he had forgotten it was there. 'I have dozens of these, which I buy to lose when I stay at my house in Brittany. It's about ninety minutes from the port of Roscoff. Do you know the area at all?'

30 – Sometimes ... crypt kickers carry sharp knives and use them at the site of a salmon leap

Lou had been working in the Exeter High Street branch of the surf gear business, as part of their new season launch, and we had arranged to meet at the Arts Centre up the road for six. They were screening a colourful and noisy Bollywood movie, with a pre-film curry, and I was excited to be going back, at least for a few hours, to the land of multi-culturalism. Growing up in an industrial city in the heart of the Midlands, I had assumed everywhere was like my home town, where we all got along and took the best bits from each other's cultures; the food being a good example. But how wrong can you be and down here in Exeter, a city not known for having people who were anything other than a shade of white, I missed it very much – especially the Asian supermarkets and Balti houses of Sparkbrook.

I walked up from the quay wrapped in my cream Barbarella coat from Barcelona and a scarf made of furry pompoms, which I took a lot of stick for on account of them looking like hamsters. It was quite mild and I enjoyed the climb up the hill, taking familiar short cuts and feeling as if I truly belonged. The lights had been on along the quay and when I arrived in town, a few of the shops were still open and lively with people bustling about. It looked vibrant and beautiful, in league with any other major European city.

I waited for her at the entrance and watched as she came strolling along, dressed in a gorgeous knee-length burgundy coat which contrasted with her perfectly groomed honey-coloured hair.

'You're glowing, Lou. What have you been up to?' I kissed her on the cheek.

'I saw Adrian last night. He was home on leave for a few days so I stayed. I'm amazed I got through the staff training after the amount of sleep I had, or didn't have more to the point,' she chuckled. 'Valentine's Day is coming up and you never know, if he asks, I could be persuaded.'

'Into what exactly?'

I had a hunch because we'd hardly seen anything of her.

'Let's just say that I might be giving my own party in a few months' time so you'll have another event to add to your growing list. I was thinking about a barn dance type of thing. Don't suppose you could suggest a venue?'

'I know the perfect spot!' I replied, thinking of Mortimer's place. 'The cider comes straight from the barrel. If Bella's band did the music, it would be the icing on the cake. Will you be needing one, a cake that is?'

I glanced casually around the bar, trying to curb my excitement.

'Not one with a bride and groom on the top, if that's what you're thinking, but I imagine a ring will be involved. I'm not saying any more because before you know it, my mother will be picking out a new hat!'

We bought a couple drinks and put our coats in the cloakroom before heading into the busy, modern restaurant with its large pieces of abstract art dotted about. A waiter showed us to a table.

'What's your news anyway, Gina, and how's Janie Juno?'

'I think the thing with Kasim has come to its natural end and though he hasn't officially been told, there's hardly any contact now. When he and I speak occasionally, the subject no longer comes up.'

'I'm not surprised. He wants a mother, not a lover.'

She looked at me directly and I saw her sensible, to the point pragmatism again.

'I agree, but it's not obvious straight away.'

'Well, the main thing is that it's obvious now, so onwards and upwards. Anyway, Bella tells me you went to a concert with Jago. How did you get on?'

'Really well, and I'm seeing him on Sunday. He's invited me to The Nobody Inn for lunch and said to ask you for directions. It seems an unlikely name. Is it for real?'

'Yes, and you'll like it. I'll email you a step by step tomorrow so you won't go wrong. I heard through the grapevine, well from Pete anyway, that he's off sailing again.'

'He's going down to Southampton early the next day, to help crew a tall ship across the Atlantic to Canada. He'll be away until the end of March.'

'Long distance relationships can be testing. Adrian and I have that problem.' She sounded wistful.

'Who said anything about a relationship?' I squeaked in alarm but she just laughed. By the time the curry came, we were already onto the topic of our rowing and how soon the clocks would go forward so we could get off the machines that Pete had us strapped to.

The film was a cheesy and high-spirited hit and we giggled about the acting as we walked arm in arm to her flat, not far from the new shopping square.

'Gina, I would invite you up but if I don't get some sleep, my career will be in serious jeopardy. Last time I spent the night with him, I over ordered on XXL pink flowery flip flops which we're now having to target at the guys. Never an easy sell to manly surfer types.'

She yawned.

'Lou, it's lovely to see you looking so happy and you can rely on me to stay schtum, but promise you'll come to the cider tasting at the brewer's place on the first of April. That way, you'll get to glug as much as you like and see what you think of the setting. I know he'd love it.'

'I promise I will.' Another big yawn. 'And thanks for the film tonight. Who said romance was dead?'

I kissed her again on the cheek and walked home, smiling at the thought of her news; holding the secret deliciously safe within me.

***

After our rowing session, Bella came to my flat and was sitting on the bed, while I changed and packed a small rucksack for the walk Jago had suggested after lunch.

'What does Janie Juno think?'

I knew her question had been phrased to ascertain what advice, if any, she had given me and how I was feeling about the date. I was honest when I said she had reassured me that I could have some male company without rushing to love or going up the aisle, and she had grinned.

'No more, and no less, than I would have said myself. Go and enjoy it and, besides, he's off the next day so you'll have the time and space to take things slowly. It looks like a good start to me.'

'Thanks, Bella, he seems to have his life nicely compartmentalised but I imagine he gets to meet some interesting women along the way and I don't think he's an angel.'

'Yes, but he's on the level, the antithesis of Max and this time round you're prepared. The change from when I first met you is over half a compass worth and look at it this way, he can't have expectations of a fast pace because it's already taken six months to get you both this far. You've had one date and it'll be another couple of months before he sees you again.' She spoke gently and firmly.

'I'd worked that out too, and it does feel like a nice slow simmer, instead of a crash and burn.'

'I agree, but if you do feel it running away from you, put the brakes on and come home.'

'I will, but his leaving is the safety net I need to spur me on, and I'm actually excited.'

'What do you know about him, Gina?' she said as she began to idly thumb the pages of Rowing & Regatta.

I sensed danger ahead and remembered their questions about Max, though I was aware that she'd known Jago, or at least knew of him, for a long time.

'Just the usual, married, divorced, children, sailing, family business. Is there something else?' I asked haltingly.

'There might be,' she laughed. 'But it'll be good, nothing like Max.'

When she spoke in forked tongues, she could be exasperating but I wasn't going to let it spoil my happy mood so carried on gathering my things and let the conversation drift out of my head.

'I'm going to buzz off now, Gina, but phone if you need to, otherwise I'll see you in the week. One last question, why are you taking clean knickers and a toothbrush?' she asked smoothly.

'In case I get run over by a bus and need to spend the night in hospital. My mother always taught me to carry these things about my person.' I glanced away quickly to hide my creeping blush.

'I see. But we both know there are no buses where you're going, don't we, Gina?'

I could have killed her, but she just stood up humming something I couldn't catch and went out, closing the door gently behind her.

***

'Glad you found it, without too much trouble. There were easier locations but there's a walk not far away that has something special I'd like to show you.'

He had risen from a table by the fire and kissed me chivalrously on the cheek as I entered.

'Lou's instructions were spot on and I've parked my car next to yours.'

'Good, we'll go in the Landie and leave yours here, then after the walk I'll bring you back. How does that sound?'

I was relieved to hear there was no hint or suggestion that I would stay the night, and I think it showed in my voice when I cheerfully replied.

'It sounds like a plan.'

We both ordered the slow roasted pork and chatted happily, while the heat from the fire made my cheeks rosy. We were perched side by side in an old fashioned settle, a bench with a built-in high back to keep out the drafts, and our shoulders and thighs brushed easily, because of its narrowness.

'Are you all packed for tomorrow? Do you have to think carefully about what to take?'

'I'm nearly there, as I keep my sailing bag to hand in case I get a call to crew at short notice. Clothes wise, I don't have much as there's a washing machine on board and the purser will normally put a load on. I mostly wear oilskins and sometimes they can be clammy, so I tend to live in tee-shirts and boxers.'

'What will the weather be like?'

'It's forecast high pressure, which means there's only a small chance of storms and icebergs.'

He remained poker faced as he said it and took a quick sip of his beer, gracefully wiping away the froth from his short beard.

'Icebergs,' I screeched with alarm, as we all know the story.

'Only joking, Gina.' he said playfully. 'We'll be fine and there's a website you can track me on. I'll give you the details and you can also send an email or better still, phone me. I'm not disappearing off the face of the earth. At least I hope not!'

He laughed heartily, reminding me again of the roguish pirate in him.

'I guess it takes a kidder to know a kidder, but you're not one of those, are you, Jago?'

I looked at him square on, and as deep into his eyes as I dared, for any sign of shiftiness at my question. When I saw only concern, I knew I had the answer.

'Not with you,' he smiled warmly.

We finished our lunch and he paid the bill at the bar whilst I went for my rucksack and changed in the toilets, re-emerging as he was getting into the Landrover.

'Throw it in the back, it'll be alright there, and climb aboard.'

I got in and sat on my side, as there was a map and a pair of gloves on the middle seat, and we set off heading west across the moor. We were soon on single track lanes and after fifteen minutes we started down a stony path. My car, for all its gadgets, would have been useless, but seeing as the Landie was more mule like than gazelle, Jago flicked it into four wheel drive and off we rocked down a steep and narrow pass.

As we jiggled and bumped our way along, with me holding firmly onto the door and dashboard for support, I asked him where exactly he was taking me, fearing as I did for my life.

'Your trouble is, you're too impatient. Wait and see.' He grinned secretively.

A few minutes later, we emerged into a small clearing and he parked up.

'This is partly what I wanted to show you.'

I jumped down and joined him as he looked out onto a high and steeply wooded valley that zigzagged away from us for miles. The winter sun was low in the far distant sky but the light it threw out made the gently snaking river glisten. It was breath-taking and I stood rooted to the spot.

'Can you make out what that is over there? See, where the clump of trees finishes.'

His voice broke my reverie and I saw what looked like a castle, far along and on the right.

'You can see why they would put it there, five hundred years ago.' I whispered.

'Actually, it was the last one to be built in England and if I told you it's much younger than that, would you be surprised?'

'I don't understand.'

My mind was still trying to absorb the majestic splendour of what I was looking at.

'It was built by Julius Drewe in the nineteen twenties, or thereabouts, and was designed by Edwin Lutyens. Mr Drewe made his money from a string of grocer's shops and was the equivalent of Sainsbury's back then. It's National Trust now but one day we'll visit.'

'I'd like that, Jago, I'm a big fan of the NT.'

'But here, I've brought my camera and I'd like to take a photo of you. Stay where you are and ... smile!'

So I did.

We also pointed it at ourselves and took one of the two of us, our heads close together. When I saw the image, I realised he'd turned towards me and it had captured him in profile, while I looked into the lens smiling. The backdrop was pure natural theatre; immense and unbridled.

'Let's carry on down the hill because the 'something special' is further along the river and we have to walk.'

'You mean, this isn't it?' I asked incredulously and he laughed.

'I've lived on Dartmoor all my life, Gina, and I still haven't got used to her wild and changeable moods, like a beautiful woman who can never be tamed.'

He glanced over mischievously.

'Hold on tightly, here we go again.'

We started further down the perilous track, the Landrover proving its worth with every lurch forward, until we reached the river plain at the bottom where the land flattened out. We pulled into a rough car park, by a delightful old stone bridge, and I spotted a pub on the other side.

'Fingle Bridge Inn. That sounds like a story waiting to be told,' I said as I zipped up my jacket.

'It keeps strange hours and I don't know why, but you can never rely on it being open. Perhaps we'll be in luck later.'

As soon as we got to the bridge, he took my hand as was his custom and once again, I felt a flood of contentment wash over me.

'This was a packhorse bridge and was built in the sixteen hundreds. Those triangular bits, that sit above the piers, are called refuges and are where the pedestrians dive when there's traffic. Like now!'

He grabbed me quickly, using his body as a shield from the huge BMW that was gingerly making its way across. The apprehension of the driver was unmistakable, and the normally perky wife cowered in her seat, shuddering at the barked instructions issuing forth from the gorilla she suddenly found herself next to.

'Grockle drivers,' I heard Jago say under his breath. With the car safely gone, we crossed over and turned left, keeping to the path by the river and went upstream. Soon, we came to a steep rock face that we had to scramble up and over and I could see he was fit when we did it with ease.

'Now, this is what I wanted to show you. Let's sit here on the bench.'

In front of me, stretching across the river, was something that resembled a weir but I could make out concrete steps and square pools. At the top, the water was still and calm but it gushed as it flowed over the damn and the waterfall effect, including the spray, was mesmerising. I estimated the height overall was about thirty feet.

'Do you know what it is?' he asked loudly over the noise of the water, opening his rucksack and taking out an apple.

'I'm no expert, but is it something for the wildlife, to help them up and down the change in level?'

'Yes, exactly. It's a man-made salmon leap to allow the fish to get upstream for spawning in October. We won't see anything today but you will later on in the year.'

He took out a sharp knife that had a bit of rope through its handle and cut the apple in half and half again, slicing away the inner core before handing me a piece off the blade.

It tasted sweet and warm and reminded me of the brewer.

'Do you perhaps know Mortimer Dunseford, by any chance Jago?' I asked between bites.

'Everyone knows Mortimer, but yes, you could say I know him and his family.'

He started to laugh.

'What's so funny?'

'Did you meet him in the course of your work with the beer festival?'

'Sort of. After Bella and I visited the venue the other day, we called in at a pub on the Valley Road and he was there. He gave us a tour of the brewery and extended an invitation to the cider tasting.'

He laughed again.

'I'll see you there then. Mortimer always appreciates the few tunes I give him on my fiddle and he plays along with his squeeze box. In the autumn, I'm part of the team that makes the cider and we use one of my tractors to run the machine that mashes the apples before they go into the press.'

'Why have you got a tractor?'

'I have a digger too. Remember, I'm in the quarrying and building business. It's essential.'

More laughter and another chunk of apple.

'Do you know anything about the family?' he was chortling now, in a way that suggested he knew something I didn't.

'Not really, but I'm puzzled as to why he calls himself Lord, and refers to his wife as Lady. Is it an affectation?' I asked genuinely.

'You really haven't a clue have you?'

He was convulsed and I was beginning to feel silly.

'He's the tenth Viscount Dunseford, his ancestor having been given a peerage for services to the admiralty at the time of Nelson and Trafalgar.'

'No!' I gasped, knowing that a Lord could be a Duke, Earl, Viscount or Baron.

'Afraid so. Would you like to know something else about his family and mine, a sort of bond that exists?' He deftly cleaned the knife on his jeans.

I was all ears, 'Of course. Tell me, tell me!'

'Gina, you are very funny.' He lifted my hand and kissed it.

'My family is the official crypt kicker to his family, which means that when any of them decide to fall off the perch it's down to me to re-open the crypt and re-close it again.'

'I've heard of crypts obviously, but only as far as bad vampire films. Where is it? Don't tell me it's in his brewery!'

'No, no, nothing like that but Mortimer would like to be buried there, if he could. It's at the edge of the churchyard in the village. There's a section of grass fenced off with low lying black railings. I dig up the grass which conceals the trap door that leads down the steps into the vault beneath the church.'

I was fascinated. 'Does it smell?'

'No, and it's very dry, but I first have to remove a block and leave it for twenty four hours because the air can be dangerous. I break down the bricked up doorway and when they've been laid to rest, I brick it back up again.'

'But, why you?'

'My ancestors, going back generations, have always done this service for the family. Remind me to tell you about the time that the previous Lady Dunseford wouldn't pay for a lead lined coffin, and another occasion when my fellow helpers brought along the cider.'

He was wiping the tears of mirth from his eyes by now at the expression on my face.

Of all the things I thought he would tell me on this walk, this wasn't one of them and then I collapsed in fits too. It was surreal.

So Mortimer really was a Lord, and that would explain the beautiful old manor house. I suppose he had to do something with his life and the brewery was a commercial success by anybody's reckoning. It seemed so unlikely and I shook my head in wonderment at the fact that Jago knew him and would be there for the tasting. It was another, in a very long line of coincidences.

He gave me the other piece of my half of the apple and we munched companionably by the river until the setting sun reminded us that we needed to get back in daylight.

'Before we go, I want to give you something, Gina. Close your eyes and hold out your hand. OK, now open them.'

In my palm was a key fob made of bright green rope that had been formed into a round sailor's knot and was about three inches long. It was a lovely little thing.

'The knot is called a Monkey's Fist and do you know how we use it?'

'No, but I'm hoping you'll tell me.'

'The rope is knotted around a weight of some sort, in the past it would have been lead but yours has a marble in it. We attach it to the end of a line we want to throw, perhaps to another ship or to someone on the dock. It's quite an art to make one.'

'Thank you. I'll use it and think of you at sea.'

'I was hoping you would.' He said thoughtfully.

We made our way back quickly and I was grateful for his help when I stumbled at the rocky part. As we approached the bridge, the lights were on in the inn and we congratulated ourselves on our good luck. We pushed the heavy door open and arrived in a cosy lounge with a roaring fire which a few of our fellow walkers were gathered around, chatting amiably. When he asked me what I wanted, it had to be Jiggy Piggy and I left him at the bar to sit down at a spare table to peel off my jacket, gloves and hat. I had started to warm my hands when the drinks arrived and he came and sat next to me.

'Thank you, Jago, for opening my eyes to the beauty of Dartmoor. The park is stunning and you are surrounded by sights to behold. The salmon leap is very special and I've never seen one before.'

'Gina,' he looked at me kindly. 'The pleasure and delight you have taken from it all has rekindled my own connection. You've made me conscious of how much I take for granted and your reaction has opened my eyes afresh. I wish I wasn't leaving tomorrow.'

I caught my breath.

'I don't want this day to end and keep putting off taking you back to your car, had you realised?'

I nodded, because it was the same for me.

'Would you like to see where I live? We go more or less past it on the way back,' he asked haltingly, unsure of whether he was overstepping the mark.

And because the day had been so easy and uncomplicated, I said yes.

31 – Sometimes ... when an owl flaps its wings you are treated to another warming fire

We chugged east, in the pitch darkness with the headlights from the car picking out the bracken that lined both sides of the old stone walls of the ancient Devon droving lanes. I was sitting in the middle seat and had a leg either side of the gear change with my right hand resting on Jago's thigh. Whenever he could, he put his own hand on top of it and we continued this way in an easy silence until we reached the outskirts of the village where he lived.

We carried on through, then out the other side, before turning down a small opening onto a gravel drive at the front of a house. A security lamp that came on with a sensor was the only light for miles. On the porch, an old tree trunk had been used as a pillar and when I looked closely, I saw that a small toy owl had been placed in a large knot in the wood. When it suddenly flapped its wings and hooted, I laughed in surprise, unaware that Jago had been pulling a cord hidden off to the right.

'Come in, Gina, I'm afraid it'll be cold because I don't have a timer for the heating, but the fire will light quickly and we'll soon be warm.'

I stood in the country kitchen while he disappeared and saw that it was large, modern and tidy with cream contemporary cupboards and a dark green cooking range. The house itself was open plan with wooden floors, but didn't look to be old, and as I moved into the lounge and dining area, I noticed the sailing memorabilia on the walls and shelves. At the far end, there was a huge granite fireplace and the beginnings of a fire he'd made from small logs while a wicker basket of bigger ones was on hand for when it got going. An old red velvet Chesterfield was positioned between two worn comfortable brown leather armchairs that sat either side of the fireplace, and the whole scene shouted resourceful bachelor.

'Come in and sit down. I've got a drop of Lagavulin somewhere. Leave your coat on until you're warm enough. I'll get the whisky.'

I heard cupboard doors opening and closing as I sat in one of the arm chairs, looking at the flames from the fire. When he returned with a small glass, I gratefully took it.

'I've put a dash of water in yours, is that OK?'

He sat down on the sofa, at the end closest to my chair.

'Perfect.' I took a sip and cradled it.

'I built this house, you know.'

'Really? From scratch?' I couldn't hide my surprise, or admiration.

'Yes, I drew up the plans and did it over three years, after my divorce. My ex-wife stayed in the one we had together because of the children, so I had to start again.'

There was no self-pity in his voice and I was reminded of Lou and Bella, who had both got on with things in the face of adversity.

'Are you warm enough now?'

I nodded.

'Come and sit next to me.' His voice was low but meaningful as he patted the seat cushion gently.

I stood up, took off my coat and bravely walked the three paces forward that would take me into his life. He put his arm around me and began stroking my shoulder while he kissed the top of my hair, as we both looked into the fire.

'God, I wish I wasn't going,' he said, almost under his breath.

'But you've been looking forward to it, you told me,' I said gently as we turned our heads to face each other.

'I was. I am. But now you've arrived, I don't want to leave you. Come with me.'

He stroked my hair and when I looked into his eyes, I saw hopefulness.

I was tempted to say yes, because it held a lot of appeal, but I was committed elsewhere and remembered what Bella had said about pace. Nonetheless, his invitation was touching because it revealed the depth of his emotions and the direction of his thoughts.

'I would love to but ... I can't,' I said slowly, with regret heavy in my voice. 'I've too much on.'

He looked back at the fire and I saw the flames reflected in his pupils.

'I know, I know,' he sighed. 'Wishful thinking on my part, but it's a wonderful possibility and I'll remember that you didn't back off for other reasons.'

I stayed quiet and he put his glass on the floor, then took mine and did the same, before cupping my face between his hands and kissing me fervently on the lips. Only the glow from the strengthening flames lit the room as we began to undress each other slowly.

When we were down to our underwear, he led me to the rug in front of the fire where we made sensitive and unhurried love. He caressed my body in the flickering light and took his time to give me an orgasm before gently placing me on my back and entering me. His body was lean and the muscles of his chest and forearms flexed taught as his thrusts grew stronger. We came in a panting rush and I kept him inside me for as long as we could. When I ran my hand along his spine, I could feel the warm sweat of his exertions. After a few minutes of us lying this way, he rolled onto his side and propped himself up on his elbow to look down at me, while he stroked my breasts and drew circles around the nipples with his free hand. As the flames threw their flickering shadows across his rugged face, I noticed his brow begin to furrow.

'Please, Gina, will you stay with me tonight?' His voice was gravelly with emotion, but it wasn't a plea and the sincerity in his tone made it easy.

'Yes, I will.'

He buried his face happily in my breasts and I placed my hands on the back of his head, letting my fingers twirl through his hair.

'But you are going to let me get some sleep, Jago, aren't you? I have a big meeting tomorrow, with an important client. Are you listening to me?'

I tugged playfully at his ear.

The reply was muffled because he had taken a nipple in his mouth, but I managed to deduce by the furious shaking of his head that it wasn't the plan.

'I'm serious. What time do you have to leave?'

More muffled replies and nipple sucking, along with a southwards straying hand, I noticed.

'Did you say five o'clock by any chance?'

More furious head movement, but nodding this time.

'I see, and I guess that means me, too, if I'm to retrieve my poor abandoned car.'

He came up for air.

'I already told Fred at the Nobody you'd be leaving it overnight, and to keep an eye out.'

'And when did you tell him this, exactly?' I feigned indignation.

'Oh, probably a few hours after you packed the toothbrush I saw fall out your rucksack, when you slung it in the back.'

This time, he got a proper pulling of his hair but it didn't bother him and a few minutes later we were panting and grinding away again for all we were worth.

***

We gathered our strewn about clothes, grabbed the whisky and the glasses, and went upstairs to the small room he chose to sleep in at the back of the house. The bed was of modern light oak and the sheets clean but not new on, signalling to me that he hadn't been out to seduce me. We jumped in at the same time from opposite sides and laughed as we collided in the middle, then cuddled again.

He switched on the low lamp, next to the bed, and poured us another small one.

'Cheers, Jago,' I held my glass aloft. 'Thank you for a wonderful time.'

'There's plenty more of those to be had, Gina. You wait and see.'

And off we went again.

And again.

And again.

To be honest, I lost count but in between our bouts of ardent love making I slept like a log and was brought to with a cup of strong tea and a slice of toast, bless him, at some ungodly hour in a strange house, somewhere in the middle of Dartmoor. I knew not where.

As I sat up in the glow from the lamp, the window at the bottom of the bed revealed twinkling lights in the very far distance.

'What's that, over there?' I gestured with my head between bites.

'The other side of this part of the valley. Difficult to see much but I promise when I get back, I'll give you a proper tour.'

'Why are there no other houses around here?' I asked yawning and rubbing my eyes.

'We're in the middle of my family's land.'

'How do you mean?'

He shook his head and laughed.

'You really are one on your own. Most women I know would have had the lowdown on me in their designer handbags.'

He was sitting on the bed, already fully clothed in his sailing gear.

'You know from my card that my surname is Clyston.'

I nodded.

'My family owns most of the land you and I travelled along, since we left Fingle Bridge.'

'Don't be ridiculous. That would be hundreds of acres.'

'Yup. I guess Bella must have forgotten to mention it.'

And in my bewilderment I laughed, too.

'I'm afraid we have to get going, Gina.'

He gently took my empty cup and plate before kissing me and going downstairs, leaving me grateful for the space to sort myself out. My hair for one thing was standing up in clumps and looked like I'd been rolling around all night.

And then I remembered I had.

I brushed my teeth and showered quickly, put on my clean knickers and was ready to go before Jago. I watched as he switched everything off and felt momentarily sad that the night was over, and the house would lie empty for months. There would be no more companionable log fires, or human voices, for a while but I consoled myself with the prospect of a formal introduction to it and its surroundings when we were reunited in a few months' time.

The sun had yet to rise as we drove east for my car and the faint drizzle caused the wipers to thurup on the windscreen intermittently. I sat in the middle again, as I had last night, and when we reached the pub my car was conspicuous in the bleak emptiness. He switched off the engine before helping me out with the rucksack and we stood in the gap between our vehicles.

He put his arms around me and kissed me firmly, then pulled away and held both of my hands in his, which he moved to his heart. He suddenly looked grey and drawn beneath his tan.

'Don't forget me,' he whispered.

'I won't.' My own voice held clear and definite.

He turned away and disappeared from view around the back of the Landrover. I heard the car door slam and the engine start before he reversed quickly and waved out the window. I stood and watched his tail lights disappearing into the early morning mist that had replaced the drizzle but was neither forlorn nor disorientated by his departure, only experiencing a happy contentment. I was glad we had this enforced separation because it would give us time for our emotions to settle, and I was looking forward to my client meeting later on.

There had been nothing to suggest that Jago had been anything more than he appeared on the surface, but just like Bella, he was turning out to be an onion, and I could only imagine the layers that were yet to be revealed.

32 – Sometimes ... being called Bubbles by your friend makes you wonder about the hole she fell into and when an emerald ring is given you need to buy a hat

'Geeeena! Geeeena!'

'I'm in the bath. What do you want now?'

'Can I come in and sit on the loo? I've got some news.'

'OK, give me a mo.'

I topped up the hot water and added more bubbles.

'I'm decent!'

The door opened and Janie Juno limped in, holding several magazines.

'Why are you limping?'

'I fell down a hole in the road but it's nothing. Anyway, that's not what I'm here for. I've found somewhere that looks perfect, well three actually. Take a look at this one first.'

She held an edition of 'French Living' magazine in front of my eyes and tapped her finger on a picture of a large Chateau.

'What do we want a house that size for?'

'No, not that one, you didn't watch where my finger was pointing properly, the one next to it.'

'Keep the page still. I can't see if you jiggle it.'

When I looked more closely, I saw what she meant. It was a very pretty off white rendered house with dark blue shutters set in a small garden. The roof was high pitched with a row of four gable ended windows protruding from it as well as a chimney. The corner stones were granite and there was more around the ground floor windows and French doors. It was difficult to tell the age but it looked in reasonable condition, and the photo had obviously been taken in the summer because there were window boxes overflowing with red geraniums.

'Where is it and how much?'

My interest was piqued.

'On the coast, thirty minutes from Quimper. Slap bang in the area we said. By my reckoning, it'll be just under two hours from Roscoff, so it will be weekendable.'

'And the price?'

I steeled myself for the catch.

'Half of what's in the kitty.'

We had each agreed the amount we would contribute, mine coming from some of my bonus and other savings and hers from a small inheritance she had received a year ago and banked.

'You're joking!' I sat up quickly and leaned forward on my knees as the deep water splashed up.

'Careful, you're getting it wet.'

She snatched it away and dabbed at it with a towel.

'What about the others?' My heart was racing.

'There's one which is stone and another that's bigger, both of which are the same price but neither of them are as close to the sea. One is twenty minutes away and the other is even further, the bigger one would you believe, but you must get more for your money because of where it is. Location! Location! Location!'

She sang it in a rising voice, which I was glad she didn't have to rely on for a living.

'What do you think we should do?'

'Aha! Now you're talking. I've been looking on the Brittany Ferries website and we can get a cheap five day break for seventy pounds for me, you and the car. The house is on the outskirts of a small town on the second peninsular below Brest, and I've found us a Chambre D'hote for fifty euros a night.'

My skin began to tingle and the goose pimples came back, not only on my neck this time but all along my spine and my hands began to shake, too, with excitement.

'What's your diary looking like? Mine is pretty empty the week after next?'

'I would need to shuffle a few things round, Gina, but it's doable? Shall we ...?'

She looked at me questioningly, but her enthusiasm mirrored my excitement and we both nodded furiously at our audaciousness.

'What shall we tell Kasim?' I asked dubiously.

'This has nothing to do with Kasim, so we don't tell him anything. Agreed?'

'Agreed, but I can't quite take it in, Janie. It's one thing us cooking up a plan, but this makes it real. Are you sure you're going to be able to get the use out of it with your business?'

'I'm certain, because a lot of what I do is internet based and I'll bunch up my client meetings and come back for a few weeks when I need to. I was going to ask you something else. Can I use your place as a base? That way, we can pool resources. The money we save can go directly into your French account which will be equal to the household bills so if we buy it, you'll have nothing more to fork out in exchange for me staying at yours.'

It was a neat idea because with the nasty inheritance laws in France, and the even nastier tax ones, we would need to put the house in my name with an agreement under English law for our joint ownership to protect it for my sons.

'It makes sense so yes, you can.'

'And how will you use a place in France, Gina?'

'Hopefully, in the same way as you but it can't be before October because I'm stuck with my project in Somerset until then, and I also have my events.'

'But by the time we buy it, if it's 'the one', October will be here in the blink of an eye and with Bella becoming a partner in May, she'll be on the ground in case of an emergency. You can do what I'm going to do and bunch your meetings together. Anything that can't wait, Bella will help with. Besides, you can be back in the South West quickly by ferry, or on the Eurostar to London.'

'You're right, and she knows I'd never treat her unfairly. We can adjust what each of us takes out of the business, depending on the work we do individually. That would seem logical.'

'It's the way forward, Gina, so there's absolutely nothing to stop us!'

She kissed me on the top of my head and then, for some reason, patted it.

I watched as she carefully tore out the picture of the pretty house and left it on top of the loo, before she stood up to gather the other magazines.

'Right then, Bubbles, I'll book the ferry and the B&B Chambre D'hote and we'll speak in French together from now on. Woohoo! Au revoir Gina, à bientôt!'

After she'd gone, I wore a disbelieving silly grin and leaned over as far as I dared to have another quick look at the picture, praying that it wasn't in need of a new roof, central heating, woodworm treatment and a host of other incidentals that we wouldn't be able to take on. The price had shocked me and there must be a reason, but the only way to find out was to hot foot it over and take a look for ourselves.

I reclined once again in the bath, and laughed out loud, before submerging my whole head and body beneath the warm frothy water and wondered briefly about the hole in the road that Janie Juno had fallen into.

***

The night before we sailed, which was Valentine's, I had invited Bella for a lasagne.

The shops had been full of cards with pink hearts and stuffed bears carrying proclamations, but I was neither lovelorn nor bitter and the day had passed in a florist's flurry of flowers ... to other people. I hadn't been expecting anything from a tall ship in the middle of the Atlantic, and I had sent nothing. For me, it was a day much like the day before but a few minutes before midnight, as we were finishing off our third bottle of red, my phone rang.

'Gina? Is that you?' Lou was crying and my first thought was that she was in trouble which sobered me up quickly.

'Lou, what's the matter?' Bella saw my concern and looked at me anxiously.

'I'm engaged!' she cried and I laughed with relief. 'That's wonderful! But stop your blubbing and tell us how he did it. I'll put you on speaker, Bella's here. Hold on.'

'I can't help it, and Adrian is next to me, say Hi.'

She was tearful and breathless.

'Hi, Adrian!' we chorused.

'Hello everyone. Tonight Lou has made me the happiest man on earth by accepting my proposal of marriage. I asked her when we got back to the flat after dinner and she said ...'

'... Yes!' we screamed, hugging and kissing each other.

'Do you have a ring?' Bella shouted over the noise.

'It's a beautiful emerald baguette with diamonds on each side. We'd seen it in an antiques shop weeks ago and he went back for it, without me knowing.' She managed between sobs.

'Gina, never mind the party in the summer, Adrian has to go to the Middle East the day after tomorrow.'

Ah, that explained a lot I thought, realising he'd brought it forward because he was off to war, but I kept my counsel because now wasn't the time.

'He's got a few days leave on the weekend of the cider tasting so do you think it would be possible for us to use it as our celebration, and invite my mum and close family. They'll be ten of us?'

'Lou, I'm absolutely certain that Mortimer will buy it.'

This was from Bella.

'I'll second that! He'll love the romance so consider it done.' I laughed.

'Oh thank you, thank you. I can't wait to show you my ring. See you soon. I love you!'

'Bye, Lou, we love you, too, and good luck Adrian overseas.' I shouted as we cheered and they rang off.

Time to open the last bottle of Harry's Bollinger that I had been purposely keeping for this very moment.

***

The following day, we caught the overnight ferry and arrived in a temperate Roscoff to blue skies. There had been a good swell on the sea but neither of us had suffered and the night had passed comfortably in our snug two berth cabin, where I had taken the top bunk.

We'd wolfed down a full English breakfast, and with her map reading and me driving, we set off in the direction of the other English cars, and the lone French one, heading towards Landivisiau. We would cut off around Quimper and go on to Audierne which, according to our guide, was a small town and active fishing port. The roads were relatively easy and as long as you stayed on the same side as the car in front, you were unlikely to come to any real harm.

As the day progressed, and the sun shone brighter, we pulled over and put the roof down, pretending to be Thelma and Louise, except we were going to something as opposed to running from it, and continued on through the fields of leafy artichokes.

At around mid-day, we entered Audierne by crossing the bridge which spanned the river Goyen, turned left at the roundabout and drove along the harbour until we found a parking space further along in a square. It was surrounded on three sides by turn of the century, elegant French apartments with iron work shuttered windows and shops that were at street level.

'Do you think we have to pay to park?' I asked, checking my mirrors for old ladies with baskets of oranges.

'No, I don't think so. There are no machines and you can stay for up to two hours, plus lunch. So civilised, don't you think, Gina?'

We walked further along the quay and stopped for a coffee at the Cafe Bourdin, sitting outside under the striped canopy. The view was of fishing boats and small yachts moored on the pontoons and there was nothing bigger than thirty two feet, which I took as an interesting sign. It gave me the feeling I was in a place of hardworking, community minded people. There was nothing superficial about any of it and I immediately felt at home.

'Café, s'il vous plaît,' I asked the waitress, who nodded to my amazement, and I understood when she told me they were on their way.

Gina Jarvie, un point; Les Francais, nil point.

'I quite like the look of that restaurant over there. Let's check it out after this. I'm going to use the loo.'

'Try not to fall down any more holes,' I quipped, as my eyes followed a small crabbing boat that was mooring up.

'Gina, you would never have known if it hadn't been for the limp, and it wasn't my fault that they'd just dug up the road. They were very nice to me afterwards and let me sit in their hut with strong tea, as well as the bandage. And the shoes were a bargain in the charity shop.'

'Yes, but they were three sizes too big, even if they were Jimmy Choos.'

'I thought if I stuffed them with a bit of cotton wool, I'd be fine, and they were too sparkly to resist.'

'OK, OK, but try to stay upright, at least.'

'That's rich coming from you. Don't go near the water, Gina!' She shouted through her cupped hands, doing a fair impression of Pete O'Mara and 'the' loudhailer.

I put on my best 'look at my face, am I concerned?' expression, but she wasn't biting.

The coffee arrived and after handing over a few euros, I sat watching the world go by. It was to be the first of many moments that I did just that, resisting the habit to fidget, phone or do something useful. As it turns out, taking the time to do nothing is one of the most useful things you can do, and I highly recommend it.

We strolled past the beauticians (I made a mental note), the Hotel de Ville where the mayor hangs out and past a small trinket shop that looked as if it had been closed for some time, but had kept its wares in the window, gathering dust and yellowing.

We stopped at the restaurant we'd been eyeing up and looked at the board.

'They do a set menu here for not very much and it's getting pretty full. What do you think?'

'Fine by me, as long as there are no mussels or oysters because of my allergy.'

Since eating a bad one in Brussels, they were sadly a no go 'danger de mort' area for me now. The waiter showed us to a table by the wall and inside was cosy and bustling with the noise of everyone's opinions on the price of fish. It was decorated in a typical French Auberge style, with dark wood beamed ceilings and exposed stone walls, low level lighting and the ubiquitous checked tablecloths.

'Here are the directions for the B&B. Chez Tante Phine's at Esquibien. Looking at the map, if you drive up there and follow the road, left by the Gendarmerie, it's on the right. She's a potter.'

'Good, not far then, after we've polished this lot off.'

The waiter brought us our starter of soupe de poisson with spicy rouille, grated gruyère and croutons, which was a meal in itself and after the monk fish tails in a light cream and wine sauce we were in gastronomique heaven, all for the price of a pub pie and chips.

'What time is the viewing at tomorrow?' I asked between garlicky mouthfuls.

'The agent will meet us at their office at eleven. We must have walked past it, according to the address, but we'll check on the way to the car.'

A couple of hours later, we emerged into the bright sunshine and needed our glasses. For the end of February, the sun was warm on our skin and we took off our thick jackets, stopping to look at the plants outside the florist and peer into the window of the bookseller.

The car was where we remembered we'd left it, and we headed out of town in search of Tante Phine's, which we easily found by the little blue sign. We pulled onto a drive that resembled the Gaudi mosaics in Barcelona. Every bit of wall had been covered and the designs ranged from a saucy mermaid, a sirene in French aptly, to a box that green frogs were leaping into.

We rang the bell and the door was answered by a stout lady with wild grey curly hair, wearing red horn rimmed glasses. She was wiping her hands on a clay smeared green apron.

'Come in, come in. I have been expecting you.' She spoke in heavily accented English but her tone was welcoming. 'I have put you in the red room, follow me, and I hope you will be comfortable. I offer normally my guests dinner but I am too busy with a work and there are many places in town. Breakfast will be at nine and if you need anything more, please do not hesitate.'

We thanked her as we carried our small overnight bags into the room, then stood gaping.

'You like?'

The room wasn't large but sun streamed through the French doors, that led out onto a black wrought iron balcony. It overlooked a small courtyard with direct views of the sea, about two hundred yards away. The walls were a deep crimson colour and the furniture was shabby chic turn of the century, with more gilt than Versailles. It was stunning.

'You like. I see. I will leave you now and come to the kitchen or studio next door if you have forgotten something.'

'Shall I pay you now?' I asked, rooting for my purse.

'Oh no, no. Just pay when you go. No need. See you at breakfast.'

With the door closed, we both jumped onto the bed and lay on our backs bouncing up and down, laughing. It didn't matter that it was a double because the room was too lovely to contemplate asking for another.

'Let's go out on to the balcony,' I said, jumping up and flinging the doors wide open, breathing in the fresh salty sea air.

'This might be our view one day, Gina. Do we dare drive around this afternoon and see if we can spot the house before we meet the agent tomorrow?'

We were standing side by side in the warm sunshine

'We most certainly do. I have an idea that it might be over that way.' I pointed down the road that led to the sea. 'Let's try it first anyway, we've nothing to lose.'

We hung up our few things and stashed our toilet bags in the small ensuite, with its tiny slipper bath and overhead shower, before driving off with the roof still down. As we got to the coast, we arrived at a junction and were about to turn left when she shouted.

'That's it! That's it! Look, over there, turn right, it's just up the hill. The sign must have blown off, but it's definitely the one.'

She had the creased and ragged picture that she'd torn out in my bathroom and was comparing it. I signalled and pulled out carefully, before doing a slow pass. It looked different from the photo because the shutters were closed, with no sign of the geraniums, but the four gabled windows were there, and it made sense that the French doors were round the back.

'Pull over, Gina. Let's park up and snoop around.'

She was jiggling with excitement so I came to a halt about fifty yards from the house and reversed into a space.

'What if someone is living there?' I asked, hesitating.

'Gina, don't be silly. Everything's shut up and if there are neighbours, they'll know we're only taking a peep because we might be interested. We're not wearing black eye masks, stripy jumpers or carrying swag bags for goodness sake.'

'OK, if you think we won't get into trouble. It looks nice though, from what I can see of it.'

'Nice! Is that all you can say? It backs directly onto the beach. Look.'

And it did.

There was a low stone wall to the front with car access onto a gravelled parking area. Because it was detached and the gate at the side was swinging on its hinges, we were able to case the back and could now see the French doors. It was in need of a coat of paint and the shutters, though they were all closed, were barely hanging on.

The small garden was overgrown, but you could forgive it anything with its set of thirty steps leading down onto a white sand bay that curved for nearly half a mile. At one end, to our right, there were huge granite boulders and at the other end in the distance, a red and white striped lighthouse stood on a concrete promontory. Beyond the boulders, I could see the catamarans of a sailing school and directly ahead, as the bay stretched round, there was a small ferry port to an island not far away.

The back of the beach was given over to natural sand dunes and grasses and, aside from this house and those either side of it, there were no others in this position. There were cafes and a hotel facing the road behind us, and some apartments further along, but the area was largely undeveloped.

Today, the sun on the water gave it a turquoise hue and if I hadn't known better, I would have thought I was in the

Caribbean. The sea was crystal clear and gently lapped against the pristine sand which sparkled everywhere we looked.

33 – Sometimes ... you pay the price for a quibble

We had all but moved in by the time we followed the agent back to the house the next day for the official viewing, but there was one thing that was bothering me and it was the cracks in the house next door. I wondered if they were due to subsidence, or erosion, because the garden wasn't big enough to withstand more of it disappearing and I wasn't into underpinning. There was nothing that stood between us and the Eastern Seaboard of the US so we'd bear the brunt of any storm, and this could be the reason it remained unsold and was relatively cheap. I wasn't going to rely on anything the agent said and would need to make enquiries of my own, but first things first, let's see inside.

We entered through the front door into darkness, while the young agent, Pierre, hastily went around opening everything up. As the light gradually came in, we were able to see it emerge. Downstairs was an open plan kitchen leading on to a lounge-diner and accept for the cast iron wood burner, everywhere and everything was blue; walls, ceilings, cupboards, floor ceramic tiles, radiators, splash backs, curtains, lampshades and the colour only added to the chilliness of the empty house.

The French doors opened from the lounge and for the first time we could get a sense of the view beyond. Small yachts were bobbing on their buoys by the port and the sailboats we had seen yesterday were out on the water in a row, reminding me of a mother duckling with her brood. I turned the handle and pushed them wide, carefully stepping down onto the small patio to take in the view. Janie Juno joined me and we squeezed each other.

Whilst the colours did nothing for the space, it wasn't anything that a lick of paint couldn't put right and even though the kitchen wasn't modern, the doors could be changed and there was room for appliances. I was looking for damp, cracks or recent repairs but there was no sign of anything. The boiler was old and German but fired up first time, and the electrics all looked new.

The agent allowed us to go up the dark wooden staircase on our own and we counted three good sized bedrooms, and a family bathroom with a white suite that was in excellent condition. There was another matching but shorter staircase leading up to a boarded attic, with three velux windows that let in plenty of light, which could be used for storage or as a fourth bedroom.

It was perfect.

We discovered it had been a holiday home, owned by the same family for twenty years but since their children had grown into adults, they had decided to travel more and had bought a campervan. There had been very little interest and the price reflected their motivation to sell as they lived in the suburbs of Paris and getting over to maintain it was proving difficult.

It seemed feasible.

Time to do a bit of sleuthing, but I would begin by asking the agent about subsidence and gauge his reaction. Unfortunately none of our French extended to structural engineering but his English was good enough, again with a heavy accent.

'It is a good question and you are right to be concerned. If you look at the house next door, you will see big cracks, yes?'

His honesty was refreshing. This was a first.

'Yes, I had spotted them.'

'There is a problem with it because it is not built on rock. Let me show you, but for this we need to go on the beach.'

With our backs to the sea, he pointed to the house on the left, a roof's height higher than ours, standing about forty feet up off the sand and showed us the clearly visible bedrock. He then went up to the end of our garden and pulled the plant life to one side which revealed ... more bedrock.

'This rock only goes half way underneath the house to the right of you and so it ... moves. You understand me? I think it is the reason this house still stays available. People are anxious, but I have lived here all my life and I know it to be true.'

'How old is the house?'

'It was built in nineteen hundred and is made of stone under the render.'

'So, if you have told this to others, why is it still for sale?'

'For the locals, it is considered to be too exposed. They prefer something inland so they don't see the storms in the winter but if you will not be here then, you will not worry too much, I think.'

'We would want to be here in the winter.'

'Well, you will need to repair and re-hang the shutters, to keep away the wind.'

'Do the waves crash up this far?'

'Oh, no. That is impossible. They stop at least fifty meters away, down there.' He pointed to the end of the line of big boulders to the right.

'Thank you Pierre. If we wanted to make an offer, how would we do it?'

'I fill in a form and ask the person selling if they accept. If they do, we fill in another form, the Compromis de Vente, where you are both bound by law unless the Notaire discovers something. How long you stay here for?'

'Until the weekend, but I will be in touch.' I already knew exactly what we were going to do.

'There is another person coming in two days who has already seen it.'

'That's useful to know but it won't affect anything. Thank you again.'

'Bon appétit and bon après midi.'

We shook hands and watched as he drove off in his little Renault. Janie Juno had let me do all the talking but now she couldn't contain herself.

'Gina, Gina. What shall we do? What about the other people?' she looked close to tears.

'Agents always say that but hopefully by then we'll know one way or the other.'

'You've got a plan, haven't you? I can tell.'

She narrowed her eyes.

'Janie, we need to knock on our neighbours' door and speak to them, the ones who are higher up. God knows, my French isn't up to it so we need an interpreter who doesn't have a vested interest, but who? We don't know anyone.'

'What about Tante Phine, the potter? She'll know the history of the falling down house and the area. She can tell us what it's like in winter and speak to the neighbour.'

'I hadn't thought of that. Let's take another good look round in case there's anything else. Help me to pull this shutter back so we can check the windows and take photos of the roof and the bedrock. I have an idea.'

***

To cut a long story short, Josephine her full name, came with us in her clay smeared apron and spoke to the neighbour, who coincidentally had a copy of the geological survey that had been undertaken when they bought theirs thirty years ago. It clearly showed the bedrock underneath their house, ours and part of the other one. I took photos of it all and after they assured us that the problem for the locals really was a preference for double glazing, modern boilers and being inland, I began to get excited.

We thanked Tante Phine and left her to her pots. I needed to find a computer quickly so we went back to the square where we had first parked.

'The Tourist office will know if there's an internet cafe. It's over there, let's ask.'

They did better than that and showed us to a bank of computers along their wall, where we set about uploading the photos onto the memory stick I always carried on my key ring. Today it was the green monkey's fist, which not only reminded me of the afternoon by the salmon leap but it had turned out to be very practical because I could see it and feel it anywhere in my bag.

I focussed on writing the email I was about to send, requesting some solid English advice, with picture attachments including the all-important photo of the geology report, and prayed that the recipient wasn't dangling from the crow's nest.

It would be to Jago.

If he had built his own house and had a tractor, and a digger, and a family quarrying business, and he was Mortimer's family's crypt kicker, he would know a thing or two about bedrock and foundations and subsidence and erosion and roofs and boilers and electrics and windows and shutters. He was the man, but though I hadn't said anything to Janie Juno, I felt time was against us. Sooner or later somebody else would do what we just did, even perhaps the people who were coming again, so we would have to be quick on our feet.

'Sent!'

The ping confirmed it.

'What shall we do now, Gina? My nerves are stretched. Do you fancy an aperitif before dinner?'

'Make it a double! I don't think we're going to get much sleep tonight.'

As it was now dark, there wasn't much we could see but it didn't stop us going back and prowling around with a torch before stopping at Les Dunes for a glass of fizz, not that we were celebrating, we just happened to see the people at the next table with one.

'How will he receive emails in the middle of the Atlantic?'

'God only knows. By satellite I guess. Harry would know all about that.'

'Harry who?'

'Oh, just somebody I met in London once. Way back, ages and ages ago. No-one you ever knew.'

I pretended to look casually around at the other drinkers, nodding and smiling at them, as I realised my slip.

'Mmmmm. I can tell, Gina, when you try to hide things from me and it's happening more and more, if you ask me,' she laughed. 'You're a bit different now to when I first knocked on your door, aren't you, Miss Uptogether?'

'I'm feeling better, that's all, and surely you wouldn't want me to spill the beans on *everything* I get up to would you? I mean, if you knew it all you might not like me, let alone go halves on a house.'

'You're right, it's best that I don't know. Do you fancy another, it's starting to wear off and I feel like I could gnaw off my own fingers, the stress is killing me that much.'

'If it's meant for you, it won't go by you, they say up in Glasgow,' I chuckled as a long buried memory of my mum repeating it entered my head. 'Be patient, Janie, that's what I'm always being told.'

'Gina, just get me a drink will you, before I poke you in the eye.'

***

The hours of the next day dragged slowly and the weather went from being calm and sunny to hostile at best, but it gave us a chance to observe first-hand the kind of battering we would be letting ourselves in for. In the morning, I looked at my email at Tante Phine's every half hour but there was nothing from him. Just before lunch we went back to the house to assess the impact of the storm and the agent was right about the waves. We had a quick drink in Les Dunes before heading back to the Auberge du Quai for some food, marking time minute by minute.

We checked on the computer in the Tourist Board and again with my laptop over the Wi-Fi in the Cafe Bourdin, but by five o'clock there was still nothing. I knew from the agent that the other people were second viewing the next day straight after lunch so if we were going to make our move, it would need to be before eleven tomorrow.

That night, we stayed in our room and Janie Juno taught me to play Backgammon. Neither of us was hungry and the idea of sitting it out in a strange restaurant, when all we wanted was our own little house, had no appeal.

After we'd polished off two bottles of wine, we were oblivious to anything and despite our nerves, we slept well.

***

'What time is it?' I yawned, stretching my arms behind my head and got up to open the curtains to the weather.

'Nine thirty. Do you think she'll have kept us any croissants?'

'Let's not bother. They do petit déjeuner at Le Bourdin and we can get our news, if there is any, in a place where we might be regular visitors, and make a memory of moment.'

'Gina, what a lovely idea. It's my turn for the shower first.'

'Mind your toe on the tap whatever you do!'

'You're forever the funny one, aren't you?' she said as she flounced.

***

It was ten thirty and we were sitting in bright sunshine once again in the cafe with my laptop whirring on the Wi-Fi connection. Someone had told me once that Brittany can have four seasons in one hour and I was beginning to believe it, with the range and change of weather we were experiencing.

'Petit déjeuner s'il vous plaît.'

'Certainement.'

I clicked onto my AOL account and slowly signed in.

'You have mail!' Joanna Lumley announced cheerfully but it could have been anything from black market Viagra to nasty payday loans so I wasn't overly excited until I scrolled down and saw one from the ship.

In the subject heading were two words.

Buy it.

So we did.

That is to say we tried.

Janie Juno had seen my expression before I had jumped out of my seat to hug her, and we stood in the thoroughfare between the outside tables hugging and kissing each other, and crying. The French, far more expressive than us, are used to public displays of emotion and didn't bat any eyelids.

Once our euphoria had subsided I looked at the time.

'Oh my God, they close at twelve and we need to get this wrapped up. We have to go. NOW!'

Janie Juno flung some euros on the table as I stowed the laptop and we ran the few meters to the agent and skidded through the door, breathless, with our woollen scarves askew.

'Welcome, welcome. I am pleased to see you again.' It was young Pierre.

'I would like to buy the house for the full asking price,' I blurted out still trying to catch my breath.

'Oh dear, I am very sorry but I think you are too late. The other people came yesterday instead and made us an offer which has been agreed to. The seller is in the area by chance with their camping van and arrives in a few moments to sign.'

Janie Juno had to sit down but for once, I was steady on my pins.

'So they haven't signed already?'

My heart was falling and rising like an elephant in a lift.

'No.'

'And is this offer less than the asking price?'

'Yes, by some distance.'

'Then you must let the owners know that I am offering the price they have asked for, without any quibble.' I spoke strongly and clearly.

'I do not understand, what is this word 'quibble'?'

'I have not tried to give them less money than they want.'

'Ah yes. I understand and it is important. Look, the sellers, here they come now.'

A couple in their mid-sixties entered through the glass doors wearing casual jeans, waterproofs and trainers, looking tanned and sprightly as if they were newly back from warmer climes.

'Monsieur et Madame Armaund. Please do come in, there has been more good news.'

He spoke in French but I understood and this sounded promising, even to my ears. I risked a peek at Janie Juno but she was pale and slumped on a yellow sofa below the window.

There was more fast conversation and, though I couldn't grasp it completely, I got the gist which was that they were going to accept my new offer and sign there and then to make it binding, because we had suggested the full amount straight away and they believed our intentions were more honourable than the other thieving couple.

Gina Jarvie, deux points; Les Francais, nil point.

Pierre came over to where I was sitting.

'I have good news, Madame. They are very happy to accept your offer and if you follow me, we will all now go and prepare the paperwork.'

He showed us into a little back office and pulled out his three part Compromis de Vente, which he began to slowly fill in. Hurry up, hurry up, I thought as he carefully took his time, writing neatly and checking the spellings of full names, addresses, national insurance numbers and everything else that the French Bureaucrats are so fastidious about, just stopping short of asking me for the name of my cousin's dog.

With each carefully written word, we were getting closer and closer to our dream and as he got near the end, I allowed myself for the first time to believe that we might actually do it.

When he asked Les Armaunds to sign, quickly followed by me, we all spontaneously kissed and hugged then myself and Janie Juno began to cry.

'Technically, there is seven days for you to change your mind but you will need to give this to the Notaire we have suggested that is next door. They will take you through the stages and I wish you all a very good day.' He handed me a copy and gave another to the sellers, keeping one for himself.

He spoke in rapid French to Monsieur et Madame who nodded and smiled and then we kissed each other one last time.

'Thank you. I am so very pleased,' I said with tears threatening again.

To my surprise Madame Armaund replied in perfect English, 'I am sure everyone will be very happy there, Gina, if I may call you that.'

I kissed her again before grabbing Janie Juno by the hand and dragged her out into the fresh air before she fainted or fell over again.

34 – Sometimes … a nervous baker has to adjust all your packages

Everyone did what they were supposed to do and eventually we were given a date to complete the sale, which was now only six weeks away, on the fifteenth of May. But before then I had Jago and the cider tasting to look forward to next Saturday, which was Easter, and the Beer Festival to worry about it.

Janie Juno had been left in charge of organising paint and was busy moving in with me. She was also looking for a van big enough to take our things over to France.

To celebrate Lou's surprise Valentine's Day engagement, I had arranged with Mortimer for Hogwash to play and he'd been delighted to accommodate her small contingency of ten or so guests, telling me that he was a staunch supporter of the institute of marriage and I believed him, despite the rumours.

Bella had known, predictably, about Janie Juno and I having bought a house and was relishing the prospect of helping us to convert the attic room. She had been a brick about our working arrangements, happily agreeing to cover things when I wouldn't be around and was looking forward to coming out with us to collect the key.

During his voyage, I had spoken to Jago on the phone twice and we had exchanged four emails, five if you counted the 'buy it'. This had suited us both and we'd kept our contact light, short and funny but he was happy at the prospect of seeing me again, and unaware that I had arranged with his son to collect him from Gatwick. Jago was expecting Joshua, but would find Gina instead.

The days leading up to it were hectic with my events work and the Somerset project, but I was glad to be occupied because as our reunion approached, I became more excited. Not heady or giddy, with my emotions running amok, but with a gentle glow of anticipation that I carried inside me.

The plane was due in at five, 1700 hours and yes, Janie Juno and Bella had both checked the time. My plan was to leave Exeter after lunch, drive the distance in three and a half hours, park, then grab a coffee.

***

I woke up at my usual time and after checking emails and sending responses over a coffee and toasted crumpets, I made a few more calls mostly to do with the festival. There were always hiccups because of the sheer number of different contributors, but on the whole it was tidy.

From my desk, I could see it was generally sunny but when I went on to the balcony, still in my robe, there was a chill in the air, so I decided to put on some jeans and a fringed wrap to keep warm. The new drop pearl dangly earrings, I'd been saving for Jago, were still in their black velvet box by my bed, and smiling, I took out my standard studs and gently fastened the new ones in. Looking in the mirror, I liked their fluidity and the way they caught the light when I moved my head.

My hair was a couple of inches longer these days, and I'd been having fewer highlights because the outdoors and

293

sunshine had brought out its natural tones. My complexion, too, was tanned and rosy and the white pastiness that I had arrived with nearly a year ago was no longer there. I always felt my blue eyes were unremarkable but because of the other physical changes, they looked bright and the colour was more defined, so I could now get away with less make-up, although I still kept my lipsticks to hand.

I took in the image and twirled so that my wrap rose up and I saw that even in my movements, I was no longer tight and rigid from where in the past I'd held myself in. As I had become more comfortable with the world around me, I had relaxed and acquired an easy grace that reflected my inner tranquillity.

'You look nice today, Gina!' I said out loud to the mirror and watched my reflection laugh as I snatched up my large shoulder bag from the bed, instantly spotting my keys by their green fob.

I locked the flat and skipped down the stairs, out through the main door and onto the quay. I was heading to Cowick Street to collect Lou and Adrian's cake for tomorrow and hoped the baker had been able to make a good job of the very specific design I had asked for. They knew about my business and could do well from it, so I was confident they would try hard.

There were a few clouds in the blue sky but the wind was blowing them steadily across, and when the sun disappeared it was only for an instant. My step was light, to match my mood, and I wanted to drop into the jewellers to show him my earrings, and thank him for the trouble he'd taken in matching the pearls to my existing necklace.

He was an older Jewish man whom I had first met when I bought some sparkly Marcasite jewellery for the various Balls and Dinners I had been invited to. He phoned whenever he came across something he thought I might like, and I had never regretted buying any of the pieces he had shown me. It wasn't a hoard by Elizabeth Taylor's standards, but I had enough to get by on.

As I walked past his window, I was glad I had taken the trouble because I spotted a small pewter pirate ship pin that would be perfect for Jago. I went in to the ding-dong of the door, as Mr Stein appeared from the back.

'Hello, Gina. Aha! I see you have on your new earrings. They suit you and I'm glad we persuaded you out of your pearl studs. I am back up in Birmingham next week and will keep a look out.'

'Thank you once again, Mr Stein. I'm still getting used to them but am very pleased, and if you do see anything else, give me a buzz. Meanwhile, I'll take the little ship pin you have in the window, please.'

The bell on the door ding-donged again as I continued on my way beneath the blackened stone railway bridge. There were a few charity shops en route and I had a quick browse, picking up a waxed jacket that I thought might be useful and a pair of good fitting jeans with the worn look I loved. The street was busy with shoppers and I always enjoyed this part of town because the shops were small independents.

I called in at the cafe next to the bakers for a quick coffee and a crispy bacon roll, then bought some sausages for the freezer from Courtneys the butcher.

My watch showed I was fine for time, so next and final stop was the cake, and when I went into the shop the baker's wife was serving.

'Hi, Gina, all ready for you.'

'Thanks, Sally, how did Russ get on?'

'It was fiddly, but I think you'll be pleased.'

Lou had specifically said it wouldn't be a bride and groom on the cake but I felt I'd come up with something that got both of them on it, without the white dress and formal attire.

'Russ,' the baker's wife shouted. 'Gina's here for the cake. Bring it through, will you.'

He appeared carrying a very large white lidded box and carefully set it on the table, next to the till.

'Did Sally tell you we had some problems?'

My heart began to sink.

'She did.'

'Well, we worked through the night and I hope it's what you want.'

His hands shook, which added to my sense of doom, and I watched with baited breath as he lifted the lid with a flourish and a nervous 'Tara!'

My request had been for a rectangular base with a separate rowing boat containing two people on top, complete with oars; Lou in her rowing gear and Adrian behind her in his naval uniform. The base was to be iced to represent the water on the river.

I steeled myself to look down, knowing there was no time to recover the situation if it was a catastrophe, but when I eventually plucked up the courage, I was rendered speechless. It was absolutely perfect, right down to the detail of the blades, the stripes on her all in one and the gold braid on his cap. I was so moved that he had taken the trouble that I couldn't speak and he mistook my silence for disapproval and began to offer suggestions.

'No, no Russ. Please, I'm sorry. It's wonderful and I can't thank you enough. A lot of work has gone into it and are you sure that the price you quoted is enough?'

'Gina, it's been a pleasure. It's not every day we get a chance to put our talents to the test like this, and Sally and I hope it's the first of many. Where did you get the idea from?' he joked.

'You'd have to know them,' I laughed, handing over the meagre thirty pounds we had agreed on.

'Would you like me to carry it out to your car?'

'It's fine, Russ, thanks. I'm walking and it isn't very far.'

'Well, if you're sure,' he said doubtfully, handing me the box slowly and adjusting my bags so I could carry it with both hands.

'Thanks once again. I'll be back!' I yelled over my shoulder as I staggered out of the door.

'Anytime.' They both chorused, watching me and their precious cake anxiously as we disappeared onto the busy street.

All I had to do now was safely deliver it.

Tottering gingerly home, I neither fell in nor fell over, and didn't bump into any little bow-legged old ladies, or come close to being mugged. I kept an eye out for cracks in the pavement, small escaped sausage dogs and boys on blue stilts, and can proudly say that the cake journeyed back without harm, but it had been close.

At one point, a man on a unicycle toppled me backwards on my final zebra crossing but luckily, he caught both me and the cake before either of us hit the ground. Sadly, his unicycle got squished by a passing Eddie Stobbard truck during the commotion, though thankfully the man escaped unhurt.

35 – Sometimes ... stepping stones lead you to a surprising journey's end

I had changed into a knee-length figure hugging, but demure, black woollen dress and put on some slingbacks to make myself nice for him, taking along my trench coat for the short walk to the terminal. The journey to the airport was uneventful, and the traffic hadn't jammed around the M25, so I made it to the airport and parked with enough time to go to the ladies before I saw on the board that the plane had landed.

I knew he would be a while longer collecting his bags, and getting through immigration, so I went to browse in the shops, allowing twenty minutes. I became engrossed in the lipsticks and was trying the samples on the back of my hand, comparing them to my last precious Chanel, when I realised that nearly half an hour had passed. I stopped what I was doing and headed in the direction of Arrivals.

On drawing closer, I saw his unmistakable back in its bright red sailing jacket but the rest of him was obscured by the pillar he was standing next to. I was ready to run up and cover his eyes with my hands, but was stopped in my tracks when, as he came in to full view, I saw him in a passionate clinch with a glamorous red head.

My legs turned to jelly and my head felt like it was being squeezed in a cold vice. After the physical shock, I panicked about what I should do and couldn't get a grip of the wild thoughts that were rattling around my addled brain. Think, I told myself, take stock, focus; use your head. He would be stranded without a lift, he would be embarrassed to see me, it would be painfully awkward but ... he wasn't expecting me and if I turned on my heel he would never know; Joshua could tell him the traffic was heavy and urge him to make his own way back.

My head was swimming, but somewhere in my confusion I knew that leaving without him was my only option so I did a one hundred and eighty degree turn and walked quickly away. My breathing was laboured and when I put my hand to my face, it felt hot and clammy. I slid my fingers into my pocket to pull out a tissue but instead, felt the box containing the pin. I carried on walking and was almost at the sliding exit doors when I heard my name.

'Gina! Gina! Is that you?' His voice held a note of desperation but I had made my decision and ignored it.

'Gina, wait. Please.'

The doors opened and I went through them, getting a blast of a welcome early evening chill. I turned to my right, in the direction of the short stay car park, without glancing behind me. I could hear the clicking of my heels on the pavement and once more fingered the small box in the pocket of my trench coat.

Panic and confusion had been replaced with anger, which was rapidly diminishing in place of apathy. I had been down this route before, but unlike with Max, I had kept my emotions in check this time and my rational self was beginning to shrug it off for what it was – a couple of dates, two phone calls and less emails than the fingers of one hand.

Jago was a man of the world and free to do what he liked, unaccountable to me or anyone. I only wished that I hadn't surprised him and had to bear witness to it, that was all.

Lost in my thoughts, I wasn't expecting the tap on the shoulder when it came and of course it was Jago, out of breath and white beneath his tan. He tried to take my elbow but I shrugged it away without looking at him until he stood in front and pinned me with both his strong arms, forcing me to a standstill. The people around us parted, ignoring the scene, too preoccupied with their own problems.

'Gina, it's not what it seems. Please, believe me.'

I shrugged and said flatly, 'It never is.'

'Is Joshua here?'

'No. I wanted to surprise you, and by the looks of things, I did. I should never have come.'

I tried to struggle free again but he held me firmly.

'I've known her for years and she travelled as the ship's doctor. We had a thing in the past, but it's over. I didn't realise she was going to be on the voyage.'

'So how do you explain the passionate clinch?'

'It was a big hug, and one kiss on the lips which lasted seconds, but critically, that's when you saw me.'

'Look, Jago, there's no need to say anymore. It is as it is. You seemed a nice guy but we barely know each other and it's a free world. Personally, I'm finding this very awkward, and I think it's best you take the train.'

'Will you be at Mortimer's cider tasting tomorrow?'

He looked his age suddenly, if not older, and had turned from white to grey.

'Perhaps. But, if I do see you there, I'll say hello.'

With a final effort, I shook myself from him. As I walked away, I belted my coat against the rain and listened to the determined click of my heels as I strode towards the

300

hole in the ground that I wanted to be swallowed up in, which for the moment would have to be my car.

***

On the drive home, I listened to the CD of arias that I had bought in Barcelona and took comfort in the cosseted luxury of my leather interior, and from the solid German engineering that protected me. I drove well and concentrated on my journey, knowing that despite my 'perhaps' to Jago, I would certainly be at the gathering the next day because of Lou's celebration and for Mortimer, whom I admired greatly.

As I had said to Jago in the impersonal confines of the busy airport, it is as it is.

I had enjoyed our dates, and the sex, but hadn't let either my head or my heart get carried away, and in the time he'd been at sea I had been productive at work, spent time with friends, and was close to completing on a house in France.

In the last year, I had shifted radically from the deluded belief that my life would only be complete once I was part of a successful couple, realising it was a status I no longer hankered for.

In terms of what had just transpired, Bella would tell me rationally that I had been shown something, and I believed I had. The proof was there that I had been correct in my assumption that he met interesting women along the way and, whilst he didn't keep a coterie like Max, he did live a full and varied life that didn't revolve around the desire, or need, for a long term exclusive relationship. The only things he could ever be wedded to now were his sailing along with his lifestyle. And why not, he'd earned the right.

What stuck in my craw was that I had seen him with her and felt humiliated, but I quickly countered it by the powerful insight it had given me into Jago's world, and a growing feeling that if we could accomplish it, we might be good friends to each other. That way, I wouldn't get in over my head or lose sleep for someone I would barely see, and we could trundle around together when it suited us. No real harm had been done and it was far, far better that I understood it for what is was than to fall for the wrong person again.

As I took the turnoff for Exeter, I glided Pilar Rodriguez out of the CD player and replaced it with The Best of The Red Hot Chilli Peppers, thinking about my outfit for the following day.

What had barely begun was over.

***

I might reasonably have been expected to have taken an overnight bag with me when I had gone to collect Jago, but strangely, I hadn't. Not from conscious choice, but from the fact that I hadn't thought about staying one way or the other. This struck me as being significant and I put it down to a deeply buried detachment, and possible indifference, that I hadn't been aware of.

When I parked my car, there was nothing to lug up the stairs and I was grateful to be back when I closed the door gently behind me and switched on the lamps. I checked my phone and saw a no-message, missed call, but even if there had been, I would have ignored it as now wasn't the time. It would be best to speak only once the dust had settled.

The sight of Lou's cake box warmed me and I lifted the lid for another peek, smiling at the expressions of the two little figures. I hoped they would like it and appreciate the sentiment of the words that Russ had so carefully iced. I wasn't in the mood to talk to anyone so while the bath was running, I went to my wardrobe to put together a barn dance ensemble, quickly realising that what I'd worn in the morning to go shopping would fit easily with my green wellies. The wrap was slate grey, light and warm, and would see me through the best, and worst, of whatever lay ahead, as far as the 'juice of the devil' went.

As I was about to switch off the bedside light and turn in, my phone rang and it was Jago. I overcame my desire to deaden it in favour of trying to clear at least some of the air between us before tomorrow, as there would be nothing worse than us having to skirt around each other in a public arena.

'Hello, Jago. Where are you?' I yawned.

'I'm at home and have just got the house warm. I'm sorry, Gina.'

'There's no need, it was my fault and I can see things more clearly now. It's fine.' I yawned again.

'You sound sleepy. You had a long drive for nothing.' He sounded dejected.

'Oh, I wouldn't say that. It helped me to understand,' I said casually.

'Understand what? You said yourself that we barely knew each other and ...'

His voice was rising but I interrupted him wearily.

'... Jago, please, let me stop you. I'm happy with my life exactly as it is, and I suspect you are too. There were times when it wasn't always like that, but I've worked hard to get myself to where I am now, and I want to keep it that way.' I tried to stifle another yawn but he heard it.

'It's not a good time to talk, is it?'

'No, but tomorrow might be difficult.'

'You're going!' He sounded surprised, but pleased.

'Of course I'm going, it's Lou's engagement celebration, and whatever has gone on between you and I is simply that, it's between you and I.'

'There are stepping stones in the river next to Mortimer's barns and we can cross them together, and take a short walk.'

The image that entered my head was of Janie Juno, and what she had told me all those months ago, but I knew with absolute certainty that the only divide I would cross with Jago would be the one that took him from lover to friend.

'OK, but Jago ...'

'Yes?' he asked expectantly.

'It's over.' My voice didn't waver as I imagined my friends at my side.

'I know.'

His tone was flat and dead.

36 – Sometimes ... a matching is combined with a hatching, but thankfully not a dispatching

Over lunch, I told Janie Juno about what had happened with Jago and she listened carefully, nodding thoughtfully as I took her through my reasoning and emotions. She had questioned me tactfully on why I was still open to the idea of staying in contact with him, and whether it would be possible without becoming too deeply or romantically involved.

When I explained that I simply liked and admired the man, but felt the side to him involving attachments was seemingly a free for all, that I wanted no part of, she agreed it might work and that I had nothing to lose in trying to steer the relationship in the direction of us becoming good friends.

Kasim had been different, as we both knew. The approach he took to attachments was the opposite, in as much as he was a one woman man but his problem was one of suffocation. We felt this was more serious in some ways and was why we kept him at arm's length, because it lingered whenever he was present. Ultimately, it had been the reason for her not going to Paris a few weeks ago.

Max, in comparison, was unscrupulous on every level so the idea of any contact whatsoever was easily dismissed.

Despite it being less than twenty four hours since what had become known as 'The Red Head Incident', I was fine, thanks to talking things through with Janie Juno. When we compared my state of mind with how I'd been with Max, she was proud of my emotional robustness and felt I'd made progress with a capital 'P', which she celebrated by producing a box of crème eggs, and laughed when I ate all six.

**

After we'd cleared away, Janie carefully carried the cake down to the car and sat with it on her lap. As we drove to Mortimer's, she went over her lists, describing paint colours and telling me about the furniture she was taking over. I was delighted because her taste, though somewhat bohemian, was excellent and I knew it would enhance the house.

'Gina, what do you think of taking your wrought iron butterfly bed and getting a light oak one to replace it here? I think it would work well in France.'

'I think so, too. It's exciting to do up a place from scratch.'

'I haven't had much luck finding anyone who'll put down a wooden floor over the horrible blue tiles downstairs. Perhaps Mortimer will know somebody. The bedrooms are fine. We can sand down the boards and use a dark varnish which will cover the worst of the marks.'

'Sounds good to me. Have we got a sander?'

'No, we ought to get some other tools, too. I'll make a list.'

As there were only so many times I could hear the 'L word', I stole a glance at her on a straight bit of road and changed the subject.

'Have you seen anything of Gaz lately?'

'No!' she exclaimed indignantly.

'The lady doth protest too much, methinks.' I smirked.

'Remember that time you let it slip out about Harry? Well, just as you don't 'fess up to everything, neither do I. All you need to know is that Gaz will never turn up in France.'

'OK, OK, calm down. Mind the cake. I only asked.'

'Humph,' was the last thing she said before we pulled into the field that Mortimer had signposted us to and I saw Jago's distinctive green Landrover parked in the corner.

***

We had arrived an hour before the official start in order to put the finishing touches to the Engagement table for Lou, which I had asked to be set up in the barn next to the cider press. It was intended for her cake and some presents so Janie Juno and I started to blow up balloons and create the display.

Though not sunny, it was dry and a warm breeze carried the scent of the early apple blossoms from the orchard, which looked a picture of pink and white as the hundred or so trees had sprung forth their bounty to the gentle call of the recent sunshine. I was tempted to snip some but couldn't bring myself to deny them the apples that would begin very soon and went in search of some early spring flowers, leaving Janie Juno red faced with her cheeks puffed out.

Mortimer was busy shouting instructions to some of the locals I recognised from the pub, who were gallantly erecting what looked like an old green canvas scout tent with thick guide ropes, wooden poles and bunting, so I left them to it. As I went in the orchard, Denzel the spaniel appeared and I began to collect daffodils that were growing at the bases of the trees, not hearing the footsteps on the grass behind me.

'Hello, Gina.'

I stood up, my arms now full, and turned around at the sound of his voice. Denzel came and sat protectively next to me.

'Hello, Jago.'

I looked him straight in the eye.

He kissed me gently on the cheek and touched my arm tenderly. His once vivid blue eyes looked red rimmed and rheumy from lack of sleep.

'I know you're busy, but can you spare me five minutes.'

He cocked his head boyishly to one side and his smile was crooked and uncertain.

'Of course,' I said easily. 'You can carry these, if you like. There are some bluebells on the other side of the river I would like to pick.'

I watched as a pair of mating chaffinches flitted about whilst a curious robin swooped down and landed by my foot. We made our way towards the noise of the babbling river and no more was said until we crossed the stepping stones to the opposite bank. The dog had followed and was shaking himself off after his swim, forcing us to stand close to avoid the deluge.

'I missed you a lot on the voyage, Gina.' His voice held deep emotion and he was struggling to go on. 'I accept I can never be the person at your side, but there is something I would like to ask you.'

He had taken my hand from beneath the flowers and I understood that the tingle of warming reassurance was there because he was someone who could look after me, not as a husband or a lover, but as someone who was practical.

It wasn't an unpleasant feeling and I let it remain where it was.

'Can we at least be friends?' He asked me sincerely.

'I think we can try,' I smiled and the relief was plain on his face.

'Really, you mean it?' he looked questioningly into my eyes.

'I do, but we can never be lovers again. I can't take the risk on you, Jago. We both have our own lives and I'm not the waiting kind.'

'I understood that, Gina, at the salmon leap. You deserve more from life than I have to offer, but I have another proposition, too.'

He smiled rakishly and I held my breath.

'I'm planting a small vineyard on some of my family's land and need help, the week after next. Will you do it with me, just the two of us, and I'll buy you lunch in the pub?'

I squeezed his hand by way of reply but I had a request of my own, and now that we had reversed back across the chasm from lovers to friends, I felt able to ask him.

'Only if you come to France to see the house.'

'Of course, I would love to.' His smile was warm and grateful.

'And ... if you could see your way to laying a wooden floor ...' I now tilted my head to one side, and grinned cheekily.

'I'd be honoured.'

We hugged, despite the flowers, to the cheerful barking of the lovely black spaniel that had begun to nuzzle my leg and I knew what I had to do.

'Take this, and say nothing.'

From my jeans I took out and gave him the small box, which he struggled to open amongst the blooms.

'I don't deserve this.' He looked at me in wonderment.

'You weren't supposed to say anything, remember? But consider it a token of our friendship and wear it at sea. The key ring you gave me is one of the most practical things I've ever owned and whatever happens ...' I shouted over my shoulder as I hopped on to the first stone to go back, 'it will always remind me of you!'

The sun suddenly burst out of the sky and I smiled at him before throwing caution to the wind and leaping wildly across, flowers and all. His laughter followed me and I was contented that we'd managed to find our own rock in the river, which by my reckoning lay somewhere about mid-way between where we both now stood.

'We've done it, Jago!' I shouted from the other side.

'I know. Thanks, Gina.'

As I strutted cheerfully back to the barns, I remembered my quip of once saying that owning a place in France was about as likely as me planting a vineyard, and promised to make mental note seven thousand and six.

***

The next people to arrive were Bella and the Hogwash guys, who appeared on the horizon from the parking field with their instruments strapped to their backs. They looked every inch like a group of travelling minstrels, complete with knotted hankies around their necks plus various assorted headgear including caps and, bizarrely, feathers. Bella's own head was bare and her thick auburn tresses hung loose around her shoulders, fluttering in the wind. Her drum was cross strapped to her back and she looked like the folk chick she was.

'Hi, Gina, is Lou here yet? How did the cake turn out? Where shall I put my present?'

'Follow me, and I'll show you. I've set up a table by the press and need to put these in some water.'

She took in my laden arms and looked over to where Jago was helping with the bunting on the tent.

'Pleased to have him back?'

'Long story, but yes, you could say that. I have news but it'll have to wait. Look, here's Mortimer.'

'Hello, ladies. Glad you could make it and nice to see the daffodils being put to good use.' He kissed us both politely on our cheeks. 'I'm sorry but you'll have to excuse me as the daughter of the house had her baby last week, a bit earlier than we were expecting, so we'll be having a hatching celebration as well as a matching. Pray to the good man above that we don't have a dispatching.'

He ambled off with the spaniel at this heel.

The cake was still in its box, to protect it mostly from the dog, and when I lifted the lid she laughed.

'Gina, it's wonderful and I love the message. Did Russ and Sally make it?'

'They did, and he told me it had been tricky, but I can't wait to see their faces.'

'I have something for you.'

She took off her drum and laid it gently down before rummaging in her bag and retrieving a small brown paper parcel.

'For me?' I asked, smiling, 'I love presents!' and ripped off the paper gleefully.

She laughed at my puzzled expression. 'I knitted them for you, it being Easter. They're supposed to be egg warmers, can't you tell?'

She sounded faintly irritated, but now she had told me, it made sense.

Nestling carefully in tissue paper were two little fawn rabbit heads complete with big floppy ears, eyes and little rabbity mouths that she had sewn in dark brown. They were cute and funny, and the image of her sitting knitting with her glasses on, along with everything else she did in her life, made me chuckle.

'They're not that funny. There's one for you and one for Janie Juno.'

'Bella, they're delightful and I will treasure mine, and you, forever and ever! Come here.'

I gave her a very big hug so she didn't see the tear in my eye.

'Happy Easter, Gina!'

'And to you, Bella, my lovely friend.'

This was how Pete O'Mara found us a few seconds later after I placed the bunnies centre stage of Lou's table, amongst the daffodils to good effect.

'Hello, troubles. I thought you lot might be here.'

Another round of hugs and kisses.

'I didn't know you would. What a pleasure. You know it's Lou's engagement party, too?' I asked him, adjusting the display.

'I did hear from her mother but I always come as a guest of Jago's. I've known Mortimer for years and he did a spot of rowing in his time, though he's grown out of it now you might say.'

'What? Mortimer a rower?' Bella asked incredulously.

'He rowed for Oxford when he was a student, and beat Cambridge.'

'Never!' We both chorused.

'Ask him, when you see him. Is Jago here?' Pete looked at me with a closed expression which left me unable to gauge whether he knew anything, so I let it go.

'He's helping with the bunting, over there.'

I pointed to the tent.

'OK, see you both later. I'm off to draw a pint of Mortimer's ale from the barrel he has so thoughtfully trammed up.'

As we watched Pete's retreating back, Bella looked closely at me.

'Are you staying with Jago tonight?'

'No. It's over.'

'Ah. I thought it might be. Something to do with a red head by any chance?' she asked kindly.

'Yup ... bang on, but we've found a way through it, and agreed on an exchange of sorts.'

'You plant the vineyard and he does the floor?'

There was no point in asking her how she knew so I turned my attention back to fiddling with the bluebells.

'Shouldn't you be with the band?' I hissed but she just smirked, picked up her drum and strode towards the tent, whilst a dozen pairs of male eyes followed her every move.

At around four o'clock, the place began to fill up and the atmosphere was one of a village fete, helped along by the juggling display from Mortimer's bearded twin sons who, by way of explanation, swore that their new hobby had given them the boost they needed to knuckle down on their overdue theses. The three brewery employees that I had met on the tour, Bob, Doddy and Binky the dwarf, whose duties I hadn't quite figured out, were on hand to re-light the flaming batons when they went out.

I could hear the band playing their jigs and people were getting stuck into the cider as the stack of jug handled glasses dwindled away. There was a BBQ going with venison steaks, sausages and burgers which Lady Dunseford, regal in tweed skirt and headscarf, was overseeing. Several more spaniels had appeared, including a lovely half grown, brown and white one called Nutmeg, and children were darting about playing with some of the balloons.

Jago had caught my eye a few times, smiling warmly, and I knew from our earlier chat that we were back on an even keel. It was a different one to this time yesterday, but it was 'even' in a calm sea, and we were comfortable with it, and each other.

When Lou arrived with Adrian at four thirty, the band struck up a few bars of 'Here comes the Bride' and she blushed for the first time since I'd known her.

She had tied up her honey hair loosely and her hazel eyes were sparkling. The shortish green tartan skirt, black tights and wellies she had on, with a baggy jumper, gave her a fresh school girl look and Adrian appeared fair and dashing in a black padded gilet, dark grey cords and checked shirt. But it was the red cap that made him stand out from the crowd.

I looked at the two of them as they accepted everyone's good wishes and although I wasn't exactly a believer, I cast my eyes upwards and asked for him to be kept safe when he went to the Middle East in two days' time.

They made their way to the table and were delighted with the cake, laughing at the words '*May you grow as you row, who said life was fair?*'

'That just about sums it up, Gina. Me doing all the hard work in front and him lying there behind, with his hands on the back of his head and feet up. I love it!'

She threw her arms around me.

'Are those knitted Easter bunnies that I can see peeping out from the daffodils?'

She bent down excitedly to look more closely.

'Those belong to Gina and Janie Juno, but I think you'll find a few of your own in one of the packages.' Bella had come to join us and smiled smugly at the delight on Lou's face.

'Oh, how lovely. I'll put them in my bottom drawer. Adrian likes boiled eggs, don't you?'

'Absolutely!' he shook his head in bewilderment, wondering if we were about to lose the plot.

'Where's Janie Juno? Is she here? I wanted to thank her for the cake.'

'Ask her to tell you about the zebra crossing because I can't go through it again. My nerves aren't up to it.' I delicately put the back of my hand to my forehead and affected a swoon. 'Here she comes, now. Meanwhile, I'm off to engage in the gentle art of chatting. See you later.'

***

I saw Janie Juno sitting by the stage talking to a young woman, who looked decidedly French, with her almost jet black eyes and casual elegance. As I approached, I saw the woman nod and stand up while my friend raised her glass and went off in the direction of the barrel.

'Hello, Gina, I have heard a lot about you. I am Francoise and I believe a house has just been bought not too far from my home town of Pont Croix.'

She kissed me on each cheek.

'I am, and it's true.' I smiled at the memory of the place that awaited us, and its 'soon to have' wooden floor.

'You like Brittany, the music and dancing and food? I do miss it but when I married David, I came to live on his farm, a few miles from here.' Her accent was there but her English was excellent.

'I know about the food but not too much more. It all happened so quickly.'

'Well in that case, you must go to the Fest Noz and learn to dance. You like the Scottish bagpipes?'

'I grew up with them.' I beamed, as they weren't to everyone's taste.

'Excellent,' she smiled warmly, 'I will write down some details for you because we have our very own version and much of our folk music is based on this. I think you will all have a very good time and I will give my family's address and you must visit them and say hello.'

I was touched by her generosity, and intrigued about the music scene which I knew Bella would love.

'Thank you, Francoise. I will definitely drop in, and if you're there visiting, please come to the house. Here's the address.' I gave her one of the useful cards that Janie Juno had assured me were not tempting providence.

'And this is my family.' She scribbled quickly on one of Mortimer's promotional Snout About Nothin' beer mats.

'A bientôt, Gina.'

'A bientôt, Francoise.'

And another round of kissing.

I would have to get used to it.

Janie Juno handed me a fresh glass of cider at the point I heard a bell ring followed by the unmistakable booming voice of Mortimer.

'Ladies and gentleman and anybody who has yet to make up their mind.' He laughed heartily, 'we are gathered here today to ...'

'Get on with it for God's sake, Dunseford. You're taking up our valuable drinking time.'

It was one of the locals.

'Eject that man!' He boomed. 'But on second thoughts better not, seeing as how he's my son in law and despite the looks of him he's been able to do the business and provide me with my first grandson.'

Everyone cheered and the beautiful days old baby was passed to Mortimer by his daughter who had come to his side. He held him high and out to the crowd. 'Welcome to the Bootley brewing dynasty, Jasper,' he bellowed and kissed the baby's forehead before handing him back to his daughter. He then dipped his finger in the pint of beer that was resting on a table close by, and dabbed it on the little chap's head.

A round of wild applause broke out, along with more cheers, and amazingly the poor baby slept through it all. The daughter wrapped him back up again snugly in a fine white shawl and went to join her mother.

'Wait, wait!' Mortimer shouted again over the noise of the crowd. 'Lou, Adrian. Get your arses over here!'

They made their way to the front, one standing either side of him and he took their nearest hands to his and raised them in the air.

'To the next generation of beer drinkers! And I hope you've given her a good seeing to before you go off to that hot place you can't tell us about.'

In keeping with the form, Adrian grabbed Lou, dipped her over backwards, brought her back up, kissed the face off her and hauled her over his shoulder, fireman style, before carrying her from the stage while beating his chest with his free hand.

The crowd erupted again and bang on cue, the band started up with a rendition of 'Always look on the Bright side ...' I looked over to where Jago was standing with Pete O'Mara and when they both lifted their glasses to me, I raised mine back.

And smiled.

At around eight o'clock, they served the hog roast that had been slow cooking for hours, and yet more venison cooked on a contraption they were calling the Heath Robinson. It was a huge flat grill over an open fire pit that Jago had made with the brewery guys. Inside the tent, people were collapsing from the cider on the various mismatched sofas that would go on to form the basis of a large bonfire later. It looked messy.

Janie Juno and I had decided earlier that we would slip away quietly, knowing that if we trumpeted our departure, we'd be coerced into staying. I for one, with the rigours of the last twenty four hours, was exhausted so after a quick pork roll we disappeared into the darkness behind the barns and made our way to the car.

37 – Sometimes ... an anniversary is marked by planting something you can drink on the next anniversary and so on ...

On the day of vine planting, I arrived at Jago's house, after more detailed directions, in time for coffee. As the weather was warm and sunny, we took our mugs outside and across a lane into the field that had already been prepared. We sat amicably at a bench set by a natural clear pond that was fed by a spring further up, and began tucking into the ice buns he told me he'd bought from a bakery on the outskirts of the village.

The field was on the south facing slope of a valley and I could see across to the other side in the far distance. The land was a patchwork of walled in fields, but on this part of Dartmoor it was green and lush with none of the harshness of the higher moor. The only sounds were the water and the noise from some crows mobbing a peregrine falcon that simply out-flew them. The sky became clear except for faint vapour trails left by jets as they ploughed their trade, with a cargo of passengers who had nothing in common except the space they would share for the duration of their journey. As I followed it west with my eyes, I took comfort from the fact that my days of executive business travel were firmly behind me.

'What gave you the idea to do it?' I asked absently, still looking up and speculating about the people as I cradled my coffee with my elbows resting on the table.

'It just sort of happened. I went on a tour of Camel Valley in Cornwall, where they make award winning fizz, and ran into someone who's doing it for themselves on a big scale, including a winery. The deal is that if I plant the same varieties as him, he'll take the grapes, make the wine, and give me a share.'

'Like they do in France?'

'Exactly, Gina. He's guided me so far on everything from the agronomist to preparing the soil, and has found the best suppliers for the fastenings and frames etc. Our job today is to plant the vines, cover them with growing tubes and attach them to the wires that run the length of the site.'

'How many bottles will you get?'

'About three thousand.'

'What? From this little patch!'

He had to be joking.

'It'll take a few years to get it established, but yes, if all goes according to plan, that'll be my share. It'll produce double that, but he'll keep the rest.'

'I'm surprised the vines are so small. This one is only twelve inches long and if you didn't know, you'd think it was a twig. It's nothing.'

'I agree. I was expecting something a bit more triffid like, too, but we stick 'em in with the waxed end showing and I'm assured they'll sprout new leaves. I'd like to think that one day I'll rival Mortimer's apple pressing.'

'Well, I hope that in return for my hard graft I'll be the guest of honour to all your annual picking vendanges and grape treading. I have the feet for it you know!' I pointed to my green wellies.

'Yours are far too small and pretty. I've seen them, remember?'

'Ah, yes.' I shifted a little uncomfortably but he wasn't flirting so much as being friendly, and I steered the conversation elsewhere.

'Was Mortimer pleased with his cider event? I haven't spoken to him, but the Beer Festival is this weekend and I know he'll be there. I think he's in with a good chance of an award for Snout About Nothin', between you and me.'

'Gina, he'd be delighted. He's got more money than he knows what to do with but that brewery is his life. Even his grandson doesn't come close, and you can see how much he dotes on Jasper already.'

I thought back to the Simba moment, when Mortimer had held him aloft, and I smiled at the memory.

'Did you know that I've been invited to visit him at his house in Brittany next month, and to a party in Brest?' I asked with my mouth full of bun.

'You're honoured. He keeps that side of his life very much under wraps. You must have heard the rumours?'

'I have, but do you think there is any truth in them?'

I wiped the crumbs away, never a good look.

'Difficult to say. No-one in England has ever seen her and Mortimer likes to cultivate the persona of being a free spirited eccentric aristocrat so perhaps it's part of his image. If he's asked you, it's because he rates you. I've never been and I'm not even sure I know anyone who has.'

'Doe his family ever go over?' I asked, puzzled.

'His son, yes, but not his daughter or wife. Maybe they have their reasons,' he said thoughtfully, rubbing his beard.

'Even if it does turn out to be the case, I'm no snitch and you will never hear it from me, or from Bella, because she's been invited too.'

'That's another thing I like about you. You're not a gossipmonger.'

'Come on, Jago, we can't sit in the sunshine all day. There's work to do, and besides, I'm up for the pint of Jiggy Piggy and fish and chips you promised, in addition of course, to my new wooden floor, at the end of May.'

I clapped my hands in happy anticipation and he rolled his eyes.

'Well, you better make sure you plant them straight then, Gina, or you can forget your pint and your dinner and your floor,' he shouted at me over his shoulder as he walked up the field carrying a pick axe.

And I saw no reason to argue with a man who could wield dangerous tools, expertly.

***

It was two hours until we opened the doors to the Festival and the queues were already around the block. This was a good sign, but I already knew from the advance tickets sales that it was a sell out. I had been working round the clock for the last few days, making sure everything was ready, and dealing with a last minute glitch with the lighting for the second marquee we had to pull in when numbers continued to swell.

Access to the site had been limited, so I had needed to co-ordinate the arrival times for the different breweries, but people were in party mood and everyone was good natured in their dealings with Miss Officious and her clipboard. I was getting used to, and enjoyed, the famous South West manyana approach to life but it was even more pronounced when I compared our laid back attitudes with some of the people who were here from 'up country' as they called it, realising how much of it had rubbed off on me.

The main marquee was lined with the stands of over fifty breweries, all with their different banners and logos, and I had organised it geographically to help visitors locate them and move about. It looked colourful and appealing.

The band was setting up in the far corner and I waved quickly to Bella when she popped her head around the flap of the tent, gesturing with my fingers that I would phone her later. It was as much as I could do at the time.

My walkie talkie in my jeans pocket was telling me that the judging had finished, and the beers had been stickered with their awards, meaning the lists were now ready for display. There were eight categories for the cask ales and five for bottled, with an overall champion, but I knew that an award of any kind would make a big difference and I wanted everyone to win.

I took one last look around before going off to see how Mortimer had faired and made my way to his corner, unable to tell from the commotion if it was good news, or bad.

On arriving, I saw him standing above Bob, his head brewer, who was lying slumped in a chair surrounded by Doddy and Binky I recognised from the brewery. Today, Mortimer had on a rust coloured sailor's smock with a big Bootley Ales logo on it, and some thick green country corduroy trousers. I noticed that the open toed sandals he generally wore, even in the winter, had been replaced with shiny brown quality brogues. The others wore jeans and Bootley tee-shirts and whilst Mortimer didn't have his beret on, the head brewer did, along with a red handkerchief that was tied around his neck.

It was this they were frantically trying to undo, to give him some air while, helpfully or otherwise, flapping his face with a copy of the judging results.

'Gina! Get over here, quick. We need some water.'

Mortimer looked worried and was pulling me by the arm.

'Bob's not well and we daren't give him any of this stuff, because there won't be enough as it is.'

He pointed to the beers.

I quickly handed over the mineral water from my bag and he unscrewed the cap and poured most of it over poor Bob, who started to splutter.

'For God's sake, Mortimer. Get 'ee away from me. You're more danger than 'elp. Just let me be!'

The Devon accent was almost comical but the water had revived him and the colour was slowly returning to his face.

'Hello, Gina. Thank 'ee maid for the water. Have you seen what we've done?'

'No, Bob. What's happened? Did you poison the judges?' I asked tongue in cheek.

'Close,' Mortimer said dryly. 'Let's just say that business will never be the same again.' He shook his head sadly and I started to feel anxious for him.

'Will you have to close down? Is it really that bad?' I gasped.

'Not that way round, you fool, the other way.'

Mortimer was rolling his eyes while Bob was trying to duck any further fanning.

'I'm sorry, but I don't understand.'

I was baffled and looked from one face to the other.

'Right then, we better put her out of her misery. Bob, you stand up and let Gina sit down.'

'But Mortimer ...'

'Never mind that. You're alright now.'

He pulled Bob out of the chair whilst the other two employees struggled to hold him upright, before pushing me firmly down on to the still warm seat.

'You first, Doddy.' Mortimer pointed at him and he stood ramrod straight as if he was about to herald the return of a conquering king, leaving Binky the dwarf to hold up poor Bob, not easy given their relative sizes.

'In the category of Cask Ales Standard Bitters, Gold went to Bootley Ales 'Naughty Porky' abv 3.5, judges notes, colour straw, aroma hoppy, full with a bitter sweet after taste.'

'Wow, that's fantastic news!'

I was thrilled for them.

'You next, Binky. Hurry up.'

Could there be more? I held my breath.

Binky passed Bob to Doddy and stepped forward, pulling himself up to his full size as best he could and announced in his heavy Devon drawl,

'In the category of Cask Ales Best Bitters, Gold went to our newest Bootley Ale 'Snout About Nothin' abv 4.0, judges notes, colour copper, aroma hoppy, malty and fruity with a dry finish.'

I clapped my hands before Mortimer nudged me to stop.

'More?' I whispered with wide eyes.

'I told you once, young lady, that you were far too impatient. Bob, put her out of her misery.'

Poor Bob was just about able to stand up unaided and was wiping his face with his red hankie.

'In the category of Cask Ales Premium Bitter, Gold went to the county's favourite Bootley Ale, Miss 'Jiggy Piggy' herself.'

He took a bow.

'No!' I screamed and covered my mouth with my hands in disbelief.

'And, the judges said,' Mortimer could barely contain himself. 'She was deceptively strong and eminently quaffable, pale and golden with a fruitiness and smooth finish. A wolf in a little piggy's clothes. Hah!'

He laughed his booming laugh as people came over to congratulate them.

'We haven't finished yet, Gina.' Bob said shyly.

'Are you serious? Let me have the last of that water. I need it.'

'Jiggy Piggy has taken Overall Champion!' Mortimer looked fit to burst with pride.

I went to lean on the stand but missed it, and fell off the chair so Bob and Doddy and Binky had to help me up and fan me this time with the judging results. Mortimer looked on with his arms folded across his huge stomach and a grin bigger than the Tamar Bridge, nodding his head in a self-satisfaction.

'So the brewery will never be the same, not because they don't want the stuff but because they won't be able to get enough of it. You're the business brains, Gina. Got any ideas, have you?'

He looked smug, as well as delighted.

***

When we opened the doors, the visitors poured in and the stack of photocopies of the award winning breweries disappeared more quickly than a hailstorm in July. The Bootley guys could barely keep up with demand, and even Mortimer was dishing it out. I took lots of photos because they didn't have time to scratch their proverbials, before going off to find Bella and tell her the good news.

People were milling around with pints and bottles in their hands and the conversations were full of abv's, tasting notes and the consistency problems facing small brewers. The crowd weren't there to glug, as much as to taste, and the Ceili music that Hogwash was banging out was perfect. A small space had been kept in front of the band, which we'd partitioned off with hay bales for people to dance and Phil had his head mic on. With his shiny bald pate and long straggly beard, Justin Timberlake had nothing to worry about as he guided people through the easy dances. He always started the music off slow, until they got into their stride, and it was great fun to watch the twirling and skipping and clapping and arm jiggling everyone eventually got into. The band were great levellers on any occasion.

We had put more hay bales around the edges of the marquee and people were sitting on these and resting their pints. The noise levels of conversations competed with the band and the whole atmosphere was celebratory and relaxed. I got called on my walkie talkie a few more times, but they were small things, and I went out of my way to help the breweries as they were the real stars of the show. I eventually bumped into Bella in the ladies portaloo during a session break, while I was refreshing my lipstick.

'Gina, isn't it wonderful news about Mortimer. It's never been known.' She hugged me.

'Have you seen them? They look like dogs with hundreds of tails, let alone two. They're beaming. Do you remember Bob, the head brewer? He had to be revived and then I fell off a chair by accident.'

'There's a surprise,' she rolled her eyes and shook her head. 'Tell me you didn't latch onto their banner and pull the whole lot down.'

How did she guess? But then again, she knew everything. Luckily, it was only the side panel that came off and Binky had stuck it back on with duct tape so everything looked fine, well almost, and you couldn't tell from a distance.

'Bella, do you think they're pleased with the organisation?' I asked nervously.

'They're raving about it, and the change from last year is marked, even the small thing of how you organised the breweries. Just look about you, and tune in to the comments.'

'I know they love the music. Thank you, so much.'

'I'm looking forward to seeing the other bands because the line-up you put together is amazing. All we've got to do is get through the full day tomorrow and half of Saturday. It'll be a walk in the park, and then ...' she clapped her hands and grinned.

'...we're off to Brittany,' I finished for her. 'That is, if I'm not dead by then Bella. God knows how I'm going to stay the course.'

'Take my advice, Gina, keep away from the beer and leave it to the pro's. See ya.'

She blew an air kiss at me as she strode back to the stage and two hundred and fifty pairs of male eyes followed her every move.

The next few days were frantic but choreographed and it was everything and more that I could have hoped for. The cross section of visitors was enlightening and I bumped into several people from the Rowing Club. Lou turned up with her mum Stephanie, and Jago wandered in with Pete O'Mara for a few hours. The County Set and Devon Lifers were all there and I recognised others from the various Balls I'd been to throughout the year. Surprisingly, they recognised me too, and some even remembered my name. When they realised I was the organiser, they congratulated me on the new feel, energy and the ideas that I had brought.

Someone asked if I had heard about the fabulous dinner that was being staged on The Salty, and when I confessed that was me, too, they were thrilled to know they were in good hands as the ticket prices had been steep in order to raise money for good causes. My business cards were asked for consistently and I ran out half way through the next day, leaving it to Janie Juno to get me some new ones. I didn't ask her how she'd managed it, but she pulled more rabbits from hats than Paul Daniels and the lovely Debbie McGhee in her role as a runner, which she had immediately offered to do at the horrible moment I realised I was short of somebody. Having her by my side when the inevitable small crises occurred had steadied my nerves and she was in line for another slap up meal at Gidleigh Park.

At the end of the festival, I was barely upright myself but it all got packed down quickly by the team and when I eventually got to bed, I slept the sleep of the dead.

The last few days had been more important than most people could have imagined because, along with Jago's vine planting, they marked the first anniversary of the new life I had made, and the first anniversary of the one I had steadfastly left behind. For good.

38 – Sometimes ... item 31b opens the floodgates to reveal a hidden truth

We had received confirmation from the Notaire that everything was in place to complete the purchase of the French house on the fifteenth of May, and an appointment had been made for us to visit his office for the final part of the process. We weren't too sure what this entailed, but the money had been sent electronically and we had received confirmation it had arrived. For the three nights in between however, neither Janie Juno nor I had slept a wink.

These days we were both carrying around lists.

And lists of lists.

I was beginning to dread the sight of the bright yellow 'sunny days' folder she was keeping, as I knew by its mere presence that I was in for an interrogation that would make the Gestapo look amateurish.

Nonetheless, I admired her thoroughness and she had picked up the ball on several occasions recently when I had been too busy. Today was bedding day, and she had coerced me into going with her to the Home section of a big department store where she was walking up and down the aisles, piling me high with towels and linen to the point where I couldn't see out.

Help eventually arrived in the form of the assistant who came when I knocked over a display of cupcake bakeware and when she suggested that we might wish to leave our things on the counter to browse in comfort, I made a dash for it before I dropped the lot on another unsuspecting little bow-legged old lady. In addition to the 'browse in comfort' comment, the assistant had also muttered something about the safety of the other shoppers, though I failed to see what danger they could have been in from a few feather pillows.

'Can we go to The Clarence for a coffee now, please? I don't see that we need all this stuff. We're not opening the Hilton, or are we? Is that the secret plan you keep hidden in your little yellow folder?'

I couldn't help but be tetchy after getting stuck on the escalator and being 'helped' to the door by a man in a uniform.

'Gina, this is supposed to be pleasurable. You're acting like somebody's grumpy husband but OK, you win. Let's cut through here and we'll see if we can get a table outside in the sun.'

We staggered along, bouncing off windows and small children whose mothers didn't notice, and found our way into Cathedral Square. We'd missed the lunch session so there were plenty of free tables and we had enough space to put our bags around us. She ordered coffee while I went to the loo but when I came back, the yellow folder was open on the table and I shuddered.

'Sit down, Gina, I need you to focus. This is what I've come up with and see if you agree.'

She pulled out several sheets of paper.

'The weekend before the Notaire meeting, I've hired a van big enough to take our stuff and booked a cheap day return on the ferry so we can keep the hire costs down. We'll make a quick dash there and back, without staying, and store everything in the garage because our neighbour has a key, and Les Armaunds have given us permission. Check?'

'Check,' I said, going along with the language.

She made a note and put a tick next to it. I noticed the sun glinting on her hair as she looked thoughtfully through her papers and saw how excited she was.

'We pick up samples of wood from the local supplier and bring them back to Jago for his advice, so we can order the materials for when he comes over. Check.'

'OK, OK, enough of the checking thing. I'll just nod.'

'Probably best. The week after, we travel overnight with Bella and arrive in the morning, going straight to the Notaire for the final part.'

She looked up at me and when I moved my head a fraction, she ticked the list.

'Bella stays the first week and helps us to settle in, then we take her to the Roscoff port and pick Jago up. Now listen, if I can't re-arrange my client meeting I'll have to go back with her but I'll know more soon.'

I decided I'd tap this time, instead of nodding, and she looked at me with narrowed eyes.

'The materials will be delivered the day Jago arrives and he'll stay for a week doing the floor.'

I poked her in the leg.

'I'll take that as an affirmative, too, but you're not going to distract me from this important work and you'll be grateful one day when we've remembered the Tetley teabags.'

I clanged my teaspoon unhelpfully against the cup twice and she shrugged.

'The week that Bella's with us, we meet Mortimer in Brest for the big party.'

'I'd forgotten about that amongst everything else. What is it again?' I drummed my fingers on the table and looked around disinterestedly.

'Gina, it was item 31b yesterday,' she sighed and I noticed the little frown marks between her eyes which made her look younger and smiled to myself.

'Ah yes, the 31b. Could you just run it past me again, please?' I said sarcastically.

Another big sigh, but I knew she had been captivated by the scant details we'd been given and loved going over it so when she began to rattle again in earnest, I let her have her moment.

She took a deep breath and took her time to locate and pull out the sheet marked 31b, smoothed it down on the table and began. I knew I wasn't giving her my full attention because the thoughts that had kept me awake last night began to slowly drift back to the fore, and her voice seemed far away as I looked out at the Cathedral.

'OK, are you ready?'

I nodded absently and folded my arms.

'It's the birthday party of an old friend of Mortimer's who he calls Claude the Crab. It's his fiftieth and will be at the Vauban in Brest, on the Avenue Georges Clémenceau. It is a recently refurbished turn of the century hotel, complete with curved brass bar and mirrors.' She stopped reading and looked up at me. 'The photos on the internet show potted palms and old wooden bistro chairs, and the walls are covered with original photos. It looks stunning, Gina.'

'What's the dress code, do you know?' I asked flatly and picked some imaginary fluff off my jumper.

'I haven't a clue, but I would guess it's not formal. though there are champagne cocktails to start with. I'm going for a plain black dress and boots. I'll show you later.

It's got square leather panels on the front and back, very sixties. I bought it in a charity shop.'

'Will there be a dinner?' I touched my right ear lobe and fiddled with the dangling pearl.

'I don't think so, but Claude the Crab is so called because he's a high-end vivier who supplies the top chefs in Paris, as well as posh supermarkets and poissoneries, so my money is on seafood. Crabs and lobsters, yum yum.'

'I'm not sure if I can be bothered to go. We'll have only just got the key, and the place will be ours at long last, and Brest is an hour away, and we'll have to stay over, and drive back, and I might get ill and ...'

'Gina! In all the time I've known you, and after everything we've talked about, I can't believe you're prepared to even think about passing this over. You love Mortimer, and if he's such big mates with Mr Crabman and he's asked you, and me by association, why would you not go? Honestly, sometimes you're, you're ...' she was blustering now.

'... a lapsed adult?' I grinned and despite her exasperation she laughed at the memory.

'Definitely behaving like a sulky child, that's for sure. Is it because you haven't got an outfit in mind? You know you always manage to throw something together and look effortlessly chic.'

She laid her hand on my arm.

'That's not me, that's you.'

'When was the last time you looked properly at yourself in the mirror, Gina, and saw what the rest of us sees?'

I thought back to the morning when I had collected Lou's cake, and the twirl I'd made with the new earrings, when I finally accepted that my emotional shift had triggered a physical one. If that's what she was referring to,

I couldn't be disingenuous, but right now, I didn't care what I looked like.

I bowed my head, staring down at my cup and felt inadequate. When she saw it, she gently covered my hand with hers.

'Look, I know what's going on here isn't about the party. You've waited a long time for this house, and everything it signifies, and you still can't allow yourself to believe it.'

I began to cry because she had judged things correctly and had seen my bad and grumpy behaviour for what it was; doubt and anxiety that I was taking another step too far by the standards of the folks back in the Midlands. I was terrified it was going to be snatched away and evaporate into thin air as nothing more than a fit of fanciful thinking. What had Gina Jarvie ever done to warrant having a second home in a beautiful foreign country?

'Remember the time you told me that it was the thought of a place in the sun that kept you going on summer days, when you were strapped to your computer?'

Her voice was gentle but her eyes urged me back to that day. I laughed and brushed away some tears.

'You make it sound like The Shawshank Redemption. It wasn't that bad, and I made good money, for my family.'

'Yes, but at what price?' she leaned back in her chair. 'You're not in that life anymore. You're in this one, and the house will be there for you, for us, when we go to Brest and when we come back, and for all the other times in our lives that are ahead of us with our family. We'll be able to row and sail, and make even more friends. Allow yourself to believe, because it's true. Hang on in there.'

It was me who collapsed into her now, the tears coursing down my face; an adulthood of pent up isolation and denial decided to pour forth in an unremarkable corner of a courtyard in Exeter, on a gloriously sunny day.

I buried my head in her shoulder and she stroked my hair.

'Gina, shush, there, there, it's OK to feel this way, but you're not on your own any more. You're not shouldering all of this. I'm here, Bella's here, Lou, we're all here. Let go of the pain, look there it goes now.'

She made a waving gesture like a bird flying gently on its wing and I looked to the sky.

'I'm sorry, I didn't see this coming,' I said wiping my eyes with the napkin from under my saucer.

'I did. Look at me, Gina. None of the items on our lists are important, we both know that. Part of the joy will be doing it up ourselves, a bit at a time, and choosing the things we want to put in it. We have no-one else to please, and no deadlines. Our work will allow us to use it, probably more than we think, and we can practise the language and explore. Just promise me one thing.'

I nodded and blew my nose.

'That you will let yourself believe ... it's OK to dream.'

39 – Sometimes … oyster beds are revealed when the tide goes out

The quick trip across the channel had been smooth in all aspects, and there were no despites to share. We'd taken across all the basics to set up home, and even managed to squeeze in my red Vespa scooter, called Valerie. I had visions of us zipping along the coast road, where the surfers caught the waves, with me driving and Janie Juno holding on tightly.

We had cleared our diaries, except for the one item she would go back with Bella for and return later on. It would mean leaving Jago and I on our own, but I was quite looking forward to helping him with the floor because we had worked companionably together on the vineyard and the guest room would be ready by the time he arrived.

My car was packed to the gunnels and we were en route to collect Bella, grateful she was slim because of the small space she was going to have to sit in. Janie Juno was in the passenger seat with the commanding yellow folder resting on her lap and it was raining heavily. The wipers were struggling to clear the screen as we pulled out into the traffic and left the quayside behind us.

'Don't do that thing that my mother always used to do,' I said, checking my lipstick in the mirror, the very, very last of my Chanel.

'What thing?' she asked evenly.

'Have you remembered the dog/cat/children/Anasol?'

'Mine used to make corned beef and tomato rolls, wrapped in tin foil, and bring a tartan thermos flask of tea that would lift the lining off a rusty pylon,' she laughed.

'I think we survive despite our mothers and not because of them, eh?' I said as fond memories of my own mum drifted in and I also thought of my boys.

'You might have something there!'

'I hope Bella's on time for once, she's a nightmare. I've taken to telling her everything is thirty minutes earlier so we have a cat's chance of being punctual, but she's too far gone now to change.'

'With your number dyslexia and her time management, you've really got the makings of a good partnership. You could both take the business a long, long, way,' she said with sarcasm.

'Thanks for your faith, but the numbers, dyslexic or otherwise, are speaking for themselves and if this continues, I can take six months of the year off. I bet you weren't expecting that.'

'Gina, frankly I'm not surprised because you and Bella were made for each other, in life and in business. You mirror yourselves perfectly. She's very proud to be your partner, she told me, and the feedback from the festival has taken you both to a different level. The national coverage has them beating a path to your door.'

'It seems that way,' I said thoughtfully. 'So did you remember to get the broadband connection up and running?'

'I thought we weren't going to do that thing, or play 'check', or look inside the yellow folder ever again so do you really want me to answer?'

When I stole a glance from the road her look was steely but I could see the corners of her mouth twitching.

'OK. I'm sorry. I know you've pulled out all the stops on this and I've not shown you the gratitude you deserve.'

'Why I can feel a hamper coming on?' she asked cautiously.

'I haven't ordered one, but seriously before Bella gets in, I want to say thank you. I know I've been remote, though I did take on board what you said at The Clarence.'

'Yes, but what did you do about it?' she asked pointedly.

'Well, it was a bit like when I first started drinking,' I began haltingly.

'OK, you're losing me, but keep going.'

And when I started to laugh she raised a questioning eyebrow.

'I've taken a few sips of journey's end, allowed it to settle to get a taste of its full flavour, and there's the distinct possibility of a deceptively smooth finish. Like Mortimer's beer.'

'Did you just conjure that up, or have you been practising?' She was looking at me closely.

'A bit of both, I think, because I knew you'd ask. But you get my meaning, don't you?' I asked gently.

'I suppose so, Gina, but after the Festival, I'll be glad if I never see another pint again!' she said lightly, trying to steer the mood.

'Janie?'

'What now?' she was feigning testiness, but it didn't fool me so I said what was really on my mind.

'I couldn't have dealt with half of what you've done, to get us this far.'

'Oh, I think you'll find that you could have, Gina.'

She turned and smiled enigmatically at me and squeezed my hand as Bella appeared at her door.

**

We arrived an hour before our meeting with the Notaire in Pont Croix which gave us enough time to walk into the square and sit outside La Galiotte, under a green canopy. We looked out on to the small market with its varied food stalls and mixture of red faced tourists and sturdy locals carrying overflowing straw baskets of fresh produce, artisan cheese and baguettes.

'Look,' Bella exclaimed pointing to the large window of the bar where I could see that the glass was engraved with the silhouettes of a couple of girls dancing, black on dark green.

'It's you and Janie Juno. That one there, with the hair slightly curling out is Janie, and the other one is you, Gina.'

Sure enough, there was no mistaking us and we all smiled happily as I stood to take a photo.

'Hallelujah! It's a sign,' Bella shouted. 'You couldn't wish for anything more convincing than that. You're on the right path and it's remarkable, even by my standards.'

'Come on. There'll be a big finger from the sky next, or a hand that pushes us to the Notaire,' I said disparagingly but remembered back to the moment when I almost didn't open the door to Janie Juno, and the 'encouragement' that had been needed, so I was no longer a hardnosed sceptic.

Janie Juno had a map in the yellow folder which guided us across cobbled streets and ancient squares to the address we had been given, and soon we arrived in front of a modern, white building. It had red windows, and big red doors, and there was no mistaking its purpose when you contrasted its nouveau defiant gaucheness to the timeless refined elegance of the charming turn of the century grand houses that flanked it on either side.

Like hospitals, lawyer's offices always turn my legs to jelly but worse, they make me feel guilty, as if I've done something wrong. I wasn't relishing the prospect of this meeting, but with Bella on one side and Janie Juno on the other, we entered and I spoke to the receptionist.

We were asked to take a seat and told that Monsieur Bavarde would be along. As we sat down, Les Armaunds came in and installed themselves next to us. We chatted a little about their latest travelling jaunts to Italy before being called into a large and expensively furnished office of wall to wall leather and a huge polished desk.

'Welcome everybody. Today is only a formality. I will go through the papers and if you have any queries, now is the time to raise them.'

He was a heavy set man of around fifty with a deep voice who was dressed casually in trousers and a blue shirt. His red rimmed glasses accentuated both his jowliness and his thick thatch of hair that I could see was dyed. Never a redeeming feature in someone you needed to put trust in, but I consoled myself with the fact that we were in another country now and they did things differently. He had spoken in French but I understood and watched as he proceeded to thumb his way through the two inch wad of papers, thinking that we were going to be in there until the next revolution.

He asked a few questions about personal circumstances and raised some queries that the survey had thrown up, but which I knew from talking to Jago, were minor. Within half an hour we had signed and shook hands. The keys were handed over in less time than it took to swallow un petit café, and we said our goodbyes and left.

We stood in a row outside in the sunshine with our backs to the red doors. It felt peculiarly anticlimactic and we struggled to move into the next moment. It was Bella who came to the rescue.

'Right then, time to check if Juno Towers is still standing.'

This was the pet name we'd given it amongst ourselves and it was enough to galvanise us into walking the few paces across the street to where the car was parked.

We took the road from Pont Croix, following the beautiful Goyen estuary where we could see the oyster beds laid out in rows on the sandbanks at low tide. The valley wasn't steep, but it was sloped, and both sides were bordered with trees whose spring leaves looked verdant in contrast to the clear blue sky.

I began to feel my excitement rise and some of the tension that I'd hardly been aware of, dropped from my shoulders at the sight of the immense natural beauty. By the time we had driven through Audierne, and out past the lighthouse, I was like a child on Christmas Eve.

Bella, who'd never seen it before, was in the passenger seat next to me, and Janie Juno was in the back going through her yellow folder.

'Gina, this is stunning. However did you find it?'

I thumbed over my shoulder to the back seat.

'We have Janie Juno to thank.'

Living it through Bella's eyes for the first time, made me see things that I'd either forgotten or hadn't noticed, and when she saw the beach, she squealed.

'Is this it? Is this the one you live by? Look at the turquoise water and the white sand. There are people swimming in it! I can see boats and the sailing school. I never thought that France looked like this.'

'Not everywhere does, Bella,' I said gently as I pulled onto the drive.

The front of the house was in shadow because it was south facing and whilst the shutters were closed, they looked tatty and in want of attention. Ivy had grown up the wall and the hydrangeas needed dead-heading. The gravel was full of weeds and the clumps of oregano and lavenders were tall and rangy.

Bella wasted no time in going round the back and I could hear her gasps from where I stood. 'You've found the steps then?' I shouted.

'Gina, you said it was by the beach. You didn't say it was on the beach!' she came rushing back round. 'I propose that you and Janie Juno hold the key together when you open the door for the first time and I'll take a photo from over there.'

With shaking hands the key got inserted into the lock and as it turned and opened we looked at each other and smiled. I let her go in first and followed, with Bella hot on my heels. We opened the shutters and the French doors then stood again in a row, facing out to sea in the small back garden where I had to shield my eyes from the sun.

'Congratulations! You're going to be very happy here. Me too, whenever there's a chance to visit,' Bella laughed heartily. 'But meanwhile, I've got something for you.'

She ferreted around in her bag and pulled out a small carved foot, made from wood, that was about eight inches long.

'This is to signify the steps you've already taken, and the footprints you have yet to make. I now pronounce Juno Towers well and truly yours.'

She presented it to us with a flourish.

Janie Juno was overcome and went off in search of something to wipe her eyes while I hugged Bella with all my heart. 'It's beautiful and thoughtful and apt and considerate and ...'

'... tell me you like it, please!'

'Oh yes, didn't I say that. I love it. Thank you, thank you.'

I kissed her on the cheek.

By the time nightfall came, we had cleaned and swept the place and made up our beds, each of us getting our own rooms ready on the first floor. I was grateful for the bedding Janie Juno had made us buy because we now had comfortable places to sleep. We were short of a fridge, a cooker and a washing machine but they were due to arrive the following day so we drank our coffee black, our wine red, and decided to go out for dinner to Le Grand Large, or The Open Sea, by the lighthouse.

In the days that followed, we scrubbed, weeded, painted, fixed, planted, chopped, sewed, sanded, filled, plastered, stained, laughed, slept, drank, ate, chatted, sunbathed, swam and were very, very happy.

The house flourished under our careful attention so that, inch by inch, the blue disappeared and was replaced with subtle tones of natural wood, cream, white and stone. We had brought over a black wrought iron patio set and with the cushions that I made, we took to sitting outside at every opportunity to enjoy the beach, and the ever changing views.

The only cloud on my horizon was Brest the next day, and I was convinced that leaving our corner of paradise was a mistake. I had no appetite for any aspect of the party, not even seeing Mortimer, but as it would be Bella's last night and she was eager to go, I really had no choice.

40 – Sometimes … when two tiny particles collide they reshape the universe around them

We arrived at the Vauban at four and checked in for the party, which would begin downstairs at six with cocktails. Janie Juno was wearing the plain dress with its black leather panels that she'd told me about and Bella had on red trousers with a black silk shirt. Her hair fell in a cascade of spirals and she'd made up her dark grey eyes carefully so that they radiated fun and confidence.

I had struggled to know what to wear and had eventually put on a black knee length swingy skirt, teamed with an off the shoulder long sleeved black top, and my slingbacks. It was nothing special because my heart wasn't it, and I hadn't even bothered to iron the skirt from when I'd unpacked it. Jewellery wise, my pearl dangly earrings were enough to set it off and I had discarded a necklace after trying it on.

My mood was mixed and alternated between begrudging, because I was away from Juno Towers, to a vague curiosity about the new French people I might meet. It was difficult to put my finger on exactly how I was feeling, but I was quiet and detached.

We went downstairs in the tiny mirrored lift, barely big enough for the three of us, and the first person we saw in the bar was Mortimer. Next to him, stood a petite and beautiful French lady who reminded me of Joanna, our neighbour back in Exeter, because visually she was of indeterminate age though her hands suggested she might be in her mid-sixties. Her blonde shoulder length hair was carefully tended and her hazel eyes danced merrily. She was dressed in a beige silk dress with a black woollen pashmina draped elegantly around her shoulders, but the thing I remember most was that she sparkled. Her ears, throat, wrists and fingers were adorned with very large and very fine white diamonds.

'Gina, come here now you silly girl and let me introduce you to someone very dear to me, Camille, Countess de Noailles. Camille meet Gina, she's the one I've been telling you about. She ran the Festival a treat, first time in history.'

He kissed me on each cheek and his voice sounded more cultured than I remembered, but perhaps it was because we were in France.

'Bienvenue, Gina, I hear that you have acquired a house.' Camille smiled and extended a hand graciously, her voice warm and refined without accent. She exuded charisma and sincerity, and though I'm not often stuck for words, I found myself mumbling and being slightly in awe.

Could this possibly be the face of Jiggy Piggy? I didn't think so but if the rumour was true, she'd been his friend since before he was married, so perhaps it was based on the younger Camille. Watching his attentiveness and radiant expression, it left me in no doubt that Mortimer was very fond of her and if the situation threw up some awkward questions, you could forgive people a lot of things when you liked them.

Bella joined us but my eyes darted around for Janie Juno, wondering where she was lurking, because I wanted her to meet Camille. As I scanned the sophisticated and elegant crowd of beautiful people, who were enjoying themselves amongst the palms and the swirling wrought iron balustrades, I eventually spotted her at the other end of the bar talking to someone.

I couldn't immediately see who it was because there were several groups between us, but when someone moved, I saw him in profile as he faced Janie Juno. He was tanned with dark hair and had on a grey cotton shirt, slightly open at the neck, and a trick of the light from the bar was showering them with a golden glow, in contrast to the people around them.

Thinking that I could negotiate the throng to reach her, I was about to squeeze through a gap when there was something about the intensity of their rapport, something about the closeness of their faces, something in the way they laughed and the way they chinked their glasses, that was enough to stop me dead.

Though I wanted to turn my head away, ashamed and embarrassed at being a bystander to a scene that was so profoundly intimate and personal, I couldn't. I looked on instead and witnessed the precise moment when kismet strikes at the hearts of two complete strangers.

He was taller than Janie Juno, of medium build with finely chiselled features and dark eyes that glittered when he looked at her, in the strange hue that shone on them and no-one else.

Never once did he take his eyes off her.

Not for one second.

I watched people going up to him to say hello and watched as he nodded, and watched him watching her.

At the same instant I realised my friend had fallen in love, I was engulfed by a crippling sense of loss, and when it was plain to see that the man in the grey shirt had fallen in love with her, it doubled.

I found myself standing in a beam of the same strange light, which brought everything around me into high definition, and found that I could pick out small details from a great distance, like his little crab cufflinks, and the way the corners of his eyes crinkled when she spoke, and the slight tremor in his hand when he touched her arm.

I saw a mixture of certainty, reassurance, shock and pleasure explode from his eyes, and knew my days with Janie Juno were numbered when hers revealed a similar whirlpool of emotions.

They had been flying through space and time, in their individual galaxies, to reach this moment and fusion had occurred on a nuclear scale when the atoms of their beings had merged, with the simple chink of a glass. Nothing had been able to stop the collision, and nothing would stop its propulsion.

What were the odds of us all arriving in Brest at the same time, on the same day, given our various ports of embarkation, adventures and voyages along the way? What forces had brought us to this point?

I shivered involuntarily as icy fingers slithered around my naked shoulders, willing my feet to move. The voices of Mortimer, Camille and Bella sounded like they were emitting from a distant tunnel, and I struggled to make out their words. From somewhere in the murky depths of my consciousness, I emerged slowly to the hand that had been placed gently on my arm.

'Let me get you a refill, Gina. You look like you've seen a ghost.'

Mortimer spoke quietly and kindly, sensing my distress at something he didn't understand as I fought to recover myself.

'Who's that man in grey down there, at the end of the bar?' I asked breathlessly, my heart pounding in my ears.

Someone had moved in front of Janie Juno so Mortimer couldn't see her.

'That's Claude the Crab, whose party this is. We'll go over and I'll introduce you, because if you hadn't already guessed, that's why you're here.' He smiled mischievously, 'I hope you don't mind, young lady, but I believe he will be as charmed by you as I am.'

He began to head over.

'No, No!' I put my hand out quickly to restrain him.

'Are you alright, Gina? Shall I find you a chair?'

Mortimer's face was full of concern.

'No, but I might get some air in a minute. Where's Claude's wife, Mortimer?'

'She might be here somewhere.'

My heart sank as I watched him looking around.

'But she's his ex. They've been divorced for five years and he's very single. We chaps have been saying to him for years that he must ease up on the business and this birthday is a milestone for him to start enjoying life again. That's where you come in.'

'Don't be ridiculous, Mortimer. This isn't a game!' I shouted and saw his look of astonishment.

I bolted for the door before he could say more, or before I fainted. Bella found me outside in a dark alleyway holding on to my stomach with one hand and a drain pipe with the other, to steady myself. She squatted down so that her head was lower than mine then looked up at me, the anguish straining her features.

'Gina, what's going on? Have you overdone it at the house? What is it? What's wrong?' She sounded frantic but I'd already made up my mind.

'Yes, I have overdone things and the champagne on an empty stomach is too much. I'll be alright, but I'm going back to the room,' I said wearily.

'And miss this fabulous party? A jazz quartet has started up and there must be more than a hundred of the French elite out there. It's exactly your kind of thing.'

She was almost pleading.

'Honestly, Bella, I think it's for the best,' I said without enthusiasm.

'Well, at least let me come up with you.'

'No, but thanks. I want to be on my own. I need to think.'

'About what? What's happened, Gina?' She spoke gently, with concern, but I'd had enough.

'I keep telling you,' I screamed. 'Why don't you listen? Nothing has happened and nothing is wrong! I just want to be on my own. Why can't you all leave me ALONE!'

I pushed by her crying, as she stared after me dumbfounded, still clutching the champagne flutes.

But I didn't care.

Back in the room, I went into the bathroom and swilled my face under the cold tap before drying it roughly on the white towel, not caring that my mascara left black smears. I lay down on the bed in the dark, fully clothed.

My thoughts were ricocheting out of control as I considered the implications of what I had seen. I rifled frantically through my raging emotions, trying to make sense of them, but struggled under the ever growing weight of confusion and conflict, feeling like an avalanche was about to engulf me.

And I wanted it to.

I wanted to be numb.

To kill the searing pain of betrayal.

And to carry on as we were before.

Falling in love with a Frenchman had scuppered all the carefully laid plans for Brittany and England, rendering the yellow 'sunny days' folder worthless, in the blink of an eye or the chink of a glass. At the precise moment we had discovered our golden nirvana, when the end of the rainbow had landed on the little house in Audierne, she was going to abandon it.

And me.

I had thought I could protect, and preserve forever, the status-quo of the life I'd fought tooth and nail for, but she was part of the equation and there was nothing I could do to stop her from extricating herself. The problem lay in the simple fact that without Janie Juno, I wasn't sure I could trust myself.

I threw back at her in my mind's eye all the baloney she'd spouted about allowing myself to believe, not shouldering things on my own and it being OK to dream. At the very point I was beginning to take my first faltering steps, she was pulling the rug from beneath me.

I could see that I had become too attached and too dependent on her, and it was my downfall because all I could do now was to watch Janie Juno walk into the future, gradually fading as she headed towards some distant desert horizon with her back to me.

Just when I'd found the best friend I could ever hope for.

She was going.

She would be gone.

She was gone.

I cried and cried, until the sound of my own sobbing became the death throes of the mortally wounded, but there was no-one there who could courageously put an end to my suffering.

41 – Sometimes ... a dove flies to the sound of a woman's voice

Coming slowly back to consciousness, I wasn't immediately certain of where I was. In the last eighteen months, I'd done more than my fair share of sleeping in strange beds so it was with a surge of happiness I remembered I was in Venice, and the reason why.

Yesterday evening, in a rush to make the restaurant for nine, I had only been able to dump my bags, hang up a dress in the dark carved wardrobe and change quickly into my black silk one. There had been no time to notice my surroundings but now, as I lay there, filled with confidence and optimism, I let my eyes rove slowly around the room.

The shutters were open and shafts of sunlight came in through the stained glass balcony doors, throwing coloured patterns onto the dark wooden floor boards. The ceilings were high and painted with scenes from a renaissance wedding where I could pick out the newlyweds as they journeyed from the ceremonial feast to the marriage bed, in a series of frescoes. I wondered fleetingly if they were original, given the age of the Palazzo.

The walls, by comparison, were plain and graced with paintings of The Madonna and Child and The Venus de Milo, amongst others. Two golden gilt chairs, upholstered in crimson satin, stood either side of the balcony doors, and a smaller version fronted an ornate dressing table where the mirror was slightly spotted with age. The quilt on my bed was of the same gold brocade as the overlong, heavy curtains that trailed elegantly on the floor, tied back with thick satin tassels. The contrast of the ostentatious furniture to the mild decay of the room, with its areas of peeling paint, made it feel like a living building from the time of the Medicis.

I sprung out of bed in my long white chemise and pulled open the heavy doors, feeling the warm breeze from the canal shimmy across my skin. The daily noises were gathering in volume and the not unpleasant but distinctly sea smell of Venice permeated my nostrils.

Scraping over an ornate black iron chair, I sat down and rested my head on my bare arms over the balustrade between the window boxes of geraniums to observe the scene below. Vaporettos, gondolas, water taxis and a barge piled high with boxes of fruit were navigating the blue green water and people shouted greetings when they saw me. I waved back with enthusiastic delight, smiling excitedly and watched the waves of their wash lap at the red and white striped poles, protruding upwards.

My thoughts, in the warming sunshine, drifted back to my extreme reaction in the Vauban, which like everything else around me today, seemed to have come from a different age. After the initial shock, I had done a good job of embracing the enforced changes because I had been sufficiently robust to deal with them, thanks to my own renaissance. The emotional vacuum in which I had barely existed a few years ago had now been filled with the love and support of friends, the satisfaction of work and two beautiful homes. As I thought about my good fortune, I smiled at the amber glow of possibility that shone within me, and pondered happily on what might lie ahead, knowing above all that my independence and new sense of self would be preserved. I saw the world very differently, but understood my place in the order of things. The only tiny cloud on the horizon was that Janie Juno and I might have some explaining to do.

Despite my earlier misgivings, I was glad I'd decided to attend and feelings of pride and pleasure enveloped me, as they had on the day when I'd made a present of the earrings to her. Life is full of people and situations that arrive unexpectedly, and the answer isn't to lock the door and hide.

The answer is to turn the handle, and open it fully.

To throw it open, as wide as you can.

With all your strength, and all your heart.

And usher the unexpected in.

***

We wore identical knee length dresses, except for the colour, and were standing side by side in front of a tall gilt mirror looking at ourselves. Mine was in a pale peach and hers was in white, both made from exquisite lace that had been intricately woven with motifs that depicted love and nature. Each time we looked, we found something new in the delicate fabric which enthralled us, and today it was me who spotted the intertwined love hearts and Janie who saw the fluttering humming birds poised in mid air, as they gathered the nectar from garlands of flowers, surrounded by angels.

Still facing the mirror, she took my hand and said gently, 'Gina, you know deep down that it's time for me to go.'

I couldn't speak and became heavy with sorrow. It brought my shoulders down and I hung my head, feeling my lips quivering as I tried to stem my grief and tears. That she had finally chosen to tell me today, of all days, was fitting; I had known it was coming but I had striven to hold on to her for a little while longer.

'You're strong enough now, on your own, and you don't need me anymore to lean on. I believe you've already worked out that I carried you when you struggled to cope; after your divorce, your move and your search for love.'

She spoke so softly and kindly that I could only nod.

'I know we'll never lose touch completely and hope I'll forever be in your mind's eye as you meander along the colourful pathways of your life, seeing the world, as you do, from your unique and quirky perspective. Please always carry me in your heart, and don't ever forget me. You'll never lose love again, Gina, I promise. I'm going to say goodbye now.'

She kissed me lightly on my cheek, and slowly let go of my hand.

And we turned to each other.

And we became each other.

And then we became the same.

The same person.

As I looked in the mirror, the image of the two of us had faded away and in its place stood one woman. My dress had turned to the colour of ivory cream and my hair was curling slightly outwards, with a few loose strands blowing gently in the breeze.

'Thank you, Janie Juno. I would never have made it without you.'

My voice, to the mirror, was softly spoken but the white dove quietly basking in the sunshine on the balustrade flew gently up into sky at the sound of it. Those were the first and only words I ever spoke out loud to her.

And then I wiped away my tears.

***

I married Claude an hour later at the Palazzo Cavalli, off the Grand Canal near the Rialto Bridge, and we emerged into the sunlight under a hail of rice and confetti. I threw my bouquet high up into the air and watched with happy delight as it fell into the eagerly outstretched hands of my two very real and living friends, Bella and Lou.

Close by, a gaily coloured troop of acrobats and jugglers, that included a boy on blue stilts trailed by a tartan-clad sausage dog, treated us to an impromptu performance for the circus that was heading to Verona.

The End